YOUNG LINCOLN OF NEW SALEM

A Novel

Sam Rawlins

YorkshirePublishing
www.yorkshirepublishing.com
Write Now

Young Lincoln of New Salem
Copyright © 2019 by Sam Rawlins.
Cover Art by Dell Harris © 2019

ISBN: 978-1-949231-95-3 (Hardbound)
ISBN: 978-1-949231-94-6 (Paperback)
ISBN: 978-1-949231-96-0 (ebook)

Printed in the USA. First edition 2019.

Yorkshire Publishing
4613 E. 91st St.
Tulsa, Oklahoma 74137
www.YorkshirePublishing.com
918.394.2665

Thanks for your interest in my new book, which was a three year labor of love in the writing, following many more years of research. May History come alive as you read the story within these pages.
-All my best,
Sam Rawlins

Dedication

For June and Mary, without whose help this book would not have been possible. June you truly are my sweet Adaline.

I also want to dedicate this work to all of those who have ever encouraged me as a writer. I treasure your support with all my heart.

Table of Contents

CHAPTER 1
A STRANGER ARRIVES
IN NEW SALEM

Walking along the time-worn path, at length I came to the primitive cabins that were remnants of a pioneer settlement. They represented a long-ago place, perhaps almost 200 years old.

Standing among these ruins I wondered, what sort of people lived here? I had a strange sensation in that haunting moment. A stirring of ghosts of those who lived in those times rose up around me. Who were they? I could shut my eyes and almost see them in my mind's eye.

Author's Note: New Salem, April 2016

… Almost 200 years ago, the land in this very spot was part of the rugged Illinois frontier. It was a wilderness, an almost impenetrable place where only the most courageous of individuals dared to live.

Eastward, a winding river worked its way through the wilderness. Twisting and turning, it was called the Sangamon River. Full of many surprises, it was deceivingly treacherous.

It was the early morning of April 19th, 1831 when onlookers high up on the bluff first caught sight of the flatboat coming around the bend of the river. It could easily be seen from a distance because it was nearly 80 feet long and 18 feet wide.

Knowing the river, many folks gathered on the bluff above sensed something out of the ordinary was about to happen. It did. Coming around the bend just below New Salem, the sudden force of the currents carried the flatboat far out onto a rock dam where it

1

got hung up. Teetering there, water began to fill rapidly into the low end of the boat. Becoming in danger of sinking, the crew immediately began to unload the boat. Among them, a tall boney stranger quickly took command. Appearing to know exactly what he was doing, he borrowed an auger from a local merchant in order to bore a hole in the bottom of the boat.

Throughout this event, a sizable group of spectators from among the townspeople gathered on the bluff above and along the river bank. Among them was a young impressionable girl of eighteen, Ann Rutledge by name. Caught up in this near disastrous event, this is what happened according to the information she recorded in her diary. She also noted that this was her first sighting of the tall stranger who would figure so deeply in her life as well as into the life of the whole town.

Meanwhile, the tall stranger directed the others in the flatboat crew: his cousin, Dennis Hanks, his half-brother, John Johnston, and even the backer of this enterprising expedition, Denton Offutt. Taking charge, the tall stranger oversaw the saving of the boat and all of its provisions. After draining the flooding water out of the boat and completely unloading it, they fashioned a makeshift wooden plug to stop up the hole they had made. Then, with the aid of some of the townspeople, they slipped the lightened boat over the dam.

Some of the more interested onlookers had come down from the bluff, gathering closer along the banks of the river. By then, it was getting into the afternoon. Noting this, one of the town's founding fathers stepped from the crowd of applauding spectators and introduced himself, "I'm James Rutledge, owner of the tavern and inn in the village above us. As it's getting into the afternoon, I would like to invite you to stay overnight in our little community."

He had been directing his conversation to the deeply tanned, tall stranger, who now could be clearly seen up close. He was a skinny fellow with several physical features that made him stand out. Many of those present immediately noticed that he had an abnormally long neck, like it had been stretched a bit too far. His angular head, together with his own life's circumstances, had worked against his facial appearance. The lack of sufficient food, or even starvation, had promoted an advanced form of deeply sunken cheeks.

Scanning the crowd, the tall stranger realized that he was their total focus now, all eyes baring down on him. Indeed, they were, as his physical appearance seemed to suggest he was so clearly at death's door. To repress this thought, he responded quickly and energetically, "I'm Abe Lincoln from Kentucky, and while I'm willing to stay overnight, that will be up to the owner of our boat."

Thereupon, a short, somewhat overweight, blustery man who had been standing somewhat behind Abe, stepped forward. "I'm Denton Offutt owner of the boat in question. Mister Rutledge, we'd be happy to accept your kind invitation to stay overnight at your inn and tavern." Then turning to Abe, he added, "We'll reload the boat in the morning."

Glancing about, Abe noticed one of the more curious onlookers was a strikingly beautiful young woman with honey-blonde hair, or so he thought. On the way up the slope to the bluff above them, Abe leaned over to their host, "Mister Rutledge, who is that young woman?"

He had gestured toward her and James Rutledge recognized her immediately, "Mister Lincoln, that's my daughter, Ann."

Ann was already some distance ahead of them going uphill and not aware they were talking about her. Ann Rutledge was indeed beautiful and Abe was not the first to notice this. It is unfortunate that no likeness of her has survived from those times before even the most primitive forms of photography. Stories though, of her beauty as told by many have survived.

In surveying the crowd earlier, Abe remembered their eyes had connected for a flickering moment. She possessed a kind, sensitive expression that seemed to welcome him, a total stranger among them. He would later find that what he surmised first for a flickering moment was absolutely true. She was indeed a warm, outgoing person in her dealings with others. For now though, these were quickly passing thoughts.

Reaching the top of the plateau, Abe got his first good look at the little settlement of New Salem. It consisted of little more than a hundred people, but seemed like a metropolis to one who'd rarely been out of the backwoods of Kentucky.

Glancing about, Abe later wrote, New Salem seemed to rise out of nature itself, carved from a surrounding wilderness of age-old trees. It was a place fresh and clean, almost like it was out of the Garden of Eden. Taking a deep breath of the freshness of nature around him, there was something almost holy about this environment. He said, "This place is beautiful, like a New Jerusalem from the Bible stories of old. If ever there was a place where one could find salvation this was it." These words were just part of his initial reaction to New Salem, but they were thoughts that would linger with him for many years.

Leading the way down Main Street, James Rutledge proudly announced, "That's my inn and tavern up ahead."

Following in the crowd, Abe Lincoln was a young man with his whole life ahead of him, his head and heart full of dreams. But, they were much more than that. They were his thoughts that would define him as a man among men who would leave his mark on the minds and hearts of so many others.

As far as Abe thought then however, he was but one small spec in the course of what was about to happen. Many years later though, he would begin to realize life is a whole lot more than mere fate. He would remark, "I believe now it was God's divine will that I came to New Salem, that I would interact with the frontier folk that lived there. They were God-fearing souls who left an indelible mark for good on humanity and left their imprint on the face of our young country."

Abe didn't know it then, but he was on far more than a flatboat journey to New Orleans. He was just beginning a spiritual journey that would reach into the rest of his life.

Entering the inn, the four weary men from the flatboat–Abe Lincoln, Dennis Hanks, John Johnston, and Denton Offutt–were ushered into the great room by the fireplace. A smiling, friendly young man approached Abe with an outstretched hand. "Hello, I'm McGrady Rutledge. My uncle owns this establishment. We're glad to have you."

"Thanks," responded Abe. "I'm Abe Lincoln, a stranger from Kentucky."

"Well, you're not a stranger anymore. I saw earlier how you saved that boat. It was quite a good job of quick thinking."

"I appreciate the compliment, but I just did what I had to do."

"Mister Lincoln, you're quite a humble young man."

"I've never been any other way. It's the way my late mother taught me to be."

Stepping to one side for a moment, Abe ran his hand through his unruly coarse hair in a valiant effort to make himself more presentable. Dressed in an old raggedy pair of ill-fitting pants and a torn, sweaty shirt, he felt exposed.

Even though his whole appearance at first glance was that of a rugged individual, he was quite self-conscious. A closer more concentrated once over would have revealed an amazingly vulnerable, sensitive young man. Inside he was desperately lonely and equally desperately lost.

Whatever voices one listens to in growing up, Abe was still trying to find those voices. When he arrived that day in New Salem, his soul was incomplete. As Abe stared into the open fireplace, these thoughts weighed heavily on his mind and were perhaps revealed to anyone really focused on him.

Ann Rutledge was nearby with her mother and sisters preparing the meal for their visitors. Even though she was busy, she caught a glimpse of Lincoln's sad face. Her own discerning intuition into other people's thoughts and feelings was a gift. Somehow, she knew there was a deep sadness and hurt welled up inside him. These were feelings that desperately needed to come out and be discussed with an understanding individual. In that brief instant she knew she was the person who could help him.

Approaching him, she got his attention, "Mister Lincoln, we need to talk."

"We do?" Abe replied, snapping out of his depression, caught quite by surprise.

"After dinner, may we step out on the porch and talk?"

"Sure." Abe responded obligingly, thinking he was looking into the face of an angel.

Suddenly, Abe's spirits were lifted. His eyes followed after her as she returned to work. He could see all the women were busily engaged in meal preparation around the large open-hearth fireplace. Using long-handled cookware, they prepared a meal, the likes of which Abe and his crew hadn't had in several days. Sitting at a long wooden dining table, the four flatboat men enjoyed every bite of it.

Even though, outside of the great fireplace, lighting was by candle light, Abe somehow managed to keep his eye on the movements of Ann Rutledge. He noticed she was thin in stature, perhaps no more than five feet, six inches in height. One more thing he picked up on, truly touched him: no matter which way she turned, her face always seemed to glow. He had seen such a face only on two other women in his entire life, his mother and his sister. They were both dead now. Somehow though, he thought God was blessing him by putting him in the presence of the face of an angel again.

Sitting there, Abe thought these New Salem folk are kind people with good hearts, something he was not used to in his upbringing. This brought him around to thinking of Ann again. He couldn't seem to get the image of her out of his head.

Presently, James Rutledge got everyone's attention, passing out cups of rum. Being a non-drinker, he quickly responded, "None for me, thanks anyway Mister Rutledge. I think I'll go outside and get some fresh air."

As Abe stood up, his eyes connected with Ann again. She acknowledged by nodding silently at him.

With that, Abe turned and left the great room. Heading for the front porch, his mind was full of thoughts of meeting an angel.

CHAPTER 2
MEETING AN ANGEL

Abe sat alone on the front porch steps of the Rutledge Inn and Tavern, gazing at the tree line which rose behind the buildings that ran along the other side of Main Street. He became lost in his thoughts.

Seeing Abe was alone, Ann Rutledge came out on the porch behind him, whispering in a low voice, "A penny for your thoughts, Mister Lincoln."

Still halfway lost in his thoughts, staring at the row of cabins running across his field of vision on the other side of Main Street, he answered her, "Life has not been easy for me. I've just been existing, struggling to live." At that point, Abe became more engaged, glancing around slightly, looking back up at Ann, he continued, "Miss Rutledge, tell me what you think. Is it wrong for me to find a reason for living?"

"No Mister Lincoln, you should find your true calling. Once you've found it, pursue it and make it part of who you are."

Abe liked what she was saying. His curiosity aroused, he asked her, "Miss Rutledge, why did you follow me out here?"

"I saw something in your eyes that made me want to know more about you."

"I'm like a floating piece of driftwood, drifting aimlessly down the river, never quite knowing where I'll wind up."

"Who are you, Mister Lincoln?"

"I've always had a hard time getting to know other people. They don't understand me. I felt uncomfortable inside, awkward around

7

all those people. Sometimes I feel more at ease when I'm by myself. Am I making any sense?"

"I think you're doing a pretty good job of explaining yourself."

Abe had felt uncommonly candid with this girl, but to him she seemed so different from a lot of people he'd met. A kindness and sensitivity radiated from her. So he continued, "You see, I left home a short while ago, striking out on my own. I was friendless, uneducated, and penniless. I've groped around since then, trying to find myself. I feel awkward at times, like I mentioned earlier."

Ann's gift, getting Abe to open up was bearing fruit. She was beginning to understand his feelings far better than most people ever would. She picked up that he had an acute sense of worthlessness about himself. Inside, he was drowning. He had been hurt by someone and hurt deeply. She felt like he wanted help but didn't know how to ask. So this sensitive young woman with a remarkable intuitive sense reached out and asked, "How are you feeling right now?"

"I'm feeling like I'm not an animal."

"What makes you say a thing like that?"

"Life has been very fortunate to you Miss Rutledge. You are the daughter of an apparently loving and affectionate father. I on the other hand...well let's just say I have experienced a life full of sadness, one that has often been cruel."

"If you will allow me to ask, how so? In what way has your life been like that?" Seeing the pain in his face, she wanted to find a way to help him. "Would you tell me more about yourself?"

Abe began to open up, "I was born Abraham Lincoln on Sunday, February 12th, 1809 in Hardin County. That was in a small cabin on a farm, a few miles south of Hodgenville, Kentucky. My family was poor. My mother was in poor health as well, passing away in 1818. It was tough on me, I was just nine years old at the time. My sister Sarah died in childbirth three years ago. That was 1828, the same year I took my first flatboat trip to New Orleans. This is my second such trip, taking cargo to sell in New Orleans. I just turned twenty-two a couple of months ago."

"I'm eighteen myself," Ann broke in. "I was also born in Kentucky, near Henderson Kentucky that is. But go ahead, tell me more about your family."

"Well," Abe tried to recall, "I know from our old family Bible. One of my ancestors, Samuel Lincoln, came from England in 1637. Among his descendants, my namesake and grandfather, Abraham Lincoln, fought to free the colonies from England during the Revolutionary War. He survived that conflict only to be killed by a drunkin' renegade Indian. So, I never had the honor of knowing someone who might have had a great influence on my life."

"What about your father, Mister Lincoln?"

"My father, Thomas Lincoln, witnessed the incident that took my grandfather's life. He was his third son and just a boy at the time. I think he may have been permanently scarred by that event. After that, as he grew up I'm told he began to drink heavily. He became an angry man, mad at the world. Nothing I ever did, no matter how hard I tried, ever seemed to please him. He liked to beat me, treating me little better than a slave. If it hadn't been for my mother, I think that he might have killed me." At that point Abe went silent, tears welling up in his visibly sad eyes.

Feeling for him, Ann came down on the porch steps, sitting down beside him. Leaning over closer to his face, her voice became genuinely caring, "I'm so sorry this happened to you. No one ever should be treated that way."

Rising above the turmoil that had risen up within him, Abe looked deep into her piercing blue eyes, asking, "Can you possibly imagine how it feels to not really have a father?"

"I don't want to imagine it."

"Miss Rutledge, your father seems like a warm, friendly person."

"He is. He's always been that way. He's not only my father, he's my best friend."

"I wish I could've had a father that way. After my mother died, it got worse. That next year my father didn't care anything about my sister and myself. He drank and drank while us kids barely survived on the dirt floor of that pathetic little cabin. We went days with little or nothing to eat and no change of clothes for weeks at a time. He treated us like two cast-off animals. We almost died."

"What saved you Mister Lincoln?"

"An angel came into my life in the form of my step-mother, Mrs. Sarah Johnston. She was a widow from over in Elizabethtown, Kentucky. Somehow my father convinced her to marry him. She was better than what he deserved. She took us kids and raised us right alongside her own son, John Johnston, as if we were her own as well. She set me on the pathway of knowledge as best she could. I call her 'mother' to this day and I always will."

"So, what will you do now since you are on your own?"

"After I finish this trip to New Orleans, I guess I'll be looking to settle down, hopefully in a nice quiet secluded place. I was just thinking about that when you came out on the porch. New Salem, being back from the bluff and almost hidden by the surrounding tree line, is sort of a secret place. Unless one knows it's here, it's out of sight from the rest of the world. Perhaps I'll find a home like this, somewhere." Glancing down, Abe was becoming lost in his thoughts again.

Ann though, was becoming inspired with an idea, "Mister Lincoln," she said, getting his attention by putting her hand on his arm, getting him to look up at her. She smiled and said, "Perhaps you might even come back here and find a home in New Salem."

"Perhaps you might be right," he said, smiling back. Then he added, "There's one more thing."

"What's that?"

"I'd be right pleased if you didn't call me Mister Lincoln any-more. Please, just call me Abe."

"Alright, Abe, but you have to call me Ann. All my friends do so."

"Ann, if I may say so, you've been so full of kindness to this stranger who knows so little and is so lacking in education." Feeling liberated by her steady gaze, he continued, "You're an angel. If there ever was such a thing as an angel in human form, it is you. Ann, you're my first friend here. I arrived here this morning a friendless young man, knowing nobody. But now, I have at least one friend in New Salem."

"You can count on that, Abe."

"I'm thanking you for that, with all my heart, Miss Ann."

Hearing this, she reached over and squeezed his hand warmly and affectionately. After that, their eyes searched each other in a wordless beginning to a friendship that would become the stuff of legend.

Even as they both parted for the evening, they both felt in their hearts there was something wonderful, even possibly spiritual about their connection. Only time would give answers to this speculation.

CHAPTER 3
FACING THE PAST

The next morning, Abe got up with a lot weighing heavily upon his mind. His head was full of ghosts from his past. They had come to him in the form of dreams that had taken him back to his childhood. Coming down from the loft, within the Rutledge tavern, he found his way to the front porch again.

It was not quite daylight as the sun was only just beginning to rise above the horizon. Ready for a new day, Abe was already staring in that direction.

"Abe, you're an early riser." The silence was broken by the voice of Ann Rutledge from behind him.

Getting his attention, Abe turned around in her direction, explaining, "I thought I might meet the morning sun right here on your front porch. I've come to believe each day is a gift from God. But, why are you up so early, Miss Ann?"

"I get up early when we have guests staying overnight."

"Truth be told," admitted Abe, "I couldn't sleep any longer. Vivid memories of my past came back to visit me in my dreams last night. Yet, even as this day is only just beginning, I feel curiously at peace already."

"None-the-less," Ann observed, "one must face the past before one can begin a new future."

"Well said, Ann Rutledge. Yesterday you asked me who I was. I guess you could say I'm the product of the losses I've suffered in life. When I lost my mother and later my sister, each time I lost part of myself. Within the downward spiral I fell into, I almost lost myself entirely. When I think about it, frankly I'm surprised that there's anything left of me."

"Oh Abe, there's a lot left in you."

"If there's anything left in me, it would certainly be due to my birth mother, Nancy Hanks Lincoln."

"You must have loved her a lot."

"All that I am, or ever hope to be, I owe to her. I've been told, as she held me in her arms after I was born, she called me 'God's little angel'. She told others that I had been sent straight from Heaven for her to raise in the ways of the Lord. Trying to do the right thing, she worked and slaved herself almost to death. What finally took her though was getting hold of some poison milk. My mother was just 35 years old when she passed away, far too young for a person to die. She never knew much happiness in her short life. In those nine years I knew her, no son ever loved a mother more. Often I wish somehow I could've done more for her. It's one of my great regrets."

"Abe, don't reproach yourself so much. I don't believe she would've wanted that. You were the son she loved and you loved her right back with the same devotion. I'm sure you will treasure memories of her forever, for the good woman she was."

"Ann, you're right again. You know, I still remember exactly what she told me the last day of her life. I was at her bedside as she looked up at me and said, 'Love the Lord and keep His commandments. Do this and surely His goodness and mercy will be with you all the days of your life.' Right after that, she took one deep breath and closed her eyes forever."

"How did your father react to this?"

"I don't know. You see, he wasn't there. He was too busy working out in the fields. He couldn't be bothered with her dying."

"Didn't he care?"

"Thomas Lincoln didn't have any feelings a day in his life, not for anyone except for himself. My sister and myself, were the only ones at our mother's bedside during her final moments."

"But Abe, after your father returned from the fields, did he do or say anything?"

"He never said a word, but at least to his credit he did do something. Being a carpenter of sorts, he fashioned a crude coffin to bury her in. I watched as he took two large pennies of those times and put them on her eyelids to hold them down. My sister and I watched as he placed her body into that coffin, nail it shut and lower it into an unmarked grave. Then, he just walked away. After our father left, my sister and I stayed there alone, overlooking our mother's grave. A multitude of feelings tore my heart out. I made sure that there was at least a simple wooden cross to mark her grave. No preacher was present to pray over her, so I prayed for her and remembered her soul to God."

"Good for you Abe, you did the right thing. God bless you for it."

"I wanted to make God the center of my life, honoring my mother's dying wish that I love the Lord and keep His commandments, but my father was against it."

"Against it! How could he be against something like that?"

"I will explain. The very night after my mother died, I prayed for His presence in my life. After falling asleep, sometime during the night a bright light appeared nearby and awakened me. From within the light a voice whispered, *I am an ever-present help in the time of your need.* I felt comforted from my grief, feeling God's presence in my life, lifting me up. I'll never forget what happened next for as long as I live."

Ann immediately revealed her own faith, "I believe it was the Lord's presence comforting you, heart and soul during the time of your loss."

"That's what I thought. I will always believe that my mother's soul went to Heaven to be with the Lord. She had been a woman of faith, who always seemed to live life with the Spirit of the Lord within her, reading stories from the Bible to us children. I like to think her angel spirit had something to do with God's words comforting me."

"Abe, what happened next, that you said you would never forget?"

"In my eagerness to help my father from the grief I believed he was suffering, I told him about my experience. Reacting, he became enraged and hit me in the face. He yelled at me, calling me a lazy dreamer. He told me God didn't talk to us humans anymore. He hit me some more and would never permit me to speak of the Lord again, that somehow what I was saying was sinful. From that day on he treated me more like his slave than his son."

Churning up memories from his past, telling Ann this story brought tears to his eyes. They so obviously matched the hurt he was feeling in his heart. Ann sensed this as she moved closer, gently touching his shoulder, comforting him. Even more so, her understanding voice comforted his heart, "You're a kind and sensitive person. In my whole life I've never met a man quite like you. Jesus said, *I am with you always.* Never believe anyone who would tell you otherwise. I for one will be praying for you. God bless you, Abe."

Silently, his eyes studied her face. The sincerity in her voice and whole expression, touched his heart again. "Back then, in 1818, I felt very much alone. I haven't had anyone pray for me since my mother passed away. Just talking to you, I don't feel so alone anymore."

"After your mother passed, didn't your father make any attempt to get closer to you kids?"

"To the contrary, he ignored me and my sister, like we weren't even there. Sometimes I wonder if he didn't wish we would die too. During the next several months, perhaps for almost a year after my mother was gone, we ate what little food we could get our hands on. We ate with our dirty little fingers as we had no baths for several months. Every time we looked over at our father, he would be almost constantly drinking, one jug after another."

"It must have been so awful to live like that."

"Yes, Ann, it was. Those were desperate times where we teetered precariously between life and death. We probably would've died had it not been for our Heaven-sent stepmother that I told you about yesterday. She cleaned us up and fed us. More than anyone else, she cared, and kept us alive."

"After your stepmother came, did your father treat you differently?"

"Yes, definitely worse. His abusive treatment of me, both mentally and physically continued throughout my youth. During those years I grew from a young kid into a teenager, reaching my present height of six feet, four inches, the last time I checked. In this same period of time my father drove me hard. He had me out in the fields working constantly often before daylight till it was almost dark again. When he could, he would 'rent' me out to others for hard labor work in the fields. He told my stepmother that every cent I made was his as long as I lived under his roof. He said, as I belonged to him, I was due nothing more than the food I ate from his table."

"How could a father treat a son like that?"

"You must remember, in his view I had become just another piece of property to him, one that he could use for whatever purpose suited him."

"What he put you through, it was hard, grueling work?"

"It was more than that, it was back-breaking. Only through sheer force of will have I survived the last few years. Being out in the hot sun, I was constantly perspiring and absolutely miserable. The sunlight was always bright and unrelenting. Constant exposure to this environment caused my skin to tan to the point it was almost brown in color and leathery in texture."

"That's how you were affected on the outside, but how were you affected on the inside? How was your personality?"

"I had no personality. I became a young man living a life of forced solitude, only confiding my most inner feelings to my stepmother. Inside, I was bursting at the seams. Desperate, I tried to figure a way out from my father's control."

"That was the case with you, but how about your sister? What happened to her?"

"My sister Sarah was treated equally bad by our father. In time, she also became desperate to escape from under our father's roof. She became so desperate that she would accept almost any way out. To that end, she accepted a marriage proposal from a rather slow-witted young man named Aaron Grigsby. They were married in 1826."

"So, your sister did escape your father's domination?"

"Yes, Sarah finally escaped our controlling father, but her happiness was short lived. Eighteen months later she died from complications during childbirth. As I said, her husband was very slow-witted. He waited far too long to get a doctor. Her baby was stillborn. My sister, God rest her soul, died on the morning of January 20th 1828, three years ago. The day she was buried, with her baby in the same casket with her, I went through the same heartbreak all over again that I did when I lost my mother. The memory still haunts me to this day."

"And your father, did he not show any compassion or love when your sister passed away?"

"No compassion, none whatsoever. As for love, I don't think my father has ever known the meaning of the word. With my sister's death though, I knew I would have to get away from him. If I did remain under his roof, I knew I would die young just like Sarah. I just knew it."

"Knowing this, there's one other thing I'm curious about. Abe, how did you wind up in Illinois?"

"By the winter of 1830, the milk sickness that took the life of my mother returned to the valley where my family lived. For the first time, real fear entered the mind of my father, I could see it in his face and hear it in his voice. He had sufficient motivation then to move from the disease infected area in which we lived. He'd heard tales from Indians of a place in Illinois they called the Sangamon which meant a land rich in food to eat. That's when my family decided to brave the winter and come to Illinois."

"After your family got to Illinois, did your father's attitude toward you change at all?"

"Not in the least. By then he was fixed in his low opinion of me. So when the very idea of this flatboat journey came up, it meant far more to me than anyone realized. It meant a chance for freedom at last. I had just turned 22 years old and when the subject of this trip came up as a very real possibility, he tried to discourage me, telling me to my face he still thought of me as worthless. He said I would be useless to the others and I would be better off just remaining on the farm. I didn't listen to him. Instead, when Mister Offutt offered me the flatboat job. I snapped at the opportunity when it came my way."

"Good for you, Abe! You will prove your father wrong. I'm glad you took the job." Ann's approval was written all over her face.

"Ann, I'm bound and determined to make the most of this opportunity and never look back." Pondering his situation for a quick moment, he smiled and added, "This has been the first glimmer of hope in my beaten down, slave-like life."

"I hope so for your sake. It's finally your chance to become a man on your own. Something else, Abe…" Her voice trailed off into silence.

"What? Please tell me."

"You ARE your own man. Despite what your father thinks, or says, you set your own destiny. I believe, even though you may not know it, the Lord has been with you a very long time."

"I believe you might be right," responded Abe, thinking about it. "What happened to me growing up is never going to happen again. I'm never going back home to that man again. This journey has been like a breath of fresh air to me, opening my mind up to new possibilities. Our conversations have got me to facing my past and more importantly to thinking about my future. I'm going to start a new life someplace else."

"I'm glad you feel that way for your sake. I want…" She hesitated, not finishing.

"What do you want, Ann?" Abe sensed she had more to say. She did.

"I want you to come back here." Ann was full of visible sincerity as she said it.

"What?" Abe wanted to be sure he understood what she said.

"After your trip to New Orleans, I would like very much to see you come back here to New Salem." Extending her hand toward him, Ann continued, "Take my hand and promise me that you'll come back."

Abe took her hand into his, and quietly whispered, "I promise."

Later, after breakfast, as the flatboat crew left the Rutledge Inn, Ann looked on from the front porch. As they departed, her father joined her. "Ann, I'm curious, what do you think of Mister Lincoln?"

"Father, I found him to be far different than most of the rough frontier folk that pass through here. He's definitely cut from a different cloth."

"Yes daughter, I agree. I could see he was a sensitive, serious-minded individual–just like you."

Walking eastward down Main Street, the four flatboat men made their way out of the little village. Getting to the bluff, where it sloped down to where their flatboat was anchored, Abe turned for one last glace at New Salem.

Denton Offutt, who was beside him, asked, "What's the matter, Abe?"

"Nothing really, I was just taking in the early morning smell."

"What smell?" asked Offutt.

Abe made a wide sweeping gesture toward the two dozen or so cabins and rickety shacks that stretched south of Main street. "Denton, there's nothing like the odor of crackling firewood on a cold morning."

Offutt agreed, "Makes one want to stay, rather than leave."

"Yes," sympathized Abe. "I'm thinking after we deliver our goods to New Orleans, I might want to come back here."

"Well, you'll have a chance to."

"How so, Denton?"

"While you were talking to Rutledge's daughter last night I was working up a business deal with Mister Rutledge."

"You did?"

"Yes, and he agreed to sell me a vacant lot up here on the bluff, where we could build a general store of sorts."

So it was, the deal was set. Offutt had shaken hands with James Rutledge on it. Furthermore, he would want to hire Abe to clerk in the store and otherwise manage it.

Denton Offutt was a man with a vision of the future as well. He saw an opportunity in New Salem. He knew the Sangamon River emptied into the Illinois River, and it in turn emptied into the Mississippi. This could build into a new shipping route to New Orleans. Offutt explained to Abe, "This very settlement could become a good stopping off place along the way. That's what got me to thinking it might be a good idea to build a store here."

Abe reacted, "That's good news, Denton." Abe knew he would be just the man to clerk and run such a store for him.

With these new revelations rolling around inside his head, Abe turned from the bluff to go down and rejoin the others on the flatboat. As they sailed away, he watched the tree line close off New Salem from view. From this distance he saw a huge shaft of sunlight break through the clouds and bless the land beneath it. He imagined that was where this little settlement would be up on the plateau. He thought to himself, the Spirit of the Lord must be watching over this place.

In that moment, a strange sense that he belonged here welled up inside Abe. Thinking about it, he whispered to himself, "This unexpected stop here is part of a bigger thing called destiny." Central to this thought was that Ann Rutledge would play an important role within that destiny to come. These thoughts stayed with him during his entire journey to New Orleans.

CHAPTER 4
FINDING A NEW HOME

Denton Offutt enjoyed listening to Abe on the flatboat journey to New Orleans. He warmed to his jokes and stories as their friendship further cemented itself. Like most everyone who grew close to Abe, Offutt found him to be an honest, well-meaning young man. Lincoln became his close confident as a shared dream formed between the two men. Offutt's vision to establish a successful store in New Salem was on its way to becoming reality.

Arriving in New Orleans, Abe saw a number of things he didn't like. What was repellent to him could be boiled down to one word, slavery. Seeing families torn apart and human beings savagely beaten, struck a nerve in his memories. Remembering the slave-like treatment he received at the hands of his own father, made him especially sympathetic to those suffering in bondage. Considering all the images, shoved in his face while he was in New Orleans, he could not wait to leave that southern city.

Seeing Abe's discomfort, Denton Offutt secured passage for him aboard a steamboat going north to Saint Louis. From there, Abe made his way back to New Salem, sometimes by stagecoach, but more often on foot. Making the long trek, one step at a time, it became far more than a physical journey. It became something spiritual. He had plenty of time to think things over. Seeing how certain experiences had completely and profoundly changed him, he now had a clearer vision of who and what were the guiding forces in his life.

Particularly from Springfield, the road became ever more primitive, sometimes just a crude path. The winding road cut through dark foreboding forests for long stretches at a time. After many miles, the thick cluster of trees began to thin out and open up to a clear, unobstructed view of what was in front of him.

A smattering of crude cabins became visible in the distance. They were almost evenly divided on either side of the Springfield Road. In no certain order, they rose from the ground among uncertain boundaries in irregular fashion.

At last Abe knew he was getting close to his goal. Even the exhaustion of such a long journey could not hold him back. Picking up the pace, he walked in a determined manner till he reached the point where the Springfield Road dead ended into Main Street. At this crossroads he froze in his tracks.

A multitude of thoughts ran through Abe's mind as he stood there motionless. As he had approached from a distance, he saw shafts of morning sunlight penetrating through the clouds above, blessing the little settlement with Heaven sent warmth. He was awe struck in that moment, feeling the presence of an invisible God watching over this place from somewhere far above. It was the brilliance of our Lord illuminating this very spot. Feeling His presence within his mind and heart, Abe was humbled to his very core, whispering, "I'm home."

Those two simple words bore a world of significance to Abe and would stay with him for years to come. It was late July 1831 when young Lincoln walked back into New Salem, keeping a promise to himself and to Ann Rutledge. Awakening him from his moments of meditation, Abe noticed movement of people nearby. Men on horseback and in horse-drawn wagons were making their way busily up and down Main Street. The sleepy little settlement had come alive and he was in the very heart of this activity.

Focusing on the Rutledge Inn a short distance away, Abe remembered the recent past of just a few months ago. Inwardly, he went through a moment of reflection. It took him a while to clearly understand what would happen next. He felt the presence of a Higher Power enter him and speak to his mind, *You belong here.*

Abe would remember what the Voice told him. It would echo in his mind for years. In that instant of time there was no more hungry soul than Abe Lincoln. He had been searching for a place to put down roots and make a meaningful life for himself. In that very spiritual moment he found a new home.

Feeling more determined than ever now, he bounded across the Springfield Road, walking at a fast clip right up to the porch of the Rutledge Inn. As fate would have it, Ann Rutledge had just stepped out on the porch. Even though it had been nearly three months, Abe immediately recognized her as he approached. "Ann," he called out, "I'm back."

"Oh, Abe!" Her whole face lit up. "I'm so very glad you came back." One could see it in her eyes and expression that she truly meant it.

"Ann, I'm home. On my way up the Springfield Road, the town just seemed to spring out of the earth, welcoming me back. Then a strange thing happened as I got closer. I heard a little voice inside my head telling me I was home."

Taking Abe's hand, she led him up on the porch, seating him in a chair there. "Now listen to me very carefully," she said continuing, "Abe, I believe the good Lord often helps us in ways we don't really realize at the time He's doing it. I've come to believe God speaks to our hearts. It's up to us if we listen, or not. I believe His Holy Spirit was attempting to give you a message for your life. I think God motivates and alters our lives in subtle ways that most of us never pick up on."

Sitting there, Abe took in every word she said. Her soft spoken, sincere voice totally convinced him. He responded quite simply, "I believe you. New Salem is such a fresh, beautiful place. I couldn't help wanting to live here and be a part of all this. I want to add something to what you said about Divine guidance. From the first time I came back in April, I felt His presence around New Salem. In fact, even now I feel it here. To my mind, it makes New Salem the special place it is today."

"God bless you, Abe. I believe the Lord wanted you here. A lot of people fail to understand that this land, this world, is His creation. We are here only as its caretakers, while we're here."

"You are so wise for one so young," said Abe, admiring her. All at once he saw not only the beauty of her youth, but also a maturity and wisdom that was way beyond her years.

Getting closer, sitting down in a chair beside him, she could not know her next question would bring back some recent uncomfortable images. She innocently asked, "How was your trip to New Orleans?"

"I didn't like what I saw there." A deeply troubled expression had formed on his face as he spoke.

"Abe, what did you see there?"

"I saw things that reminded me of my past. I saw cruelty and human suffering. I saw slavery in its worst form, poor pathetic people being savagely beaten and treated like animals. Seeing so many human beings completely devoid of any compassion for their fellow man seemed so wrong. More than that, it was a sin."

"It must have seemed like a nightmare."

"Only it was real, the worst reality I've ever seen. Ann, it's not right. All men are created equal, at least in God's eyes."

"If you feel that strongly, maybe you ought to do something about it."

"Perhaps one day I will." What Abe had seen in New Orleans were among the worst examples of the slave trade, images that would burn deep into his mind and memory, things he would never forget. Immersed in his deepest thoughts, he added, "I don't like to think about it, but here I am talking about it."

"Maybe it'll do you some good to get it off your chest."

Looking into her kind, receptive face, he reacted, "It already has."

"Abe, I'm glad you talked to me."

"Maybe that's why the Lord brought me back here, so that I could see you and talk to you again."

As they studied each other silently, Abe extended his hand toward her, taking her hand into his, squeezing it affectionately. He had opened up his heart to her again, revealing his deepest feelings.

In turn, Ann revealed herself again, to be truly a good person, something that emanated from a place down deep within her heart. At this point, knowing something, she spoke up about it, "I understand from my father that Mister Offutt is buying a business lot here in New Salem."

Abe recognized the importance of Ann's statement, immediately responding in the affirmative, "Yes, it's true."

"That's wonderful news!" Ann reacted obviously pleased.

"I'm very happy about it," he added. "It looks like I'm going to manage the store for him."

Denton Offutt had already followed through on his promises. On July 8th, 1831, the County Commissioners Court of Sangamon County had granted Offutt a business license to sell merchandise in a retail store in New Salem. The license fee at the time totaled the sum of five dollars in 1831 money.

Denton Offutt was an old-fashioned Kentucky horse whisperer, sort of like a P.T. Barnum wheeler-dealer of his time. Chubby and blustery, he was also quite a jovial character. At times he was a little too fond of drink, as many who knew him remarked. Though much about him has been lost to history, much is known through his connection with young Abe Lincoln.

Upon his return from New Orleans, Offutt secured lot 14, North of Main Street, from James Rutledge. It was his express purpose of building his store there. The purchase price for the lot was ten dollars.

The Offutt store was a primitive affair for those times. Consisting of a small one-room building with one off-center front door with just one window facing the street, the building had little storefront appeal. Inside, the layout of its one little rectangular room was quite simplistic with just one long counter running parallel to the walls. Yet, despite these limitations, curiosity brought customers inside, at least for a while. It would be up to the store manager's charismatic personality to keep them coming back.

It was within this little store that Abe had his first extended contact with the citizens of New Salem. He was outgoing, personable, and honest. This led very quickly to the frontier people living there taking him into their hearts as one of their own. This acceptance, cemented Abe's feelings that he truly was home. Like no other time in his young life, he no longer felt like he was drifting aimlessly. That sense of internal struggle was fast disappearing, rapidly being replaced by a measure of new-found confidence.

From the beginning, Offutt realized that both he and Abe were strangers in New Salem. He began a search with the intention of hiring young Lincoln an assistant who was knowledgeable of the folks who lived in and around the area. His search led him to just such a person, a young 19-year-old who lived on his father's farm about a mile southwest of New Salem. William G. Greene–or just Billy Greene as he was known by everyone–turned out to be perfect for the job of assistant clerk.

Billy Greene proved to be an invaluable help to young Lincoln. He easily took on the role of properly introducing Abe to his customers. Billy was aware of everyone's credit worthiness and would frequently pull Abe aside, whispering to him if the customer's credit was any good.

As the hours of work were long and tiresome, Billy would often stay overnight at the store. At least at first, as Abe had no money, he slept in the store as well. Thrown together under such circumstances, the both of them having rural backgrounds and similar outlooks on life, grew to confide in each other and become fast friends. Abe and Billy would often–after hours–play checkers well into the night.

The bonds of their friendship quickly grew, to them becoming almost like brothers. Abe felt like he could tell him his deepest secrets. Abe revealed to him what he had to few others, his lack of formal education. He had attended school less than one year in his whole life. Beyond being able to barely sign his own name, he was only barely able to read the most simple of children's stories and a few simple Bible verses. Beyond what his birth mother taught him as a child was beyond him.

"I want to change all that," Abe said. "Billy, I would like to be able to sign my own name. That's why I sign things just as 'A. Lincoln.' It's too many letters for me to remember. I want to be better than myself. Is that not possible?"

"Of course it is, Abe." Billy wanted to help his new friend. Having lived in Illinois for the past ten years, he had attended school as taught by the local Scottish school master, Mentor Graham. Billy had acquired a working knowledge of reading and writing and now wanted to pass on what he knew to Abe. During their off time, Billy would spend many hours every day helping him learn to read and write. Billy's help in opening up new worlds of knowledge for him was something Abe never forgot.

It was now mid-September 1831 and every day seemed to bring someone of worth and value into Abe's life. In that first week they were opened, a very well-dressed man entered the store, gazing around, till his eyes fell on Abe, where they remained.

Abe felt as if he was being sized up. He was right. Almost at the same time he felt a nudge from Billy. Leaning over to him, Billy whispered, "That's Doctor Allen. He came to town about a month after you came here, back in April."

Walking with a very noticeable limp, which he never discussed, Doctor Allen approached the counter. Stopping directly across from Abe, he extended his hand in an offer of friendship. Identifying himself, he said, "Mister Lincoln, I'm Doctor John Allen. I just want to say, I'm glad you decided to come here, because the town needs more people like you."

"Thanks Doc," responded Abe, shaking hands with him. "But, if I may ask, what type of person am I, that the town needs more people like me?"

"Miss Ann Mayes Rutledge spoke highly of you. She thought we ought to meet."

Hearing this, Abe studied the young doctor more closely. Tall, over six feet, but not as tall as Abe, he was a clean-shaven young man of about thirty. The feature that really stood out through was the doctor's piercing gaze that really seemed to analyze a person.

Taking the doctor's words in, Abe replied, "Well, if Miss Ann thought we should meet, I'm glad you came over." Abe's winning smile and outgoing personality really shined in that moment. Still though, a lingering curiosity within him caused Abe to ask, "If anything, what else did Miss Ann say about me?"

"Mr. Lincoln, Miss Ann says you're a man of faith and deep convictions. So am I. I understand we're both newcomers to New Salem."

"Yes, that's correct."

"I came all the way from Chelsea, Vermont, hoping to start a new life here in the West. I was hoping to find the essence of God's country. I believe I found it when I arrived in New Salem. Almost immediately, I decided to stay. I bought vacant lots, 3 and 4, near the Rutledge Inn, where I'm building a home and office for my medical practice. Miss Ann also said you had a similar experience in coming here."

"Yes, I very much did. I felt like the Lord wanted me here. For what purpose I do not yet know."

"Only the future may tell, Mr. Lincoln."

"Please Doc, call me Abe. I hope very much that we can be friends."

The two men would become friends and would remain so through some of the most trying times that would be interwoven through both of their lives. The good Lord sometimes works in mysterious ways. Perhaps he wanted these two men of faith to be close in the trying years to come.

The next day in the store, in walked a man with a shock-wave of unruly bright red hair. Again, Billy was at Lincoln's ear. "Abe, that's him, that's schoolmaster Graham, the man who taught me to read and write. You need to meet him."

The red-haired man had a distinct twinkle in one of his eyes as he approached the counter. Yet, he stepped back and watched how Abe handled other customers. Finally, the store cleared, leaving just Abe, Billy, and Mentor Graham. He had listened carefully to Abe and his conversations with customers. Coming up to the counter opposite Abe, he introduced himself, "I'm schoolmaster Graham at a little school just outside of New Salem, that is when we have enough pupils. Billy here used to be one of my students. On the other hand, I've always been available to do some tutoring on the side."

Abe glanced over at Billy, referring to him, "Billy's been telling me what a wonderful teacher you are."

"Educating others is something I wanted to do from a very early age. I've devoted my life to that end."

"Teaching is a wonderful thing," observed Abe. "There's no more noble profession than being a school teacher, expanding the minds of others."

"That's so nice of you to say, Mister Lincoln."

"I'm just plain Abe to my friends. I just want to be considered a friendly neighbor by everyone."

"Abe, I think you'll succeed at it. Watching you earlier, I was impressed."

"Thank you, Mister Graham. I appreciate your kind words."

"Abe, you're a 'people' person. It's a rare gift, actually very few possess. I noticed you're outgoing to the customers and accommodating to them. Keep it up and they will think of you more than a store clerk. They will embrace you as a friend."

"I want that also. But I want to learn more, get a better education and improve myself."

"Whenever you're ready to learn more, come and see me. I live out a little west of town. Billy will tell you how to get there."

After Graham left the store, Billy said, "Abe, I think he likes you."

Mentor Graham did indeed like Abe Lincoln. He thought of him as a bright young store clerk with a thirst for knowledge. There was more though. He sensed an invisible spark of something unknown that would arouse his interest in Abe, time and time again. And too, there was something familiar about Abe that he couldn't put his finger on. For now though, he would ponder it only as a passing thought.

In those first two weeks the store prospered, keeping Abe and Billy busy. Unfortunately, Denton Offutt had nothing to do now, but just watch his two clerks work. This did not suite him at all. He was bored. Very shortly his old bad habits would come back to haunt him. He would succumb to a major weakness of his. That is to say, he had a deep and abiding love for corn whiskey.

It was only 30 short steps from the Offutt store to Clary's Saloon. More often than not, Denton Offutt could be found there getting very liquored up. Little did he know it, but one day soon he would become like 'Daniel in the lion's den.' He was going to be baited by William Clary for spiteful reasons.

Up to now the Clary saloon had enjoyed business dominance in the area. Bill Clary was the sole proprietor of a saloon for the hard drinkers of the county who would come from far and wide to spend their money in his establishment. It had been the sole business up on the bluff. But now, here was another business so very close to his own. It was a place where the frontier folk could spend their monies on more useful things than hard drinks.

Bill Clary saw his money-making business of the past three years drop significantly in three short weeks. He had seen young Lincoln standing outside the Offutt store, luring customers inside– potentially his customers–with his gift of gab. They would come out of the Offutt store, carrying arm loads of farm tools and supplies. Then they would have no money to spend on drinks. Clary was furious, ate up with jealousy. It was HIS money, or so he thought. Now it was being stolen by this hick from the backwoods of Kentucky. Something had to be done.

So Clary worked up a plan to take Lincoln down and put him out of commission. Part of what he would do was a plan of entrapment of unsuspecting Denton Offutt. On one afternoon of what had become a daily ritual, Offutt came through the saloon doors, bragging as usual.

"So how's business?" Clary asked him, with his ulterior motive in the back of his mind.

"My business is going through the roof. I'm making money hand over fist."

"But Denton, you're over here most of the time. What's your secret?"

"My secret is the best head clerk a business could have. You see, I have such a man in young Lincoln."

Clary paused, just long enough to refill Offutt's mug clear to the top. Then he continued, "I've got several good bartenders working for me and I've still been losing a lot of money the past two weeks."

After taking another huge gulp of whiskey, Offutt continued to boast, "Clary, the reason you're losing money is because my man Lincoln is a better clerk than anybody you've got working for you over here. In fact, he's better than all your people combined."

Upon hearing this, it was all Clary could do to contain himself. Turning red-faced, he was fuming underneath. He formed his mouth into a fake smile and asked, "Mister Offutt, is your man Lincoln good at anything else besides clerking?"

"Yes, of course he is," fired back Offutt without batting an eyelash. Now he was off and running in his boasting, "Abe's a man of tremendous physical strength. He can whip anybody, anywhere!"

A cunning smile flickered across Clary's face. He could spring his trap now. "I bet you my man Jack Armstrong can take him. He's county champion."

Offutt couldn't stop himself then. "Clary, Lincoln can whip any man alive! I'll bet you ten dollars that Abe can whip him."

"Done! I'll take that bet." Clary was smiling ear to ear.

Offutt was thunderstruck in that moment. He began to think about what he'd just done. Hearing laughter off to one side, he turned around to see it was coming from the table behind him. There sat three men drinking heavily, laughing at him. Offutt reacted, "What's so funny?"

"You are, Offutt," answered one of this rowdy group. "Don't you know who Jack Armstrong is?"

"Not really."

"Well, I'll tell you who he is. In all the matches he's fought, he remains undefeated. His physical prowess is unequalled. Jack Armstrong is not going down easy. Your man is not going to be too happy when he finds out you've put him in a fight without his knowledge or consent."

The man beside him at the table, laughed as well and added, "Offutt, you've really shot your mouth off this time. With friends like you, young Lincoln doesn't need enemies."

The laughter that followed grew louder and hit Offutt like a hard slap in the face. Awakened from his drunken stupor, Offutt staggered back to his store with what had just happened. It weighed heavily upon his mind. He knew one thing for sure, he would have to face his head clerk with some unwelcome news.

This careless wager could have far-reaching consequences. Young Lincoln had found a new home in New Salem, but now would he be able to keep it? He might even have to stand his ground and fight for it, or be ran out of town. What should he do? What would he do?

CHAPTER 5
MEETING JACK ARMSTRONG

Back in the general store, Denton Offutt had just explained the situation:

"You did what?!" Abe reacted with indignation and surprise. "Mister Offutt, you made this bet without asking or telling me anything about it. I don't fight a man without good reason. No, I won't have anything to do with it."

"But Abe," Offutt protested, "I'll lose my ten dollars. After all, we've been through so much together. I've helped you when you've needed help. Now I need your help in this one little thing."

"Fighting another man is more than just a little thing."

"There's one more thing you're not considering," added Offutt, taking a slightly different approach.

"What's that?" asked Abe.

"This Jack Armstrong, he's the Clary's Grove champion. Those Clary boys are a bunch of hard-core ruffians. They'll be coming to town looking for a fight. If you don't fight this Armstrong fella, they'll think you a coward. Worse, they will probably run you and me both out of town."

"Then I guess I have no choice. I'll have to fight him, that is if I want to stay here in New Salem and be left alone."

"Oh thank you, Abe!" Offutt appeared visibly relieved, wiping a bit of perspiration from his forehead.

"One thing though," added Abe, "don't you ever volunteer me to fight someone again. Is that understood?"

"Understood, never again." Trying to make a quick exit before Abe changed his mind, Offutt started edging toward the door.

Abe was curious. "And just where are you going, Mister Offutt?"

"Oh, I uh," Offutt was trying to think quickly. "I guess I'd better go and tell Bill Clary the fight is on."

"One minute, Mister Offutt. Just when and where is this fight supposed to take place?"

"Right outside, halfway between our two stores, this Saturday, twelve noon straight up."

"That means I have only four days to prepare for this fight."

Sensing Abe's rising anxiety again, Offutt thought it best to make an immediate exit. "Well, I better go and make the arrangements with Clary." With that, Offutt left the store to avoid any further questions from Abe.

Abe turned to Billy Greene who'd been standing nearby the whole time. "Billy, what has Denton Offutt just gotten me into?"

"You've known Offutt a lot longer than I have."

"I've been in a few fights in my time, but should I really fight this Armstrong fella?"

"Abe, I know this Jack Armstrong and I've watched him fight many times."

"What's he like?"

"He's shorter than you, only about five feet, nine inches tall. Stocky built, muscular, he's as strong as an ox. But, if you move around a lot and avoid his crushing bear hugs, you just might wear him down. I'll teach you some of his moves to avoid."

"But Billy, do I stand a chance against him?"

"Well, maybe. Try not to get too close to him and you just might come out of this okay."

"You're not offering me much hope, are you?"

"I'm just being honest when I give you my opinions. False hope is not worth a plug nickel. Truth on the other hand, may be worth something to you."

"It is, Billy. You're a good friend."

The prospect of meeting Jack Armstrong weighed heavily upon Abe's mind. Early the next day, he was alone, getting ready to open the store when the front door opened. One anxious person entered to confront him.

It was Ann Rutledge. Concern was written on her face before she ever opened her mouth. Abe knew what had happened. Overnight, news of the upcoming fight had started spreading throughout New Salem.

"Abe, is it true?" She asked, her voice full of worry.

"Yes, it's true." Abe could only tell the truth.

She explained her concern, "I know of Jack Armstrong. I've seen him be a tough, brutal troublemaker and a bully to others. When challenged, I've seen him lash out at others and hurt them badly."

"Ann, I'll be careful. Armstrong's reputation precedes him. When I meet him Saturday, I may have a few surprises for him."

Abe's words did not relieve her this time. The aura of fear remained clearly visible, surrounding her. "Please listen," she urged. The sound in her voice became increasingly more caring as she spoke. "If you get hurt, I don't know what I'll do. Two of the Clary Grove boys were eating breakfast at the Inn this morning. They were saying how Armstrong was gonna kill this Lincoln fella Saturday morning. It really and truly scared me."

Abe took her shaking, cold hand into his. Gazing into her eyes he saw the image that had come to mean so much to him. Looking up at him again was the face of a caring angel. "Ann, Ann," he whispered softly, "I can take care of myself, I'll be okay."

"I'm gonna pray for you anyway, Abe."

"Bless you Ann. God willing, I'll be coming out of this fight okay, that is as long as I have someone like you saying prayers for my safety."

Abe squeezed her hand warmly. Having reassured Ann, the aura of worry finally seemed to slowly fade from her face, at least for now.

Billy Greene, who had been cutting firewood outside, stepped back into the store, quietly and largely unnoticed. Eventually though, his steps across the plank floor alerted Ann of his presence.

All glanced over at him and he responded, "Good morning, Miss Ann."

"Good morning, Billy." Turning back to Abe, she announced, "I really must be getting back to the Inn. Take care of yourself, Abe."

"I will," he answered softly as she left the store. Abe, who was unsure of how much of their conversation Billy Greene had heard, glanced over at him.

Billy was a very understanding young man who always seemed to know more than he let on. Coming up close beside Abe, he whispered, "I believe that girl genuinely cares for you."

Abe whispered back, "I know she does and it means a lot to me." Still Abe wanted to know more, "Billy, what else can you tell me about Ann Rutledge?"

"Just what you probably already now."

"Tell me anyway," pressed Abe.

"She has a gentle heart, full of outgoing kindness to most everyone in New Salem. She's sort of like an angel."

"She is an angel, Billy. She is." With that thought lingering on Abe's mind, the store suddenly came alive.

Other customers entered and the two men got busy. It was only later, in the early afternoon when the store's activity quieted down, Abe noticed a single very interesting looking person come through the door.

Abe, who was at the very back of the store, leaned over to Billy, asking in a low voice, "Who's that?" The object of his curiosity was an enormous fat man, white haired with an accompanying white beard, looking quite similar to the very vision of what Santa Claus might look like. When he spotted Abe, he smiled and his rosy cheeks stood out.

At the same time, Billy leaned in close to Abe and whispered, "That's Judge Green, the Justice of the Peace around here. He's also my wantabe cousin."

"What?"

"I'll explain later."

"While the two were talking, Judge Green wandered through the store toward them. The Judge was not tall, yet he weighed almost 300 pounds. Abe would soon find that he was a jovial, good-humored man whom he would feel quite comfortable around.

As he got closer, Billy introduced him, "Abe, this is Judge Bowling Green, the Justice of the Peace here in Sangamon County. The Judge came to the New Salem area from Tennessee about ten years ago."

Standing right across from him, Abe got a good up close look at the Judge, who was wearing a large pair of spectacles. Adjusting them so he could see better, he began, "Mister Lincoln, I presume?"

"That's right, Judge, but just call me Abe."

"How wonderful, a humble newcomer to New Salem. Billy, I like this young tall drink of water already."

"Thank you Judge, it's an honor to meet you."

"I'll get right to it young fella, I will be the referee at the fight between you and Armstrong this Saturday. Rumor has it the Clary boys are gonna run you out of town after the fight. I can tell you right now, that's not going to happen. I won't allow it."

"Thank you, Judge."

"Before you thank me, you might as well know something else, cause you're gonna hear it sooner or later. I'm Jack Armstrong's half-brother."

"Oh really." Abe immediately became visibly guarded, pulling back from the Judge.

"Now just hold on young fella. There's something else you should know. Jack and I haven't really spoken for at least a couple of years. If any a man ever deserved being taught a good lesson for his wrong-headed ways, it's Jack. In my view, actions have consequences. I hope you're the man to teach him that lesson."

"Why do you say that, Judge?"

"I never thought I'd say these words about my own kid-brother. You see, Jack used to be a God-fearing, family man. Then, the more he hung around those Clary boys, he started drinking and bullying others. Sometimes his victims would be honest, descent folk. I told him what he was doing wasn't right, that one day he would meet up with a better man than he was. It was over two years ago when I first spoke to him about this. Abe, I can't explain it, but when I first saw you, a little voice inside my head said you might be that better man."

"Judge, there's something I want you to know about me. I'm a man of peace. Yes, it's true, I'm gonna fight your brother, but I take no satisfaction in that."

"I know that, my boy. I could see that in you from the moment we met. But sometimes matters are taken out of our hands. There's something about to happen that I think is God's will being done."

"Judge, I think I'm gonna like you. I just hope I can measure up in your eyes, come Saturday morning."

"Don't worry, you will."

Abe had gotten an almost instant feeling that the Judge was someone he was going to look up to in the future. Mind you, he hadn't an inkling what that future might be, but he was already beginning to have a strange feeling that Fate was taking an active hand in his life. To that end, it now made him curious. "Judge, if I may ask, do you have any thoughts about what I should do when I fight your brother?"

"Yes, I do," he responded definitely. "There are a few things you must do, that is if you're going to win."

"What are those things?"

"The first thing you probably know already, but stay out of his reach. He's got a crushing bear hug that can break a few ribs if he gets hold of you. Working against him is the fact he has short arms with a short reach. Make him move around a lot, trying to get to you. This will wear him down. I've watched Jack fight, and if he can't get an immediate advantage he will get careless. When this happens, his short fuse gets the best of him. He becomes a dirty fighter and will try to hurt you, deliberately committing a foul. Above all, just remember when fighting Jack, you must have quick reflexes to counter his every move."

40

Abe took all these pointers to heart. He was beginning to realize he'd have his hands full come Saturday morning. After the Judge left, he reviewed everything in his mind.

Turning to Billy, Abe agonized, "I tried to be outgoing and friendly to everyone. How could all this have happened?"

"Through no fault of your own. But it's your very nature of being kind to others that make you stick out like a sore thumb to the Clary clan. They're nothing but a wild, hateful bunch looking for someone to pounce upon."

"So I became their target?" Abe asked.

"Your honest, clean ways are so opposed to the Clary boys' way of life. It's like the Judge has said, they're nothing but a pack of ignorant troublemakers."

"Sounds like it's a lot for me to contend with, going against their set ways. But you know something, I'm not budging. I'll fight Armstrong if I have to, cause no pack of bullies are gonna run me out of this town."

"I'll stand by you Abe, but I'll be honest with you. I wouldn't want to be in your shoes for the world."

"Billy, the truth be told, I'm not wanting to be in my shoes either."

Thinking about it some more, Abe realized Offutt had become the unwitting catalyst of this whole mess. His bragging attitude had been the spark that lit this fire in the first place. The more he brooded over it, Abe came to believe things would never be the same between him and Denton Offutt.

As all of these uneasy thoughts rolled through his head, Abe fell into an uneasy sleep. He awoke before the crack of dawn Saturday morning pondering something Judge Green had said to him. The more he focused on it, the more he began to believe it: this was indeed God intervening in Jack Armstrong's life and he would be the Lord's instrument this day. Believing it, made Abe stronger inside himself. He had found the perfect frame of mind to be in for what was to come.

At 8 A.M., Abe went outside to the well out back of the store, washed his face and whispered a prayer, "Thank you for another day of life, oh Lord. Please be with me and help me to do the right thing, whatever that may be."

Feeling the presence of God all around him, he went back inside and further prepared himself in the hours leading up to noon.

About 11 A.M., with no one in the store, Billy went up to him, asking, "How are you doing, Abe?"

"I'm feeling fine now. I was outside earlier and overhead some of the Clary boys out back of the saloon. They were pitching horse shoes and laying bets on how badly Armstrong's gonna beat me."

"Pay'em no mind, Abe. You're a better man than the whole lot of them."

"You're a good friend. I'm thank'n you, Billy."

At 12 noon, when Abe stepped outside to face the Clary mob, he did so in the right frame of mind. Beside him, Billy Greene accompanied him every step of the way as they walked to a level patch of ground between the Offutt store and the Clary Saloon. This was where Denton Offutt and Bill Clary had agreed the match between Lincoln and Armstrong would take place.

News of this match had spread rapidly throughout New Salem's population. The entire Clary clan from nearby Clary's Grove, located about three miles southwest of town, had made the journey to witness this fight. It was no secret among the Clarys that this would be Bill Clary's get back at Denton Offutt for stealing business from him the past several weeks.

Bill Clary had been the first settler in the county, years before when the town of New Salem was but a dream. He married his wife, Sarah, back in Tennessee before moving here. From that union he induced the rest of the Armstrong family and the Clary clan to move with him. It would not be a stretch to say Bill Clary considered New Salem his town. In his mind, this match would prove it, seeing Lincoln and his competition soundly defeated.

From the gathering crowd came a roaring cry from the Clary boys for the fight to begin. "Settle down men." The booming voice of Judge Bowling Green immediately silenced them as he emerged from the surrounding crowd. "Okay men," the Judge began, "this is going to be a fair fight according to the rules." Pausing, he looked directly at his brother as he said, "No fouls will be permitted, and if observed by me, the match will be over. The guilty party will be disqualified and his opponent will be declared the winner. Is this understood?"

Both men, from opposite ends of the crowd, nodded they understood. Verifying this, the Judge announced, "In this corner we have the fighting champion of Menard County, Jack Armstrong!"

Abe would now get his first look at his opponent. Armstrong stepped forward, taking his shirt off as he emerged into the open space. His upper torso revealed he was a heavily muscle-bound example of a fighting man. As he turned in Abe's direction, Armstrong's intense stare searched the crowd for his opposition.

In a matter of seconds, the Judge turned in Abe's direction, announcing, "Now comes the challenger, the pride of Kentucky, young Lincoln."

Acknowledging the Judge's introduction, Abe stepped into the open space from the opposite end. Taking his shirt off as well, he too revealed something, a much leaner, extremely thin torso, more deeply tanned than his opponent. In a sense, Abe appeared to be barely skin stretched over bone. Though he'd missed more than his share of meals, his extremely long-arms were quite muscled as well, but in a much different way from Armstrong's physique. Abe's body was more the result of heavy, hard labor over long hours.

The Judge continued, "Both men being present, let the match begin!" With those words said, he quickly stepped back into the surrounding crowd. Almost simultaneously, the roar of the spectators exploded as everyone became excited.

Seeing that Abe appeared to be no weakling was perhaps the first sign to Armstrong that this Kentuckian could perhaps be a worthy opponent after all. As he advanced toward Abe, he made a reference to his height, "Perhaps I'll have to cut you down to size."

"Never mind that Jack," answered Abe. "Perhaps I'll have to make you even shorter than you are."

Jack Armstrong, being a master of this type of fighting, had been brimming with a certain amount of over confidence. As they circled each other, things became different. Abe was fast and agile. Because of this, Armstrong decided to move more cautiously.

This was alright with Abe, forcing Armstrong to not be so aggressive. He was keeping the county champion on his toes. No matter what maneuvers he used from his fighting experience, Abe managed to stay just outside of his reach.

These moves were rapidly frustrating Armstrong. So it became time for him to try all manner of dirty tricks. These all proved to no avail.

Reaching his breaking point, Armstrong gave a knowing glance to two tall Clary boys who were standing on either side of the much shorter Judge Green. They understand what he meant, immediately pushing in front of the Judge, obscuring his view of the match. Sure of this, the dirty fighter quickly made his move.

Armstrong charged Abe, rushing in low, almost hugging the ground. Getting in close, he committed a deliberate foul, coming down hard, mashing Abe's foot. Catching Abe by surprise, he followed this up by delivering a fast hard fist to his groin area.

Abe was hurt for sure, but he contained the pain through sheer force of will. During that quick agonizing moment he heard the Judge's words in his head, *Jack will try to hurt you.*

Then something happened that the Clary boys champion hadn't expected. Instead of toppling over, the tall Kentuckian became enraged, fighting back in like style. Being within striking range, in mere seconds, Abe thrust his left arm straight at Armstrong's throat, rapidly wrapping his long fingers around his neck. Clamping them down, digging his fingers deep, he rapidly cut off his oxygen. Armstrong was now powerless in young Lincoln's vice grip.

Adrenalin surged through Abe, momentarily giving him almost super human strength. Lifting Armstrong off the ground with his long left arm, Abe shook the bully quite violently, like a rag doll, as he flailed about helplessly.

The pro-Clary crowd reacted in an uproar at this development. They were all yelling foul. "No choking! No choking!" Never mind that Armstrong had committed the first foul by mashing Abe's foot, their man was on the receiving end now.

Abe ignored them. Having Armstrong in a choker hold with his left hand, he now reached in with his right hand, grabbing hold of the front of his pants. With this leverage, Abe swung Armstrong's body further upward to a point where the bully was momentarily above his head. In this one quick move, like lifting a large bale of hay, Abe held his opponent in this airborne position. Now with all his force, Abe flung Jack onto the earth below.

Armstrong hit the ground hard. The loud sound told the story at the same time. The impact was so great that the wind was completely knocked out of Abe's opponent. He lay there, knocked almost senseless, gasping for breath.

The Clary boys among the spectators were shocked at first. They instantly became inflamed, shaking their fists and yelling at young Lincoln. Foremost among them was Henry McHenry, one of Jack's close friends. Like all the rest of the Clary boys, they were related in some fashion or another. In Henry's case, he was married to Jack Armstrong's sister. "Foul!" He yelled from the top of his lung's, "Come on boys, let's get him and teach him a real lesson!"

Abe slowly backed across the level patch of ground till his back was almost up against the Offutt store. At the same time–in mass–the Clary clan followed Abe, shaking their fists at him. Big trouble was about to happen if someone didn't interrupt.

Meanwhile, Jack Armstrong was pulling himself up, coming to his knees at the same time. Unnoticed by the crowd, Armstrong looked up into the face of his brother, Judge Green, who was standing above him. "Jack," he said, "though your friends tried to block my view so you could hurt that boy, I believe in the end you got what you deserved! Now, that young fella is going to be badly hurt if you don't rein in your cronies. You used to be a pretty decent fella yourself once upon a time. Why don't you, for once in your life, do the right thing?"

"But Judge, you're my brother," Armstrong pleaded.

"Jack it's getting where I'm ashamed to call you my brother!" The look the Judge gave Jack Armstrong in that moment was intense. It was also the truth.

"But Judge!–Judge!" Armstrong called after him.

Judge Green didn't respond, already headed in the direction of the Offutt store in an attempt to diffuse a situation that was rapidly coming to a boil.

Jack Armstrong was left alone with his thoughts. What they were, only Abe would know later.

"Men, stop it! Young Lincoln won the match. Accept it!" Judge Green yelled at the Clary boys gathering in front of Lincoln, getting their attention.

Henry McHenry turned sharply, facing him, "Judge you were the referee of the match. This however, is beyond the match. It's none of your business!" Ignoring the Judge, he once more refocused on young Lincoln, drilling a vicious stare into his face. "You dirty choker!" He yelled on, filled with rage, "We're gonna teach you a lesson for what you did to my brother-in-law. We're all gonna rush you at once!"

"Men, hold on!" yelled Billy, as he stepped in between Abe and his would-be attackers. "Henry, you and the rest of you Clary boys should fight fair and square?"

"Billy, this ain't any of your business." Henry was not going to listen.

"You're wrong Henry." Billy got his attention once more, continuing, "Lincoln is my friend and I'm standing with him."

"Get out of the way!" Henry angrily shoved Billy aside.

"Wait just one minute!" Abe demanded, getting the attention of over a dozen Clary boys gathered in front of him. "Henry, your brother-in-law and I had a no holds barred match today. Now, for whatever reason you think you might have a grievance against me, I'll gladly fight you. I'll fight all of you, but one at a time."

Henry was still white-hot with anger, bent on hurting Abe, "Lincoln, we'll come at you all at once and see how you like it! There's no one going to stop us either."

"There's one person going to stop you! There'll be no more fight'n today!" The familiar roaring voice of Jack Armstrong could be heard from behind the Clary boys as he pushed his way through the crowd till he was face to face with Lincoln. Jack's piercing eyes studied Abe closely for a long moment. Then, turning to the Clary boys, he brought the heat of the moment down a notch or two, "This man threw me fair and square. Fight's over boys."

"That's the truth of it?" Bill Clary still questioned. He'd been standing to one side, silently observing everything, secretly hoping for a far different outcome.

"That's the truth of it Bill." confirmed Jack Armstrong.

"Hey Clary," came the familiar voice of Denton Offutt, the man whose abrasive bragging started all of this. Emerging from the crowd, he confronted Bill Clary, "You heard it, my man Lincoln won fair and square. Now pay up." Offutt couldn't hold back a visibly obnoxious grin as he shoved his open palm right up in front of Bill Clary.

Quite reluctantly, Clary withdrew a ten-dollar gold piece from his pocket. "Alright Offutt, a bet is a bet." Slapping it into Offutt's hand somewhat begrudgingly, he started to walk off.

"Wait, Clary," Offutt called after him. "Just to show you my heart's in the right place, I want to buy drinks for every man here. Henry, that means you and all the rest of you Clary boys."

"All right," echoed all of them at once.

Turning to Bill Clary, Offutt slapped the gold piece back into Clary's hand. A rare smile formed on his face as he reacted, "Denton, you're an okay fella after all."

The fight that had begun with such bitter feelings now ended in a truce. The whole crowd headed for the saloon, with the exception of four men: Billy and the Judge, as well as Abe and Jack Armstrong.

The Judge commented, so Jack could hear it, "Billy, I think my brother did the right thing for the first time in a long time."

His brother did overhear him and said so, "Thank you, Judge." Jack was grateful, really wanting the Judge's approval.

As they walked back in the Offutt store, the Judge leaned over and whispered to Billy, "I think–in time–I may yet get my brother back."

Meanwhile, Abe was picking up his shirt from where he had left it when Armstrong called after him, "Wait up, Lincoln. I'd like to have a private word with you. Please."

"Sure, Jack," responded Abe, feeling, inside himself this would be more than a casual conversation.

The two men stayed outside stepping to the back of the Offutt store where they could both talk freely. What was said was meant for no others to hear.

Jack Armstrong opened up with his most private feelings. "Lincoln, when I came face to face with you a few moments ago, I found myself staring into the face of a man with strength. I saw you stand up to my friends, but it's not physical strength I'm talk'n about. It's something else, something more that I can't put my finger on right now. My brother told me, one day a better man would come along and lick me. I think you're that better man."

As Jack was completely sincere, it moved Abe to respond with equal sincerity, "Thank you, Jack. Sometimes it takes a real man to speak honestly about what's in his heart."

This comment was well received by Jack Armstrong as he immediately extended his hand toward Abe in friendship, saying, "I think I'm gonna like you."

Abe accepted Jack's hand, swallowing it up inside his own long bony grip. A warm friendship that would last the rest of Armstrong's life, and even beyond, had begun.

Jack continued, feeling truly humbled, "I want to apologize to you. I'm sorry for fouling you during the match. It was wrong of me. I shouldn't have done it. I deserved what you did to me. All I can say is I've never been thrown like that before. This was something new for me. There comes a time in life when we all have to eat humble pie. I guess this was my time. Anyway, after you bested me I laid there think'n, how did I wind up in that position? Now I know. Abe, I'm a blacksmith by trade. So, when I moved out to Clary's grove, all my neighbors started coming to me to shoe their horses. That led to other things. They got me to drink'n and hang'n out with them instead of stay'n home with my family. More and more, I started living my life inside a bottle. Well, I want that kind of life to stop, and I mean right now."

"Only you can make that happen."

"You're right. I'm starting right now. I'm face'n the truth. There's better things in life for me to do than hang'n out with a bunch of hot-headed drunks."

"Good for you, Jack."

"By the way, Abe, you don't drink, do you?"

"No, I do not. I've had one bad experience with a drunk in my life. That's enough."

Listening to Abe, something in the way he spoke struck a positive chord inside Jack. "Abe, I admire a man like you. If it were possible, I'd like to start this day over."

"Then let's do just that," responded Abe, feeling the same way.

"Hello, I'm Jack Armstrong," announced the muscle-bound blacksmith, eager to erase the friction of the morning.

Shortly, the two went back into the Offutt store where to both Billy's and Judge Green's amazement, the two *fighters* of the morning acted like they were life-long best friends.

Much later that day, when the two were alone in the store, Billy remarked, "Abe, it's amazing what happened between you and Jack Armstrong. By the time he left the store he was polite and respectful, not the drunken hot-head I've always known. I just know you had something to do with it. How on earth did you ever accomplish it?"

"There's nothing to it Billy. Just be real to people, sincere and honest."

"That's it, you're honest Abe." Before long, what Billy started calling him was picked up by everybody in New Salem. The legend of *honest Abe* had begun.

CHAPTER 6
THE BEGINNINGS OF HONEST ABE

After the Lincoln-Armstrong match, it was a new day in the Offutt store. No one was saying anything about running Abe out of town. The attention toward him was more friendly than ever before.

People started noticing there was something special about young Lincoln that set him apart from others. He seemed to glow from within. When he spoke, everyone listened. When he entered a room, he brightened it up with his warm personality. It became the essence of who he was.

Most folks in New Salem came to like Abe enormously. There was no in between. Those who disliked him were decidedly in the minority. One such person who was quite bitter was Bill Clary. His feelings would soon be made public.

A few days after the match, the early morning store hours found Billy Greene looking out the front door when he saw two men headed for the store. Reacting, he quickly turned to warn Abe, "We've got company coming!"

"That's good Billy. We can always welcome customers."

"Not good! It's Armstrong and his brother-in-law, Henry McHenry!"

"Calm down, Billy. Remember the fight's over with. They're probably want'n to just be friendly."

Before anything else could be said, they were almost at the door. Billy quickly headed behind the counter next to Abe. As the two entered, Jack took his hat off, nudging Henry to do likewise.

"Abe," he asked, "is it alright if we come in especially this early in the morning?"

"Yeah, sure. Jack, customers and friends are always welcome."

"Well, Abe, uh," Jack began haltingly, "my brother-in-law, Henry here, has something to say to both you and Billy." Glancing over at him, he continued, "Okay Henry, you've got the floor."

Henry felt all eyes on him as he began, "Mister Lincoln, Billy, I just want to apologize for my rude ways during the match the other day. I just got excited, too excited. I was out of line. I'm sorry for yelling at you, Mister Lincoln. Billy, I'm sorry for shoving you around. It won't happen again."

"Henry, it's just Abe, not Mister Lincoln. I'm just one of the boys. We all get excited about things we really believe in, and you believe in Jack here. If the day ever comes when someone's got me down, I hope I'll have a friend just like you come to my aid."

Henry's expression changed from guarded to outgoing in an instant. "Jack was right about you, Abe. You're a real okay guy. I'm man enough to admit when I've been in the wrong. I'm, uh hope'n I can be your friend too."

As Henry offered his hand, Abe accepted it in warm friendship, adding, "Henry, you're welcome in here anytime."

Billy, who had been a little more guarded, finally spoke up, "Yeah sure, we can all be friends."

"Billy," Henry said glancing over at him, "I've been need'n to get some new tools for my farm. Jack's been tell'n me to spend my money on something more useful than drinks over at the saloon."

"We've got some farming tools in the back," Billy responded. "Come with me and I'll show you what we've got."

As Billy and Henry left for the back of the store, Jack leaned across the counter and spoke to Lincoln in a low voice, "Abe, you're like my brother."

"How so?"

"He knows how to set people at ease, getting down on their level when he talks to them. You're the same. I will always look up to you for that."

"I hope to never disappoint you, Jack."

At that very moment, a rare visitor entered the store. It was Bill Clary, owner of the saloon. "I happened to be outside and thought I saw both you and Henry come in here. I didn't know you'd even consider associate'n yourself with the likes of Lincoln, especially after the way he humiliated you the other day." As he spoke, the smell of liquor was heavy upon his breath.

"Now listen here, Bill." Jack spoke as he turned around in his direction, explaining, "Abe and I were just having a nice quiet, peaceful conversation."

"Oh," Clary reacted, trying to think through his drunkenness, "Well, ain't you come'n over for drinks later? After all, I've got a few more matches lined up for you."

"Bill, I'm through fight'n. Those days are over with for me."

"What?"

"And, I'm through drink'n."

"What!"

"There comes a time when a man has to put his family first. I've got a wife and a little boy to think of. They need me more than a bottle over at your saloon."

"That's the way you want it, Jack?"

"That's the way I want it."

Bill Clary looked like he'd just been slapped in the face, reacting angerly, "Then when you need money, don't you be come'n to me, cause you won't get it! Not now, not ever!"

In a rage, Clary started for the door, but stopping right in the doorway, turning back around, he glared at Abe, shaking his fist at him. "You know," he continued angrily, "somehow I think you had something to do with this, Lincoln. Someday you're gonna get what's come'n to you!" With that said, Clary barged through the doorway, heading back to his saloon in a huff.

Abe did not respond angrily, only quietly observing, "I think he's in a bad mood."

"Bill Clary is a proud, vein man with a very large ego," Jack explained. "I didn't intend to hurt him, but that man can't take no for an answer. Abe, I'm changing. The whole town's changing."

"Jack, I hope it's for the better, for all of us."

"Abe, if you ever have occasion to come out to Clary's Grove, please come by and see me. I'd sure like you to meet my wife Hannah and our little boy."

"I'd like that too, Jack."

Shortly after Jack Armstrong and Henry McHenry left, the well-dressed doctor, John Allen entered the store. Spotting Abe behind the counter, he went over to him. "I came in here specifically to see you."

"What's on your mind, Doc?"

"Abe, let me start by saying you are definitely making a difference in New Salem."

"How so?"

"Word has it about town you've got a couple of the Clary boys to stop drinking. That's a good first step in getting the rowdy weekend crowd to settle down from the way they come into town, tearing things up."

"Well Doc, I didn't really have much to do with it, except around the edges."

"I'll say it again, Abe Lincoln, you're a very humble man. Do you remember, about a week or so ago saying to me you thought the Lord wanted you here, but you didn't know for what purpose?"

"Yes Doc, I remember saying it."

"Well now I know for what purpose."

"I'm all ears. Please tell me."

"You're here to make a difference in other people's lives."

"You really think so?"

"Abe, what more noble thing can a person do than bring people into the ways of the Lord? In your own way you're helping to bring those that are like lost sheep back into the fold."

"Yes, I'd kinda like for that to be true," admitted Abe, beginning to like the idea of what Doc Allen was saying.

"You've inspired me," continued Doc Allen, "to want to do something myself that'll make a difference, something positive."

"What are you thinking, Doc?"

"You might as was well know a few more things about me. I've been a life-long Presbyterian. I don't drink, smoke, or curse. I've never tried to impose my beliefs on others, until now. I've got this idea of trying to form a temperance society among the good people of New Salem."

"Good luck in that. Most of the frontier folks I've come in contact with around here are good, honest people. But, some of them do like an occasional drink."

"I've got to try. I feel like it's what the Lord wants me to do. Our little town doesn't need to have that saloon. I for one believe it's a place of evil, a threat to families raising their children near that sort of environment. I'm going to try to get people to picket the saloon and drive Clary out of business."

"Going up against a man like Bill Clary could be asking for trouble. But Doc, good luck to you anyway. We need a clean town for the future."

"Thanks Abe, but even more, I'd like to have your prayers."

"You've got'em in spades."

As Doctor Allen left, Abe looked around. He'd been so totally focused on his conversation with the doctor, he hadn't noticed Ann Rutledge had slipped quietly into the store and had been standing off to one side. For some time she'd been listening to at least part of their conversation.

She approached the counter opposite him, speaking up, "I came to tell you why I wasn't at the fight the other day. First, I couldn't bear to see you hurt. I was coming anyway though. But then, my father wouldn't let me. He kept me working at the Inn all day. But even as I stayed there, my thoughts and prayers were with you."

"I felt them. They kept me strong."

"They will always be with you."

As she said these words, he could see the same very deep and sincere feelings mirrored in her face. "Ann, just you saying it means the world to me."

Without looking back, she could sense other customers entering the store, behind her.

"May I help you?" The voice of Billy could be heard ushering them across the store, away from Ann and Abe, so they could continue their conversation.

Ann spoke up again, "I noticed you talking to Doctor Allen."

"Yes, I was."

"He's a good man, a man of faith who needs our prayers and support."

"Yes, he's a man of sincere beliefs."

"Abe, what do you believe in?" Her eyes searched his face for an answer.

"I love the Lord. I don't believe I would be here now if it wasn't for Him. But yet, I'm still searching."

"Searching for what?"

"Searching for a sign from Him, I know He's out there. Sometimes I feel His presence, as I've told you. I feel Him knocking at my door, especially when I'm around you. Yet, something inside me is holding me back, still waiting for a sign I haven't received."

"I have no doubt about it, Abe. One day in the Lord's own good time you'll receive that sign. I'm sure of it," Ann said reassuringly.

"I guess for now, I'll just have to wait."

"For now I feel like God is with you, far more than you know."

"Ann, I'll say it again, you have a lot of wisdom stored up inside yourself. I hope to learn more from you as time goes by."

"Speaking of time! Talking to you, I lost track of it! I have to get back to the Inn."

Even as she said it, her eyes told a different story to Abe–that she wanted to stay.

"See you later, Ann." Abe whispered, as his eyes remained locked on her, following her out the door and beyond.

"Abe–Abe," a voice called to him again.

Abe shook his head for a quick second, coming out of his trance.

"Young fella, I'm trying to get your attention." The familiar voice of Judge Green brought him back.

"Oh sorry, Judge," Abe said, refocusing on him. "How can I help you?"

"Young fella, from the looks of things, you mean how can I help you?" As the Judge spoke, the familiar Santa Claus smile crossed his face, rosy cheeks in all.

"Okay Judge, how can you help me?"

"While you were talking, first to Doc Allen and then to Ann Rutledge, I couldn't help but hear your conversations while I was looking around."

"I'm sorry, Judge. I guess my mind got a little too pre-occupied with what they were saying. I never really saw you come in. My apologies."

"That's alright, Billy offered to help me, but I became far too interested in your conversations."

"How were they interesting to you?"

"My boy, you seem to be far too concerned about receiving a sign from God. I'll tell you, at least from my own experience, if you keep your heart opened up to receiving Him, He'll come into your life when you're least expecting it. Faith is a curious thing. It works differently on each of us. Just remember, never close off your mind to the Lord. I've seen far too may who've gone through life that way and became hard, bitter souls. It's a terrible thing to see."

"Yes, I know exactly what you're talking about. I've seen it myself. I'll tell you about it sometime, but not now."

Judge Green pressed on, "Another thing I heard you talking about was being noble. In my office out at my farm I happen to have a fine collection of Shakespeare's works as well as a wonderful Bible with commentary. These books thoroughly explore the nobility of man, or lack of it. Also, if you're interested, I have a set of law books that discuss the right and the wrong of all mankind down through the pages of history."

"I'd sure like to look at those books." Immediately, there was an excited look on Abe's face, as if Pandora's Box had just been opened. The Judge could see it too.

"My boy, come out to my place anytime. You'd be welcome." He could see the hunger for knowledge in Abe and added, "When I was your age I wanted to read everything I could get my hands on. You're welcome to borrow any of my books you might have an interest in."

"Oh, thank you, Judge!" responded an excited Abe.

Continuing, the Judge switched his focus, "As to Doc Allen and Bill Clary: William Price Clary is a very stubborn man who won't be taken down easy, Doc may not know what he's up against. On the other hand, even though Doc Allen walks with a limp, I've noticed he does not let anything cripple his defiant spirit. So, it will be an interesting test of wills to witness, which sort of brings me back to you."

"How so, Judge?"

"I know you talked to my brother after the match, the other day. Earlier, I just happened to see him leaving town with some farming tools he acquired here. I also noticed he hadn't been drinking either. Abe, I may yet get my brother back, and for whatever part you had in that, I'm thanking you."

"I've only done what I thought was right."

"My boy, you're an honest person with a good set of values you live by. I hope more people see that in you as time goes by."

"After the Judge left, Abe remarked to Billy, "You know, the Judge is a very good man."

"He's a fine decent man," Billy added, "who happens to like you. I think he sees you as a kindred spirit who shares many of his interests."

Over the next couple of weeks Doctor Allen followed through on his idea of a temperance society. It caught on. Doc and his supporters picketed the saloon heavily, carrying signs, they marched around it all day, for weeks.

Potential customers were discouraged from going inside. The decent folks of New Salem were on the march, bound to rid their town of what they saw as an undesirable element. In short order, the saloon's clientele dwindled into nothing.

As time passed into early November, William Price Clary sat alone inside his once profitable business, a broken man. Brooding and depressed, he knew it couldn't survive the coming winter. He reasoned, civilization and morality had destroyed his livelihood. Yet he was only 31 years old at the time and he could start anew elsewhere. Being a stubborn redneck, he would figure a way out of this mess. By the summer of the next year he would move west to Texas, where the wilder frontier atmosphere was more suited to his taste.

At the same time, another prominent citizen of New Salem was contemplating pulling up stakes. During the second week of November, a concerned Denton Offutt entered his store early one morning. Catching sight of young Lincoln, he called out to him, "Abe, step outside with me for a moment. I'd like to have a word with you."

Abe stepped out on the store's front porch to see what his boss wanted. Thinking it was uncharacteristic to see the heavy drinking Offutt before noon, he asked, "Denton isn't it awful early for you to be up?"

Offutt spoke in a low voice, "Abe, I've come to a painful decision I've had to make."

"What could that be?"

"It's been weighing heavily upon me. I've decided we're going to have to close the store. Sales have dwindled to nothing. In a few days I'm going to be flat busted out of money. I'm get'n out of this town while I still can, before the winter sets in."

"Is there no other way?" This was crushing news to Abe, even though he knew in his heart, this time Offutt was right. Customers had stopped buying. There was no money to be had in New Salem, at least for them.

"Abe," Offutt explained, "look down the street and tell me what you see."

Abe looked down Main Street to the west. On the north side of the street, across from the Rutledge Inn, stood the huge McNeil mercantile store. It was a building almost four times the size of the little Offutt store.

"The McNeil store is taking in what little money there is in New Salem. They are bigger than us with much more inventory. Down here on the bluff we can't compete with them. With winter coming, the Sangamon River is going to freeze over. That means no boat traffic. I'm just seeing the writing on the wall. We've got to get out of here while the get'n is good!"

"I'm sorry Denton, but I'm staying."

"Abe, I was kinda hope'n you would come with me. You see, I have this knack with horses, which I believe is a genuine gift. A lot of people have told me horses listen to me.

"Oh really," reacted Abe, immediately suspicious.

"Yes, really. I can get horses to do a lot of things other people can't. I think that there will be a real demand for my type of horse whisperer. I just know we could get rich together.

"A horse whisperer? What's that?" Abe was full of questions.

"It's someone who whispers to horses, soft and gentle like, getting them to do what a person wants them to do. So I'm going back to Kentucky and see if I can make a go of it as a business. I was hope'n you'd come along with me as my assistant."

"No Denton, I feel in my heart my future lies here in New Salem."

"If you mean that Rutledge girl, I hate to poor cold water on your dreams, but–"

"What do you mean?" Abe interrupted.

"Have you ever met John McNeil?"

"I've seen him from a distance, but I've never actually met him."

"Well, he's a right handsome man, something you're not. But more to the point, he's well to do and got plenty of money. Staying over at the Rutledge Inn, I've noticed him eyeing Ann."

"He can look all he wants, but when it comes down to it, it's up to what Ann wants."

"Not exactly, Abe. James Rutledge is hurting for money too. A wealthy son-in-law could help him out. Don't you know, if he tells her to marry him, she'll have to do what her father says?"

"Denton, I don't know that. Anyway, I'm staying here."

"Then I guess we've come to a parting of the ways, Abe. I'm leaving here by tomorrow. I'd appreciate it if you not tell anyone."

"What'll happen to the store?"

"Well I guess, Abe you'll be in charge of paying my creditors with what money the store takes in, till they decide to close the doors."

Later that afternoon, Denton Offutt slipped out of town and into the pages of history. No one knows for sure, but it was rumored he did go back to Kentucky for a while. Then he pushed further south to New Orleans. But for the most part, all record of his life after New Salem has been lost to the memoires of man.

As for Abe, despite the fact of Offutt skipping town, his reputation for honesty overrode that of his shady boss with the store's creditors. Abe and Billy would be around to keep the store open, at least through the coming winter.

CHAPTER 7
THE WINTER OF THE DEEP SNOW

As if Offutt had been some sort of fortune-teller, the winter from mid-November 1831 through mid-January 1832 came in all its fury. The 'winter of the deep snow', or so it was called, overwhelmed New Salem with no letup. Abe understood very quickly, as more than three feet of snow piled up in places. It was so deep that many animals could not reach their food supply. Hundreds of such animals, outside in the elements, perished in the extreme cold.

It was not much better for humans either. Starvation ran rampant that winter. Many people–especially the older ones–simply ran out of food and starved to death.

Such thoughts were very much on Abe's mind. Since there was no business for long stretches of the day, he and Billy stood around shaking. The persistent biting cold penetrated the interior of the pathetic little store. There seemed to be no escaping it. Yet, the force of will within Abe's mind was strong enough to keep the flicker of life alive inside him.

In a story that Billy Greene often told, it was during this particularly dark time that an elderly widow came in the store to buy provisions for the winter. She only had a couple of dollars to spend. Abe took note of her near poverty state, whispering to Billy, "I'm not going to let that poor woman starve." After she had spent her two dollars and hadn't got near what she needed, Abe allowed her to charge several more dollars' worth of provisions in order to survive.

After she left, Billy said, "You know she may never have enough money to pay the store back."

"It doesn't matter. I won't have that woman's life on my conscious. After all, there's more important things in life than making money."

"The voices of our creditors might say different."

Abe reflected, "I've thought about that. But there's something I want you to remember, something more important than the voices of mortal man. The Voice of God sometimes speaks to our conscience about the right thing to do."

"Are you saying the Voice of God spoke to you?"

"All I'm saying is when that little old lady came in here, weak and trembling, a Voice spoke to my mind, *Do the right thing by this woman.* Sometimes a cup of kindness is worth more than all the money in the world."

"God bless you, Abe." Incidents like this stuck in Billy's mind as he would later write, it was little nuggets of wisdom like this that were the beginnings of the Abraham Lincoln the world would come to know.

It was only a few minutes after the woman left, Abe realized he had overcharged her twenty-five cents for what she did pay in cash. Without hesitation he withdrew a quarter from the cashbox, bundled up, and took off in the snow to catch up with her. Not only did he return the overcharged amount, but helped her safely home. From where she lived, south of New Salem, and then back to the store, was over a mile in the bone-chilling cold.

Getting back, Abe was near frozen. Shaking and trembling, he could barely put one foot in front of the other. Helping him to a chair by their small fireplace at the back of the store, Billy stood by him for a moment. Looking on admiringly, he said, "You truly are honest Abe."

"Thank you, Billy. No matter what I do, I'm always gonna try to live up to those words."

Even though Billy brought him blankets to warm him, it was several hours before Abe stopped shaking from the cold.

Outside, the weather evolved into a near whiteout blizzard. The cold air swept through New Salem, slamming every cabin with its full penetrating force. The snow and sleet was beginning to drift down the store's crude little chimney, leaving a thin white glaze covering the floor.

As the day progressed into evening, it became a test of wills against the elements for Abe and Billy. They found themselves huddling together trying to get warm and stay alive. Hanging onto life by the slenderest of threads, it would take a miracle for them to live. That miracle came.

After a while there was a loud pounding, coming from the outside. Inside, the two men were beyond the ability to answer. A very strong man out there was able to break the door free from the clutches of freezing ice that that were holding it shut.

Abe and Billy sat rigid in crude chairs with the store's blankets wrapped around themselves. At that very moment they were about to lapse into unconsciousness. With only a flicker of life left in them, both men had not heard the front door fly open. Two heavily bundled up figures entered, closing the door firmly. Abe strained to look up and see who they were. He recognized both of them. It was Ann and her cousin, McGrady Rutledge.

Looking down at him, an expression of extreme concern formed on Ann's face. "My God!" Her words were full of alarm, "Abe, you're near frozen."

"Ann, help. Billy and I need help." It was all he could say. Abe's mind as well as his body was becoming dangerously close to being terminal victims of the freezing cold.

"Quick McGrady, the soup."

McGrady Rutledge immediately understood Ann. The two had braved the blizzard winds and brought hot soup from the Inn for Abe and Billy. Pouring it into two crude cups, they administered it to the near frozen men.

Ann held it, giving it to Abe a little at a time. His own hands were too stiff to hold anything at first. The hot soup felt good to him, restoring warmth and feeling after a while. Only then could he hold the cup as he drank some more. Ann though, still steadied him, gently guiding his shaking hands. The warmth of her own hands sent revitalizing heat into Abe's flesh.

Becoming more aware, regaining his focus, he declared, "Miss Ann, you truly are an angel in the flesh."

Coming around, Billy Greene agreed, "Miss Rutledge, you are our savior." Then looking up at McGrady, who was pouring hot soup down him, he added between gulps, "You too, McGrady. You're the assistant savior."

"Hey fellas, give Ann all the credit. She got concerned about you two, so we got bundled up and come over to check on you. She brought along the hot soup, while I used my strength to get the door open. It had become almost frozen shut. But it was Ann's urgings that brought me along, and that's the truth of it."

Abe leaned over to Ann, who had pulled out another chair from the back of the store, and was now sitting next to him. Whispering, he asked, "Is that really the truth, Ann?"

"Yes," she explained, "when you truly care for someone, there's nothing you won't do to help them."

"Ann, you're wonderful, just wonderful." Inside his mind though, Abe was thinking much more than that. He truly did see the face and figure of an angel sitting right next to him. After a brief moment of silence, he added, "I'm more than grateful. You saved our lives. I owe you my life. It belongs to you."

"Abe, I only did what the Good Book teaches me to do. If I didn't, I wouldn't be able to stand before the Lord when my time comes and say I did all I could with my life."

Billy Greene marveled, "Miss Ann, there's something really special about you that makes you stand apart from others."

"Billy, that's something I've known since my first day in New Salem," observed Abe, while maintaining a steady gaze of admiration as he said those words.

McGrady interrupted just then, "Alright, enough from you two. You young men need to shut this place down right now. It's too cold for you to survive in here."

"Father sent us to fetch both of you back to the Inn," Ann explained. "He's got a warm fire going within the fireplace in the great room. You can make pallets on the floor there and stay the night, or until this blizzard blows over."

"That sounds pretty good to me," Billy responded, gulping the rest of his hot soup down.

Abe knew this was the only way they were going to survive. Getting up on his feet, he urged Billy, "Come on, let's batten down the hatches here and follow Miss Ann and McGrady back over to the Inn."

As the legend grew, it was on one dark evening during the winter of 1831 this young angel of New Salem saved the lives of Abe Lincoln and Billy Greene, leading them back to a place of hope and salvation in the form of the Rutledge Inn.

For the next couple of weeks, the crude thermometers in New Salem rose no higher than just a few degrees above zero. For almost two months the surrounding countryside remained snow covered. It might be said the elements of the harsh winter brought Ann and Abe together in ways they wouldn't have anticipated.

With the Offutt store closed down, Abe was out of work, but not for long. Ann talked to her father about letting Abe board at the Inn during the winter while he sought out his future.

Being the man he was, Abe went up to him, making things clear, "Mister Rutledge, I'm not a free loader. While I'm here, I want to earn my keep."

"Abe, I appreciate that, but what do you think you can do here?"

"Even though I personally don't drink, I know my way around a saloon from living with a heavy drinking father. For you, I will gladly tend bar in your tavern."

"I appreciate that, son. Ann told me about your father and your feelings about him. I want to assure you I'm not that type of man."

"Well then, if you'll let me, I'll gladly work in your tavern."

"Okay, is there anything else you can do?"

"Yes, I noticed you're running low on firewood. Before this winter is over with you'll be needing more, a lot more."

"But son, with it being so bad outside, I can't ask you to do that."

"You don't have to ask. I'll do it, and willingly so. For you and Mrs. Rutledge, and your family, it's the least I can do."

One thing Abe was allowed to keep from the Offutt store was the store's axe. Having a certain talent born out of necessity from his youth was that of being an accomplished rail-splitter. He knew what he could do and would make good use of his expertise with an axe now.

True to his word, Abe tended bar for long hours and then went out in the bitter cold for long periods of time and chopped firewood for the huge fireplace. Coming in from the bone chilling environment outside, Ann never failed him. She always had hot meals for him. Often, she would sit alone with him and talk for long periods of time. Their conversation, while warm and friendly, has unfortunately been lost to history.

James and Mary Rutledge did notice their daughter's growing closeness to young Lincoln. The tender feelings that passed between them were also noticed by Ann's cousin, McGrady Rutledge. As time went on, her brother David also took note of what was happening. They both expressed their support for Abe, liking and admiring him. During the next two months it seemed as though whenever he spoke, the entire Rutledge family listened.

As days passed during the winter months, one thorn did raise its ugly head. Among all the good feelings for Abe, there was one mean-spirited, self-centered person who harbored ill will against him, one John McNeil. He would come in for the lunch or dinner meal and sit alone in a dark corner, staring at Abe and Ann, smoldering with jealousy inside himself. Within this one particular man was a selfish soul who wanted to possess Ann.

On one such afternoon, after becoming overwhelmed with jealous rage, he quietly rose from a shadowy corner of the great room, leaving the Inn for his mercantile store across the street. His barely visible irritation had gone largely unnoticed except for the careful observation of one witness to his behavior. Later, that one person would quietly pull Abe aside and warn him.

"Abe, I need to talk with you alone," whispered Billy Greene, stressing, "It's important."

"Okay Billy, let's find a place where we can talk privately."

The two men went over to a darkened corner in the great room. There, they sat alone, conversing freely in the shadows.

"Abe, I have to warn you about John McNeil. He has very bad feelings against you."

"Billy, how do you know such a thing?"

"I know this because I have to work too. You see, he offered me a job over at his mercantile store, at least for the next few months. We got to talking and all of a sudden, he just blurted out how much he hates you. I asked why?"

"Billy, I've given him no cause to hate me."

"Well, to him you have. He thinks Ann is going to belong to him."

"What makes him think such a thing?"

"Before we came over here to stay the winter, he'd already been laying the groundwork with James Rutledge. He seems to know Mr. Rutledge is hurting for money. McNeil has become quite wealthy in these parts and is known to have a lot of money. He's in a position where he could help Mister Rutledge, but there's one catch."

"What's that?"

"Ann has caught his eye. He sees that she has the potential of being the type of wife he wants, and he wants her."

"Does he think he can buy a wife?"

"Frankly, yes. McNeil is the type of person who eats, breathes, and lives money. So now we come to the problem concerning you."

"What problem is that?"

"You're in the way of the natural course of events as he sees them. Ann has become infatuated with you. He said that you are not of his social stature and therefore you are unworthy of her. He firmly believes with you out of the way he can 'convince' Mister Rutledge to persuade Ann to marry him."

"Billy, you know you're beginning to sound a little bit like Denton Offutt. He said something similar to me just before he left town."

"Well, I'm decidedly not Denton Offutt. I wanted to tell you what I've been hearing because you're my friend, probably the best friend I could have."

"Billy, I appreciate what you're saying, but nothing and no one is ever going to change my feelings for Ann Rutledge."

"Good for you, Abe. I just hope you know what you're doing."

"To tell you the truth, I'm not really sure. It's just, sometimes I feel there's a guiding force outside myself, leading me on, often times telling me what to do. What about you?"

"I'm only going to stay here through the spring. Then when the weather is better, I'm going back to my father's farm, a few miles south of here."

"Well, it sounds like you've got your life planned out."

"Just for the near future. I'm going to take your advice, Abe. I'm eventually going back to school, maybe even college."

"Good for you, Billy. I don't know how just yet, but I'm going to better myself too." Holding out his hand to Billy, he felt the urge to shake his hand, having a sudden feeling he might not see him for a while. Abe added, "Maybe we'll see each other in better times."

"Just maybe," responded Billy, smiling as he got up and left for work over at the McNeil store.

Abe glanced after him till he was out of sight, whispering to himself, "I guess we're never completely sure about the future. It's all in the good Lord's hands."

Later that night, Abe ascended the ladder into the upstairs loft at the Rutledge Inn. This is where he was sleeping now, since he was boarding at the Inn. Laying down on his pallet, he felt eyes were studying him. They belonged to the man sleeping on the pallet next to him.

Finally the voice of that person spoke up, "Abe, how do you feel about my cousin?" It was the voice of Ann's cousin, McGrady Rutledge.

Abe answered, "McGrady, you know what I think about Ann. She's a beautiful woman who has the appearance of an angel. There's only one problem."

"What's that, Abe?"

"I believe I'm falling in love with this angel."

"I know she cares for you a lot. Why don't you tell her?"

"I want to, but–"

"But why?"

"I'll tell you why. I've agonized over this. Believe me, McGrady, I want to tell Ann how I feel, but one thing holds me back. I have nothing, actually less than nothing. In fact, I am nothing. Everyone tells me John McNeil wants to marry her. He's rich and handsome, all the things I'm not. How can I compete with him?"

"You say, you're nothing. Nothing could be further from the truth. You're far greater than John McNeil could ever be."

"Tell me. In what way?"

"I've talked with John McNeil at length. He's a self-absorbed human being, who thinks nothing of others. He only thinks of what he wants. He's a taker, never a giver. You, on the other hand, are the total opposite. You're kind and considerate, thinking of everyone but yourself. You have all the qualities that Ann looks up to. McNeil is nothing in comparison to you. So don't sell yourself short. Tell Ann how you feel and she will run away with you in a minute."

"You really think so?"

"I know so."

Abe thought about this conversation all night, agonizing over what he should do. Come morning, he would speak to Ann. With that resolution firmly embedded in his brain, he finally drifted off to sleep for a few hours.

Getting up early the next morning, he realized his self-worth had been challenged. He knew he had to do something, but as so often happens in life, fate would deal him a card that was unexpected.

Coming down from the loft, he searched out Ann, who was already up and fully dressed. "Ann, I need to talk to you about something important."

"Funny you should say that, I was just fixing to come up to the loft and get you. There's someone waiting in the great room who's desperate to see you."

"Who on earth could that be?"

"Henry McHenry, Jack Armstrong's brother-in-law. He said it was urgent to speak with you. He looked to me like he had the weight of the world on his shoulders."

"But Ann, I wanted to talk to you about us and how you might feel about me."

"Why, Abe Lincoln, after all this time you should know how I feel about you. Just look into my face and tell me what you see."

Concentrating, he focused on her expression, then telling her, "I see a face full of caring feelings."

"And these feelings are for you," she explained, adding, "only for you."

Her words impacted Abe deeply. "Ann, you mean the world to me."

She reacted, receiving his words just as deeply into her heart. But glancing past Abe, she sensed a very concerned man in the great room who had come all the way in from Clary's Grove. "I think for now, you should go talk to Mister McHenry. We can talk more about ourselves later. There'll be plenty of time for us. After all, you and Billy have spent the last two months here. It's near the end of January already."

"Time has passed so quickly," acknowledged Abe, thinking about it. Constantly working around the Rutledge Inn, he had lost all track of time. "I hadn't thought about it, but it's a new year. It's a time for new resolutions in our lives."

Ann leaned in closer to Abe agreeing, "You're right, but those new resolutions can wait till later. We'll have plenty of time to talk about us and our future."

"Plenty of time," reflected Abe, thinking out loud. "I guess as you say, we'll talk more later. For now, I'll go talk to Henry." Abe smiled at her as he turned, heading from the front hallway into the great room.

Entering, he immediately encountered Henry McHenry, most anxious about something.

"Henry, what on earth brings you into town? I imagine it's still quite bad out your way."

"It is, Mister Lincoln. Even though it's cold and miserable out, this has been the first break in the weather since mid-November. I had to come. Us folks out at Clary's Grove are in a bad way." He paused for a moment, being visibly upset. Like Ann had said, worry was written all over his face.

Seeing this, Abe invited him to take a seat at a nearby table. Sitting down, Abe put a comforting hand on Henry's shoulder, "Now Henry, tell me all about it."

"I got up before the crack of dawn, got my wagon hitched up and set out for New Salem. You see, everything is in short supply out at Clary's Grove. With many of our farm animals outside, they froze to death during the blizzard last month. With what little we have, we're in critical need. When I got here I went down to Mister Offutt's store on the bluff, only to find it's all closed up. So I came up here to the Inn looking for you."

"Well you found me. But I hate to tell you this, the Offutt store is out of business. We had to close its doors when the blizzard hit in mid-November.

"Then, what are we going to do? Our families are starving." Tears of desperation were forming in his eyes. "I stopped at the McNeil store across the street and he would give me no store credit. That man has the coldest heart I've ever seen. If you don't have cash money, you're out of luck with him. I don't know what to do. I need help."

Abe thought for a moment, looking into the pleading man's face. Then he knew what he must do. "Henry, I'm not like John McNeil, I can help you," Abe declared with firmness. "The store may be closed up, but I can still get in. We can take your wagon down there and load it up with whatever inventory is left, can goods, other necessities. Whatever you need, take it."

Henry was profoundly moved, "You mean you would do that for us?"

"Of course, I would," declared Abe. "The Good Book teaches us, *Do unto others as you would have them do unto you.* I can do no less."

"God bless you, Mister Lincoln. I wish more people were like you and we would have a lot better world."

"Henry, let me get my coat and I'll be right with you."

As Abe got up, he noticed that Ann had been standing over by the fireplace listening to the conversation. Following him out of the great room to the main hallway, she whispered, "I'm so very proud of you. Not everyone is big-hearted as you are."

"Ann, I'm just doing what I believe is right. I'm going to help Henry and those folks out at Clary's Grove."

"I just have a feeling," Ann revealed, continuing, "that you should go out there. Knowing you as I do, you might make a difference if they live or die."

"Very well, I'll go, because it's the right thing for me to do. But, even more so, I trust your feelings that I should go. Ann, I don't know how long I'll be gone."

"Just remember, Abe, my heart is with you, no matter how long you're gone."

"I'll remember," Abe said, turning to ascend the ladder to get his coat and other things in the loft.

Later, as Abe and Henry were loading his wagon, he asked, "Henry, as a matter of curiosity, how's Jack Armstrong doing?"

"He's doing right poorly."

"What happened?"

"Jack was shoeing a horse, when it got excited and kicked him hard, right in the stomach. That evening he started spitting up blood. That was a couple days ago. He's been laid up, hurting ever since. I'm worried, because I don't know how his family are going to make it till spring without help."

"Well Henry, help's a coming."

"How do you mean, Abe?"

"I mean I'm going with you back out to Clary's Grove. I'll stay as long as I'm needed, helping the Armstrong's and everyone else out there."

"You really mean it, don't you, Abe?"

"Yes, I'll help as much as it's humanly possible for me to do so."

"I'd heard from others you were like that. Abe, you truly are a good man."

By 11 AM that day, late in January, 1832, Abe and Henry left New Salem for Clary's Grove. It was a small settlement, about three or four miles to the west.

After several hours travel over rugged terrain, Henry halted the wagon, pointing to eight or ten primitive cabins in the distance. "Abe, there she is, Clary's Grove. All the cabins were sort of built close together."

"Henry, I'm anxious to check on Jack Armstrong."

"Okay, we'll stop there first. Jack's place is the far cabin on the right, straight ahead."

Pulling up in front of the Armstrong place, Henry brought the wagon to a halt. As he did so, a slender young woman came out to see who it was.

"Hannah, it's me," announced Henry. "I'm back from New Salem with some provisions."

"Oh thank God!" She uttered, a feeling of visible relief written across her face.

"No, you can thank this man," Henry spoke up, correcting her. "This here is Abraham Lincoln. You may have heard Jack speak of him."

"I certainly have," Hannah responded in recognition. "Mister Lincoln, I'm so glad to finally meet you at last."

"It's all my pleasure," replied Abe, who could not help staring at her. "I don't know what it is, but you remind me of someone who was once close to me." The young twenty-one year old, Hannah Jones Armstrong, reminded Abe very much of his mother who passed away when he was nine years old. The resemblance was startling, a face he never forgot.

"Please, come in," she said. "Jack will be most anxious to see you."

Hannah led the two men inside to see her ailing husband. Immediately, Abe saw that the interior of the Armstrong cabin was a simple affair. It was essentially a two-room home–very meager– very humble in appearance. With one medium size fireplace and very little fire wood remaining, Abe quickly knew they were in desperate straits.

Hannah did not let on about this, being a very brave, strong-willed woman. Beyond the physical resemblance, her whole attitude and behavior again reminded him of his late mother.

Both Henry and Abe followed Henry to the Armstrong bedroom. Hannah announced, "Henry's back." Henry went on in while Abe remained just beyond the bedroom door, not quite in view from the inside the room.

Jack, laid up on their crude bed, managed to look up at Henry, asking, "Did you have any luck in New Salem?"

"More than luck, Jack. I talked to Mister Lincoln and he practically emptied the store, filling the wagon with all the provisions he had left."

"But Henry, all of us folks put together in Clary's Grove couldn't pay for a wagonload of provisions, at least not right now. Doesn't Abe know it?"

"Yes, he knows. But it didn't matter to him. What did matter was that we not starve to death."

"God bless him," said Jack, tears forming in his eyes as he added, "Abe's truly a good friend."

"Thanks, Jack," acknowledged Abe, entering the room.

"Abe? You came way out here?" Jack could hardly believe he had come out to Clary's Grove in the cold weather.

Abe explained, "I heard you were laid up, so I decided to come and check on you."

"Mister Lincoln sure didn't come empty handed," Hannah added, speaking up. "He brought as many provisions as Henry's wagon would carry, just for us folks out here."

Jack looked up at Abe from his bed, not hardly believing it, "You did that for us?"

"Yes, I did. When Henry told me how bad things were out here–well–I had to help. One thing I've been learning in life is to follow the golden rule: Do unto others as you would have them done unto you."

"I'm grateful, Abe, most grateful," replied Jack deeply moved as he extended his hand toward the tall Kentuckian looming over him.

Abe took Jack's hand into his, receiving it in warm friendship, commenting, "You know what this means?"

"What?" asked Jack.

"It's much more than just a handshake," explained Abe. "It means we're gonna be friends for life."

"Mister Lincoln," broke in Hannah, getting his attention. "You truly are a good Samaritan."

"Hannah, I hope I will always be able to live up to your kind comment. But I'm just a humble guy trying to be the best person I know how to be to others. So, I'd be right proud if you just call me Abe."

"Then you just keep on calling me, Hannah."

"No disrespect, but I think I'd be more comfortable calling you 'Aunt Hannah'. You see, you remind me of someone who–"

Just then their conversation was interrupted by baby-like, young laughter coming from somewhere in the room.

Glancing around, Abe wondered aloud, "Now who is that?"

Pointing past Abe, Hannah identified the source of the sound, "It's our little boy, Pleasant, asleep in his bed."

Abe glanced at the baby boy, not quite three years old, in a little bed across the room. "Pleasant, you call him?" Abe asked.

Jack explained, "He never cries. He's always happy. So Hannah and I decided to call him, 'Pleasant.' He's such a good boy."

Eyeing him carefully, Abe commented, "He appears to be a growing boy."

"He is that," Jack seconded. "He's growing like a weed. In fact, I'm gonna have to build him a bigger bed as soon as I can get up and around."

"Well for now, Jack, you stay in bed and get well. While I'm here, I'd be right grateful if you folks would let me help out with the chores."

"Abe, thank you a lot. I ain't never go'n to forget this."

"Well then, I better go help Henry unload all the provisions we brought out here."

Thus, on a wintery afternoon in late January 1832, a bond and life-long friendship was made between Abe and the entire Armstrong family. Shortly though, Abe would become fast friends with all the folks in Clary's Grove. The very individuals who had wanted to run him out of New Salem soon accepted him as a good Samaritan. More importantly, in their hearts and minds, they started accepting him as one of their own.

As Abe returned from helping Henry distributing the remaining provisions to other needy families in Clary's Grove, Hannah Armstrong came outside, waving him down.

"Abe, where were you going?"

"Oh, I was going to check out your barn and see if I could sleep there"

No, you won't, not in this cold. Jack and I want you to come inside and stay in our little home, for as long as you're in Clary's Grove."

"Thank you, Aunt Hannah, that's real nice of you."

Reacting, she came closer to Abe, "Okay, I want to have a private word with you."

Stepping into their nearby little barn, just behind the Armstrong home, looking him square in the face, she was curious, "I want to know why you're calling me 'Aunt Hannah.' After all, I would guess we're about the same age."

"Just between you and me, Hannah, you look so much like my mother, you could be her sister. If that were so, it would make you my Aunt. So–to me–you've just gotta be 'Aunt Hannah.' My mother was a very beautiful woman whose looks and expressions you possess."

"WAS?" asked Hannah.

"She died way before her time, working and slaving herself to death. I was only nine years old when she passed on. After that happened, in my mind, I heard her voice saying *I'll always be with you, watching over you.* When I saw you this morning, it shocked me because you looked so much like her. It was like she did come back, only inside you."

"Abe, bless you for telling me. If she were here, I think your mother would be mighty proud of you. Somehow, I think she knows how you've turned out."

"Thank you for saying it. You're most kind–Aunt Hannah."

"One more thing, Abe. I want to thank you for your part in helping to restore my husband to me. I thought I had lost him to the Devil."

"To the Devil?"

"Yes, to booze and violence. Those fights he engaged in were taking him over, turning him away from the kind and gentle man he once was, turning him into someone I did not recognize."

"But Hannah, he's changing back, right before our eyes."

"Abe, that's what I want to tell you. He's stopped drinking and fighting, right after that fight with you last year. It was right about then he started thinking more about me and little Pleasant, becoming the man I fell in love with once again."

"Inside himself, he was always that good man, Hannah. He just needed to come back into the light from the dark place he had fallen into."

Hannah looked at Abe with an unusual, all-knowing expression filling her face, as she continued, "I believe the Lord works His wonders in strange ways, sometimes. Looking at you just now, I could see a glimmer of the Spirit of the Lord working through you. I know now you had something to do with bringing Jack back into the light. Abe, just so you know it, I'll always be grateful to you for that."

It had been happening all day, but especially after those few minutes alone with Hannah Armstrong in the barn, Abe quite literally became part of the Armstrong family. He would remain so for almost the next seven weeks. He would chop firewood for them, do repairs inside and outside their cabin, attend to the few farm animals they still had out in their little barn, and even make that new larger bed for little Pleasant.

Inside the Armstrong cabin, Jack slowly recovered, regaining his strength, little by little. As for Hannah, she looked after Abe like a real 'Aunt Hannah', mending his torn clothes, and keeping him fed.

During those weeks in Clary's Grove, as the weather got better, Abe also helped the other residents there. Already an accomplished rail splitter he helped with the construction of new fences, more clearly defining the boundaries of everyone's farms. For others, he helped construct new, more solid roofs for many individual's cabins. In doing so, he was honest and fair, looking out for each person's interest.

Even as he worked helping others, he didn't neglect the Armstrongs either. He still found time to chop plenty of firewood for their fireplace during the still chilly months of February and March, keeping them warm within their cabin.

Jack was slowly recovering from his horse shoeing accident. Watching Abe, he saw how he treated everybody, kind and gentle like.

As Abe sat by the fireplace one evening, Jack moved his chair over by him. "Abe," he revealed, "I've been watching you while I've been recovering. I've noticed an inner light within you seems to come to the surface and reveal itself as you work with others. You project a warmth that seems to leave a good feeling with whomever you're conversing with."

"Jack, I believe somewhere in the Bible it teaches that we should let our own inner light shine to the rest of the world."

"Well, you've taught me something. I see there's a lot more to be gained by treating people in kinder, gentler ways. Beginning with Hannah and Pleasant, I've been practicing your example. I want you to know everything has become a lot happier since you came here. You've helped to make it so."

"Thank you, Jack. I've been noticing your progress too. You've become a far happier man."

"Speaking of happiness, Hannah and I've been growing closer than we've ever been. We've been talking, and have decided Pleasant needs a brother. So we're going to try to make that happen."

"Good for you Jack. I hope it works out for you and Hannah."

It may have been partly because of that conversation, no one really knows, but the next morning, Abe and Jack moved Pleasant's new bed into a corner of the living room. This is where Abe would tell him stories by the fireplace and rock him to sleep many a night. The tall stranger soon became 'Uncle Abe' to the little boy. This was something he would also become to the new baby, Duff, when he came along in 1833.

Toward the last few days of March something happened to alter this idyllic existence. A knock at the door one morning would change things yet again. Jack opened the door to a familiar face. It was Santa Claus all over, in the form of Judge Green, Jack's half-brother.

"Come on in Judge. Have a cup of coffee with us, over by the fireplace."

"I'd be happy to."

"It's good to see my brother come into my house once again," said Jack welcoming him in.

Sitting down, the Judge continued, "The nature of my business concerns young Lincoln here. I'd hope you wouldn't mind. I'm here to fetch him for a job over at my place."

"It's up to Abe," Jack explained, "I have no hold on him to stay here."

Abe had been listening carefully since his name was mentioned. "I'm all ears. What do you have in mind Judge?"

"I'm just returning from New Salem where I learned the Offutt store is closed up and you're out of work," explained the Judge. "Well, I'm in a position to offer you a job that pays real money for your services, that is if you're interested."

"I'm interested," responded Abe, giving Judge Green his full attention.

As it turned out, the Judge had seen Henry McHenry in New Salem a day or two earlier. Henry had told him about Abe coming out to Clary's Grove, helping Jack and other residents make it through the winter.

After a few hours visit, Abe realized the Judge and Jack were becoming really close again. Jack was nearly well and ready to get back to work. It was a good time for him to move on, go help the Judge and eventually get back to New Salem.

Right after lunch, that day in late March 1832 Abe set out with the Judge. Riding in his buggy, the two men headed for the Judge's farm, which was about two miles due north of Clary's Grove.

On the way to their destination, about a mile into their journey, Abe noticed something setting in the distance, along the western horizon. He was amazed, as it was his first look at a large two-story full brick home. Having never see such a home, let alone one that was totally brick, he got excited. "Whose place is that?!"

"Why, Abe," the Judge explained, "that's Mentor Graham's place, the only brick home in these parts."

"It's right pretty in fact," added Abe, admiringly. "I've never seen such a place." Indeed, Abe had spent his whole life living out in the wilderness or small settlements of little more than a hundred people. Up to that time, New Salem with its 125 residents had been the largest town he'd ever lived in for any length of time. It had only been on the flatboat journey of 1831 that he had finally seen large cities like St. Louis and New Orleans. As he put it, "I was 21 years old before I finally got out and saw the world."

Another hour of travel, and Abe caught sight of the Judge's farm for the first time. Up ahead was his residence, a large two-story frame home, containing many rooms. As his family had grown, many rooms had been added on over the years. His farm with several out-buildings was equally impressive, sprawling over nearly a hundred acres.

"Impressive!" Abe reacted out loud. "Your farm compares in size with all of New Salem."

"Well, Abe, it didn't happen all at once. It's the result of many years hard work. That's something I want you to remember."

"What exactly is that?"

"That nothing in this life worth achieving is easily achieved. It's usually the result of many years hard work."

Stopping at a hitching post near the front of his home, the Judge announced, "We're home."

Getting out on the passenger side of the buggy, Abe went around to the other side, helping Judge Green down. As he did so, he glanced back down the rough road they had traveled on from Clary's Grove. Noticing the absence of something, Abe remarked, "It's gone, all the snow's gone."

"That's right, Abe. The winter of the deep snow is over, thank God. We've got about a week or so to go then there'll be a lot of work to be done around here. For now though, let's go inside. I want you to meet some of my family."

CHAPTER 8
AT JUDGE GREEN'S FARM

Standing in front of Judge Green's two-story farmhouse, Abe noticed it was a multi-chimney mansion of sorts, with chimneys at each end of the house. That meant multiple fireplaces upstairs as well as downstairs. It also indicated that Judge Green was a man of means and one of the wealthiest persons this side of Springfield.

Inside, Abe followed the Judge down a short hallway, bordered by his office on one side and a greeting parlor on the other side. The end of the short hall opened into a large family room, where the Judge's wife and children were gathered.

"Abe, I want you to meet my wife, Nancy."

"I'm so glad to meet you, Mrs. Green. Nancy was my late mother's name."

"I'm sure she was a very good woman, Mister Lincoln."

"She was–she is. You see, I feel like she's my guardian angel in Heaven."

"Speaking of angels," broke in the Judge, "here are my five little angels." Pointing, he preceded to introduced them, "Elizabeth, Jane, Amanda, and baby Delilah are the girls, and this is William, my son. They are all under ten years old."

"Amazing," responded Abe, surveying the gathered group of youngsters. "They are a fine group of young people."

"Thank you, Abe. I'm pretty proud of them," echoed the Judge.

"As a matter of curiosity," Abe wondered, "If you don't mind me asking, just how old are you Judge?"

"I know, the white hair and beard makes me look older, but I just turned 46 January 25th. Now it's my turn, how old are you, Abe?"

"Let me think a moment," he said, scratching his head. I've been so busy I haven't had time to think about it. I just had a birthday February 12th, so I'm 23–at least for the rest of the year."

Pleasant conversation went through dinner and on into the late evening, ending with the Judge offering Abe a spot near the fireplace in the great room. It was there he would make a pallet and sleep the first night. He agreed to meet the Judge in his office the next morning for what he assumed would be a discussion of what he was to do on the farm. In that assumption he would only partly be right.

An hour or two before daylight, an intense headache penetrated Abe's brain as he slept. The pulsating pain impacted him right above his left eye. Without realizing it, he moaned aloud, reliving an old nightmare from his long ago past. As he lay there trapped within restless turmoil, he felt a compassionate hand invade his nightmare world, gently shaking his shoulder.

"Abe, you're having a nightmare," announced a voice.

Abe snapped up to a sitting position, quite startled. "What? What is it?" Shaken from his nightmare, he found himself staring into the face of Judge Green as he loomed above him.

The Judge pulled up a chair next to Abe, who remained sitting up on his pallet. As the two men sat in the still darkened great room, they began to talk. Only illuminated by the crackling fire from the fireplace, the Judge explained, "I'm an early riser, usually getting up way before daylight."

"I'm sorry Judge, I sometimes have a recurring headache above my left eye, and a nightmare that goes along with it."

"Abe, what do you think causes it?"

"I know exactly what causes it. Right after my mother died, I was taking my dad's work horse to the fields the next morning. I was just trying to help him out with the day's work, but he was drunk and reacted violently…"

"What did he do to you, Abe?"

"Let me explain something. He'd been drinking heavily all night after my mother died. I didn't know it then–I was just nine years old–but he was an alcoholic. Well, he came up behind me, cursed me, and grabbed me by the back of my shirt. Yanking me backwards, he jerked me off his horse. I hit the ground hard. It must have excited the horse, because it kicked me in the head right above my left eye. It was like a sledgehammer hitting me full force. Everything went black and I passed out."

"He did that to you! What happened after that?"

"I only know what my cousin, Dennis Hanks, has told me, as he was there and witnessed the whole incident. He said I lay there still, all death-like. Dennis started to check on me but my father yelled at him, 'Leave him be! Don't touch him. If he's dead in the morning, we'll bury him by his mother.' Dennis tried to explain to him, that I was only try'n to help him with the chores since mother had just died. My father answered him, 'I don't need his help, not now, not ever. Besides, no one rides my horse unless I give'em my permission.' According to Dennis, he went back inside and drank heavily until he passed out at the table."

"What kind of man was your father to treat his own son that way?"

"When you're deal'n with a drunk, I have since found out, you're deal'n with someone who has no common sense, no reason."

"Well, what happened to you?"

"My cousin was too scared to do anything at first. So I was left laying there till my father passed out. Then, Dennis dragged me inside, where he and my little sister Sarah cleaned me up and put cold rags on my forehead to take the swelling down. I must've slept all night, but before I woke up the next morning, I saw this vision of my mother surrounded by a brilliant light. She said, 'Never fear, I'm gonna be with you always now.' Then I woke up, all healed. It was like my mother came down from Heaven as my guardian angel, and the good Lord healed me."

"That's a remarkable story, Abe."

"I guess the only after effects I've had is my lazy left eye affecting me sometimes when I can't quire open my left eyelid all the way and occasional headaches and dreams, sometimes very bad dreams. But all in all, I count myself pretty lucky to be alive."

The Judge shook his head and concluded, "None of this should have ever happened to you, but perhaps there's some Divine purpose yet to come."

"I still don't know the ending of my story, Judge. To my way of thinking, I figure there has to be a reason for which I was healed."

"Well, my boy, I believe sometimes the Lord does things we don't understand right then, but in the fullness of time, maybe we learn. After breakfast, I want you to come into my office and let me show you some books that may help you."

"I'd like that Judge."

"Oh, one thing, I was wondering. Whatever happened to your father? Has he gone on to meet his Maker?"

"Oh no, he's not dead. He's still alive and still drinking, at least that's what I heard in a letter from my cousin. He said my father told him I was worthless and a good riddance."

"My boy, he doesn't deserve you as a son."

"I haven't seen him in almost a year and a half now. I don't think he knows exactly where I'm at. Anyways, if I ever see him again in this life, it'll be too soon."

After breakfast, Abe did meet with the Judge in his office. In a sense, this day would become the first day of a new life for him. For within the walls of this little office would be the building blocks–the very essence of all knowledge–that would begin to change his life forever.

"My boy, have a seat. It's time we had a heart to heart talk, about your future."

"Well, Judge, I'm anxious to know about my future." Abe didn't realize his comment was a bit prophetic, as the Judge was already formulating a plan in his mind concerning him.

Seated behind his desk, he explained, "Abe, I'm a man of vision, only the vision I have now concerns your future. I've been watching you."

"And what have you seen?" Abe questioned from his chair, sitting on the opposite side of the desk, facing the Judge.

The Judge studied him closely for a moment and told him, "I see in you a young man who possesses enormous potential."

"Potential for what?"

"For anything. I've seen you accomplish everything you've put your mind to do ever since you set foot in New Salem. You could barely read when you started at the Offutt store. But you hung in there and mastered elementary reading and math. I know this because Billy told me so."

"What exactly did Billy tell you?"

"That he helped you with your studies at night. Now he says you can run circles around him."

"I had to, Judge. I just had to. I have this deep hunger inside me to learn, not to be illiterate like my father. I won't be like him."

"While you're educating yourself, I wish you would help my half-brother. Jack can barely sign his name."

"He can do more than that now. While I was at his place, with him laid up, I've been helping him in that regard. He can even write a letter now. It's simple, with some misspellings, but he can do it."

"Amazing."

"Something else. He even kept a little diary, sort of a record of what happened while I was out there these past seven weeks. You ought to ask him to show it to you the next time you're over there."

"Oh, I couldn't do that."

"Yes you can, Jack's pretty proud of it. You may not realize it, but he really looks up to you and admires you. This rift of the past few years has really weighed heavily upon his mind. Being ill has made him take stock of himself and his life. He loves you Judge. To him you are HIS brother, not just a half-brother. He wants to tell you, but he doesn't know how."

"Thank you, Abe, for telling me this. It means a lot to me. You know, there is something about your personality. You have a knack for being able to draw the best out of a person. For instance, those Clary's Grove boys were ready to run you out of town a few months ago. Now, they love you and accept you as one of their own. Henry McHenry told me that when I ran into him in New Salem, while I was looking for you."

"Now you're making me feel good, Judge. In my whole life, I've always wanted to feel needed, to *belong* somewhere. At least I've accomplished that somewhat in New Salem and out at Clary's Grove."

"See Abe, that's what I've been saying. You can achieve anything you put your mind to do."

"You're right, there's a lot more for me to learn."

"What do you see around you in my office?"

"Bookcases that go all around the room, full of lots of books."

"These books are very special, Abe. They contain the knowledge I've accumulated over a lifetime. They are about the history of our country, the history of the world, about religion, about the Bible and how we came to be children of God."

"All the things I ever wanted to learn and know about."

"Well now you can, Abe."

"I can?"

"Yes, while you're here at my farm you may read and study whatever you'd like to in here."

"Why would you be doing that for me Judge?"

"Abe, do you know what it is to mentor a person?"

"No, not really."

It means to teach, to help you learn and acquire knowledge, so you can grow into the man you were meant to be."

"Judge you can't possibly imagine what this means to me."

"I've got a pretty good idea. I started my family later than most people do. My son is only seven years old, a small child yet. I'm not getting any younger, but I'm wanting to impart my knowledge to someone while I still can."

"Thank you, Judge, for whatever you see in me."

"Right now, my boy, I have plenty of time to show you. For instance, that bookcase behind you contains all my law books and everything I've ever learned about the law. They have led me here to become Justice of the Peace of this county."

"There's so much knowledge here-so much to learn," marveled Abe.

Over the next ten days it was as though a miracle happened. Abe quickly became a part of the Green family, far more than just a visitor. Abe became like an older son to Judge and Mrs. Green, something the couple had always wanted. To Abe, on the other hand, he saw Judge Green as a surrogate father figure, like the father he'd always wanted and never had. He felt like the Judge really understood him. To the Judge, the young Kentuckian became like a gift from God that he and his wife took great pride in.

During those ten days, Abe could often be found in the Judge's office where he would sit at an old school desk, reading and studying one book after another, learning whatever he could comprehend. From early hours of the morning till late into the night, Abe was getting a crash course in education. Things went along wonderfully with Abe soaking up knowledge like a sponge.

Then came the morning of April 5th, 1832, the day an excited rider could be seen emerging from the northern horizon at a fast gallop. Abe and the Judge had been outside that morning, looking over the farm. All that was within their field of vision included several outlying buildings and cabins spread over the Judge's property. Nearer to the house was a large barn, where the Judge's horses, his buggy, and two wagons were kept. The way the Judge had been talking, he was wanting Abe to help him oversee the farm and its half dozen farm hands who were presently out in the field. All of those plans were about to change very quickly as Fate was to rule otherwise.

The excited rider was getting closer, but they still could not make out what he was saying from a distance. Moments later though, he reached the farmhouse, riding into view right in from of Abe and Judge Green. He was yelling at the top of his voice, "It's war!" Without dismounting he yanked a pamphlet from his saddle bags. Handing it to Judge Green, he added, "You'll probably be needed in New Salem." Without another word, he rode off in the direction of Clary's Grove.

Not quite comprehending or understanding what was happening, Abe asked excitedly, "What war?!"

Having just read the pamphlet, the Judge answered, "I'll tell you about it on the way to New Salem. Abe, go to the barn, hitch up the buggy and meet me back here in fifteen minutes. While you do that I'll have to warn everybody of what may happen."

Turning around, the Judge eyed a large bell hanging near the hitching post. Going over to it, he pulled the rope, ringing the farm's alarm bell several times. This was the signal for all his workers within earshot to come to the farm house immediately.

After sounding the alarm, the Judge stepped back inside, retrieving two Kentucky long rifles with powder horns for himself and Abe. While inside, the Judge also drew his family close, hugging and telling them, "I'll be back, but just when, I can't really say. May God bless and protect all of you in the meantime."

Nancy Green replied, "I love you. May God be with you."

Hearing some of this as he brought the buggy up by the front door, Abe knew the situation was serious. As he waited on the Judge, anxiety filled him with the feeling his world was about to be turned upside down.

CHAPTER 9
THE BLACKHAWK WAR

Turning the reigns over to the Judge as they left the farm, Abe became a passenger in the buggy once more. He was a man with questions and proceeded to ask, "Judge, who was that horseman who rode up earlier?"

"He was a courier from Governor Reynolds over in Vandalia."

This aroused Abe's curiosity. He was full of more questions. "Why was he so anxious? What's happening?"

"The man was anxious because he was on an urgent mission. It could be a matter of life and death."

"A matter of life and death?" Abe repeated him, except more serious, even grave.

"Yes, the pamphlet he handed me back there brought home some of my worst fears."

"Judge, what are some of your worst fears?'

"A few years ago, back in '27 we had an Indian uprising here, I was Captain of the militia from around here. The Indians were driven west of the Mississippi. We put the uprising down, but it left a lot of bitter feelings among the Indians. I've always feared those feelings might catch fire again."

"So those feelings have become a reality?"

"Yes, Abe, I think they have. That pamphlet was calling every able bodied man to arms and unite as a state-wide militia to repel the invader."

"The invader?"

"It seems that Chief Black Hawk with over 500 of his warriors have invaded the entire state demanding their ancestral tribal lands be returned to them."

"Was the treaty unfair to the Indians?"

The Judge glanced over at Abe as he asked this question. Thinking about it, he answered truthfully, "Frankly, yes. Squatters have moved in, taking the land guaranteed under the treaty. Chief Black Hawk is 65 years old with a long-standing sense of right and wrong. He is willing to put his life on the line for what he believes in. His people agree with him and think they have been wronged. For them the time to talk is over with. They have come back into Illinois armed to the hilt. There have already been some initial hostilities. Innocent civilian blood has been spilled. Since this has happened, I believe it will be very difficult to put a lid back on what is about to happen."

"What is that, Judge?"

"I think more blood is going to be spilled. A war that nobody wants is about to take place."

As they headed on to New Salem, the two men grew quiet. Dark thoughts of what might happen filled their minds with apprehension and concern.

After a while, they finally caught sight of New Salem up ahead on the horizon. As smoke from fireplaces drifted lazily into the sky above, the town appeared quiet and undisturbed.

Abe reacted, a bit relieved, "It looks peaceful as usual."

"So it appears, at least for now," added Judge Green. "But let's see how the townspeople handle the news."

As they came into New Salem from the west, everybody seemed to be going about their business as usual. Entering onto Main Street, the Judge steered his horse-drawn buggy, urging the horses toward a hitching post near the Rutledge Inn. Nearby was a large alarm bell, that if rung could be heard within a quarter mile's distance, all over town.

"Abe," instructed the Judge, "go and ring that bell for several minutes. I want to get everyone's attention so I can read this pamphlet to them."

Abe complied, pulling on the bell for a full ten minutes or more. Sure enough, the loud clanging got everyone's attention. Coming out of stores, and even from nearby cabins just south of New Salem, the whole town gathered near Judge Green who was now standing on the front porch of the Rutledge Inn.

Just about the same time, there was a loud commotion from the west as about a dozen mounted horsemen, followed by many wagons, came barreling down Main Street at a fast pace. Stopping in a cloud of dust near the Rutledge Inn, one almost immediately could tell it was the Clary's Grove boys and many of their families.

Coming across the street from his store was John McNeil, with a deadly serious scowl on his face. Seeing it was Abe clanging the alarm bell, he proceeded straight toward him in confrontational fashion. "Lincoln, what is the meaning of this?!"

Overhearing him from the porch, the Judge broke in, "Not now, McNeil! Whatever is on your mind will just have to wait. I have an urgent matter of the gravest importance that will have to come first. Understand!"

The Judge had spoken with such commanding authority even the high-handed McNeil had to back off. "Sure Judge, of course I understand." His voice wavered, becoming considerably more meek, as he saw the glare coming from the Judge's face.

Returning his focus to Lincoln, he edged closer to him till they were right in front of each other. McNeil whispered to him, but still in his ordering tone of voice, "Lincoln, I have to talk to you after the Judge is finished, inside the Inn"

Not flinching a bit, Abe fired back, "Anytime, McNeil–only later."

While the Judge was waiting for more townspeople to join the crowd of listeners, Jack Armstrong, Henry McHenry, and other Clary Grove boys encircled Abe, glad to see him. As Jack put it, "It's mighty good to see our savior from the winter of the deep snow again." Then getting more serious and with a tone of worry in his voice added, "Governor Reynolds' courier stopped in Clary's Grove. Our women folk are really worried. The courier told us to evacuate to New Salem, that the Judge would tell us more here. So I came to hear what my brother has to say."

With an enormous crowd of New Salem citizens, dismounted horsemen and wagons full of women and children from Clary's Grove gathered, Judge Green addressed them all in his booming voice, "Men, citizens of New Salem, a grave emergency is about to befall us." Waving the pamphlet, he explained, "I hold here a message and a call to arms straight from Governor Reynolds announcing a war is coming soon. Chief Black Hawk and over five hundred of his best mounted warriors have already put several cabins to the torch and murdered civilians. We must get prepared to protect our women and children."

"We'll be ready, Judge." Jack Armstrong spoke up, waving the Kentucky long rifle he was holding.

The Judge explained further, "The Governor is asking all settlements and towns in Illinois to form their own local militias to be our first line of defense against this invader and to protect our homes. I will have more information and instructions shortly, perhaps by tomorrow. So, in the meantime, secure your homes and get prepared for what could be war, very soon."

As soon as Judge Green finished, Henry McHenry, who was standing close to Abe, spoke to him, "I've got something to tell you, something important."

Abe acknowledged him. "Okay Henry, what is it?"

"Do you remember while you were out at Clary's Grove the first part of March, I mentioned I'd gotten some cash together to come back into New Salem and see if I could pick up a few more supplies at McNeil's store?"

"Yes, I remember you saying something about it, but that's all I remember. Why? Did something earth-shaking happen?"

"Yes, Abe. Something pretty important did happen. Well, I figure I outa tell you since you'll probably find out, sooner than later."

"What happened, Henry?"

"When I entered McNeil's store this time, he took a great deal of interest when I told him I was your friend. We got to talk'n and he said there's go'n to be an election this fall for a new representative from these parts. He asked me who would be a good candidate to represent New Salem? I answered Abe Lincoln, of course. So with Mister McNeil's help, we filled out the nominating papers so you could run in the election to represent us in the state house."

"You did what?!"

"We sure did. Mister McNeil thought it was a great idea. He was so generous to help me fill out the necessary papers, even sign your name for you. He was so helpful."

"I'll bet he was." Abe was immediately suspicious, knowing if he won the election, it would take him out of New Salem for months at a time. Just what McNeil wanted, so he could make a move on Ann. Abe wasn't sure how he'd deal with it, but he would figure out something.

There was no more time to think, as Jack Armstrong and all of Abe's friends had gathered around him, yelling, "Lincoln for office! Lincoln for our representative!"

Backing up toward the front door of the Rutledge Inn, Abe was feeling pressure closing in all around him.

Moving toward Abe till he was right in front of him, Jack noticed something uncomfortable in his expression. He then sought to somewhat soften the emphasis of the situation. Turning to the crowd, Jack broke in, "Wait a minute men. We're forget'n why we're here. A war's fast come'n in our direction." But, turning back to Lincoln, "Abe, if you could say a quick little something to those who've always supported you."

The Judge, who had heard everything, whispered in Abe's ear, "Whatever you say, speak truthfully from your heart."

With this advice, Abe knew what to say, and said it, "Men, you honor me far more than I deserve. I am humble Abraham Lincoln. You, my friends have made me a candidate for public office. If elected in the election later this year, I will honestly and faithfully serve you with all of my heart. If not elected, it'll be all the same. For by nominating me, you have, already honored me more than I could ever hope to have been."

"You're an honest man, Abe Lincoln," spoke up Doctor Allen, who had just joined the crowd.

"Thanks, Doc," replied Abe, giving him a glance full of honest appreciation in his face. "Now men, let's join Judge Green inside, in the great room. I'm sure he'll have more to say about the coming emergency."

As everyone followed Judge Green inside, he managed to lean in close to Abe and whisper, "My boy, good speech, short and to the point."

As everyone entered the great room, Abe stepped to one side, his eyes adjusting to the darker candle and lantern lit setting. Looking around, he spotted the one person he'd hope to see from his first moment back in New Salem. It was Ann. Illuminated, by the flames from the nearby fireplace, her eyes were fixed squarely on him. He immediately went over by her while everyone else followed Judge Green, gathering around him in another part of the great room.

Having a brief moment to themselves, Abe and Ann faced each other for the first time in over three months. Ann opened up, "I've missed you a lot, but a lot has happened since you've been gone."

"A lot has happened," agreed Abe, continuing, "and now I fear our world is about to be turned upside down once again."

"It already has. While you've been gone, my father has almost lost everything."

"How can that be?"

"The winter hit my family hard, financially. We were about to lose everything and be homeless. But something happened."

"What happened?"

"John McNeil approached my father, made him an offer of a loan and even a place to live if the Inn went out of business."

"I didn't realize McNeil was so charitable."

"The price of his charity is more than I can bare." Ann suddenly went silent, about to cry.

Abe persisted, "What is his price?"

"He insisted my father pledge–in writing–that I would marry him, that I must comply with this agreement or my family would become penniless, without any hope of survival. I was his price for helping my family. Abe, I don't know what to do. I don't love him, but I don't want to see my family become homeless."

"Ann, listen to me." Abe said those word with all the authority he could summon into his voice. "I'll talk to John McNeil."

"Oh Abe, you must not," she responded, looking both worried and frightened.

"Don't worry, Ann. He wants to visit with me anyway."

Ann looked very surprised, still questioning, "He does?"

"Yes, he does," Abe reconfirmed, glancing around the great room. Finding the object of his search, his eyes fell upon the face of McNeil. He had been staring at Ann and Abe from his table across the great room.

Reacting, Abe returned to his conversation with Ann, "In fact, I do believe McNeil wants to talk to me right now."

"Oh, Abe."

"Don't worry, I'll handle this."

Turning in the direction of McNeil, who was seated at a little corner wall table across the room from the fireplace, Abe approached him with forceful determination in his every step. Stopping right in front of his table, Abe's voice became more forceful than usual, "So you wanted to talk to me."

"Lincoln, I told you earlier, I wanted to speak to you! That meant right away!" McNeil could barely contain his exploding temper as he glared at him the same time.

"Listen here, you may have noticed I am not one of your employees, nor am I at your beck and call." Abe immediately took a disliking to John McNeil thinking he possessed similar personality traits to his own unbending father, Thomas Lincoln.

At the same time, McNeil quickly appreciated that this tall Kentuckian was not a man who would easily cow down to his demands. This was something he was not used to dealing with. Seeing the determined expression in Abe's face, he decided it best to start over. "Lincoln, please, sit down. Much has happened. We need to talk."

"Very well then. I'll talk with you for a bit." Sitting down, across the table from him, Abe added, "Mister, where I come from, most people get a lot further with me by being more cordial, not by issuing commands."

"Lincoln, you're not like anyone I've ever met. Perhaps that's because I'm from New York and you're from the Kentucky frontier. We were brought up in two different worlds. Perhaps that has something to do with the fact I've never liked you."

"Well McNeil, maybe you're right to a certain degree. You, in your fancy eastern clothes, make quite a contrast to me, in my homespun frontier clothes. Yet, I think it goes deeper than that. We think differently. Maybe, you don't like me because I put the value of people's feelings above the value of money."

"See, that's what I don't understand about you. Having money is the answer to everything for me. Money is power. Money gives me control."

"How do you mean that, McNeil?"

"With money I can buy anything I want. You see, I have bought Miss Rutledge."

"Your money can't buy her love."

"What does that matter? She can bare children and she will bare mine."

"You assume too much. She hasn't married you. She's not your wife yet."

"You're correct Lincoln, but she will be my wife."

"What makes you so sure of that?"

"Oh, Ann didn't tell you? Well maybe she didn't know. Her father has already signed a contract with me. As his daughter, she has to honor the terms of that agreement."

"I'm not so sure you can make that stick in a court of law."

"Who are you, Lincoln? What do you know about the law?"

"I'm someone whose learn'n more about the law all the time. Someday I might even become a lawyer myself."

"That'll be the day. But enough of this for now, what I wanted to talk to you about has to do with this war coming on. While you and all those rowdy friends of yours go off to fight it, I'll organize the citizens that stay here and arm them with rifles from my store."

"It sounds like you've got it all figured out."

"This much I've got figured, if you don't upset Miss Rutledge or her family, they will find a friend to help them, with money and a roof over their heads. On the other hand, if you make trouble for me, they may find themselves with no money to keep this place open. They could even wind up out on the street, homeless."

"Would you really do that to people?"

"Lincoln, I'll do whatever it takes to get what I want. Now if you'll be reasonable and march out of here with your little militia, I'll see that Miss Rutledge and her family are well taken care of while you're gone. In fact, I'm going to see that my clerk and your old friend, Billy Green, joins the militia and goes along with you. This way it'll be seen as me doing my patriotic duty for the war effort."

"Very well, I won't cause you any trouble–at least for now. But when this war is over, I'll be coming back to revisit this situation with you."

"There won't be anything to revisit. You see, Lincoln, by then you'll be out of the picture for good."

"Don't be too sure about that. One thing life has taught me is sometimes Fate has a way of intervening and changing over lives completely, especially when we least expect it."

"Abe Lincoln! Where are you?" The booming voice of Judge Green could suddenly be heard all over the great room, fast becoming very crowded.

"Right here, Judge," replied Abe, standing up, waving his hand.

Leaving McNeil with his thoughts of possessing Ann, Abe began working his way through the crowd toward two huge tables pushed together and the Santa Claus figure standing behind them. The Judge had been surrounded by not only the Clary boys, but by members of the Rutledge clan as well. Ann's cousin, McGrady, along with her brothers, John and David, were all eager to join the proposed New Salem militia.

Joining the group, Abe quickly noticed he was the center of attention. Everyone just happened to be suddenly focused on him. "What's happening men?" Abe asked, becoming very curious.

"What's happening involves you," explained Judge Green. Glancing over at Jack Armstrong, who had worked his way over next to Abe, the Judge called on his brother, "Why don't you tell Abe?"

Having Abe's full attention, Jack told him, "While you were talking to Ann and Mister McNeil, we all got together and decided something very important about you."

Abe searched the faces of the entire group. They were all grinning big. Shooting a quick glance over to the Judge only brought a short response from him, "Just keep listening to Jack here."

Getting his attention again, Jack continued, "Abe, as I was say'n, all these men here look up to you. So, all of us here took a vote and chose you to be our leader and command the New Salem militia."

McGrady added, "That counts for all us Rutledges too."

Abe was completely surprised at this turn of events. "What about it Judge?"

"Under Illinois law each local militia can elect their own officers. The men of New Salem have chosen you."

Jack extended his hand, shaking hands with Abe, "Congratulations, Captain Lincoln, you are now the commander of our local militia."

Abe was genuinely moved. "Men, you've done me a great honor. This is so unexpected. I'm surprised."

The Judge added, "My boy, the men of New Salem have complete faith in you."

"Whatever happens, I promise to do my very best for everyone here. I just know a good captain must have a good first sergeant to carry out his orders, so I'd like to nominate a born leader as my first sergeant, Jack Armstrong!"

Everyone seconded that nomination with an uproarious hurrah. Abe and Jack warmly shook hands again in what would cement a friendship that would last, the rest of their lives.

Plans for war progressed with each passing hour. Going over maps that Judge Green had spread out across the two tables, everyone talked till late in the evening.

The next morning, a new courier arrived with news from Governor Reynolds. It was confirmed that Black Hawk's band of warriors were already in the western part of the state. United States army troops stationed in Illinois would not be of sufficient members to repel the invasion. All local militias were to form, begin training at once, and await a call to action that could come at any time.

A vacant field just south of downtown New Salem was selected as the place to gather at straight up noon that day. At the appointed time it was evident the word had spread. Rugged looking frontiersmen from the surrounding area had gotten the word and were already spilling into New Salem. Dressed in home spun clothes and buckskins, they were armed with all manner of weapons, Kentucky long rifles, muskets and flint-lock pistols, as well as wicked-looking Bowie knives. Gathering together, they had the look of a gang of ruffians that nobody would want to tangle with.

Judge Green stepped forward to address the crowd, soon getting everyone's attention, "For those that don't know me, I'm Judge Bowling Green, Justice of the Peace of the county. I'm here to inform all of you of dire news. Governor Reynolds is calling every able-bodied man between the ages of eighteen and forty-five to serve for the duration of the coming emergency. Black Hawk has an army of mounted warriors–Sauk and Fox Indians–that have crossed our borders into the western part of the state. It is the Governor's goal to raise at least a thousand man fighting force to face this threat. Those of you that have not done so already, should go see Billy Greene in the great room of the Rutledge Inn. He has an enlistment roll for all of you to sign. Once you've done that, report back here to Captain Lincoln and Sergeant Armstrong for further instructions."

As the newcomers in the crowd headed down the Springfield Road to enroll, one of them looked familiar to Jack Armstrong.

Getting Abe's attention, he told him, "Here comes someone I think you should meet."

Waving down the young man headed in their direction, Jack called out to him, "Bill step over here, I want you to meet someone."

Complying, the young man joined Jack and Abe, off to one side of the road. "Why Jack Armstrong," he said, recognizing him, "something looks different about you."

"I am different. I woke up and stopped drink'n. But, I haven't seen you in over a year. You used to come into New Salem and party with us every weekend."

"Yeah, I guess the ways of sin sort of caught up with me too. I've had to stay home and work my father's farm since he's out preaching the word of the Lord all the time."

Gesturing to Abe, Jack introduced the two men. "Bill, this is our leader and my friend, Captain Abraham Lincoln. Abe, this here's Bill Berry from Rock Creek, a little settlement about four miles south of here."

The two shook hands and Abe inquired, "You say your father is a preacher?"

"Yes, he's been a circuit riding preacher in Sangamon County for about ten years now. When he's not on the road, he's got a little church down our ways, the Rock Creek Presbyterian Church. When we heard about Black Hawk's invasion, he told me I had to join up, that it was my patriotic duty. You see, my father was with Andy Jackson at the Battle of New Orleans in the War of 1812. While there, he had the honor to personally lower the British flag and raise the American flag back over New Orleans."

"We're glad to have you with us," Abe said, welcoming him. "Any son of a true American patriot is always welcome in our militia."

"Thank you, Captain Lincoln, but in a way, just maybe the experience will help me escape the shadow of my father."

"I kind of know what you mean," agreed Abe, reflecting, "there comes a time when most young men have to escape the shadows of their fathers."

Nodding in agreement, young Berry switched subjects with a curious question that struck another cord with Abe, "Since I haven't been in New Salem for over a year, may I ask, is Miss Ann still at the Inn?"

"She sure is," broke in Jack. "She's there right now help'n Billy Greene sign people up for the militia."

This news seemed to encourage him as a big smile broke out across his face, "Then I'd better go and have her help me sign up right now." With that remark, Bill Berry took off in the direction of the Rutledge Inn.

After he was out of ear shot, Abe leaned in close to Jack. "Tell me more about Bill Berry."

"I'd forgotten, Abe, he used to be sweet on Ann. But she started avoiding him when he started hang'n out with me and the Clary boys. He got to drink'n heavy and became what we call a bad drunk. I'm ashamed of having been a bad influence on him. I know it really hurt his father to see his son become a drunkard. Rev. Berry is a non-drinker and a very spiritual person. Bill is basically a good person, one who is tempted too easily. I think being with us in whatever comes, might be the best thing that could ever happen to him."

"I'll be glad to help him too. I think we all need a helping hand at one time or another in our lives." Abe was thinking of more than just Bill Berry as he said those words.

"Abe, I think I'm beginning to really know you. Helping people is what you do best anyway. You really do practice what you preach."

"Jack, I try. I really try."

Just then, some rowdiness among the men across the road got both men's attention. "I'll take care of this," Jack announced. Headed across the road he yelled, "Alright men, straighten up! Act like real militia veterans."

Abe was alone now, watching his new sergeant straighten out the formation of those already signed up. Jack was already doing his part of turning these frontiersmen into the beginnings of a fighting force.

105

As he observed the men, thoughts of all that had happened over the past year ran through Abe's head. He was quickly drawn out of his thoughts though when he suddenly felt a firm hand on his shoulder from behind. "Lincoln," a familiar voice announced itself. Abe turned around to see the stern figure of a heavily bearded man with blazing eyes facing him. It was William Price Clary.

"What do you want?" Abe asked, almost defensively.

"I didn't come here to fight you. I just want to talk."

"You've got my attention, Bill Clary. Talk."

"We haven't seen each other since before I had to close my saloon last year. I know, I said and did a lot of things to hurt you. I tried my best to run you out of town, but you wouldn't be run out. Well, I've had time to think about a lot of things these past few months. My kin told me how you went out to Clary's Grove and helped them make it through the winter. I just wanted to say that you're a lot better man than I thought you were."

"I'm thank'n you for saying that, Bill."

"I couldn't live with myself if I didn't try to set things right with you, Lincoln. Now with this Indian emergency, I wanted to volunteer the services of myself and two dozen of my kin that live a few miles south of here."

"I must confess to you," Abe revealed, "I didn't know who was going to watch out for the women folk here and out at Clary's Grove."

"We will, Lincoln. I'll see to it. You have my word of honor on it."

"Well, Bill, maybe we can be friends after all of this is over."

"I'd like that Lincoln, but as I said I've done a lot of think'n about my life. I've come to the conclusion, I'm just not used to the civilized way of life you and others are bring'n to New Salem. I came here almost twelve years ago when it was a wild rugged frontier. What I'm used to is more of a hard drink'n, hard fight'n life style. No, when all these Indian troubles are over, I'm take'n my wife and family, and all who'll go with me, southwest to Texas. I'm hear'n that my type of environment exists there."

"After these troubles are over with, wherever you go, I wish you luck, Bill." With that, Abe offered his hand.

"Thank you, Lincoln. I kinda see why Jack likes you so much." Bill Clary shook hands with Abe for the first and only time. True to his word, Clary would move to Texas after the Blackhawk War, and live out his life there on the Texas frontier.

Events moved quickly during the next few days. Judge Green took charge of making sure all militia men were armed and had a horse. A flurry of messages came into New Salem by courier from Governor Reynolds in Vandalia to the Judge's headquarters at the Rutledge Inn.

Finally, the orders came down for the New Salem militia to report. Pulling Abe aside, Judge Green wished him well, "God bless you my boy. I'll be praying for your safety and for that of all your men."

The local company was to be dispatched to Beardstown, some forty miles to the northwest. Preparing for their departure, the militia was gathering at the far east end of town near the old Offutt store. The plan was they would march down Main Street heading west to the road that would take them in a north westerly direction to their destination.

The Judge walked with Abe down Main Street to where everyone was gathering by the boarded up Offutt store. As they went along, the Judge said something to Abe in a low voice, "I want you to know I'll be personally looking out for your interests while you're gone."

"I'm not sure I follow you Judge," questioned Abe.

"Before you ride out, I want you to go check something out on the far side of the Offutt store. Then you'll understand what I mean."

Abe complied with the Judge, not fully understanding. Walking in that direction, he knew the other side of the Offutt store was presently out of sight from everyone else. He thought to himself, very mysterious, but he knew not to question the Judge. Turning the corner, heading to the back side of the Offutt store, he stopped dead in his tracks.

107

Standing immediately in front of him was the figure of Ann Rutledge. Clutching something in her hand, she's stepped closer to him. "Oh Abe, I couldn't let you leave without seeing you. I had to tell you, there's only one man I love on the face of the earth, and it sure isn't John McNeil." Opening her hand she revealed a bright red bandana. Reaching up, she placed it around his neck. "I made this for you. I pray this might help keep you safe and bring you back to me." Taking his hand, she kissed it gently, lovingly.

Emotions taking him over, Abe drew her close to him, underneath the wide-brimmed felt hat the Judge had given him.

Not knowing what was keeping him, Jack Armstrong and Billy Greene had dismounted and were about to round the corner of the old store when Jack motioned Billy to stop. They could plainly see something, but Abe's wide-brimmed hat was blocking their view. Jack whispered, "Billy, let's go back and tell the men our leader is tending to important business."

"Yes," agreed Billy, "but I believe our Captain has a sweetheart."

Momentarily, Abe returned, his face reflecting something had boosted his morale. Whatever happened between Ann and him, no one would ever know as they had been out of sight from the entire town. Even Jack and Billy could never be completely sure, as Abe's hat had hid their private communication from History's prying eye.

As Abe mounted his horse, Judge Green looked up at him, and said knowingly, "Just remember, Abe, it was like I was telling you. I'll be looking out for your interest while you're gone."

Abe nodded silently, fully understanding him now. Wheeling his horse around, in a raised voice he gave the order, "Forward men, to Beardstown."

As the mounted militia proceeded westward down Main Street, a swelling crowd of citizens on both sides of the street cheered them as they left town.

On the front porch of the Inn, James Rutledge stood with John McNeil beside him. Leaning over to McNeil, Rutledge wondered out loud, "I wonder where Ann is. I would've thought she would have liked to have seen her brothers ride out of town with Captain Lincoln."

"Captain Lincoln!" McNeil reacted in a belittling tone. "She's better off remaining inside doing women's work in the kitchen."

The two men would remain completely ignorant of the secret farewell meeting that had taken place. Only many months later, Ann would reveal what happened to her cousin, McGrady, and her brothers, John and David. Little by little, the rest of the Rutledge clan would begin to realize that Ann, in her own quiet way, was a person of independent will and inner faith.

From town, the mounted militia headed across country, stopping only at Richland Creek, a small community about nine miles northwest of New Salem. There on the farm of Dallas Scott, a group of volunteers had gathered, wanting to join the mounted militia. Again, the swelling band of militia put the question of leadership to a vote. Abe was elected captain by over 75 percent of the vote. It was another morale booster to 23-year-old, young Lincoln.

Early the next day, this all volunteer group arrived in Beardstown, where they were officially sworn into service by officers of the U.S. Army. One of those in charge was Colonel Zachary Taylor, who would become a future president of the United States.

One might say, in one of those ironies of History, the assembling of fighting men at Beardstown was a gathering of presidents. Colonel Taylor ordered his son-in-law, who was a young lieutenant under him, to swear in and administer the oath of allegiance to young Lincoln and his group of volunteers. The young lieutenant was Jefferson Davis, who would become President of the Confederacy during the Civil War. It was there, at Beardstown on April 22nd 1832, that he and young Lincoln met for the first time.

After administering the oath of allegiance, Lieutenant Davis announced, "It is official now, you are Captain Lincoln in the 31st Regiment of Militia from Sangamon County. You and your men will comprise a rifle company within the 4th Regiment of Mounted Volunteers. Congratulations, Captain Lincoln."

"Thank you, sir," answered Abe, proudly shaking hands with a man, who years later he would try to remember exactly what he looked like. As the two men saluted each other, Colonel Taylor, who'd been looking on, was said to have commented to a friend, "Look at my son-in-law, I think he's a born leader and you know something, I wouldn't be surprised if that young militia captain doesn't amount to something too. He handles himself well."

April 22nd 1832 was also a fateful day in another way. After drawing supplies, the 4th Regiment of the Mounted Volunteers were setup in tents on vacant land just outside of Beardstown. Abe had just got situated inside his officer's tent when Sergeant Jack Armstrong entered, a bit on the anxious side. "Abe, there's an officer outside, a major who says he wants to talk to you."

"Calm down, Jack. Just properly announce him as you bring him in."

"Abe, I'll do my best."

As the tent flap opened back, an impressive looking major entered. Jack came to attention, announcing him, "Sir, this is Major John T. Stuart."

"At ease Sergeant," responded Major Stuart, continuing, "that will be all. I have something for Captain Lincoln."

Saluting him, Abe responded smartly, "Captain Lincoln at your service sir."

"At ease, Lincoln. You are Abe Lincoln from New Salem?"

"Yes sir, I am that Abe Lincoln." He wondered, he knows my name, but how? He would quickly find out.

"Lincoln, we have a mutual friend."

"We do?"

"Yes, Judge Green, Justice of the Peace of Sangamon County. He spoke highly of you and said I should meet you."

"I appreciate Judge Green's kind words, Major Stuart."

"Lincoln, the Judge is more than a friend. He was my mentor. I was a struggling law student when he encouraged me. Without his help, I don't know if I would have made it. But I did. Now I'm a full-fledged attorney in Springfield. Before these Indian troubles started, I got to this place in my life thanks to the Judge. He saw something in me, just as I suspicion he sees something in you. He wrote to me, that you were interested in history and the law, and liked to read."

"That's true, sir. I devour every book I can get my hands on."

"So do I! Lincoln, if you find the law has a place in your future and you decide to pursue it, come and see me if you're ever in Springfield."

"Thank you, Major Stuart. That's very generous of you."

"Let's just say, I'm trying to follow the Judge's example. After all, I owe him a very big favor. He helped change my life."

"In a very short time the Judge has become like a father to me, the father I wished I always had."

Stuart studied Lincoln silently, carefully listening to him. "Lincoln, I think I'm going to like you."

As the Major started to leave, he remembered why he first came to see Lincoln. "I almost forgot. I was supposed to give you something. This is for you." With that, he handed over a bright sword contained within a leather scabbard and belt. Presenting it to Abe, he said, "It's standard army issue for officers. While it's in your possession, use it wisely."

"Thank you, sir. I will wear it with honor."

After Major Stuart left, Abe thought, here was a man he liked. He would remember him and years later they would become close friends in Springfield.

Every day that followed brought signs the Indian war was heating up. It soon became the primary goal to make contact with Black Hawk and stop his reign of terror. Abe and the 4th Mounted Militia departed Beardstown on April 28th. Attempting to find Black Hawk became sort of a cat and mouse game, chasing after shadows that turned out to be nothing but shadows.

Moving across open country toward Rock Island, Abe found himself in at least one predicament. Even though he'd become a quick study of military commands, he clearly saw he was about to have a big problem. Seeing they were fast approaching a long fence with only one narrow gate as a means to reach the other side, he racked his brain for the correct command.

Needing help, he glanced over at Jack Armstrong riding beside him. Jack understood Abe's silent plea, but quickly shook his head that he too was ignorant of the proper command.

Abe immediately decided that desperate situations such as this required desperate solutions. He would resort to creative commands not found in the rule book.

Pulling ahead of his men, he wheeled his horse around, facing them. Raising his voice, he shouted with authority, "Halt! Men, dismount! Company will pass through the gate and reform on the other side of the fence in two minutes!"

Jack Armstrong and Billy Greene came up beside Abe commenting in low voices. Jack said, "Abe, I knew it, you're a born leader." Billy agreed, "There's no one quite like you, Abe."

"My friends," Abe explained, "sometimes a leader has to be different and break the mold in order to succeed." He would often remind himself of this advice throughout the rest of his life.

At Rock Island, the 4th Mounted Militia joined with other units with Whiteside's brigade and advanced along the Rock River, chasing after Black Hawk's band. After a forced march, 40 miles upstream, they finally did make contact on May 14th near a place called Old Man's Creek, where it was rumored the Indians were gathered in force.

The violent clash that followed was called the battle of Stillman's Run, named after Major Isaiah Stillman, who had led 275 militia men into what became a disaster. Black Hawk knew they were coming and lured them into a trap. Before they knew it, Stillman's forces were receiving incoming fire from all directions.

Lincoln and the 4th Mounted Militia were in the rear guard when they heard sounds of massive musket fire and ear-piercing screams of the dying and wounded. Abe ordered, "Forward, men!" Even as they advanced, dozens of dismounted militias were running past them in the opposite direction. The fleeing men were in full panic mode, their faces full of fear. Hence the name of the battle became 'Stillman's Run.'

One man in particular, stopped right in front of Lincoln, yelling, "You're going the wrong way. Flee for your life! Those savages are murdering everyone in sight! They have no mercy!" After these words, sheer horror seemed to overwhelm him again, and he rejoined the other panic-stricken soldiers who'd ceased to be an army.

Abe glanced back at the other members of the 4th who'd remained close behind him. Ignoring the warnings of what was happening up ahead he gave the order, "Forward, ride to the sound of the battle!" Without hesitation, his men followed him. They did so, not because he was their captain, but because they genuinely believed in him.

As they pushed forward, getting closer to the battle, all sounds of the fighting went completely silent. Riding through a wooded area, the trees finally gave way to a small open clearing. It was there, Abe and his men reined in their horses, stopping them cold in their tracks.

Sprawled about this open area were the lifeless bodies of twelve of their fellow comrades. Seeing they had all been mutilated in the worst way, Abe wheeled his horse around, facing his men. "This is the work of animals," he declared.

Jack agreed, but having known some of the victims, he became emotional as he spoke, "It's more the work of butchers. I knew some of these men. Now I can barely recognize them." Gesturing to one and then another, he identified them, "There lies Joe Draper, and over there is John Walters and Gideon Munson. Those men had children who'll have to grow up without their fathers now. They didn't deserve to have their lives end like this. Abe, I can't go back and tell their grieving widows that I just left their bodies out here to rot. We've got to bury them."

"And we will," responded Abe, reassuringly. "It's the right thing." That said, he assigned a dozen men to stand guard, positioned at key points in all directions around the clearing while the rest of his company formed into one huge burial detail. He said,

"Burying the dead is the saddest thing in all the world to me. These men received death at the hands of devils. It seems the least we can do is give them a Christian burial at the hands of God-fearing men."

The burial took the rest of the day until late in the evening. At almost sunset, Abe and others of the 4th Militia gathered around the grave site. With bowed heads, they prayed. Abe said a few words, "Dear Lord, we herewith commend these souls of our fellow kinsmen and friends to Thee. May their bodies rest in peace forever." Of all the rugged frontiersmen present, without exception, there was not a dry eye among them.

As there had been no further attacks or any other signs of Black Hawk's warriors, Abe elected to make camp for the night right where they were. They would make no fires and remain as quiet as possible. It would be far too dangerous to be moving around in the dark, especially in unfamiliar territory. Abe concluded, "We will move out in the morning, returning to our lines as quickly as possible."

At the first signs of the rising sun above the horizon, Abe led his company from the clearing, each man riding past the row of graves. In this way each man paid their own silent respects to the fallen, making this place all the more sacred.

Returning to the base of their operations by the next day, May 16th, Abe found that morale was not good within many militia companies. Failing to capture or corral Black Hawk and his warriors was reason enough for discouragement among these men.

Later on that evening, a group of his men approached Lincoln in front of his tent. Pulling Abe aside, Jack Armstrong felt it was urgent to have a few words with him, "Abe, most of the men are pretty demoralized. I must tell you, I agree with most of what they are saying."

"What are they saying, Jack?"

"That this is work for the regular army boys. We're not Indian fighters. We're mostly farmers."

"You're thinking of those men we buried back at Old Man's Creek."

"Yes, I am. Those men were family men with wives and children, like most of us. The men are really getting angry with our army superiors."

"Why are the men upset with the army boys? Tell me, Jack."

"Those army boys broke and ran from the battle. They left it to us farmers to do their fighting. Our men aren't calling it the battle of Old Man's Creek, they're calling it 'Stillman's Run' because Major Stillman and his men turned and ran."

"I agree, Jack. What the army boys did was both disgraceful and unacceptable. I think I should talk to the men."

Later, Ann's brothers John and David Rutledge came to Abe's tent. Echoing Jack Armstrong, John spoke for both of them, "Abe, you know we look up to you like an older brother, but like most volunteers, we only signed up for one month's service in the militia."

"I know, I'm grateful. I can't ask for more than what you've already given. But, at the same time, I promised both your sister and Judge Green, I'd see this thing through, until Black Hawk is killed or captured."

At the mention of his sister, John blurted out, "We don't like what McNeil is doing to our sister and our father. We know she really loves you and she shouldn't have her life made unhappy. David and I have talked this thing over and we can take care of our mother and father. When our enlistment is up in a few days, we're going back to New Salem and do what we can to help our *brother*."

"Your brother?"

"Yes–you, Abe. As far as David and I are concerned you're already part of the Rutledge family."

Abe was deeply moved. "All my life I've wanted to belong somewhere and be accepted by others."

"Abe, you're accepted by us."

As John said this, his words brought tears to Abe's eyes. In the privacy of Captain Lincoln's tent that night the three men hugged each other like brothers.

Ten days later, John and David Rutledge were mustered out of militia service. Before he left, John went to Lincoln's tent to bid him farewell. "Abe, I just wanted you to know, I think you're one of the finest men who ever lived."

Abe felt deeply humbled. "John, your words are more precious than gold to me."

John Rutledge was true to his word. Actually, both he and his brother urged Ann to break off the engagement to McNeil and go ahead and marry Abe. For the rest of his life, John, who was almost two years younger than Abe, continued to love him like a big brother.

With a heavy heart, Abe hated to see the two brothers depart camp on May 27th 1832. There were other reasons for Abe to be depressed though. Many more one-month enlistments expired and several more men close to him left camp that day. Jack Armstrong, Henry McHenry and other Clary boys left as well.

Even Abe's old friend, Billy Greene, chose not to re-enlist. Seeing Abe, he told him, "My father's been alone on his farm while I've been gone over a month. I must go back and check on him."

"Billy, I can't fault you for that. One who loves his father should go and check on the man's well-being. You're truly fortunate to have a loving relationship with your father."

"Thank you for saying that, Abe, but there is another reason as well. You have inspired me to do something."

"What could that possibly be?"

"Seeing you, in spite of the odds against you, to get as much education as you can has instilled in me the same desires. I'm gonna go back to school and try to better myself in life."

"I'm proud of you Billy."

"So you don't fault me for going back? We're still friends?"

"Of course I don't fault you. We're friends forever," Abe answered, warmly shaking hands with him.

After Billy left, walking through camp, Abe was feeling quite alone. Then he spotted young William Franklin Berry. Abe thought of him as young, even though he was only two years older than Berry. In life experience though, Abe's life had been full of trauma, in almost overwhelming episodes, coming one right after another.

On the other hand, the preacher's son had barely been away from home his entire life. Berry had grown up in sort of a protective bubble where most everything had been handed to him. Still though, he'd become a good soldier, serving bravely during his one month's militia service under the watchful eye of Jack Armstrong. But now Jack was gone.

"Bill," Abe called after him, getting his attention. "I suppose you're going home too."

"No sir, Captain Lincoln. I was just going over to re-enlist, that is if they'll have me."

"If that's what you want to do, you've got my recommendation. I'm curious though: Bill, you could return home now and nobody would fault you."

"Nobody but myself. You see, it's like I said, I've been living my whole life in the shadow of my father, a veteran of the War of 1812. I see this as my opportunity to make something of myself. So far, I've kept it together and haven't broken under fire."

"Bill, you've been a good soldier and you're gonna keep on being a good soldier."

"Captain, how do you know that?"

"Because I'm going over and re-enlist right along with you. We're going to stick this war out together."

"Thank you, Captain Lincoln!"

"Oh Bill, ease up on that *Captain Lincoln*! We're both re-enlisting as privates, so just call me Abe from now on out."

"You mean we can be like friends." One could hear the hero worship in Bill Berry's voice.

"Bill, we ARE friends."

From that day forward, Abe would take this young man under his wing. They would be the best of friends throughout the rest of William Berry's short life.

On May 29th, Abe and Bill Berry were integrated into a company of mounted volunteers under Captain Elijah Iles. The army was reorganizing after the debacle at Stillman's Run, preparing for a new offensive against Black Hawk. Again though, for several days it became a game of the cat chasing after the mouse. Only the mice were just a little bit quicker, staying ahead of the cat. But in time, the mice would run out of steam and have to turn and fight. This would happen soon.

Abe and Bill Berry were part of the new offensive that departed Dixon's Ferry, hot after Black Hawk giving chase along the Galena Trail. It was there they made contact with hundreds of Indian warriors in mid-June.

Again, Abe and Bill found themselves part of the regiment pulling up the rear guard. They could hear yelling and screaming coming from up ahead. This time the army boys didn't run. They stood their ground against what eyewitnesses said were vast numbers of half-naked warriors who came at them with a barrage of spears and tomahawks. Some of them came charging into the militia's ranks, cutting and slashing with large wicked looking knives.

Advancing, getting ever closer, Abe and Bill could now hear volley after volley of large amounts of musket fire, followed by bone-chilling screams. At length, they rode into Kellogg's Grove where a large part of the battle had taken place. What met the relief column was a bloody mess. Men gushing blood from horrible wounds.

It was then, Abe and Bill, and other mounted militias were ordered to ride up a little hill just ahead of their position to search for any more wounded or dead. Up that little hill, every member of that patrol saw something they'd never forget for the rest of their lives.

As they reached the top of the hill, the glare of the morning sun met their eyes, casting a reddish hue that seemed to envelope everyone and everything. As Abe's eyes began to refocus, he realized he was looking at a scene of horrible reality. Men had been hacked to pieces, the victims of their enemies' furiousity.

What every member of that patrol saw was seared into their memories for years to come. The expressions of unspeakable horror were on the faces of all the dead.

Affecting Bill Berry immediately, he asked Abe, "Why do they all look that way?"

Somehow Abe could visualize what they saw, "To a man this was their final moment of life. Those moments were when they looked directly into the face of death itself. For perhaps just a brief instant, I think they all realized they were about to lose their most precious possession, life itself."

After burying these poor souls as best they could, Abe and the other members of his patrol rode back to the little cabin-like fortress at Kellogg's Grove. The mood among all of them was somber and quiet. Even as they rode back, Abe was silently praying for the souls of those victims. It was all he could do for the moment.

By late evening, Abe and Bill found themselves gathered around a campfire. Bill was shaking, as the demons of fear were slowly taking hold of him. Putting a comforting hand on his shoulder, Abe tried to console him, "Bill, no matter how bad it feels, those feelings will pass. Those men aren't suffering anymore. They're in the hands of the good Lord now."

Though still shaking, Bill looked up into Abe's calming face. He opened up, "It's hard. I knew some of those men: Marcus Randolph, Ben Scott, Jim Black and Abner Bradford. Fine descent fellows, everyone. All of them were young men. They didn't deserve to die."

"Perhaps not, but they had become soldiers. In war, I guess we all have to come to expect things like this will happen."

"Abe, I don't care what my father says, I hate soldiering now."

"I sort of agree with you. After today I know something now. I hate war and just about everything about it. It's left an awful feeling inside me. There's just too much death and heartbreak. It's more than a man can stand."

What Abe saw at Kellogg's Grove would stay with him forever. Many years later, when Abe walked the fields of Gettysburg after the great battle there, he came across the bodies of dead soldiers still unburied. A sad haunted expression filled his face and he was heard whispering "Just like in the Black Hawk War. When will men ever learn?"

In late June of 1832, Abe was back in camp at Dixon's Ferry, where on the morning of June 29th he found himself confronting a familiar face, Major John Stuart. "Good morning, Lincoln. So you're still with us. How is army life treating you? Are you going to stay with it?"

"I don't think so. I've seen too much killing, enough to last me a lifetime."

"Yes, I heard your company had rather a bad time of it at Kellogg's Grove."

"Major, it was much more than a bad time. It's been two weeks now and I still can't get it out of my head. I remember everything I saw in vivid detail, just how those men looked, their bodies laid out on the ground, blood streaming from their heads. They all had been mutilated and scalped by those redskins. It was frightening, probably the most grotesque thing I've ever seen."

Looking at Abe knowingly, Major Stuart reflected, "No I don't guess army life would be in your future. You know, I don't think it'll be in my future either. As soon as I can, I'm going back to my law practice in Springfield." Starting to walk off, in almost an afterthought, the Major turned back to Abe, "Say Lincoln, have you given the idea of the law any more thought since we talked last?"

"Not really, too much soldiering going on. But," Abe paused for a moment of reflection, and then explained, "I've thought about it this much: It's really more of a dream right now, but with more education, perhaps one day, I might become a lawyer."

"If your dream could come true, what kind of lawyer would you want to become?"

Abe didn't have to think. He responded immediately, "I would want to become a good lawyer–an honest one."

"Lincoln, you just might have promise. If ever that dream comes true for you, and you happen to be in Springfield, look me up."

A few days later, on July 10th, most of Abe's entire company was mustered out of the service. The numbers of regular army units had increased so much, it was decided they had sufficient forces to pursue Black Hawk and put an end to the Indian war.

When Abe and Bill got the news, they had been part of the army's pursuit of the Indians. At the time of their discharge, the chase after the enemy had taken them to Whitewater Wisconsin.

Processing their discharge papers was young 2nd Lieutenant Robert Anderson. "Thanks men for being part of the mounted militia. Here's payment for your service."

Abe was appreciative, "Thank you sir, this money will help me a great deal." Abe was paid $80.00 for his one-month service as a captain and $7.66 per month for his two-month service as a private. In addition, Abe and Bill were paid 40 cents per day of their entire service for providing their own horses as part of the mounted militia.

As they started to leave, Abe had one nagging question on his mind. "Lieutenant Anderson, do you think the army will ever catch Black Hawk?"

"Yes, I do. As we speak, Lieutenant Davis is on his way with a sufficient force to encircle and capture him."

"Would that be Lieutenant Jefferson Davis?"

"Why yes, do you know him?"

"Yes sir, he's the officer who officially swore me in three months ago."

"Lincoln, he's a good man, one who won't underestimate Black Hawk. I've heard Lieutenant Davis say you can never underestimate an enemy who's passionate about their beliefs."

Abe would hear those words about Jefferson Davis again. Many years later, he sought to understand this man he'd only met once–ever so briefly–in his life. Abe would often think about Fate and life's little ironies throughout his life. In fact, the same 2nd Lieutenant Robert Anderson would rise in rank over the years and become the Major Anderson who commanded Fort Sumter, whose surrender of it to the Confederacy would ignite the Civil War. On April 15th 1861, Abe was heard saying, "Major Anderson, I knew that man during the Black Hawk War."

As to Chief Black Hawk himself, Lieutenant Davis and the army finally did capture the Indian leader. Defiant to the last, the

65-year-old warrior was reported to have said to his captors, "I've done nothing but fight for what was ours. Year after year, the white man has stolen our lands. You know this was the cause of our making war. For this and starving my people, you ought to be ashamed."

Later, Abe would hear a report of this old Chief's statement. Abe would take his words to heart; seeing what was good in the hearts of all men, even his worst enemies. He would grow to become a seeker of truth and justice in every matter that crossed his path.

During the past three months, the experiences of the Black Hawk War had awakened in Abe an even more conscious appreciation for the value of human life. Embracing this, he resolved to improve himself in every way possible and to make every moment of the rest of his life count for something.

CHAPTER 10
FINDING THEIR WAY TO
NEW JERUSALEM

It was now late evening, July 10th 1832. Abe and Bill Berry had decided to sleep near their horses that night and depart the army camp early the next day. They woke up as planned only to discover their horses had been stolen during the night.

Resolving to begin their long trip home anyway, they set out on foot. July 1832 was a particularly hot and humid summer month. The weather lent itself to a mosquito outbreak. They were blood thirsty and aggressive.

In the depths of their discomfort, Abe tried his best to lift Bill Berry's spirits. "Bill, in spite of our unpleasant situation, we're actually pretty lucky."

"How can you say that?"

"Cause if the Indians had been as blood thirsty as these mosquitoes, we'd already been goners for sure."

"Only you could've said such a thing." Berry was already used to Abe's sense of dark humor.

Far from being irritating, Abe's gift of conversation helped alleviate the miserable conditions they were in. Beyond the insects, constant exposure to the elements further weakened them. Having ran out of food and water, these additional factors were fast bringing on dehydration and collapse. They knew they would have to stop soon, as they were well past being ready to drop.

They were both praying for a miracle, and as nightfall was closing in on them, the Lord answered their prayers. The ability to put one foot in front of the other was giving out within both of them. Yet, up ahead was God's answer to their prayers.

An abandoned cabin suddenly became visible, just a few feet right in front of them. Abe and Bill could hardly believe their eyes. It was fully stocked, packed to the brim with food, water and beds to sleep on. The two men were able to prepare their first decent meal in days.

"Thank you, Lord," said Abe, uttering his sincere thanks out loud. "You know, God sure does work in mysterious ways, actually more often than we realize."

"Why do you suppose this place is abandoned?" Bill wondered, asking Abe.

"Whoever lived here, left pretty quick." Abe reasoned, "It had to be because of the Indian raids in these parts. Many peace-loving settlers have been murdered around here."

Being the type of person Abe was, he left a note with some money, paying for the food they took. The note said: 'Your food was ate by two starving militia volunteers. Knowing nothing in life is free, we are forever grateful. Here is payment for the provisions we partook. In humble gratitude, A. Lincoln of New Salem.'

Traveling further south, they reached Peoria, Illinois within a few more days, completing two hundred miles of their journey. Peoria was a small settlement at the time, with a population of under 200 people. It was there, Abe and Bill were able to purchase a canoe. Going down the Illinois River, they were able to travel the 45-mile distance from Peoria to Havana, Illinois within another day or so. There they were able to sell the canoe and reimburse themselves.

Now they were less than 30 miles to New Salem. But it was late in the evening, so Abe and Bill decided to camp out that night, near the banks of the Illinois River. As they relaxed by their campfire, the two men talked for a while.

Abe was in a reflective mood, revealing his deepest thoughts, "I feel like I'm finding my way to New Jerusalem again."

"Could you explain that?"

"Bill, New Jerusalem is talked about in the Bible. It is often described as a Heavenly place. For me though, it's sort of a holy place on Earth. In so many ways, New Salem is the New Jerusalem for me."

"Abe, you're sounding a bit like my father and the Christian beliefs he teaches."

"He sounds like someone I'd like to meet, someone who lets God guide him."

"He does, Abe. My father's often said the good Lord guided him to Sangamon County before there was any such place as New Salem, and had him build his church along Rock Creek."

"I can relate to your father. I feel like the Lord is leading me back to New Salem for a reason and a purpose. Deep down inside of me, in my heart, I feel like the Lord is telling me it's a spiritual place. It represents a coming together of all that is good and decent for me. In the book of Revelations it says New Jerusalem will be lit by the glory of God. As I was leaving New Salem on the flatboat to New Orleans last year, I looked up and saw a large shaft of light break through the clouds and bless our little town with God's heavenly glory. It felt like the Lord was telling me this was where He wanted me to come back and live."

"Abe, I think I understand you a little better now."

"Bill, I'm a simple, God-fearing man. Something else though," Abe continued, "if New Salem would stay just like it is now, I think I wouldn't mind living out the rest of my natural life there."

"You really mean that?"

"Yes, now more than ever."

Bill had listened intently and completely. Hearing him out, he thought of Abe as one of the most honest and sincere men he'd ever known. Even after they parted company later, Bill had already decided here was the man he would want as his best friend in whatever he would do for the rest of his life.

Before the crack of dawn, Abe and Bill got up, preparing for the final leg of their journey. The two men set out across country in a southeasterly direction that would intersect with New Salem.

They proceeded all day at a determined pace. As darkness came upon them, the full moon rose, clear and bright in the night sky. They could see the outline of a small settlement in the distance. Both men knew–it was New Salem. Picking up their pace, both men realized they were home.

Stopping at the edge of town, Bill Berry had a word with Abe, "I'm not going to stop here, I feel my father's spirit calling me home. So I'm going to take the Springfield Road turn off and head on home to Rock Creek."

"But Bill, don't you want to stop off at the Rutledge Inn and see Ann before heading on home?"

"No, I fancied her once, but a blind man could see she's clearly in love with you."

"You see that?"

"Listen Abe, I've never had a friend like you. I feel like I have my scalp and my life thanks to you. You deserve every good thing that happens to you. You're like an older brother to me. I won't get in the way, you deserve Ann. She's a fine woman and will make you a good wife. If you love her, don't hesitate, go after her."

"Thank you, Bill." The two men shook hands warmly, before they parted.

As Bill took the Springfield Road turn off, he turned to Abe a final time, "I'll see you real soon, my friend."

Responding, Abe waved farewell as his young friend disappeared into the darkness.

As Abe was alone now, his original goal came springing back into conscious thought. Up ahead was the heart of New Salem, his New Jerusalem. Even though it was late at night and most lights were out in New Salem, he had to see Ann. Advancing on down Main Street, he could see a single flickering light from within the front window of the Rutledge Inn.

Reaching the Inn, Abe stepped quietly onto the porch and, ever so slightly, opened the front door. As he entered, he could see the flashing light was coming from the crackling fire within the great room's grand fireplace. No one appeared to be awake, so making as little noise as possible he stepped into the great room. Only then did he realize a lone figure was sitting on a bench in the shadows, near the fireplace. The figure looked up in his direction, emitting one word, "Abe?" It was Ann's voice.

Standing up, Ann Rutledge was fully bathed in the revealing fire light. It was obvious she had been crying as tears were rolling from her eyes even then. Struggling, she managed to say the words, "Oh thank God you're alive."

Rushing forward toward Abe as he advanced toward her, they went into each other's arms. Clinging to each other, Abe whispered, "Oh Ann, it's so good to be home and have you in my arms."

"I'm so glad to be in your arms. It's something I've always wanted."

In the full firelight now, Abe could clearly see her face. "You've been crying. Why?"

"Judge Green, Jack and his wife Hannah, Billy Greene, others, and myself, we've all been grieving for you. They were beginning to think you might be dead."

"But why would you think that?"

"Judge Green's horse, Diamond, the one he loaned you for the mounted militia, well one night about a week ago he showed up outside the Judge's farmhouse, riderless. We all knew that the horse would never leave you willingly. So, everyone had begun to think you might be dead–that is everyone but me. I've been praying for you, every day and every night. I haven't been able to sleep. Then I heard a Voice speak to my mind last night. It said that you weren't dead, you'd be home soon."

"Oh Ann, I wish I could've somehow contacted you. Diamond was stolen by someone the first night of my discharge from the militia. I guess he must have gotten away from whoever took him and by some miracle found his way back home."

"Abe, all I know is God told me you'd be coming home. Rather you know it or not, the good Lord has been watching over you."

"Ann, I feel so humbled. You're such a wonderful, wonderful person." The honesty and purity of what she was saying reached directly into his soul, making Abe feel the presence of God was all around him. More than ever, he believed it was Ann's prayers that made a difference for him, his life, and his future.

In that moment, two souls came together, drawn into each other's loving arms once more. Neither one wanted to let go, wanting instead for these feeling to last forever.

Looking up into his face, Ann managed to whisper through her tears, "I'm so glad to be here to welcome you back home. Knowing you're safe means the world to me!"

This was all Abe needed to hear, for it was then that tears welled up in his eyes as well. He thought, I'm truly home, back in my New Jerusalem.

Twenty-four hours later, news had traveled fast and a crowd of well-wishers and friends gathered around Abe in the great room, late the next evening. There was Jack Armstrong and several Clary's Grove boys, Ann's cousin, McGrady and her brothers John and David, Judge Green and the dedicated physician of New Salem, Doctor John Allen. Everyone's spirits were lifted to see the safe return of New Salem's favorite son. They were also emotionally moved because he was a man they had all come to love and respect.

Doctor Allen was first up on his feet, "We are all thankful to God for the return of our hometown hero, Captain Abe Lincoln."

Jack Armstrong seconded that comment, "I'm thank'n the good Lord for bringing the man back so many of us served under in the war. Abe, I'm not only speak'n for myself, but for all the Clary's Grove boys when I say you have all our heartfelt thanks for having been able to be under your leadership."

Henry McHenry agreed loudly, "Here! Here!"

Jack continued, "After the disaster at 'Stillman's Run', Abe successfully brought all of us here back to safety, avoiding Black Hawk's plans to ambush us."

"Yes, surely the Lord was with all of you," observed Doctor Allen.

Judge Green took the opportunity to break in at this point, "As Justice of the Peace of Sangamon County, I think I speak for the whole town when I say we are proud and honored to know you."

Abe stood up interrupting, "No, I must object. All of you have made me feel like a brother, a son, one of your family. No, it is I who feels honored just to know all of you." As Abe set back down, everyone could tell he had meant what he had said, because every word had been uttered with such feeling, straight from his heart.

The Judge who had been sitting beside Abe, stood up again, patting him on the back and continuing, "Everyone here came up with the idea and we all think you richly deserve something. So Abe, we came up with an idea of a present for you."

"This is unexpected," said Abe, quite surprised. "I don't deserve a present."

"Yes, you do, my boy."

"But Judge, what could it be?"

"Son, you'll have to wait till morning, then I can show you."

As Ann brought food to the three tables butted together for the celebration, she broke in with a question, "Abe would you tell all of us folks here who didn't serve, what was the Black Hawk War really like?"

"Yes Abe, tell all of us," seconded the Judge, Doctor Allen and Ann's father, all at once. They all seemed very curious.

Abe took on a serious expression as he spoke, "Before I get into this, I want to say at the outset, I don't like war. It leaves an awful feeling inside you. Fighting was all around me, often within earshot, a lot of shooting and killing, but in all of the months of that war I never saw a live, fighting Indian up close. Instead, I saw a much more fearsome foe."

Wide-eyed, Ann asked, "What was that, Abe?"

"It was the most relentless enemy of all frontiersmen, a truly blood sucking foe. No matter how many times I'd hit these creatures, they kept on coming."

Having her rapt attention, Ann asked, "Were they cannibals?"

Considering her question, Abe answered, "After a fashion they were probably cannibals, only considerably smaller. They were mosquitoes."

His answer brought considerable laughter from the entire crowd.

As the humorous moment died down, the Judge sought to refocus everyone's attention on an upcoming important matter, "Abe, you're probably forgetting something important. Before you left for the war, you were nominated for public office, to represent the good people here in the state legislature. That election is coming up shortly."

"It had slipped my mind," Abe acknowledged. "The truth of the matter is with the war and all, I've been thinking only about keeping my scalp, surviving, and coming back here to my home."

Doctor Allen spoke up, "No one can fault you for that. The good Lord brought you back, safe and sound. I, for one, believe he had a purpose in doing it."

"Thanks Doc, all of you have flattered me by putting me up for office. If elected, I'll serve all of you to the best of my abilities. If on the other hand, I lose, it'll be just the same, because you've already flattered me beyond reason by nominating me. That is something, come what may, I will always feel greatly humbled about. The very fact that you are all my friends is something I'll treasure always."

Abe's words were truly sincere, spoken from his heart. They elicited an applause and roar of approval from his friends around him. Looking into their admiring faces, he was truly moved. It was a good feeling welling up inside him. Inside, he felt more than ever, he was back in his own New Jerusalem where everything was coming together in a positive way.

Later, after everybody left, Judge Green took Abe aside, whispering, "Something has come up. I'll need to talk to you about it in the morning."

"What is it, Judge?"

"An important matter that I'll need your assistance in."

"You can count on me, Judge."

Judge Green would say no more for now, instead waving good-night, heading for a room within the Inn where he'd been staying.

Alone in the great room now, Abe still felt the presence of some-one else. Glancing around, he saw Ann's smiling face over by the fireplace. As he walked across the room toward her, he had a good feeling inside his heart and soul. It was good to be home.

CHAPTER 11
A FUTURE IN NEW SALEM

The next morning found Abe meeting with Judge Green out behind the Rutledge Inn, in the vicinity of the barn and stables.

"Abe, I wanted you to meet me here so I could give you the surprise we talked about last night."

"What could it be?" Abe inquired with mounting curiosity rising within him. He eagerly followed the Judge toward the barn.

"My boy, I've been awfully concerned about you."

"How so, Judge?"

"Having no means of transportation, you haven't been able to get around very well."

"Having so little money I haven't been able to afford even a horse."

"Son, that's not going to be the case anymore."

"It's not?"

"Since Diamond found his way home, he's been worthless to me. He just mopes around, like he's lost his best friend. Abe, what did you do to that horse while you had him?"

"Oh, I guess I fed him a few apples every now and then."

The Judge didn't quite believe it. "I suspect you fed him more than just a few. You spoiled him."

Abe hung his head and replied, "Guilty as charged. I'd look in his eyes and couldn't help myself. I guess I love that horse."

"I know he loves you."

As they advanced into the Inn's barn, both Abe and the Judge heard an excited snort, followed by the distinctive sound of a horse whinnying.

"That sounds like Diamond!" Abe's voice rose in excitement.

"It certainly is, my boy. I want you to have him, my present to you."

Looking around, Abe quickly spotted him in a nearby stall. "Oh Diamond, I've missed you."

One could almost see the love in the horse's large all-encompassing, expressive eyes. As he nuzzled up against young Lincoln, Abe hugged his neck gently.

The Judge could see there was great love between these two. Thinking to himself, the Judge knew he'd done a good deed. Shaking his head to that effect, he commented, "If ever there were two that belonged together, it's you and Diamond."

"Thank you, Judge."

"You've been needing a horse. Now you've got one."

"Diamond's not just a horse. He's the best! How can I ever repay you?"

"You can start by helping me with a rather confidential matter."

"Oh yes," acknowledged Abe, "you said something about it last night."

"I think you might especially be interested in this. It involves John McNeil." The Judge's expression became very serious.

This got Abe's full attention. He knew anything concerning John McNeil might eventually involve him.

An hour later the three men would meet very privately, all alone, inside the now rather barren old Offutt store. Except for a few chairs and a small table, it was empty. As soon as McNeil entered, his eyes locked onto Lincoln. Neither wanted to be there, but sometimes the elements of necessity and inevitability coupled together have a way of bringing out one's deepest secrets. With these factors in play, each man took a seat around the small table.

McNeil immediately reacted to Abe's presence, "I didn't know he was going to be here."

The Judge explained, "For your business transaction, in order for me to notarize it, you need a witness of good character to authenticate and witness your signature. Now if you have some objection to a war hero of good reputation witnessing this document, we can just forget the whole thing till you bring in another suitable witness."

McNeil shifted about, appearing physically uncomfortable. "Then I couldn't complete this matter today? It would mean a delay?"

"That is correct, Mister McNeil."

"Then I suppose Mister Lincoln will have to do as a witness," McNeil relunctantly conceded.

With that settled, Judge Green explained to Abe what was going on, "Son, Mister McNeil is in the process of selling his store and all the assets within it. I have drawn up all the documents necessary to complete the sale. Now all that's needed is Mister McNeil to sign it and you provide a witness signature. Then I can legally notarize this bill of sale as Justice of the Peace of Sangamon County."

Surprised, Abe looked at McNeil, "You're selling your store?"

"Yes, Lincoln, but only out of necessity. I have to return to New York immediately. My father is desperately ill, and my mother is not in the best of health either. I need money for the trip."

Abe pressed him for more information, "Will you be returning to New Salem?"

"Yes, as soon as my parents are able, I'll bring them back with me." McNeil paused for a moment becoming irritated at Abe's curiosity. "Lincoln, I know this will disappoint you, but I intend to return in about three months to marry Miss Rutledge."

At this point, the Judge broke in, "Gentlemen please, let's return to the business at hand." Having the bill of sale and a pen on the small table, he indicated, "McNeil, sign right here."

After signing his first name immediately, he hesitated, glancing up. "Judge, in order for this sale to be legitimate, I have to sign my full legal name?"

"Yes, of course, McNeil."

"Looking down, he continued his signature. That finished, the Judge turned the document around in Abe's direction, passing the pen to him. "Abe, just sign next to where it says witness."

Abe, being the forever cautious man, he was, it was inevitable he would read the document first. As he did so, Abe hesitated, seeming to scrutinize McNeil's signature. Looking up at the Judge, he declared, "I can't sign this."

McNeil getting upset, yelled, "Lincoln, just sign it!"

"He signed it alright, but not as John McNeil," Abe pointed out.

Looking at the bill of sale more closely, the Judge could also see something was wrong.

John McNeil saw clearly in the Judge's expression that an explanation would be necessary. It was time for McNeil to be honest and tell the complete truth. His face became ashen as he attempted to explain, "I must ask you to keep what I'm about to tell you completely confidential."

"That depends on what you have to say," Abe responded, immediately suspicious.

A look of desperation, uncommon to him, filled McNeil's face as he continued, "Then I guess I have no choice. First of all, the man you know as John McNeil does not exist. I have been living here the past several years under an assumed name. My real name is John McNamar. That is my real name on the bill of sale."

"Mister McNamar," the Judge asked, "why have you been living here under an assumed name?"

"My parents and entire family back east are all heavily in debt. They continue to be harassed by bill collectors. When I came to New Salem in 1829 I had little money. During the past four years, without being harassed by those attempting to track down John McNamar, I've been able to amass the funds necessary to help my family pay their bills. This is why I need the sale of my store to go through as soon as possible."

"This is the only reason?" questioned Abe.

"I assure you, Lincoln, I only want to help my family out, get my father and mother well, and bring them back here in approximately three months."

"Are you going to be honest with Ann and tell her all this before you leave town?"

"If all goes well with this sale, I'll be leaving New Salem in the morning. I promise you, I will see Miss Rutledge later this afternoon and tell her everything."

Satisfied, Abe agreed, "Very well, under these conditions I will go ahead and provide a witness signature on your bill of sale, Mister... McNamar."

"Thank you, Mister Lincoln."

Abe had grudgingly earned a bit of respect from John McNamar, who would never view him quite the same again.

After Judge Green put his notary seal on the document and McNamar had left, he and Abe sat alone in the old Offutt store.

Abe asked, "What do you think, Judge?"

"I'm thinking if he's not back here in three months, we'll know if John McNamar is telling the truth."

The next morning, Abe was sitting in the great room of the Rutledge Inn having breakfast when he happened to look up into the familiar face of someone entering the room. It was William Franklin Berry.

"Hello Abe. I bet you didn't think you'd see me so soon?"

"Bill, to tell you the truth, I hadn't thought much about it."

"Well, I have," said Berry, sitting down directly across from Abe. "After we parted the other night, I haven't thought about much else. You see, when I got home I found my world had completely changed. It's like Fate has directed me to this moment."

"Bill, I'm a strong believer in Fate. What exactly happened?"

"My father was overjoyed and grateful to see me alive. So much so he went ahead and gave me my share of the inheritance he had planned on leaving me. He said he felt like my military service with you has given me the maturity and judgement to strike out on my own. Of course, he prays I will use my inheritance wisely, and that's what I'm trying to do."

"I'm glad for you Bill, but what has this to do with me?"

"A lot!"

"How so?"

"I can think of no finer, more honest, person to help guide me through the business world here in New Salem."

"What exactly are you proposing, Bill?"

"I'm proposing that we become business partners. I have the money and you have the experience."

Abe was listening, but still questioning, "What sort of business are you proposing?"

"An opportunity has opened up and I took advantage of it. Two of the smaller stores on Main Street closed up while we were away in the Black Hawk War. With the inheritance I got, I went ahead and bought up their inventories yesterday. What you may not know is John McNeil sold out his entire inventory yesterday."

"Actually, I did hear something about that."

"You probably haven't heard who the buyer was."

"Not really."

"Abe, the buyer was his chief clerk, our friend, Billy Greene."

"Billy Greene! How did he manage it?"

"With some money from his father and other investors. I think, perhaps Doctor Allen, Mentor Graham, the schoolteacher, perhaps Judge Green and others."

"I always thought Billy had the potential to be a smart business man."

"Abe, he was able to buy McNeil out for a small fraction of what his inventory is worth. It seems McNeil is having to leave town in a hurry, needed cash, and was desperate to make a quick deal."

"Oh really?" Abe didn't want to let on what he knew about the situation.

"Anyway," Berry continued, "here is the opportunity: Billy doesn't want a store. He wants to go back to school."

"Yes, he's told me he wants to get more education."

"Well, I just came from talking with him. He said if you go in partners with me, he will accept a small quick profit up front and our note for the balance over time. He says your word is better than any man in Illinois."

The more Berry talked, it was obvious he was bubbling over with enthusiasm. It quickly became infectious and shortly Abe was caught up in this dream. In a matter of hours, Abe became Billy Berry's partner.

This new venture found a home in a vacant 18 x 12 building near the juncture of where the Springfield Road merged into Main Street. As Abe looked up at the structure, a surge of hope and self-confidence filled him. He was full of new found optimism that this mercantile store was not going to be a failure like the Offutt store. He was in charge here and his sheer force of will was going to make his vision a successful reality.

Abe was full of ideas as he stared at the store's front door and single window to the left of it as they stared back at him.

"We're going to have to add something here," he remarked to Bill Berry.

"What's that, Abe?"

"A sign to the right of the front door that says: Berry-Lincoln Store. What do you think?"

"Sounds terrific, in alphabetical order." Berry smiled, obviously satisfied.

Staring at the building a little closer, Abe added, "Let's do an add on to the back of the store, an 8 x 12 back room to be used as a combination storeroom and sleeping quarters."

"Perfect," agreed Berry, "let's do it."

After all the work was done, Abe stood outside and whispered to himself, "Just maybe, I'll have a future in New Salem."

Before grand opening day, Abe wanted to get a feel of the place. Walking inside, feeling the plank floors beneath his feet, he stepped behind the counter. From there he could see out the front door and window, and have a clear view of the Springfield Road, which it faced. Walking back outside, he could see the side of the Rutledge Inn, which stood just across the Springfield Road to the East. He could also see Main Street, running past, just to the north of his little store.

Crossing the ground from his front door, he walked over and stood beneath an enormous shade tree, which was located close to the corner where Main Street merged into the Springfield Road. From this vantage point he could watch the general public, traveling in their wagons and such, up and down Main Street. Since they moved along at such a slow pace, he could perhaps lure some of them to stop and come into his own modest store.

Shortly after the store opened, the first disappointment to Abe was only a minor bump in the road. Since he had only made a half-hearted attempt in running for the state legislature it did not surprise him that he lost. Then too, the Black Hawk War had intervened and made it impractical for any serious run for office.

His first time in the new Berry-Lincoln store, Judge Green had come in town to check it out and give Abe the election results, "Out of thirteen candidates running, you finished in eighth position. Not bad for a first-time candidate who only ran part time. Maybe you'll do better next time."

"Maybe, reflected Abe, "if there is a next time."

"There is some good news in all this," the Judge pointed out. "You received 277 votes out of the 300 votes east in the precinct here. That includes New Salem, Clary's Grove, and all the other farms and settlements close by, south and west of here."

"I guess it shows there were at least 23 people around here who didn't like me."

"Not necessarily, Abe." Judge Green explained, "Out of the 23 votes you didn't get, ten voters refrained from voting for state representative. Only thirteen voters in this precinct voted against you. That's not bad at all."

"Who won, Judge?"

"The four top vote getters out of the thirteen candidates get the privilege of serving in the next state legislature. The big winners were from the precincts in and around Springfield. One of them is a young attorney friend of mine, John Stuart, with 991 votes."

"I met him during the Black Hawk War. He seemed like a good man."

"He is, Abe. He can also be a good friend to you if you pursue the law as a profession."

"Perhaps one day," considered Abe, "but for now maybe I should try my hand at something else, like being a blacksmith."

"That's nonsense!" declared Billy Greene, who'd just entered the store. "Just about anybody with a strong arm, can learn to be a blacksmith. I know you, and you have the mental capacity for greater things. Abe, I say this as your friend."

"Billy, I take it as coming from a friend."

Mentor Graham, the Scotch-Irish schoolmaster was there and had been listening to the whole conversation. He broke in at this point, "Mister Lincoln, I'll tell you honestly, if you ever hope to seek a higher position in life, more education would be both helpful and necessary in my view."

"My boy, he's absolutely correct in what he says," the Judge agreed.

It was a lot for Abe to ponder. For the present though, the success of the Berry-Lincoln store was the most important thing on his mind. For what remained of August, September and October, he poured all of his energies and every waking moment into making that success happen.

Abe was busy selling to all the well-wishers who came into the store, wanting to shop with the man they all deemed a war hero. He seemed honest to a fault, always warm and friendly. Added to these qualities, he was often modest and self-effacing, a decent human being.

To all but a very few, did he ever reveal the deep emotional scars that he kept hidden just below the surface. Ann knew about them and so did Judge Green, but these were treasured friends. They were also the people who loved him.

For the time being, Abe did not allow himself to think about those times that traumatized his early life. His whole conscious thought was wrapped up in selling the store's hot ticket items: calico fabrics, cotton thread, and candle molds to the ladies; gunpowder, axes, shovels, saws and all manner of farming tools to the men.

Yet, there was one item he preferred not to sell at all. High market demands forced him to sell large containers of whiskey. He soon realized many of his male customers, the rough frontier folk, who lived around New Salem, would either buy it in his store or take their business for it and other store items as well, elsewhere. To stay in business, he had to concede in this matter.

About the same time as this concession, something else began to bother Abe deeply. At first, it was just a feeling in the back of his mind, then later a more pronounced suspicion. He couldn't let go of it. Something Jack Armstrong had once told him about Bill Berry's drinking came back to haunt him. Increasingly so, toward the end of September, Abe began to notice, rather than staying behind the counter, Berry would retreat to the back room. Often, it would leave Abe having to wait on all the customers by himself.

One evening, Abe went to the back to check on Berry. What he saw reminded him of forgotten memories of his father. There was Berry, fully engulfed in a severe case of tremors and pronounced shaking. In his hand was a nearly empty jug of the store's whiskey.

"Bill!" Abe reacted. "What do you think you're doing?"

"Don't look at me!" Berry snapped back in a raised voice partly angry, but even more ashamed.

Abe ignored him and persisted, "What's happened to you?"

"Abe, I couldn't help it," Berry answered in an emotional, almost crying voice. "Every night this past week I've been having dreams, really nightmares! I was back in the Black Hawk War, reliving what we saw at Stillman's Run and Kellogg's Grove. I had to have a drink to erase those memories. When one drink wouldn't do it, I had to have another and another."

"Stop it, Bill. Stop it! I saw the same horrible things you saw."

"I'm not like you, Abe. You've got an internal strength like I've never seen in any other man. Don't you know that's why so many of us looked up to you? But I'm weak. Weak, I tell you!"

"Bill, listen to me. You can overcome this. You were doing so well. Your father was proud of you again."

Bill Berry heard him, yet he resisted. He had fallen into the grip of depression, continuing to protest, "I'm no good. I shouldn't have ever come to you to go in business with me. Abe, I feel like I deceived you."

"Bill, quit running yourself down. Fight it. You can overcome this, but you've got to try."

Berry looked up into Abe's pleading face, giving a half-hearted answer, "Very well, I'll try. I'll try... I guess."

On that uneasy note, the conversation ended. Abe had hopes for a positive outcome, but it was not to be. Soon after, business seemed to dry up all over New Salem. Whether was a short depression or something more permanent, no one seemed to know. Even more so, all the negative factors were taking their toll on the Berry-Lincoln store.

The downward spiral continued unabated as Berry started having all his old drinking buddies drop into the store. They turned it into a saloon, running off customers. Abe acquired sleeping quarters back over at the Rutledge Inn. Meanwhile, Berry descended into alcoholism, drowning himself in a continuous sea of alcohol.

During those troubled days, an incident occurred in which two ladies of New Salem came out of the store looking very disgusted. They came upon Abe who was stretched out under the shade tree at the edge of the property reading a book. "Mister Lincoln," one of the ladies called out, getting his attention. "We were highly offended by those drunks in your store."

"I'm highly offended too," replied Abe. "I can't stand to be in the same room with them. That's why I'm out here, reading a book."

Abe was much more depressed than he let on. What little business the store still had was being driven away by the drunken Berry and the company he kept. Abe could see it clearly now, the store was fast going under. Since most of the money invested had come from Berry, he felt powerless to do anything about it. He asked himself, *What have I gotten myself into?* It was like he was reliving something out of his father's drunken past.

Abe continued to lie under the shade tree reading a book most days. It was his way of escaping the reality that was fast closing in on him. He felt like he had to get away from the smell of whiskey and the smell of those who drank it.

Instead, Abe much preferred the outdoor smells of New Salem. Sitting there, underneath his favorite shade tree, he looked around and could see cattle and goats grazing on the hillsides in the distance. Closer, he could hear the sound of hogs wallowing in the dust of the Springfield Road, just south of the store. It was within these sights and smells of the countryside he sought to lose himself. It was a far simpler, uncomplicated time and he embraced it.

From the front porch of the Rutledge Inn, Ann could see Abe sitting underneath the tree. Even from that distance she could see the sad, sinking expression in his face. As he returned to the Inn during the evening, she could see the depressed expression still lingering in his face. At the same time, she was well aware that he was quiet, un-talkative, as if the weight of the world was on his shoulders. At the first opportunity, when Judge Green was in town, she pulled him aside and alerted him about Abe's condition.

That very evening in mid-October 1832, Judge Green sat down with Abe in a secluded corner of the great room. The Judge immediately inquired, "What's wrong Abe?"

Abe immediately opened up about Berry's alcoholism and how the store was fast going under.

The Judge got no objections from Abe when he said he would take his buggy down to Rock Creek in the morning and see Reverend Berry about his out of control son. The Judge concluded, "Abe, we'll talk more tomorrow evening after I return."

About noon the next day, the Judge came back to New Salem with a proud looking, distinguished white-haired passenger in his buggy with him. This was the Reverend John McCutchen Berry.

Stopping near the shade tree where Abe happened to be standing, the elderly man asked, "Is my son in your store?"

"Yes sir, he is."

"Mister Lincoln, is he drunk?"

Before answering that question, Abe could see tears forming in Reverend Berry's eyes. He knew he had to answer, no matter how painful the truth was. He said simply, "Yes, he is."

"Mister Lincoln, I'm sorry for any shame or humiliation my son has caused you. Judge Green told me you're a non-drinker and a man of good moral character."

"Yes sir, I try to be." Abe wanted to say more and did, "Reverend Berry, your son is a good man who served well with me during the Black Hawk war, but right now he needs help. I tried, but could never quite seem to reach him."

"Well, that's all one can do, is to try. Now it's my turn. I'm going in there to get him. I'll take my son back to Rock Creek and try to help him myself."

Judge Green rented a wagon at his own expense and between the three of them laid an almost unconscious Bill Berry in the back of the wagon.

As the wagon was about to pull out, Reverend Berry leaned over to Abe almost without warning and said, "God bless you for being a friend to my son." With that, the wagon headed south, down the Springfield Road toward Rock Creek. Bill Berry would never return to the Berry-Lincoln store throughout the rest of his short life.

After cleaning up the mess in the store, Abe joined the Judge for dinner over at the Inn. After dinner the Judge spoke frankly, "My boy, it doesn't look good. I know, because I witnessed the signatures on several of those notes you co-signed with Berry. With him unable to pay the money back, you will be held liable for those debts.

Abe took it hard, "Those notes come due between spring and summer next year. I won't be able to pay; the store will go into default. So, I guess my life is over with."

"My boy it's not all that bad! I'll try to work something out with your creditors so you can keep the store open for a while and liquidate your inventory. This way you'll be able to pay your creditors something."

"How much do you think I owe them?"

"From what papers I've seen, you co-signed with Berry for several hundred dollars, maybe even over a thousand dollars."

"That's like the national debt! For me that's a fortune." Abe thought a moment and added, "I was caught up in a dream and dreams seldom come true."

"My boy, in the meantime I'll try to figure out how you can make some extra money."

"As slow as business has been, at least I'll have plenty of time on my hands. I'll be able to read some more books."

"While you're at it, figure out what you want to be, get some more education."

"I will Judge, I'll think on it."

During the next week, Abe made a few sales. The store became more inviting as all of Berry's drunken buddies were gone now. A few sales were not enough though. They were few and far between. There was far too much quiet time. Total and complete silence, the kind in which he allowed his mind to wander. In such a state he rebuked himself many times over. He thought himself a failure. In the prolonged silence of one late afternoon the store's four walls seemed to close in on him. He could hear the intrusive words of Thomas Lincoln burrow deep into his mind, ridiculing him, "You're never going to amount to anything. You're a failure and you'll always be one. A failure! A failure!"

"No, no, NO!" Abe refused to listen to those words, but before he could shake off the feeling they brought, he heard another voice, vastly different.

"Abe, what's wrong?"

"Looking up, he saw the face of Ann, starring across the counter at him. Her quiet figure had stepped into the store while he had been lost in thought. Her face was so full of strength and truth.

Still trying to get over the negative spirit of his father, Abe couldn't maintain eye contact with Ann. He hung his head, glancing down at the counter.

"Abe, I ask you again, what's wrong?"

146

Shaking his head, he answered, "I can't talk about it right now. I'm being haunted."

Ann wouldn't hear of it. "Yes, you can. Look at me. Abe, right now."

Abe slowly raised his head until his eyes met hers. "I'm looking," he answered.

She insisted, "Now tell me, what's haunting you."

"I was sitting here thinking about the store going under and all of a sudden I could hear the voice of my father telling me I was a failure and would never succeed at anything I tried to do."

"Abe, listen to me. These were the words of a ghost, a person who never loved you or ever even tried to understand you."

"Then what words should I listen to?"

"Listen to the words of every one of us who is trying to help you. You can overcome this setback and do anything you set your mind to do. I, for one, have faith in you."

Abe took heart in what she was saying, feeling her words lift him out of his depression. "God bless you Ann."

Taking his hand, she gently squeezed it, further demonstrating her declaration of support, "You can become the man you dream of becoming. I know you can do it."

It was then Abe really knew in his heart how deeply Ann cared for him. He was about to say more to her when he noticed a certain well-dressed man standing in the doorway. It was Doctor John Allen. Abe welcomed him, "Come on in Doc, I'm still open."

Ann excused herself, "I'd better get back to the Inn, I have work to do."

As she walked past him, Doctor Allen spoke up, "Good day, Miss Rutledge."

"And a good day to you Doctor Allen," Ann responded, smiling in his direction as she left the store.

Approaching the counter, the good doctor observed to Abe, "She is a warm and wonderful girl, one of the most outgoing persons in all of New Salem. Anyone who has her friendship is indeed fortunate.

"Oh yes, I totally agree, though I believe she is so much more than just an outgoing person," replied Abe, coming very close to revealing the degree of his feelings for Ann.

"Now, you've got me curious." Doc Allen inquired, "What else do you see in Miss Rutledge?"

Feeling like he could open up to the good doctor, Abe told him, "I see something of the Spirit of Heaven all around her. Even more so, I see the spirit of an angel in her, something God has put here in the flesh to bless all who know her."

"There's something I see in you too," observed Doc.

"Oh really, what's that Doc?"

"You have an aura of goodness all around you. Abe, you're someone whose blessed this community by your presence."

"Doc, that's mighty nice of you to say."

"I mean it, Abe, because it's the truth. Now, as to why I'm here. Oh yes, I'm about to do something that's new for me. I'm going to plant a little garden out behind my place. So I figured I could use a rake and a shovel."

"Well, you came to the right place to get them."

As Abe handed him the tools and he in return paid for them, the Doctor observed, "I know these are hard, desperate times for you. I just want you to know I'm praying the good Lord's going to see you through this."

"Doc, I'm thanking you for your prayers. With Ann, you and the good Lord on my side, it sure lifts my spirits."

As he started to leave, Doc wondered out loud, "I guess we might see you over at the Inn for dinner?"

"No, I won't be there. I can't afford it, or to stay there any longer. With times as hard as they are, to save money I'm sleeping in the back of the store now and fixing my own meals over by the fireplace here."

Even though it was late October, going into the winter of 1832 was nowhere near as severe as 1831's winter of the deep snow. It was still uncommonly warm till late in the evenings. Abe continued to read his books outside, under the mighty oak tree a few hours a day. In the evenings it remained warm and cozy inside the little Berry-Lincoln store. One thing about it, before moving in, Abe well insulated the store. The walls were covered with black walnut boards for weather protection while the roof had been secured with sycamore boards. From floor to ceiling, up front the store reached a height of no more than ten feet, while in back the ceiling was not quite nine feet. The large, robust fireplace seemed to put out enough heat to adequately warm the interior of the entire structure.

It was during this time that lady luck, or perhaps Doctor Allen's prayer had some effect on Abe in another way. One day, as a traveler was turning his wagon slowly onto the Springfield Road, he sought to lighten his load. Stopping, he offered Abe a large barrel full of odds and ends for fifty cents. Abe stored it next to his bed in back of the store and forgot about it till early November 1832.

Having plenty of time at this point, Abe finally decided to empty the barrel, only to discover a hidden treasure. Getting to the bottom, there in plain sight were several books. Retrieving them, he found them to be a complete set of Blackstone's Commentaries on the Laws of England. Abe devoured this four-volume set during the winter of 1832, the books becoming his first law books.

Just beyond the end of the counter there were two chairs near the store's large fireplace. A few days before Thanksgiving, business had completely dried up, so Abe took the time to sit there and get lost within the pages of his new books.

About then, Ann entered the store. The creaking floor boards near the door alerted him. Abe looked up, seeing her.

"What are you reading, Abe?"

"I'm reading some books that were buried at the bottom of a barrel I purchased. They are fascinating, at least to me. Perhaps it's because I have so much time on my hands, but never in my whole life have I become so totally absorbed in something I've read."

"What are they?"

"They're a set of books on the very foundation of English law. These are the basic laws used in America right now. I believe it was by some act of Fate I accidently got them."

"It was no accident. Abe, I believe it was an act of the good Lord, that you got those books. I think God takes a more active hand in our lives than most people believe. Don't you see it? I believe God knows your heart more than you realize. He's pointing the way for you. I can see it, almost as if in a vision. He wants you to become the lawyer you've always dreamed of becoming.

"You really think so Ann?"

"Yes, I do, with all of my heart."

"Anyway, to become that lawyer would take a lot more education than I have right now."

"Then go out there and get it."

"What?"

"If you don't try to get that education, you won't have a future in New Salem or anywhere else for that matter."

Her words were the blunt truth. Looking over at her, she came closer and sat down in the other chair near him. He studied her resolute face for a moment, finally responding, "Of course, you're right."

"That's the spirit. Go back to school and get more education. Mister Graham would teach you grammar and mathematics. Judge Green would help you with your law studies. They both want to help, but you have to be willing and apply yourself."

"Maybe, but would Mister Graham take a class of one?"

"How about a class of two?"

"What do you mean, Ann?"

"I mean I would go to school with you. I need more education before going on to finishing school."

"Two students might make it worth his while. He just might consider it."

"Of course, he would," Ann said, encouraging him.

"Wait a minute," Abe wondered out loud, "how can you take off from your work over at the Inn to go to school with me?"

"That's why I came over. I have both good news and bad news."

"Oh no, what happened?"

"The Inn has finally gone under, but the new owners want me to stay on, board there, and work two to three days a week. The other four or five days a week I'll be free to do whatever I want, and what I want is to go back to school, with you."

"You would do this to help me?"

"I would do this to help us."

For a long moment he was silent, his eyes searching her face. In that moment Abe was reminded of one more truth. Ann had always been steadfast as his primary supporter. She was his rock.

Abe would spend Thanksgiving day at the Inn with the entire Rutledge family. It was a happy day, full of warmth and love amidst a sea of hard times. The day after, Abe would help Ann's brothers and cousin pack up two wagons to take with them to new lodgings north of town. Meanwhile, Ann would remain in town as she had said, working for the new owners.

Without saying it, Ann had tied herself to Abe's future. He thought about this as he prepared to leave town the last day of November, to go see Mentor Graham. Mounting Diamond, he set out riding west.

Abe's mind was filled with a lot of thoughts and a wide range of possible outcomes. For a while it appeared he had no future at all. Now though, there was a chance he might yet have a bright future in New Salem. With God's help, just maybe. As he rode, he whispered aloud, "Thank you Lord."

CHAPTER 12
THE SEARCH FOR KNOWLEDGE

A s Abe crossed the rolling land, he came to sort of a plateau where he could get a clear view of Clary's Grove up ahead. Getting closer, he could see it somehow looked different. It appeared to be about half abandoned. Many cabins were deserted. What happened? To get answers, he urged Diamond forward, in the direction of Jack Armstrong's place.

Coming around the corner of one such lifeless cabin, Abe came face to face with a smiling Jack Armstrong, standing outside, near the front of his own home. Their eyes meeting, Jack spoke up, "Howdy, Abe. It's good to see you–mighty good."

Dismounting, Abe shook hands and repeated the greeting, "It's mighty good to see you Jack, but," he was immediately curious, "what's happened to Clary's Grove?"

"In a way it was Bill Clary's doing. When he left for Texas after the Black Hawk War, two-thirds of the Clary clan that lived here pulled up stakes and left for Texas with him."

Abe was amazed. But before he could say another word, Jack's wife, Hannah, appeared in the doorway, "Abe Lincoln, is that you? Come in and stay for supper."

Abe responded, "That's right kind of you, Hannah. I'll be happy to oblige."

Later, inside at the dinner table, Abe got a clear, up close view of Hannah. She was heavy with child.

Jack could tell he noticed and commented, "Abe, you had a hand in this."

"How so?"

"You helped bring Hannah and me closer, back together. I'll be forever thank'n you for that. Besides, little Pleasant needs a baby brother."

"When is the baby due?" Abe asked.

Hannah spoke up, "Jack thinks it's going to be a boy, but no one really knows. We think the baby's gonna be born sometime after the first of the year."

"After that, what's gonna happen to you all? Are you gonna stay here in Clary's Grove?"

"As soon as Hannah's had the baby and gets healed up, I think we're gonna move."

"Where to, Jack?"

"About six miles north of here, to some property my brother owns in a little farming community near Sand Ridge. The Judge says we can share-crop it for a couple of years, then buy it from him."

Hannah added, "I hope you'll come and visit us after we get moved."

"More than that," volunteered Abe, "let me know when you get ready and I'll help you move."

Jack asked, "How can we reach you? Where will you be?"

"That's what I came by to tell you, about me and all the New Salem news. I'm headed over to Mr. Graham's place to see if he'll take me as a pupil and see if I can't get some more education."

"'What about the Berry-Lincoln store?"

"Jack, that's part of the sad news. Business has about dwindled away into nothing, sort of winked out. A depression has hit all the business in New Salem, the Rutledge Inn, everything seems to be on the verge of going under. As for me, my creditors are going to let me stay there and sell what I can, at least for the time being."

Hannah spoke up, "Well, if you get kicked out, you can always come and stay with us, wherever we're at." As she was very definite, Jack was nodding his head in agreement as well.

154

Abe was sincerely moved, "Thank you both, I'm right grateful. You're the best friends a person could have."

They continued to visit till it was quite late. Abe found out that Jack's brother-in-law, Henry McHenry had already moved north and was share-cropping on the Judge's hundred acre farm and helping to manage the farm for him.

An attentive listener to all this conversation was the Armstrong's three-year old young son, Pleasant, who was re-acquainting himself with Abe. After a while, he kept interrupting the adult conversation, "Uncle Abe, Uncle Abe, please tell me a story, one about you and Daddy in the Black Hawk War."

"Fine, I'll tell you how your Daddy and I fought off an army of savages, known as the deadly mosquitoes."

Jack whispered to Hannah, "Now we're in for one of Abe's whopper stories."

Abe heard them and said, "Now Pleasant, this story is more true than any story you've ever been told."

They all laughed and had a wonderful evening renewing friendships. Abe slept well that night, his first in a long time, letting go of his past for at least one night.

The next morning, as Abe mounted Diamond to head on up to the Graham home, Hannah came out to wish him off. "Abe, I have to say it, you're gonna get the education you want and make something of yourself."

"You really think so, Hannah?"

"I do, because you have the will and desire to make it happen. You're a strong-willed person, deep inside yourself. Jack and I have both been picking up on this for a long time now."

"Is it really so, obvious? How do you know all of this?"

"I don't know how I know all of this, I just do. Maybe that's what any person sees that really gets to know you, Abe."

"Hannah, I'll tell you what I see: a strong-willed person in you. Take care of yourself and have a strong healthy baby. I'll be coming around and rock him to sleep just as I used to rock little Pleasant.

One more thing, bare what I tell you, Pleasant is going to grow into a man just like his father and live a long healthy life."

By then, Jack and little Pleasant had come outside and were all waving goodbye as Abe and Diamond disappeared over the horizon. Getting closer to his destination, Abe was focused on visiting with Mentor Graham about his future. His mind was firmly set on his search for knowledge.

Approaching the two-story brick home that stood majestically on its owner's forty acres was a little intimidating to Abe. He did not have much time for reflection as the home's owner had emerged onto the front porch, having a clear view of the approaching rider. The owner's flaming red hair easily identified him as the 32 year old Scotch-Irish schoolteacher, Mentor Graham. "A fine morning to you, Mister Lincoln," he announced as Abe dismounted Diamond.

After Abe tethered his horse to a nearby hitching post, he opened up, "Mister Graham, I've had a lot on my mind lately and wanted to get your advice."

Graham could see by the serious expression that filled his face, young Lincoln would have a lot to talk about. "Come sit with me on the front porch and let's talk."

"Thank you," responded Abe, instantly feeling welcomed by the school teacher's cheerful disposition.

After filling the two chairs there, Graham's eyes scanned the eastern horizon, as his home faced the East, and commented, "Here it is December, and it's uncommonly warm, almost like springtime, not like last year's winter of the deep snow."

"Thank God for that," observed Abe.

"Yes, Abe, thank God." Graham's face took on an expression of grief as he recalled a sad time, "Before you came to Sangamon County, the day before Christmas in 1830, our first son was born. My wife was weak; our little child was even weaker. He had beautiful blue eyes, thick black hair, but was incredibly thin. We took care of him the best we could, but his little heart wasn't strong enough, and he passed away within a few days. I made his coffin with my own hands. After we buried him in the graveyard a half mile from here, my wife and I prayed for our baby's soul. We still do, even today. I guess the Lord knows best in His Divine Wisdom. Since then, I haven't been able to teach small children. In fact it's been over a year since I've taught school."

As he looked over at him, Abe could see the tears welled up in the schoolteacher's eyes. "I'm very sorry. To lose a loved one is heart breaking. I understand as much as one can, having lost my mother and my sister. You have my prayers for what it's worth."

"It's worth a lot. You're a good man, Abe Lincoln."

"I try to be. I'm always trying to be better than I am. That's why I'm here today. I've begun to formulate a plan to achieve a series of career goals. I've been talking to Judge Green and he's been encouraging me, loaning me some of his law books. Now I know I want to become a lawyer someday. But before I can even consider it, I need more education. It was not by choice I was born into rugged frontier life. It is my choice to educate myself and try to escape it."

"Abe, I admired you running for public office, so soon after returning from the Black Hawk War. Even though you were ill-prepared, you pushed ahead and did it anyway. I, for one, liked what you said and voted for you."

"Thank you, Mister Graham, it means a lot to me just hearing you say that. It's hard to explain, but there's something inside me pushing me forward. It's like a thirst I can't satisfy. I have this desire to do something meaningful in this life. Then it came to me like a revelation. I believe with all my heart, it is through the law I can accomplish my goal. I thought to myself, where do I begin? I listened to myself and realized it begins with my speech. I have a notion of studying grammar."

"Abe, I think it is the best thing you can do, a good place for you to start."

"If I had a good grammar book, I would commence studying right now."

Graham thought for a moment. "I believe I know where you might get one. There's a farmer, John Vance by name, who lives six miles straight south of here. He has a copy of an excellent book by Samuel Kirkham, entitled *Kirkham's Grammar*. It's the much improved 1828 edition, which is what you will need. I believe he will sell it for a price."

"I still have some money saved back from my service in the Black Hawk War. I'll pay whatever price he asks."

"Abe, I admire your enthusiasm, but before you go see Vance, let me write a note that may help convince him to sell you the book."

"Mister Graham, your helping me means more than I can say."

Just then, the school teacher could see something truly remarkable in Abe's face. A thirst for knowledge was clearly visible, like an aura of light surrounding him. It was there ever so briefly, then it was gone. To Graham, it seemed to be some form of positive energy, existing just below the surface inside Lincoln. Reacting to what he'd seen, he added, "Abe, I'll do anything to help you."

"If I'm able to acquire this book, will you tutor and help me to learn what I need to know? As I said, I have a little money, so I'll be able to pay you. If you will consider taking a second pupil as well, Miss Ann Rutledge would like to make it a class of two. I'll pay for both of us if you will accept us."

"Of course, I will. Getting two serious minded students who want to learn is something I believe will be a good thing for me. You may not know, but Miss Ann was a student of mine when she was younger, before she went to work in the Inn. I remember her as a bright girl, very intelligent. Having both of you here should prove very interesting."

"Thank you Mister Graham. I'm very grateful."

"Abe, as I think about it, I can't help but feel the hand of God at work here, not only helping you and Miss Ann, but also helping to lift me out of the state of sadness I've been in."

Abe agreed, "Miss Ann's been telling me for a long time, God works in mysterious ways helping us, even when we don't quite realize it."

Mentor Graham listened, a good feeling going through him. Realizing someone very important to him would find it a very positive experience to meet Lincoln, he spoke up, "Abe, I'd like you to come inside and meet my wife Sarah. She's an excellent cook, and I know she's fixing breakfast right now. Would you join us?"

"Of course I would, I'm right grateful."

Going inside, Abe immediately found himself in a nicer home than any he'd seen in all of New Salem. With much of its furniture being imported from back East, it was more lavish than even Judge Green's large farmhouse. Graham commented, "Though I have occasionally fancied myself something of a carpenter, most of the furniture was hand made by master craftsmen, true artists whose families came from Europe in the last century."

"I've never seen such beautiful work," marveled Abe.

"Now, I want to introduce you to a person, much more beautiful than any of these pieces of furniture."

Mentor Graham led him into an impressive formal dining room where he came face to face with the radiant 29-year old lady of the house, Sarah Rafferty Graham, Mentor's wife. She was Irish and equally red-headed. "So, this is the Mister Abraham Lincoln I've been hearing about for over a year," she said.

"It's an honor to meet you Mrs. Graham, but I'm just plain Abe Lincoln to my friends."

"Well, I'm just Sarah to all of my friends. I do hope we can be friends, Abe."

"So do I," replied Abe, feeling the warmth and goodness of these two people who had suffered loss, just as he had. It seemed like he'd just fallen into the midst of a new family who were immediately making him feel like one of their own. Their friendliness lifted his spirits and warmed his heart.

Over breakfast, they became acquainted and revealed to Abe their complete family history. Sarah Rafferty had married Mentor in 1816 when she was thirteen and he was almost sixteen. Over the many years they were married, Sarah would give birth to fifteen children, eleven of whom would survive past infancy. The Graham's marriage was an excellent example of the way of life during America's westward expansion in the 1800s. Mentor and

Sarah were among the lucky ones who truly became partners in both love and life, being married over fifty years.

As they continued their discussion, Mentor told Abe, "I got to America by way of my ancestors. I can trace them all the way back to Scotland and the deeds of my Scottish clansman, Lang Willie Graeme. It was said he had no rein on his tongue and no sheath to his sword. That got him into trouble with the English King, James of England. His descendants left Scotland in 1701 for the great land of America. My kinsmen moved around from North Carolina, fought in the revolution against King George, eventually settling in Kentucky."

"Why that's where I'm from," interrupted Abe. "How could you possibly know all of this history?"

"It's all recorded in our family Bible, the deeds of my family members. Proud of all of them, I am."

"As you should be, Mister Graham. In the same way, I am proud of my grandfather, my namesake, Captain Abraham Lincoln. He served on General Washington's staff. Though I never met him, I feel as though I know him through his deeds."

After breakfast, Abe and Mentor walked outside toward the west, where the open land of the Graham property met the tree line in back of his home. Turning to Abe, Mentor Graham admitted a surprising revelation to him, "Abe, while I'm proud of my ancestors, I'm not proud of some of my actions, or lack of action in my past."

"Mentor, you're a good man as far as I'm concerned. I'm not so sure I'm the person you need to be talking to about this."

"I'm sure, because it deeply concerns you."

This got Abe's attention. He reacted, "I'm listening."

"It was nine years ago, Abe, when you were living in Kentucky. You were fourteen years old, I was twenty-three. Even today, the memory of what I saw that morning and later the same afternoon is just as real as the two of us talking right now.

"Mentor, what did you see? What happened?"

"I saw you Abe. I was living in Kentucky, near where you lived for a brief period of time. I was walking down a country road when the screaming of a man out in a nearby field got my attention. It was your father, Thomas Lincoln. He was beating the back of his fourteen-year-old son with a large stick, yelling that he was too slow, not working fast enough. Your father appeared to be a mean, vicious man. At first, I wanted to interrupt, but then I told myself not to get involved, this was none of my business. That boy was you Abe. I didn't get involved then, but I am now. I'm going to help you all I can now."

"Thanks Mentor, for telling me this. My life was a living hell back then."

"I know, there's more to my story, Abe."

"More?"

"Yes, don't you remember what happened later that afternoon at the tavern?"

"I'm not sure," Abe said, trying to review his own past inside his mind. "My life was such an unending flow of unhappiness back then."

"As I said, I know. I was there," persisted Mentor Graham.

Abe strained, trying to remember a long-buried memory within the inner recesses of his mind. Slowly it came back as he recalled that awful afternoon, if it were playing out all over, perfectly visualized in his mind:

Abe's Flashback

My stepmother had sent me to the tavern to fetch my father home for dinner. I walked in, getting a massive whiff of the whiskey odor there. Spotting him, I saw my father was drinking heavily and already quite drunk.

He turned and glared at me, his eyes full of hate. "Boy, what are you doing here? I've told you never to come in here!"

"Momma wants you to come home. Dinner's get'n cold. Sis and I both want you to come home. Please…"

"Stop your whimpering boy. When are you ever going to be a man? Not another word!"

Before I could say anything else, he slapped me hard across the face, knocking me to the floor.

Back To The Present

Looking back up at Mentor Graham, Abe added, "All I remember was more pain after that."

"I remember the rest. I've never forgotten it all these years later." Mentor recalled the rest of that brutal afternoon:

Mentor Graham's Flashback

After your father knocked you to the floor, he continued yelling, "Don't you ever come in here again, shaming me in front of my friends!" Then he started kicking you in the side, again and again.

Somehow, you managed to roll out of the way. Looking up at him, you begged, "Daddy, please! Please stop!"

Your father became enraged again, yelling "Don't you ever call me Daddy in front of my friends!" He then kicked you in the mouth and above your eye in the forehead.

You pleaded, "Daddy, not in my forehead! That's where it hurts!"

"Then you need to hurt there again," he yelled back.

That's when I could take no more of this abuse. Your face was bruised and bloodied. The back of your shirt was wet with splotches of blood from where he hit you earlier in the day. Seeing this up close was when my Scottish temper got the best of me and I grabbed him by the arm, telling him, "Enough! The boy has had enough!"

Full of anger myself, I pushed him backward, very hard. Losing his footing, he stumbled backward, crashing into the bar.

It was then, he started yelling at me, "You can't tell me what to do. He's my son!"

I answered, "Then treat him like he's your son!"

In his drunken stupor, he started to come at me, but I held my hand up in defiance and warned him, "You beat up young boys, but if you come at me you'll be fighting a man." I guess he had second thoughts because he turned around and started drinking heavily again.

Then I went over where you lay crumpled on the floor and helped you to your feet. You could barely see me through your tears and blood. I said, "Go home boy, have your Mom help clean you up."

After seeing you out the door, I went back over to the bar to have a word with your father. I asked him, "What kind of man treats his son like a slave?"

"I do, he answered, "because he's my slave! Scotsman, you'd better wake up, you're in Kentucky, a slave state!"

"I guess I know that," I said. Thinking about it later though, this fact weighed heavily on my mind.

Finishing my drink, I vowed never to have another drink again. Seeing your father drunk, cured me in another way. Since that day I have never set foot in another tavern.

Back To The Present

As Mentor finished his story, Abe snapped out of his vision of those long-ago events. Reacting, he said, "I remember now! You were the red-haired man who stopped my father, only you were younger then."

"Yes, it was me. I wasn't sure if I should remind you. Sometimes such awful memories should stay repressed. For a long time, I've kept silent about it, ever since you came to New Salem."

"Thomas Lincoln stopped being a father to me when I was nine years old. He may have sired me, but that was as far as it went. You know, he got his wish in one way when I walked out of that tavern. I never called him 'Daddy' ever again. In his mind he was firmly convinced it was pre-ordained that children were to bare and suffer without complaint in whatever situation they were born into. I most profoundly disagreed with him."

"Did you ever attempt to discuss this with him?"

"Yes, we clashed more than once. I didn't fit into his pre-conceived notion of what a son should be like, so I was forced to bend to his will, be beaten into submission and become like a slave."

"The way he treated you wasn't right. Every man is born with free will and should be allowed to carve out his own future."

"I tried to discuss this very point with him and he told me in no uncertain terms that his children were born to be little more than slaves, living out their lives in hard labor on his farm. When I reached twenty-one my mind was already made up. I struck out on my own, having had enough of that way of life. That's why I come to you, to help me find my own destiny, whatever that may be."

"You can count on me, Abe. Perhaps, we will find your destiny together."

Looking around, from where they were standing at the western edge of Graham's property, Abe noted, "Speaking of destiny, this is such a beautiful place, when did you first come here, Mentor?"

"Strange to say, something your father said about Kentucky being a slave state got me to thinking. When we found out that Illinois was far less a slave state than other states, Sarah and I decided to move here. When we got here in the fall of '26, there was no New Salem in Sangamon County. It was just a thickly wooded area. There was only Judge Green's farm about a mile north of here. Otherwise, there was only a handful of rugged frontier folk living throughout the county. When I acquired these forty acres, it was all a densely wooded area at first. It took over five years of hard work to turn it into what you see now. Within my story is a lesson for you, Abe. To achieve your dreams will require you to use some of the same tools I have used."

"What might they be?" Abe was eager to know.

"Have a clear vision of the goal you want to accomplish. Then using that as your guide, apply hard work and your own sheer force of will to reach your goals."

Abe became excited, "Mentor, I can do it. I can do this!"

"Of course, you can, but Abe I have a few words of advice for you. I want you to do a few things in the learning process with me.

Make a real effort to learn something new, each and every day. Never go to sleep at night without having doing this. If you do this for as long as you live, you will find yourself becoming wise and more intelligent."

Taking in every word, Abe promised, "I will do it, every day for the rest of my life."

"Just remember, there's a whole world of knowledge out there, many things to learn about life, as you make your journey through it. Hopefully, you will become a little wiser with each step forward."

"Hopefully I will," said Abe, having a lot on his mind to think about.

After their conversation, the two men went back inside, having taken the first step in establishing what would be a life-long permanent bond of friendship. They would be on a first name basis from then on.

Back inside, Mentor wrote a short note to farmer Vance that would prove helpful in procuring the grammar book. Abe felt like he was gathering momentum as a man on a mission now. Shortly thereafter, he left on Diamond, heading due south to Vance's farm.

Two days later, Abe arrived back in New Salem. Entering the closed-up Berry-Lincoln store, he sat down by the unlit fireplace, resting for a moment. He wasn't alone very long when Ann entered, sitting down beside him.

"Abe, I saw you ride in. I've been keeping an eye out for your return every day. How did the trip go?" She was immediately anxious and curious.

Smiling, he looked over to Ann and said, "Mentor Graham agreed we could start classes together just as soon as we could make it out there."

"Oh Abe, I knew you could do it!" Her face lit up with joy from ear to ear. Then almost as an afterthought, a question overtook her joy. "But what will we study from when we get out there?"

"From this," Abe answered, holding up the book that was in his lap. It was labeled on the cover: *Kirkham's Grammar*, the improved 1828 edition.

"How on earth did you get this book?"

"Mister Graham directed me to a farmer who lived a few miles south of him, who just happened to have this book."

"Just how did you manage to get it from him?"

"The old farmer needed more wood for his fireplace, so I spent half a day, chopping firewood for him. Fortunately, it's still dry and warm enough so I could do it. That, together with a letter from Mister Graham about our sincerity to learn and two dollars cash, bought the book."

"I'm so proud of you. If there's a way to do something, you will find it."

"There's one more thing left to do. Come with me."

Ann followed Abe, over to the counter where he had a pen. Writing on the cover of the book, he wrote:

Ann Rutledge is learning English grammar with me. – A. Lincoln

He then, handed the book to her, where upon she held it close to herself for a moment. Shutting her eyes, Ann said, "I pray to God that both of us will get full value out of this book. Thank you, Lord for bringing it into our possession."

"What?"

"From this day forward, we're in this together, getting an education, everything."

Ann was correct in a sense. After being kept for many generations within the Rutledge family, this grammar book representing Abe's bond with Ann, still exists today.

For Abe and Ann back then, in December 1832, their search for knowledge had only just begun.

CHAPTER 13
LEARNING, REVELATIONS, AND BECOMING POSTMASTER

To begin the first phase of their learning experience, Abe rented a buggy for Ann and himself. Within days they showed up at Mentor Graham's front door. Standing before him in his living room, Mentor immediately picked up on something in both their facial expressions. In their whole manner they both displayed a great degree of sincerity and determination. Then too, he was surprised at the speed with which Abe had acquired the *Kirkham's Grammar* volume from farmer Vance. He could immediately tell they already had begun studying it. From this beginning he knew they were committed.

Through the rest of December, on into January and February 1833 Mentor proceeded to guide Abe and Ann through a thorough understanding of grammar, broadening their range of knowledge. Making detailed notes about the progression of his students, he was becoming more impressed every day by their ever-expanding intelligence.

One evening after they had left, Sarah questioned her husband, "What do you think of Ann? How are they doing with their studies?"

Mentor answered, "Ann's a bright girl and tolerably good scholar. I see in both of them that burning spark of desire to learn, deeply embedded within themselves."

Coming out a few days each week, as the weeks turned into months, Mentor soon became aware he had two very gifted students under his tutelage. In late February, Sarah Graham had begun to take Ann more under her wing, teaching her more of the things she would need to know about managing a home, things she would need to know in finishing school. At this same time, Abe had evolved to the point where Mentor gently guided him through a rudimentary knowledge of mathematics.

Abe's mind could not rest. Out of this, a strange fascination with surveying grew within him. Trying to wrap his mind around the subject, he sought Mentor's help. To appease Abe's unquenchable thirst for knowledge, he acquired another book, *Flint and Gibson's Treatise on Surveying* for his student. Studying day and night, some days without any sleep at all, Abe mastered all the books he could find on the intricate subject within six weeks. Normally it would have taken the average student several months, if not years, to acquire the working knowledge Abe had. Seeing this progress, Mentor commented to Judge Green, "Abe is no average student."

With what little money he had, Abe bought a compass, chain, and other surveying instruments and obtained several surveying jobs. The results were attested to be amazingly accurate and correct. He eventually would make the unheard-of sum, for those times, of three dollars per day for his surveying assignments. It was the most money he'd made in his life up to that time.

This achievement notwithstanding, Abe's major goal to become a lawyer remained. From that position he was dreaming of an even larger goal, wanting to accomplish something for the greater good of all mankind. Along with this ever-expanding goal, his interest in the deepest, most profound subjects that have challenged man grew within him. He was reaching his limits of comprehension and understanding, but yet he wanted to learn more. The time had come again to seek Mentor's advice and counsel.

"I'm trying to learn more," Abe complained, "but I can't seem to contain it all in my head."

"Avoid distractions, solitude and quiet may help your concentration," advised Mentor. "Whatever your having problems with, read it aloud in small sections when you are alone. Then put the book away and write your own interpretation of what you've read.

Do your studies in this manner until you completely comprehend what you've read."

Abe found this method especially helpful when he strove to understand scriptures from the Bible. On their way back to New Salem one evening, Abe told Ann, "In my thirst for knowledge I want to read as much as humanly possible that would give me a complete understanding of the Bible."

On one day in late February, when Ann had to work at the Inn, Abe stayed overnight at the Graham's residence. Combining his grammar and surveying studies, he now added law to the mix. Reciting his studies from memory, Abe was becoming better and more fluent with each day's passing.

Mentor marveled at Abe's improvement, "In all my years as a schoolmaster, I've seen no student accomplish what you have done in so short amount of time."

"Really," Abe replied, "I'm grateful for the compliment."

"It's a compliment you deserve. Here you have mastered the rudiments and rules of English grammar and are already writing deeds, contracts and other papers for people."

"Yes, but I couldn't have done it without both you and Judge Green helping me."

"I still find your progress nothing short of amazing."

"Mentor, I'm mighty grateful for your support, beyond words. The man I am becoming, I owe to you and the Judge."

After dinner that evening, the two men continued talking by the fireplace in the living room. At some point in their discussion, they veered off into the subject of theology with Abe expressing his concerns, "Mentor, I need guidance in understanding the deeper meanings of God's word. There's something going on within myself that I don't understand."

"Abe, I'll help you if I can."

"What I'm about to tell you, few people know. Sometimes I hear voices and see visions, not often, but as I say, sometimes... Maybe God can help me."

Mentor studied him for a moment, then asked, "How long has this been going on?"

"Since right around the time I was kicked in the forehead by a horse. I was nine years old at the time, and my mother had just died."

"Who else knows about this?"

"Around here, just Ann and Judge Green."

"You say it doesn't happen much anymore?"

"But when it does happen, it's usually preceded by blinding painful headaches. My head feels like it's going to explode."

Realizing this was reaching beyond his own understanding, Mentor said, "With your permission I'd like to discuss this with Doctor Allen in the greatest of confidence."

"Yes, Mentor. Of course, discuss it with him. In the meantime though, would you pray for me?"

"Of course I will, my friend." Mentor Graham felt humbled that Abe had brought him into his confidence. Knowing Abe's history and how he evolved, Mentor had begun to appreciate the growing genius expanding inside him. Despite any potential handicaps, Mentor was committed to helping Abe reach his full potential.

The two men continued talking until way past midnight. That was when Sarah Graham came downstairs, only to find Abe and her husband still actively engaged in profound conversation. It was then she made an extraordinary offer, "Abe, since your studies bring you out here so often, why don't you just move in till you complete your schooling?"

Abe was moved by her honest and sincere offer. He then glanced over to Mentor.

Feeling all eyes on him, Mentor responded, "If Sarah says it's okay, it's an acceptable arrangement with me. After all, we have an empty guest bedroom upstairs."

The decision was made and Abe came to live with the Grahams for the next several months, excepting for the days he had to be in New Salem, until his schooling was complete.

This worked out till one such day in late April when Abe had to go to New Salem to meet with Judge Green at the closed-up

Berry-Lincoln store. "I have very good news for you," announced Judge Green. "Abe, I told you I would find a way for you to make some extra money to live on, yet still not interfere with your schooling."

"Yes, I do remember you mentioning that possibility," recalled Abe.

His all too familiar Santa Claus-like smile beamed from the Judge's face. "I've found something I think you'll like."

"That's most excellent news!" An excited Abe responded, knowing full well any extra income at this point in time would be a God-send. Burning curiosity brought on the obvious question, "But Judge, what kind of job would it be?"

"My boy, how would you like to be the new Postmaster of New Salem and all the surrounding area?"

"I would like it fine, but I thought New Salem already had a postmaster and a post office."

"It's sort of had both, but the situation has changed. Our first mail service began back on Christmas day of 1829. A fellow named Harvey Ross was our first mail carrier. His route began north of Beardstown, down to Springfield and over to New Salem on his way back up. As you can imagine, his stops here were infrequent, usually no more than two to three times per month. About a year later we got our very own post office established right here. Recently though, the post office duties wound up with Sam Hill, who owns a tool store on the other side of Main Street."

"I know Sam," acknowledged Abe, "but I thought he was basically a whiskey dealer."

"You're exactly right," agreed the Judge. He explained, "That's why I got drawn into this matter. Many of the good ladies of New Salem came complaining to me. It seems more than once, Sam was much too interested in selling his whiskey wares to his other customers, rather than taking care of his post office duties. I questioned Sam about this and he told me quite frankly he had no interest in continuing as Postmaster."

"So, what's going to happen?"

"Abe, if you're in agreement, I'll proceed with my petition to get you the appointment."

"Sure, Judge. I'm honored you would consider me for this position."

"My boy, I know you'll work hard and justify my confidence in you."

True to his word, Judge Green's petition produced successful results. Abe Lincoln was appointed Postmaster on May 7, 1833. On that day, Abe and Billy Greene carried the 'official' post office file cabinet across Main Street, setting it up behind the counter in the former Berry-Lincoln store. Abe would be a success in this position, getting well acquainted with almost every citizen in New Salem and the surrounding area.

A few days later, a white-haired, bearded stranger rode along Main Street looking for something. Seeing the new post office sign tacked over the old Berry-Lincoln sign, he came to a stop. Tethering his horse to a nearby hitching post, the seemingly old man entered and announced in a booming voice, "Captain Abe Lincoln!"

From behind the counter, Abe looked up and recognized him, "Uncle Jimmy Short!"

Though the white beard made him look much older, this man was only two years older than Abe. No matter, Abe had already tagged the nickname on him. "Uncle Jimmy, I haven't seen you since the Black Hawk War."

James Short had gotten close to Abe, being a very good Indian scout for the 4th Mounted Militia during that brief war. He had helped Abe save a lot of lives. Jimmy never shied away from his opinions that the Indians had their lands stolen from them. He'd always said: "A lot of blood shed during the Black Hawk War could have been avoided had the Indians been treated fairly." Abe always valued Jimmy's opinions. In turn, Jimmy liked Abe a lot.

Complimenting Abe, he said, "Now with you Postmaster, maybe I'll get my mail where I'm living at now."

"Jimmy, where exactly is that?"

"Up north of town, out on Sand Ridge, about a half mile from where the Rutledge family lives now."

This got Abe's attention. "Now Jimmy, where exactly did you say the Rutledge family lived?"

"They're living on John McNeil's farm, about half a mile from me. I hear they have some kind of arrangement with McNeil to live there while he's gone."

"I'd heard something about it," Abe replied, not letting on how much he knew.

Jimmy continued, "You know, Sand Ridge is becoming quite popular of late. Sergeant Armstrong came up to visit me last week, checking out a homestead near me. I think he's got a mind to share crop it for its owner."

Happy to see Abe again, Jimmy said he'd be back in a few weeks to pick up some mail he was expecting from back East. As the two men parted, they shook hands warmly, promising to see each other again.

The function of a post office and mail delivery were quite different in the 1830s than they are today. The mail was delivered to New Salem by coach or on horseback once or twice a week. As Postmaster, Abe only had to work one to three days per week. With such a light workload, Abe and Ann were still able to go out to the Graham home once or twice per week. When Ann had to work, Abe would continue to stay overnight with the Grahams.

Abe soon learned which days the mail would arrive in New Salem. First, he would sort out the mail that he knew customers would come to the post office to pick up. Then he would set aside the other mail he knew he would have to deliver himself. Often, this would take what would be a very long day. Frequently, Abe would be seen carrying the mail in his hat. As he delivered mail in this manner, he made small talk with his customers, getting to know each one of them on an intimate basis.

Taking his job seriously, Abe's caring ways proved to be a positive factor with everyone. Over time, all the frontier folk around New Salem and the surrounding area began to think of him as another member of the family. Everyone responded positively, even growing to love him.

One of the benefits of being Postmaster was that he would get first chance to read all the newspapers of the day as they came in. This enabled him to be well informed and up on current events. Among those he was known to have received and read were the *Sangamo Journal*, the *Missouri Republican*, and the *Louisville Journal*.

Popular as Postmaster, Abe would remain in that position as long as it existed. Though he gave his all, remuneration for his efforts was quite modest. Seldom did he earn more than twenty-five to thirty-five dollars per year.

Even as he was struggling to just hang on, those economic forces that had brought down the Berry-Lincoln store were once more rising to put pressure on Abe. One day in early June, Judge Green entered the post office with a grim look on his face. Abe immediately knew bad news was in the air.

"What's wrong, Judge?" Abe asked, just sensing something unpleasant.

"Abe, let's sit down over by the fireplace and talk a bit." The Judge paused for a moment, then stressed it even more, "It's important you hear what I have to say."

"Sure Judge," Abe replied immediately, wanting to be accommodating. After sitting down, he asked, "What has happened to bring you into the post office with such a sad expression on your face?"

"What has happened is that bad luck has continued to follow you, even to the point of coming right in here after you."

"How so, Judge?"

"Son, you might recall I told you I would try to work something out with all the store's creditors so you could pay them back over time."

"Yes, I remember you telling me that last fall."

"Every one of your creditors has agreed to those terms–that is save one. The one hold out is a man you do not know, one you've never met."

"I thought I knew all of the store's creditors?"

"You do, except for one investor from Springfield who loaned Bill Berry some two hundred dollars. The agreement that Berry signed clearly states that in case of the store's failure and Berry's inability to pay off the loan, the debt falls to you as the surviving partner. The debt went past due after January 30th, over four months ago. With everything else that has happened, I thought it best not to tell you at the time and try to work something out."

"Judge, am I liable for this two hundred dollars?"

"Yes, my boy, I'm afraid so. You may remember Berry had you sign several papers when you became partners, papers that I witnessed."

"Yes, I remember initialing several papers, A. Lincoln, but I thought that Berry was fully liable along with me."

"Not the way this creditor had his lawyer draw up the loan papers that you and Berry both signed. This creditor, Peter Van Bergen, from Springfield, is a hard-nosed businessman. I tried to negotiate a pay out over time, but he wouldn't hear of it. Despite my best efforts, he brought suit against you in Springfield and won."

"What does this mean, Judge?"

"Van Bergen was awarded a judgement by the court in Springfield. This allows the legal seizure of your assets that he can then sell to recoup all or part of his loan."

"Judge, I have no assets!"

"He can't take the post office. It's no longer the Berry-Lincoln store."

"Thank God, I'll still have a roof over my head."

"He can't take your books. I've already told him they're my property on loan to you."

"Thank you for that, Judge."

"Unfortunately, he can take Diamond. When I gave him to you, the records were changed to reflect I deeded the horse over to you. Also, he can take your saddle and all your surveying equipment, your compass and chain as well."

"When will all this happen?"

175

"This afternoon. Son, I'm here in my official capacity as Justice of the Peace to see these items are delivered to Van Bergen without incident. I hope it goes without saying, I wouldn't be doing this unless I hadn't been ordered to by the law I'm sworn to uphold."

"I know that Judge, but thanks for saying it anyway."

After the Judge left, Abe felt greatly humbled by his own shortcomings and weighted down by a sense of failure closing in all around him. Becoming very discouraged, sitting there, he stared at nothing for hours. Finally, he spoke out loud to a Higher Power, "Lord, I don't know what to do. Please help me find a way out of this."

"A way out of what?" A loud questioning voice spoke up from behind Abe, startling him.

Jerking around in his seat, Abe rose to his feet, immediately recognizing the source, "Uncle Jimmy, what brings you to town?" It was his grizzled Indian scout from the Black Hawk War.

"Abe, I told you I'd be coming back in to pick up my mail."

"Oh yes, I remember." Going over to the mail cabinet, Abe pulled out two letters for James Short. "Here's your mail, Jimmy."

"Thanks Abe, but now tell your old friend what's wrong."

Abe told him the whole sad story of his conversation with Judge Green earlier. It was impossible to hide the depression that had crept into his face.

Jimmy commented, "It's not right, taking a man's horse and all his surveying equipment, depriving him of his livelihood. Even more so, how are you going to continue studying out at Mister Graham's place?"

Abe seemed lost as he replied, "I don't know. I can't imagine my future now."

"Abe, I'll say it again, it's just not right breaking a man that way. There just has to be a way for you to bounce back from this setback."

"Jimmy, I keep hoping."

"You were praying earlier."

"Yes, I was."

"Well, keep praying. There's one thing I've learned in this life–and not everyone agrees with me on this–the Lord does answer prayers."

After Jimmy left, Abe did keep praying. It was hard, but he also kept delivering the mail. Over the next nine days, walking many miles per day, carrying the mail inside his hat. He did so until late one evening when a loud knock at the post office door got his attention. Opening the door, there stood Jimmy Short in front of him. "Come on in Jimmy. What brings you to the post office so late?"

"Business with you, Abe. I told you to keep praying."

"I have, Jimmy, I have."

"Abe, it's just like I said. Your prayers would be answered."

"What do you mean?"

"I attended the auction of your horse and other property earlier this afternoon. The high bid on the whole lot was $120.00."

Abe was now curious about one point. "If I may ask, who bought my horse?"

"I did, Abe. Diamond and all your belongings are right outside. I told you I didn't think it was right what Van Bergan did, so I bought it all back for you."

"But Uncle Jimmy, it was a $120.00 of your money."

"That's not what matters. You're my friend, Abe. Besides, it was only part of the money paid me for Indian scout'n in the Black Hawk War."

Abe was profoundly moved by his unselfishness. "Jimmy, you're one of the kindest, most honorable men I've ever known. You're a true friend. When I am able, just as you have today, I will do as much for you sometime."

Abe never forgot Uncle Jimmy. Many years later, in the midst of civil war, he heard about his old friend being in financial trouble. James Short was living in California at the time when he was notified that he had been appointed Indian agent for the Round Valley Indian Reservation out there. It was an important position with a good salary. Abe told others, "I can think of no fairer man to take up the Indian's cause." In this way, he was able to repay Uncle Jimmy's kindness many times over.

Getting Diamond back, Abe could resume classes with Ann out at the Graham home as well as being able to run the post office in New Salem. This was a good thing, now more than ever, as Ann was at the center of his conscious thought.

On one such day in late June 1833, Ann came to the post office, just as she had for several days in succession, enquiring about any mail addressed to her. "Abe, have you received any letters from a Mister John McNamar?"

Before he answered her question, his eyes formed into a fixed, almost concentrated stare, studying Ann for a long moment. Increasingly so, Abe had not been able to think or do a thing that he didn't dream of her. It had gotten to the point where he was becoming consumed by the very thought of her. Just hearing McNamar's name caused him to blurt out, "Don't you mean McNeil?"

"How did you know?" She asked, surprise written all over her face.

"I've known since the day before he left town. I had to witness a document before Judge Green so he could complete the sale of his store. He told me he would tell you the truth that very day. He also said he would be back within three months to marry you. Now, another month and it'll be a full year since he's been gone."

"You knew all this time and never said a word."

"Yes Ann, I did. It tore me apart not being able to say anything, but you see he got me and the Judge to promise we wouldn't expose him."

"Abe, I don't know how it's happened, but somehow the word got out. Some say he must've been some sort of criminal to live here under an assumed name. Now, some people have been looking at me and saying, 'Look at the poor Rutledge girl, she's been lied to and abandoned.' He wrote me one letter about two weeks after he left town. Since that time, I've heard nothing, not a word from him. As you know, I was forced into this arrangement. I gave my word to him only to help my parents. I feel so shamed, hurt. I don't know what to do." At this point, tears filled her eyes, her voice going silent.

The one thing Abe could not stand was knowing Ann was hurt. Seeing her in the clutches of a broken heart, he reacted, "He's not worth it, you know."

"What?"

"He's not worth your feelings, even thinking about him. After all, the man was an imposter and a liar!"

"A liar?"

"Yes, he lied about who he was and lied when he said he'd be back within three months. Who knows where he really is or if he'll ever return to New Salem? Besides, there's someone right here in New Salem, right now that really loves you."

"Who?"

"Me!"

A whole range of emotions passed over her face in a matter of seconds as she searched Abe's face, taking in the full meaning of what he had just said. "Oh Abe, you're such a decent caring man."

"Ann, I think I started falling in love with you that first night we spoke on the front porch of the Inn. But then, I thought how could such a beautiful angel fall in love with such an ignorant boy, having such a homely face like this?" Abe gestured toward his face as he hung his head in low self-esteem.

Ann stepped closer, taking his hand, squeezing it, until his eyes came up, meeting hers. Then, she told him, "I didn't fall in love with your face, I fell in love with your mind and heart. You're different than any man I've ever known. You're good, honest and kind. It's because of these qualities–and so much more I can't put into words–I love you." Her face revealed the truth. She had laid open her own heart and soul.

Her hand still in his, Abe spoke words straight from his own heart as well, "The goodness and beauty I see in you is far more than skin deep, it's part of your soul. When I say it right now, I love you, I mean it forever, and ever, and always."

179

In that moment of confessed truth, they both went into each other's arms. Within the privacy of the New Salem post office, they kissed and embraced each other, revealing the love they had held within themselves for so long.

After that afternoon, nothing would ever be the same between Ann and Abe. Their feelings were coming out into the light of day as their mutual destiny was fast overtaking them.

CHAPTER 14
TRUE LOVE FOUND

Abe got up the next morning, his mind full of thoughts about Ann. With each succeeding day, he felt the positive aura she projected, surrounding him.

Those first three days of July found either Ann coming to the post office or Abe visiting the great room of the Inn quite frequently. Coming into contact, they would stare at each over for long periods of time. In those unspoken moments they seemed to be searching for something in each other, far more than skin deep. They both picked up on a sense of goodness and purity in each other. Seeing those qualities were fast leading them into a permanent commitment that summer of 1833.

Late in the afternoon of July 4th, Abe was behind the counter in the post office. He could hear laughter and high spirits coming from the Inn. He thought many of the townspeople were celebrating the 4th. Looking up, there was Ann, standing in the doorway.

She spoke first, "You know, I look for the *inner light* in people. When I see it, I know those are the special people."

"Is that what you saw in me?" Abe asked.

"Yes, I saw it in you when I first met you. Your father had almost killed it in you, but there it was, still flickering, struggling to come to the surface."

"You're right. I had been beat down so much by the cruelty of my father. I was smothering in a very dark place. If I hadn't met you, I don't know what would have happened. But how did you see anything in me?"

"I saw it in your humanity and kindness to others."

"Ann, that's what I first saw in you. As I think about it, I believe it was the inner light of my angel mother that saved me from death so many times as I was growing up. Then when I met you, it was your inner light that saved me all over again."

"Abe, you might say I'm here to save you again, right now."

"You are?"

She explained, "I thought I might come over and celebrate the 4th with you. How about we go outside and visit under the shade of our favorite tree?"

Going outside, Abe and Ann got under the shade of the expansive oak tree on the corner, overlooking Main Street. There was still ample daylight as it was one of those long summer evenings.

Looking at each other as only two people who are in love can look at each other, Ann said, "Let's talk about our future…together."

Abe was completely caught up in the full meaning of those words, immediately expressing his feelings, "It's about time we become officially betrothed."

"Let's announce it to the whole world," Ann said excitedly.

Abe thought for a moment, coming up with a solution. "Let's do it in such a way that everyone who passes this tree will know it."

Ann agreed, "Yes, I want everyone in New Salem to see it."

Abe looked around spotting a large stone nearby. With a bit of effort and a lot of adrenalin, he was able to move it over and position it in such a way that anybody passing by on Main Street could easily see it. If a passerby stopped and stepped a little closer, one could clearly make out the words etched deeply into the stone's surface. They read, *A. Lincoln and Ann Rutledge were betrothed here July 4, 1833.*

In following days, the stone was almost immediately noticed by Abe's old friends Billy Greene and Jack Armstrong, who'd come to town looking for him. They both swore to its authenticity. They noticed the hand writing matched perfectly with an inscription on an axe handle of a certain axe known to have been in young Lincoln's possession around that time. On the axe handle inscription read, *A. Lincoln, New Salem 1833.* Also, there was more than a passing similarity to the writing on the cover of a certain grammar book known to have belonged to Ann Rutledge then.

Looking down at the stone first after positioning it, Abe's expression reflected how he was feeling. He was happier and more satisfied than any time in his life.

At the same time, Ann's face was glowing in approval as she grabbed Abe's hand, looking up at him with her penetrating blue eyes. There was no mistaking how she felt.

For several minutes, they both were frozen in silence and in time. At length, Abe finally spoke, "The way you're looking at me does give me hope…for our future."

"Abe," she said, "I look the way I do because I love you."

Hearing this, he was filled with emotion, "That you could love me…"

"Yes," she said, reassuring him, "I do, with all my heart."

Standing there, their eyes transfixed on each other they both saw something special. As they went into each other's arms, they both could feel it as well. It was as if some invisible aura was surrounding them with warmth and love. Perhaps without either one of them knowing it, the light and love of Almighty God was bringing them together. They kissed in a moment they both would remember as the defining moment of happiness in both their lives.

Shortly after July 4th, Abe and Ann were back in classes out at the Graham place. Almost immediately, Mentor noticed they couldn't keep their eyes off each other. His observation was quick, "Since you two were here last, something has happened."

Abe confessed, "Something has happened. Our relationship has changed. We are now engaged to be married."

Mentor turned to Ann, "What say you?"

"It's true, absolutely true!" She answered, bubbling over with happiness.

The schoolmaster was elated, "I'm so happy for you both, yours' is an ideal match!" then thinking as only a school teacher would, he added, "After all, you both like to read books!"

Later that evening, Mentor Graham would record this conversation of Abe and Ann's intentions in his journal-diary which survived for many decades.

On the following day, Abe and Ann would journey a mile north to Judge Green's farm. The Judge was at his desk in his office when his wife, Nancy Potter Green, stuck her head in the door. "Judge, you have visitors, very important visitors."

Looking up, he immediately saw Abe and Ann, coming hand-in-hand into his office. "This is a surprise!" He reacted in his big booming voice. "What brings both of you way out here?"

Abe told him the good news, "Judge, we wanted you to be among the first to know: It's official, we are engaged to be married."

"Oh joy!" The Judge responded loudly, as a rosy smile erupted across his face. "What great news!" He said, standing up, coming around his desk to face them, continuing, "It's so wonderful when two young people like yourselves can find that one special person you're meant to be with."

Facing him up close now, Ann was grateful, "Thank you Judge, that's exactly how I feel."

Abe added, "It's important to me–more than you know–to have your blessing!"

Looking at him, the Judge could see the heart felt honesty and sincerity in his face. "Son, you both have that and my prayers for a long happy life together." Then turning to Ann, the Judge felt like he had to ask her, "What about John McNamar, Miss Ann?"

"He promised, he'd be back within three months. It's been almost a year now and I have heard not a word from him in more than ten months. Since he does not care to write me, I do not care about his plans any longer. I'm going ahead with my life."

"Bless you child. If that man ever comes back here, refer him to me. I will set him straight about the consequences of his broken promises."

"Thank you Judge," added Abe. "If it ever comes to that I will appreciate your help."

Now, taking in the wider view of Abe and Ann together, the Judge addressed his questions to both of them, "What are your plans for the future? When will this marriage take place?"

Abe answered first, "I want to finish my education and become eligible to practice law in the state of Illinois. Then I will be able to support Ann and, God willing, our family to come."

"While Abe is doing that," broke in Ann, "I want to finish my own education so I may be a good wife to the finest lawyer in the whole state." As she spoke, her eyes revealed nothing but admiration for Abe.

The Judge could easily see they were deeply in love and said, "Bless you both, may every happiness come your way. But, how long do you think it will take you to accomplish your goals?"

"We are in July," Abe responded, thinking on his feet. "It'll take the rest of this year, all of 1834 and some of 1835."

Ann added, "We hope to marry in the late fall of '35, or by Christmas of that year."

The Judge thought for a moment, and then gave his approval, "It sounds like a good plan to me."

"Whenever the time comes," explained Abe, "we want you to marry us."

"My boy, Miss Ann, it would be my honor to do that. Whatever happens, I pray the good Lord will be with both of you."

Headed back to New Salem in their buggy, Abe and Ann were leaving with their hearts uplifted after visiting with Judge Green. Now with a vision of their future firmly embraced within themselves, they set out to make it a reality.

While Ann was back working at the Inn, Abe kept true to his promise to the Armstrongs to help them move. Hannah had regained her strength after giving birth to another baby boy. His father proudly named him Duff Armstrong.

Almost from the first, every time Abe would go near the baby he would stop crying and be fascinated with the tall stranger. Jack rendered his verdict, "Abe you're stuck with this baby. You're going to be his Uncle Abe."

"I'll be proud to be his Uncle. But Jack, I feel more like I'm his godfather."

A light seemed to come on inside Jack. "Abe," he said, "if anything ever happens to me, promise me you'll take care of Duff."

"I promise. Jack, you have my word of honor, but nothing's going to happen to you."

It was then, Jack Armstrong said something very profound, "My friend, none of us know what the future holds, none but the Good Lord."

Over the next few days, Abe would help the Armstrongs move several miles north, to a small place owned by Judge Green. Actually, it was up on Sand Ridge, near where both the Rutledge family and Uncle Jimmy Short were also living.

Returning to New Salem, Abe picked up Ann. Once again, they resumed their studies with Mentor Graham. Throughout the rest of 1833, Abe would continue the delicate balance of his post office duties and continuing his education.

Expanding his studies, schoolmaster Graham added additional books for Abe to absorb. They included: *Adam's Arithmetic*, *Woodbridge's Geography*, and *Worcester's Ancient and Modern History*.

Abe found himself struggling to process this wealth of new information, but he was determined to break through the dark ages he grew up in, actually beginning to achieve the level of intelligence he had dreamed. One day he said to Mentor Graham, "I owe you so much, for pushing me forward, not allowing me to settle for less. I remember telling you I could read and write well enough, and cipher a bit, thinking I could go it alone then."

Mentor recalled, "And I remember telling you, "Yes you could do that, but you have only just begun, receiving only the building blocks of what all knowledge is built upon. If you want to become the man you envision, you have a long way to go."

"Yes, I remember your words," acknowledged Abe. "My friend, I'm so grateful to you for helping me stay on course to accomplish my goals. Before, I was less than nothing. Now, I feel like I'm slowly becoming the man I want to be."

For the rest of 1833, Abe took advantage of every opportunity to be with Ann. Outside of going to school together, they went to church and social functions together. These included Abe accompanying Ann to Quilting Bees and Sunday services at Doctor Allen's home, often listening to sermons delivered by Bill Berry's father, the Rev. John McCutcheon Berry.

Abe spent the entire week leading up to Christmas 1833 out at Sand Ridge. After dropping off Ann at her parent's place, he back tracked, spending a couple days with Jack and Hannah Armstrong. While there, he assisted Jack with some of his blacksmith chores and tell his whopper stories to little Pleasant in the evening. Then later he would set up with their new baby, rocking his cradle.

Jack would say, "I hear little Duff."

"You mean, baby William," insisted Hannah.

Jack whispered to Abe, "Hannah insists on calling him by his given Christian name, but for me he'll always be my little Duffer."

Abe sensed Hannah was trying to listen in, so trying to head off a dispute, he spoke up just so she could hear, "Alright, I hear him, Hannah please pass me 'baby William' and I'll rock him to sleep."

Feeling appeased, she smiled and chastised Jack a little, "See their Jack, let this be a lesson to you. This is why Abe is so popular, he knows exactly how to please people.

"Anything for the lady of the house," conceded Abe.

More agreeable now, Hannah passed the infant, William 'Duff' Armstrong, to Abe. As though it was by some strange spell, the baby immediately stopped crying and in Abe's arms became more relaxed. In no time, he was cooing and drifted off to sleep.

Jack whispered, "I don't understand how you do that."

Abe explained, "You just have to have a soft voice and a tender touch."

From then on, whenever Abe visited the Armstrongs, he was entrusted with rocking little Duff. As the baby grew into a boy, and later into a man, Duff always referred to Abe as 'Uncle Abe'.

After leaving the Armstrong place, he journeyed back toward the Rutledge home, stopping just a half mile short of it at Jimmy Short's place. Jimmy told Abe, "Mrs. Rutledge–Ann's mother– comes over about once a week and cleans house for me. It's a perfect arrangement. I pay her a weekly salary and she keeps my place straightened out and looking nice."

Abe and Uncle Jimmy swapped stories for two days. As Jimmy would recall it, "Abe's conversation was always cheerful and full of fun, making him an especially good companion for me, being the lonesome old bachelor, I was. Nearing Christmas that year, Abe seemed more upbeat and positive about life than I had ever seen him. But of course, back then I had no knowledge of his relationship with Miss Ann. Three days before Christmas he left for the Rutledge place, telling me his life was about to change forever, in a good way."

Arriving at the Rutledge place about mid-day, it was obvious to the rest of the Rutledge clan, that the language of love had permeated the hearts and souls of both Ann and Abe. At one time or another over the next three days every member of the Rutledge family saw them in affectionate embrace, kissing each other.

Finally, after Christmas dinner, her brother David and cousin McGrady confronted the two of them. David spoke first, "I know what both of you said, but you really should go ahead and get married as soon as possible." He paused for a moment, then added something very prophetic, "After all, life is all so fleeting."

"Yes," agreed McGrady. Then speaking directly to Ann, he said, "Cousin, this may be your one chance. Grab at happiness with Abe while you still can."

David appealed to her once more, "Ann, please listen. You should marry this man. If for no other reason, he possesses honesty and integrity to his core. There's no finer man in my opinion."

Ann eagerly agreed, "You'll get no argument from me on that account." Pausing, she looked over at Abe, continuing, "He is the finest man in all of New Salem. I'm truly the luckiest girl in the world."

Abe quickly added, "She may be the luckiest girl, but I am by far the most fortunate man in the world to have earned the love of your angel sister. I know you both mean well, but Ann and I both want to complete our education so we will be a little better off than where we're at right now. This above all, I want you to know I love Ann and we truly are looking forward to–"

Smiling, Ann broke in at that precise instant and completed the thought, "We are looking forward to a lifetime of happiness with each other."

Looking back on it, many years later, Abe recalled, "Christmas of 1833 was one of the happiest times of my life. If things had gone the way of dreams, I would've wished to remain happily buried forever in the New Salem of those wonderful days."

Time marches on though, and the new year–1834–seemed to come all too quickly. It would be a year of new opportunities, new challenges, and new accomplishments.

Through his duties as Postmaster, Abe continued to be in constant contact with the public. This led to an inevitable deepening of friendships with most everyone who lived in and around New Salem. Abe's personal happiness seemed to become a part of his outgoing personality. He never met a stranger. Before long, everyone accepted him with open arms, sharing their most intimate stories with him.

From a friendless loner when he first came to New Salem, Abe evolved into a person that many had honestly come to love.

In this process, he found within his own self a growing heart full of love for the decent frontier folk that had become his family.

Seeing this ever-growing connection with others, coupled with his budding fascination with politics, it becomes easier to see why Abe did run for political office again.

So it was, in the early days of 1834 a dream filled Abe's head: He would become a candidate for the state legislature a second time.

After he filed as a candidate, Abe was asked why he was running for office. He answered, "Because I believe in equal justice for everyone. You see, I was born the poorest of the poor and will forever remain from the most humble walk of life. If that's all I ever have, my life will be full and complete to the end of my days. But if I am elected, I will stand for everyone's right to equal justice. On the other hand, if I am not elected, I will still stand for equal justice for all, right up to the last breath of my life."

After one such speech, Ann pulled him aside, telling him, "Abe, I'm so proud. You express your feelings so well. I feel it, truth and honesty is in your every word."

"Ann, I've learned so much this last year, that out of it comes something I want to hold to forever. The words that come to me are what I believe with my whole heart and soul. In all things, this above all, to thine own self be true."

Abe campaigned right up into the summer of 1834. Before each speaking event, he would shake hands with everyone in his audience, 'pressing the flesh' as he called it. Seating young children in his lap, he would take the time to tell them whopper stores, to their obvious delight. In doing so he endeared himself to their parents. Then, taking still more time, he would even help others split rails for their fences, illustrating he was not just another politician, but one of them –a man of the people who would listen to their concerns. When it finally came time for him to speak, they listened. Many of the voters were deeply moved by Abe's speeches even saying this man knew more than all his opponents put together.

By the time of the election, Abe had become well known throughout Sangamon County as well as other parts of Illinois. On August 4th, out of thirteen candidates running, the top four were elected according to state rules. At 1,376 votes received, Abe came in second, with only 14 votes separating him from the number one vote getter. He had been elected to the Illinois House of Representatives, representing Sangamon County.

All the returns in and verified, Judge Green made the official announcement from the front porch of the Inn in New Salem to a large crowd gathered in the street and all around the building. "It is with great pride I present the first person ever elected to the State

House from New Salem, Mister Abe Lincoln!" The whole crowd roared their approval.

Abe emerged from the Inn, hand-in-hand with Ann Rutledge. Smiling, both of their faces beamed with joy. Mentor Graham, who was there that day, said both of them appeared positively radiant.

Abe introduced Ann as his fiancé and future wife. In a sense, this was their moment of triumph together. Everyone in the crowd could see it too. The language of true love found, the kind that comes from the heart, had added new meaning to their lives and changed everything.

Since the next session of the legislative did not begin till late in the year, Abe and Ann went about their lives, spending as much time as possible together, fully committed to each other. They had begun to attend regular Sunday church services in Doctor Allen's home. At one such service in early November, Rev. John M. Berry was preaching the sermon. After the service, Rev. Berry mentioned to Abe and Ann that he wanted to speak with both of them privately. He told them, "My son is gravely ill. He's been asking for both of you. Is it possible? Would you come and see him?"

"Yes, of course," said Abe. No matter what had happened due to Bill Berry's drinking problem, he and Ann both knew that Bill had always been a good person at heart.

Sometime before Thanksgiving, Abe and Ann took the buggy on a journey a few miles south to the Berry farm along Rock Creek. Visiting Bill Berry at his bedside, they only had to take one look at his pale countenance to know his days were very definitely numbered.

Bill asked if both Ann and Abe could forgive him for the wrongs he felt he had committed against them, and following that, wished them every happiness together.

Ann could tell his words were sincere. Taking his hand, she responded with equal sincerity, "Of course, we will forgive you and pray for you as well."

Bill also apologized to Abe for getting him involved in the Berry-Lincoln store, leaving him this way. Taking Abe's hand with what little strength he still had, Bill managed to whisper, "Abe, you're the finest man I've ever known."

Later, on the buggy ride back to New Salem, Abe was profoundly bothered, seeing the wasted shell of a man that Berry had become. "I pray to God I may never end up like him."

"You won't," reassured Ann, "because you have too much force of will and drive to succeed." Abe felt, better for a brief moment, until Ann continued, revealing what she had been pondering, "On the other hand, I'm profoundly worried about one thing."

"About what?"

Ann explained, "Bill's so young, cut down in his prime before his life could amount to anything. It makes me worry about us. Are we safe from being cut down like him? Abe, will we have enough time?"

"Who can say? Only the good Lord knows the answers to those questions."

A sudden gust of cold air passed over them. It was going to be a cold winter, far colder than the previous winter of '33. Ann spread a blanket over her lap, one they had brought along in the buggy. Feeling the need for more warmth, she moved over closer to Abe. It was though he were an extra layer of insulation against the cold. She felt a certain sense of security just being close to him. Expressing her feelings, she said, "In a way, I wish you didn't have to leave at all for the new legislature in Vandalia. I wish you could stay right here with me. But on the other hand, I'm proud you won. It means our dreams are one step closer to coming true."

Abe let her know how he felt, "I'll be thinking of you every day I'm gone. After all, the dream you're talking about is my dream too. I want you to remember something."

"What, Abe?"

"Every day I love you. I always will."

"Oh Abe, that helps me." Her spirits lifted, her whole face turned into a glowing expression of hope towards Abe.

After that, they both went silent, with just an occasional glance toward each other. Abe concentrated more on the reins of the horses as they made tracks, carrying the buggy down the Springfield Road toward the hoped for feeling of a warm fireplace back in New Salem. At the same time, they were leaving the cold of Rock Creek behind, trying to shut its sadness out of their minds.

CHAPTER 15
LOST DREAMS

Back in New Salem, Abe was preparing for his eminent departure for Vandalia and the fall session of the State Legislature. To reach the capital in time, he had to depart on the Saturday morning stage. He planned to meet it at its usual stop in front of the old Rutledge Inn.

Emerging from the Inn, Ann was beside Abe as they encountered a small crowd of well-wishers. Surprised, Abe said, "I didn't expect this."

Ann leaned in close and whispered, "They're here because they love you. We all love you."

Setting his traveling bag down, Abe turned to Ann having eyes only for her. "You're so wonderful. I can't wait till I can return."

"How long will you be gone?"

"Let's see," Abe considered her question. "Opening session begins next Monday, December 1st. I'll miss Christmas and New Year's. I'm not going to like that, but by going straight through, the legislature should adjourn by sometime in February. I'll be back as soon as I can after that."

"Well, let's see," considered Ann, "just what kind of salary will my favorite assemblyman be making while he's gone?"

"I believe my salary will be three dollars per day for every day the legislature is actually in session."

"That's good!"

"Yes, it's good but I'm not keeping it."

"But why?"

"Because it's going to be my first deposit toward our future."

"Oh, Abe." Her face filled up with love.

"Ann, I'm going to be thinking of you every day."

Just then, Ann didn't care what anyone thought. On impulse, she went into Abe's arms. They kissed each other as only two young people in love would show such affection.

"Well done, son," said Judge Green, who witnessed the embrace.

"Yes, very well done," seconded David Rutledge, who was going to be running the Post Office with Billy Greene while Abe was gone.

"Here comes the stage!" Someone in the crowd spotted the stagecoach coming down Main Street.

Climbing aboard, Abe began a life-changing journey. One might say that November Saturday witnessed the beginning of young Lincoln's entry into public service. Dressed in a new suit, bought by a group of his New Salem friends, Abe looked every bit the successful politician he was on his way to becoming.

So it was, on December 1st, 1834, Abe joined the Illinois State Assembly, comprised of 55 representatives and 26 senators. During the first session, Abe learned the ropes observing his fellow members with more experience. By mid-February though, he was more than anxious to return to New Salem. He had become homesick and desperately wanted to see Ann again.

On the afternoon of February 17th, 1835, the stage pulled up in front of the Rutledge Inn. From it emerged a distinguished passenger. Abe had returned, receiving an awaiting Ann Rutledge into his arms.

Going inside, sitting down in the great room, they were joined by Jack Armstrong, as well as Ann's brother David and her cousin McGrady Rutledge.

Abe was thrilled to see all of them. "This is great! My old friends, it's like a reunion of the old 4th Mounted Militia from the Black Hawk War."

"It sorta is," answered Jack, "but we have some bad news."

Suddenly you could've heard a pin drop. The smile disappeared from Abe's face as he noticed the grave expressions on everyone. He asked, "What's happened?"

Since he was sitting closest to Abe, Jack answered, "We've lost Bill Berry. He passed away January 10th, while you were away in Vandalia. His father, Rev. Berry, sent word that he wanted Bill's friends from the Black Hawk War to be pallbearers at his funeral. So David and McGrady here, along with Henry McHenry and myself carried his coffin from the Rock Creek church to the family cemetery nearby. He was laid to rest beside his grandmother."

"I didn't know, I would've been there had I known," Abe said, obviously saddened. "Even though I only saw him once last year, about a week before I left for Vandalia, I still cared for Bill. I was shocked at his appearance then."

"We were all shocked," David Rutledge broke in, adding "He had suffered from intermittent fever and chills for almost two months. Along with that, he suffered from long bouts of vomiting, not being able to keep his fluid down. He suffered so much…it finally broke him in the end."

McGrady added, "We thought it best not to let you know. We knew you would've given up your seat in the legislature and come home right away. You'd worked so hard to get where you're at now. If Bill could be here right now, I feel certain he would say: 'Leave Abe where he is, besides I know how he feels about me'."

"Mac, perhaps you're right. But how did his funeral go?"

"It was a beautiful funeral," answered Ann. "As you know, Mentor Graham is a wonderful carpenter. He called a halt to whatever he was doing and went to work–day and night–fashioning the most beautiful coffin for Bill. Rev. Berry preached his son's funeral. How he was able to do it, I'll never know."

"Miss Ann, I know." Jack revealed, adding his insight, "He did it with the Lord's good help. I have to say something though."

"What, Jack?" Ann asked.

"I can't help it," he said, shaking his head, "I've done a lot of soul searching about this: If, back in my wilder days, I hadn't taken

Bill down the drink'n path, things just might have turned out different for him. After we carried Bill's coffin out to the frozen earth of
that cemetery, I stayed, watch'n Mister Graham place that walnut
marker he'd carved, into the earth. I read the inscription, it said:

WILLIAM FRANKLIN BERRY
Born January 8, 1811
Died January 10, 1835
Age 24 Years, 2 Days

I thought, only 24, that was too young for him to die. I told his
father how I felt partially responsible. But instead of rebuking me,
he told me I should try to live a better life, and in doing that I would
honor the memory of his son. So I've been read'n the Bible every
day, try'n to live the better life Rev. Berry spoke about."

Ann took Jack's hand into hers; "God bless you Jack Armstrong.
You must not blame yourself. The good Lord doesn't want you to
feel so guilt ridden."

"Thank you, Miss Ann." A grateful Jack Armstrong, connecting
with Ann's penetrating eyes, saw the angel that Abe was always
telling him about. He said, "I think I see why you and Abe are just
right for each other."

Abe added, "I think all of us gathered around this table are right
for each other. Through the growing bond we all have I believe we
have blessed each other's lives. As for Bill, I mourn his loss, cut
down in his prime the way he was. I always will pray for his soul."

Jack agreed, "Here, here. Please God, be with Bill's soul."

Everyone sitting at the table in the great room agreed and felt
better that February afternoon. Even so, 1835 was going to be a
rough year ahead. It had started in death and tragedy, leaving feelings that would linger on, spiraling out of control in ways none of
them could ever imagine.

As spring time came, so did new challenges. Abe went back
to being Postmaster, studying Judge Green's law books more than

ever before, and continuing his studies with Ann out at Mentor Graham's place.

It was one day in April though, when Doctor Allen came into the Post Office, that Abe received his first inkling about something unsettling, something that could be in New Salem's future.

Doctor Allen inquired, "Any mail for me?"

"No Doc, not today," answered Abe. "Are you expecting something?"

"Yes, matter of fact I am, a book on infectious diseases and their causes. Doctor Gershom Jayne, a Springfield physician, is sending it to me. Would you let me know just as soon as you get it?"

"Sure, Doc. Infectious diseases? You've got me concerned. Is there any such thing around here?"

"Abe, what I'm about to tell you has to remain in strict confidence."

"Sure, Doc, sure. We can't have any undue panic getting started around here."

"Very good. Abe, I will tell you. I'm getting seriously concerned about something. It all started back on December 7th. I was contacted to come out and examine Bill Berry and see if I could help him. When I first visited with him, he told me that back in late September he had been bitten or stung by a nest of mosquitos and other insects along the waters that flow by Rock Creek. That information stuck in my mind. As Bill's condition worsened I contacted Doctor Anson Henry from over in Sangamon Town to consult with me. Then later, Doctor Jayne consulted with me. All of us reached the same conclusion: There could be a very real infectious insect connection."

"If this be true," considered Abe, "could this spread and turn into something a lot worse?" The question turned out to be very prophetic.

"I don't know, Abe. A lot will depend on the weather and the growing insect population around here. In the meantime I'm trying to learn all I can. Do let me know when that book comes in."

"I sure will."

As Doctor Allen turned to leave, Abe thought of one more question. "Oh Doc, is there a cure for what might be coming?"

The question gave Doctor Allen pause. He stopped in his tracks and turned to answer. "I don't know, I just don't know. The whole medical profession is still learning. This is 1835, and there is so much we doctors don't know. Perhaps in a hundred years or more we'll crawl up to that level of knowledge where we can answer most any medical question. But right now so much is unknown to us."

The amount of uncertainty in Doctor Allen's voice lingered on with Abe. For weeks after, it stuck in the back of his mind as a form of dark foreboding.

About one month later, in early May, Ann stopped by the Post Office with some important news. She told him, "Business has dropped way down over at the Inn. They no longer need me, even part time."

"What are you going to do?" Abe asked.

"My Mom and Dad can always use me out at the Sand Ridge farm, at least until Fall. I'm still planning on going to finishing school in Jacksonville in September. I've been saving my money for it, so I can be a worthy wife to my lawyer husband."

"Ann, you're so much more than worthy."

"I would still like you to be proud of me."

"I am now and always will be proud of you. More than that, I'll always love you, Ann."

She moved closer, taking his hand, looking up into his face with her piercing blue eyes, and made an important request, "Promise me, you'll say that when we're old and gray."

"I promise." Abe grew silent after that vow, completely transfixed by her. Taking her into his arms, he held her close and kissed her, again and again.

The next morning, Abe rented a buggy and took Ann out to her parent's farm on Sand Ridge. Staying only a few hours, he headed back to New Salem and his Post Office duties. On the journey back, he noticed how it was already oppressively hot and humid, and not even June, yet. For one brief moment he thought, could this be the type of weather Doctor Allen was concerned about? That thought would be a harbinger of events to come.

So far, the spring and early summer of 1835 had become like a wonderful dream of hoped for happiness for now and for the future. Sadly though, coming events which the mind of man has no control over, nature versus man, would turn everything into lost dreams.

The summer of 1835 would be remembered most for its unending spurts of unbearable heat and humidity followed by equally unending heavy rainfalls. It was turning out almost as Doctor Allen had predicted. The weather was fast turning the whole area along the Sangamon River into a perfect breeding ground for disease carrying insects.

One farmer after another reported their crops in ruin. With the disease carrying mosquitoes and other insects everywhere, more and more people were beginning to fall ill. Before anyone quite realized it, an epidemic from which there was no cure had roared into the entire area. As conditions worsened, death seemed to be knocking at every door, in and around New Salem.

All around him, Abe saw people dropping in the wake of what was happening. At least at first, he seemed incredibly untouched. Perhaps due to his excessive exposure to disease carrying mosquitoes during the Black Hawk War, some sort of body immunity had built up within his bloodstream.

Shortly, everyone's friendly Postmaster became a tower of strength and their best friend as he helped as many people as he could. Rather it was helping a much-overworked Doctor Allen or out helping Mentor Graham with the construction of much needed caskets, Abe seemed to be everywhere at once.

But every man has his limits, no matter who he is. Abe found his limits in early July. It was July 3rd, and he suddenly realized he hadn't heard from Ann in several weeks, tomorrow would be the second anniversary of their engagement, he thought. So early the next morning, he took Diamond and rode out to Sand Ridge to check on her. What he would see at the Rutledge farm would shake him. For the first time since the epidemic had begun, a bit of doubt and negative thinking got into his subconscious. Some of his force of will and strength began to seep out of him, only to be replaced by a good measure of worry and concern.

Standing before Abe was not the Ann he had known, but rather a washed-out shadow of her former self. She smiled bravely but could not hide the truth from his discerning eyes. There was sickness and disease among the Rutledge family. Like the angelic person she was, she'd tried to minister to one sick person after another. Becoming worn down in the process, she was approaching the point of collapse.

Barely able to stand, it took all of Ann's effort to just put one foot in front of another and walk across to a nearby shade tree in front of the farmhouse. In doing this, she walked with Abe mostly supporting her every step of the way. Stopping at the tree, she was winded and wringing wet with sweat. In this light her exposed arms were clearly visible, covered with insect bites.

Fearing the worst, Abe asked her, "What's happened here?"

"It's my little brother, William, he's only nine and he's come down with the 'sickness'. My sister Nancy and brother Robert are both sick too. Mom and Dad are getting weaker by the day. If it wasn't for my older sister Jane, and brother John, I might not be able to make it either. Truth be known though, whenever I feel like I'm going to lose it and collapse, I think of you. Abe, you are my strength and my rock–you and the good Lord above."

Moving closer, he reassured her, "Like I said before, I'm here for you. I will love you always."

Looking up into his face, a wordless expression of her feelings formed on her face. "Abe, your words are more precious than gold to me."

"You know," he said, "today is the second anniversary of when we became engaged."

"It was the most important day of my life," she revealed. "I want to re-pledge those words with my everlasting love for you right now."

Once again they kissed. Embracing and holding onto each other, it was though their combined energy reinforced the waning strength that had been in both of them.

With the unbreakable bond of love renewed, Abe and Ann went back into the farmhouse to visit the rest of the Rutledge family. Inside, the farmhouse was a large three room building: a good-sized living room centered between the two bedrooms, which were at each end of the house. Presently, the three oldest, John (age 24), Jane (age 26) and cousin McGrady (age 20) occupied one bedroom. The three sick ones, brothers William and Robert, and sister Nancy were bedridden in the other bedroom. Their parents, James and Mary Rutledge, were not doing well either, being made as comfortable as possible in the living room.

Abe went to see the three sick youngsters first. Telling them a story, he tried to lift their spirits as best he could under the circumstances. Ann's baby sister, Nancy, who was fourteen at this time, had always liked Abe and laughed hard when he told one of his whoppers. Seeing her spirits lifted, Abe concluded, "Now you get to feeling better real soon. Annie needs you to be well."

Going back in the living room, Abe went over to see Mister Rutledge who said, "Thank you, Abe, for coming out and checking on us. It's right kindly of you to do that. I think it's time I told you something. I think you're one of the finest young men I've ever met. I know John and David think so, and I just want you to know I feel that way too." Glancing over at Ann, he added, "I know Annie is glad you came too. It means a lot to her."

"Thank you, Mister Rutledge. Coming from you, those words mean a lot. But you have to know, I came out here to see the whole Rutledge family. Things aren't the same in New Salem without you running the Inn."

James Rutledge became sad, "Bless you for that Abe, but those times are passed now. Dreams die hard. The Inn was my dream, but it's lost forever now." He grew quiet just thinking about it. Caught up in a world of his own lost dreams, this man looking far older than his fifty-four years, would never be the same again.

Abe looked around, spotting Ann sitting at a little desk over in a corner of the large living room. She was reading the family Bible, praying. He went over by her as she was lost in thought. Turning the Bible's pages, she pulled out a letter she had placed there. Reading it, she smiled and looked up, seeing Abe. "I'm sorry, I didn't notice you near me. I guess I was lost in this letter. It's from David."

Abe had wondered where her younger brother was. "How did you get a letter from David? Where is he?"

Ann explained, "While you've been so busy helping everybody this past month, Billy Greene's been helping you, taking care of the mail at the Post Office."

Abe admitted, "Yes, I guess I've let that slide. Good old Billy, he knew I needed help."

Ann continued, "He gave this letter to Cousin McGrady when he was in town, since it was addressed to me. You must've known how much David has always admired you. After all, he followed you off to the Black Hawk War when he was only seventeen."

"Yes, I know. He'd come over to the Post Office and crack the law books and read them with me."

"That's right, Abe. He told me if you were going to become a lawyer, he wanted to as well."

"Good for him, he's a smart young man."

"Yes, Abe, he's always known what he wanted. He wants you to be proud of him."

"I am. He's like the baby brother I never had."

"While we were off taking classes with Mentor Graham, David was saving his money and applied to the law school over in Jacksonville. He got accepted. He writes me that his grades are good and he wants me to join him in September. He says, so I can go to the finishing school there for young ladies. He says, 'sis, so you can be a proper wife for a certain young lawyer from New Salem'.–I haven't had the heart, or the strength, to write him about all the sickness here. If I can just get everybody well here, there'll be no need to write him. Then I can join him in September. That's what I was praying about just now."

"Sure, everyone's going to get better here and then this will all seem like a bad dream."

Ann smiled, "Oh Abe, you work on me like a tonic, a good tonic that is. Every time we talk, I see a ray of hope and feel better."

"That's the spirit, I see a bright future for us." Abe lied, for he could see how ill she was becoming, but for her sake as well as his, he didn't want to admit it. At least for then, he did a pretty good job of hiding his concern. Taking her hand gently, he kissed it and said, "I'm going to go now. You don't need to see me out. I want you to sit right here for a while and regain your strength."

"I will, for you, Abe," she promised.

Outside, Abe spotted Ann's older brother, John, who'd been working out in the fields and Cousin McGrady, who'd also been working out back. Telling them of his concerns, Abe said, "I'm going to get Doctor Allen and have him check on everybody here. In the meantime, John, please take all of the hard work off of Ann. She needs rest, a lot of it, immediately. Please, will you do this for me?"

"I will, Abe. I promise. You have my word of honor."

Turning to McGrady, Abe admitted, "I'm deeply worried about everyone in there. Mac, will you take your horse and ride over to Jacksonville? Let David know just how bad things are here."

"I will, Abe. I'll leave within the hour."

"Thanks Mac," Abe said as he mounted Diamond, heading back to New Salem. On a mission, his mind full of worry, he searched for Doctor Allen until he found him.

Doctor Allen agreed to head out to Sand Ridge immediately. But studying Abe carefully, he could see he was wearing down as well. He said, "I'm concerned about you as well. You've been taking too much upon yourself lately. Why don't you stop and rest for a while?"

"I will Doc, I've got just one more trip to do. I promised Mentor Graham I'd be coming back to his place."

"That's a good idea. Sarah Graham will fix you something to eat and you can get some much-needed rest while you're there."

"Thanks for your concern, Doc. I promise I'll take better care of myself."

"And I promise you, I'll be leaving shortly to make my rounds at Sand Ridge. I'll join you at the Grahams in a few days and let you know how things are going."

"Thanks Doc, God bless you for all you're doing."

Doctor Allen appreciated those words, being a very religious man. "Abe, that's why I'm in the practice of medicine, to do as much good as I can, with the Lord's help as He sees fit to give it to me."

Sometime later that evening, Abe rode up to the Graham place. Sarah Graham noticed his worn-down look right away. "Abe, wash up right now. Then come inside and I'll have something for you to eat."

"Thank you, Sarah. I'm right grateful."

She knew he truly meant it, because his humble sincerity was always reflected in the sound of his voice. She told him so, "You're a good man, Abe Lincoln, one who is always welcome under our roof."

Later, at the dinner table, the three talked about the 'sickness' that had engulfed the area. As they ate, both Sarah and Mentor studied Abe closely. They came to the same conclusion: Abe had been burning the candles at both ends far too long. It was time for him to stop and get some much-needed rest. For the next four weeks he did just that, sending written messages to Ann by way of either Doctor Allen or McGrady Rutledge.

The 'sickness' that hit the New Salem area was what we today might call a typhoid fever epidemic. In 1835 there was no known cure and the mortality rate was often 50 percent, sometimes even more.

Doctor Allen reported back to Abe: He had ordered Ann to bed with complete bed-rest. Knowing she was such a force of nature, as she had almost worked herself into the grave, he gave strict orders to make her stay in bed. Her brother David–whom McGrady Rutledge got to take a break from school–had come home and was waiting on her, hand and foot.

After Doctor Allen left, Abe remained in the living room of the Graham home, talking with Sarah and Mentor. Sarah let out her frustrations, "This 'sickness' or 'brain fever' as some call it, is worse than a plague of locusts, fever and chills, vomiting and dysentery. It just means death and more death."

"Yes, Sarah Rafferty," agreed her husband Mentor, adding a humble plea, "May God help us all. In so many ways, it's truly a bad year."

Abe had just sat there, silent and brooding, his head full of so many grave thoughts. Finally, he stood up and said, "I think I'll go outside and walk out back to the tree line."

"Why, Abe?" Mentor inquired.

"A full moon's out. I think I'll look up at the stars and say a prayer hoping it'll reach God in the heavens above. I want to say my own prayer for Ann and all the poor souls suffering right now."

Mentor stood up, giving Abe a firm pat on the shoulder, "My friend," he said, perhaps that's the best thing we humans can do right now, to put this matter into Divine hands."

By now, Abe had let his studies go. He couldn't concentrate. He almost couldn't function. Conditions worsened throughout the area, with more and more reported deaths. Abe still managed to hold it together just enough to help Mentor in the construction of more coffins. Even so, the constant thought of death was becoming more and more troubling to him. The headaches were coming back. He was hearing voices too, especially of those people who had already died during the last two months.

About the third week of August, just before dawn, Abe was just waking up, only to hear the clear voice of Ann, pleading, *Hurry, come quick because I will die soon.*

Abe bolted up, startled. He dressed quickly, ran downstairs and out to the barn where he saddled up Diamond.

Mentor Graham, always an early riser, thought he'd heard Abe. Dressing fast, he followed him to the barn. "Abe, what's the matter?"

207

"I heard Ann calling for me, just as if she were in my room with me."

"Abe, just think about this. It's not possible."

"Perhaps, just perhaps," Abe reasoned, "the Lord sometimes allows such things to happen."

Mentor had no immediate answer, but as they were walking out of the barn into the first light of day, they both looked up to see a lone rider coming over the horizon at a fast gallop. Coming to a halt almost right in front of Abe and Mentor, it was Doctor Allen.

An immediate growing premonition nagging away inside him, Abe had to know, "Doc, how's Ann?"

The expression on Doctor Allen's face mirrored many words, none of them what he would want to hear. "Abe, it's not good. I've just come from her bedside where she's been calling for you."

Hearing this, Mentor Graham placed a hand on Abe's shoulder. "I guess sometimes the Lord does allow strange things to happen."

Not understanding, Doc asked, "What?"

"Nothing, Doc. Mentor will explain later," answered Abe, brushing his question aside, still pressing for information, "How's Ann? How's she doing?"

"She's in the grip of the brain fever."

"What's happened?"

"She's taken a turn for the worse. As she was calling for you, it was though she somehow knew she didn't have the strength to recover."

"How long, Doc? How long does she have?"

"A few days at best, maybe just a day or two, or maybe just a few hours."

"Oh God! Oh God!" At the same time as the anxiety in those words escaped his lips, Abe's face turned almost ashen white. The pain he felt from Doc's dire prediction was more severe than a hundred beatings from his father.

Sensing his pain, Mentor went to his side, bracing him up, as Abe almost collapsed. Doc came up on the other side, placing a firm hand on his shoulder to steady him. "Abe," he said, "it deeply saddens me to bring you this information."

Getting some of his strength back, Abe agreed, "I know, Doc. You're just doing what you have to do. I'll be okay." Pulling away, taking a step backward, he addressed both Mentor and Doctor Allen at the same time, in a voice filled with desperation, "I've got to go to her! Now!"

Mounting Diamond, he took off at a fast gallop. As Abe rode hard and fast toward Sand Ridge, his mind was consumed with thoughts of Ann, for she was his whole world. During that long ride, the true meaning of those words 'lost dreams' hit him hard like a sledgehammer blow.

CHAPTER 16
TIMES THAT TRY ONE'S SOUL

As he reached Sand Ridge, Abe urged Diamond forward, and headed straight for the Rutledge farmhouse. Dismounting, he rushed toward the front door. It was though a powerful force was pushing him forward. He didn't bother to knock, just opened the door and entered. In the living room were Ann's brothers, sisters, and parents all gathered together. All of them sensed Abe's commanding presence and inner will that could not be stopped.

David, home from law school, reacted first, "Abe, thank God you've come. Ann's been asking for you."

"David, where is she?"

Gesturing toward the bedroom nearest him, he said, "In there."

No one said a word as Abe walked past all of them. Quietly opening the door, he entered Ann's bedroom, closing the door behind himself. Remaining frozen in his tracks, his eyes adjusted to the dim light of her room.

His first glimpse of Ann told him her body must be ravaged with fever as she was sweating heavily. She was sort of propped up in bed but did not notice him at first as she seemed to be talking to someone hovering above her bed. As Abe took a few steps toward her, she caught a glimpse of him and broke off eye contact with her invisible guest. "Oh Abe," she spoke in a washed out, weak voice, "I was just hanging on, hoping to see you one more time."

He could clearly see she was pale and emaciated from the toll 'the sickness' had taken out of her. It was a miracle she had lasted this long, he thought. Just seeing her this way, it felt like his heart was being ripped out.

Looking up at him, Ann managed a faint, flickering smile. "My Abe, I knew you'd come."

"Not anyone or anything on the face of the earth could stop me."

Extending her hand upward, she reached for him. "Abe, please, hold me."

Sitting down at the edge of her bed, gently and tenderly, he slid his arms around Ann, drawing her closer to him. Their eyes locked on each other and her life extended for a little while longer. It didn't matter about anything else. The whole world could be slipping away around them, because to Ann and Abe the precious moments they had then was their world. It was though his strength became her strength. Later, Abe thought it was because God wanted them to have this little bit of extra time together.

"I would like to see sunlight," she pleaded, "where the earth meets blue skies rising into the heavens, just one more time." Abe complied, cradling Ann in his arms, he carried her over by the window where she could see out. She marveled in awe, "Isn't it beautiful, God's creation?"

"Yes, it is. I wish we could watch things like this together, always."

Looking at him, she reached over and touched his forehead above his sensitive left eye, answering him, "We will be able to look at things together now. I'll be right here in your mind, watching with you."

They enjoyed the beauty of nature a few more minutes, then carrying her back to the bed, he cradled her in his arms, next to him.

Staring deeply into his face, it was though Ann could see his soul. She asked him, "Do you know who I was talking to when you came in here?"

"I have no idea, but I felt more than a human presence when I came into your room."

"What you felt was the presence of the Lord. I was talking to God and His angels. I was dreaming of you and they said you would come."

"You saw them?" Abe questioned.

"They are still here: The Lord's angels and His Holy Spirit. Don't you feel them?"

Abe considered the question as he glanced about the room, coming back to Ann. Focusing on her, he saw an aura of light cast upon her surrounding her bed, yet it came from no visible light source. "I feel something. It's warm and comforting, yet it's cool and healing."

"It's the energy of our Lord. His Holy Spirit is in this room."

"If He is here, why doesn't He heal you?"

"He has healed me. Though my physical body is dying, He has strengthened my soul and healed me spiritually. I'm not hurting any longer."

Hearing Ann mention death brought a flashback into Abe's mind: He saw his mother and sister dying all over again. Sadness and turmoil filled his mind. He could not hide the tears that were filling his eyes and spilling down his face.

Ann saw this. Even in those moments of her waning strength she sought to comfort him. Extending her hand into his, she tried to console him, "Abe, my Abe, the Lord wanted you here because He wanted me to tell you something."

"What's that?" He asked, raising his head, wiping the tears from his face with the back of one hand.

"He wanted me to tell you how I feel, how I've always felt." As she told him, she opened up her soul with all the feelings in her heart, "My love will never leave you. Every time you think of me, you will know I love you. I'm going to love you always, right on up and into the hereafter, forever."

"Ann, it's your love and encouragement that's helped lift me up to what I am. You are my life. What can I ever hope to be without you?"

"You'll do what I always knew you could do," she whispered in an ever weakening voice."

"I'll do anything for you. I'll be anything you want me to be."

"Dearest Abe, if you do just one thing I'll be proud."

"What thing is that?"

"In everything you do, live an honest and upright life."

"I will. I promise before God, I'll always make you proud of me."

"I've always been proud of you. You're one of the most truly good men who's ever walked the earth."

"If I can just measure up to half of what you think of me, I'll be doing something."

"You will, and so much more…"

Her body's weakness had forced her into silence for a few moments. Squeezing his hand, her eyes searched his face as she was about to exact one other commitment from him, "Abe, please say a prayer for me after I'm gone."

"Of course, I will, but shouldn't I say it now?"

"Wait till after I'm gone because though my body be dead, I will still be alive in your mind. The Lord is listening to all our prayers, whenever they're said. I found that out when I prayed for you. He spoke to my mind, answering me."

"You prayed for me?"

"Ever since the day we first met, I prayed for you and your soul."

"I felt something unspoken, drawing me back to New Salem. It was you."

"It was me."

"Oh Ann, I love you with all my heart."

"I know Abe, I've always known."

Every word that passed between them that final afternoon was said with complete unconditional love from both their hearts and souls. There was no human witness to their expressions of everlasting love, sacred promises and commitment. But there was one witness: The Holy Spirit was present, bearing witness of what was said for all time.

A short time later, Ann slipped into a deep sleep, as her whole body was beginning to shut down. Abe bent over and gently kissed her limp hand, whispering, "I'll love you forever." A tidal wave of intense grief engulfed him in that moment.

As Abe stood up, it was as if all his inner strength had drained out of him, leaving him little more than a weak shell of a man.

Opening the door of Ann's room, Abe stood before the Rutledge family with tears streaming down his face. It was as if his whole body was dragging as he staggered across the living room and out the front door, without uttering a single word.

Barely able to walk, Abe collapsed into a chair on the Rutledge front porch. Almost in shock, he buried his tear-stained face in the palms of his hands.

After a few moments, Abe felt a comforting hand on his shoulder. He looked up to see that it belonged to Ann's brother, David. In an emotion filled voice, he said, "Abe, you know how I feel. You're the finest man I've ever known. Sis loved you and so do I."

Hearing those words, Abe rose from the chair and embraced Ann's brother. In their mutual grief, the two men supported each other.

"If it were humanly possible," Abe told him, "I would've given up all the strength left in me to keep her alive. But of course, such miracles are reserved for the Creator."

"God bless you, Abe. I believe the good Lord knows your heart. Sis knew it too. That was one more reason why she loved you."

"Thank you, David." Abe was grateful for his friendship and support, but was once more feeling exhausted to the point of collapse. Slumping back down in the chair again, David sat down in the chair next to him.

As the two men talked, Ann's younger sister had come out on the porch, looking up at both of them. Nancy Rutledge was only fourteen at the time, but very intelligent for her age. Like David, she had always liked and admired Abe. Keeping a diary record of these events, she recorded her own thoughts and impressions of what happened. Observing Abe, she recorded: As long as I live I'll never will forget how Abe looked when he came out on the porch. I've never seen such a sad and broken-hearted expression on any man.

Young Nancy finally asked him, "Did Annie say anything to you, Abe?"

Taking her hand, Abe had her full attention as he answered her, "Nancy, she told me to always live an honest and upright life. I promised Annie I would, for the rest of my life."

Relinquishing the young girl's hand, he lowered his head once again. He knew he was losing Ann and felt nothing but sadness and depression. As he could no longer contain his grief, his whole body shook as he cried aloud. Abe was caught up in the clutches of overwhelming heartbreak that was closing in all around him.

Without saying a word, to escape in a sense, Abe walked out in front of the farmhouse to where the beautiful shade tree stood. This was where he and Ann had shared so many of their feelings with each other. In a strange way he could still feel her presence there. As a breeze passed over him just the thought of her being there with him was of some comfort. "Oh Ann," he whispered to himself, "I need you so."

A vain hope passed momentarily through his mind that Ann might yet wake up from her deep sleep. But that was not to be. She had slipped into the depths of a profound unconsciousness that there is no waking up from. The unbreakable bond of physical commitment between Ann and Abe was about to be broken by the laws of life and death.

"Ann's life was too short," Abe whispered to himself. "She had only turned 22 on January 7th. We were planning a whole lifetime together." To have her life snuffed out in this way was more than he could take. Feeling like his own life essence was draining out of him; he went to his knees by the shade tree.

A strange quiet came over the whole farm. Something happened, Abe was sure of it. Then it came–a loud piercing scream from Ann's mother, who was inside her room. Then came her voice, just as clear as if she had been right next to him, "She's gone! My baby's gone!"

Abe glanced back toward the house. David and Nancy, crying out loud, rushed back inside from the porch. The screams and crying from everyone inside reached his ears. Yet, Abe remained on his knees, riveted to the tree. A powerful surge of grief went through him as he cried unashamedly. His whole body shook with emotion as he managed to whisper, "Oh God, oh God…" At 26 years old, his whole life had been a string of misfortunes and tragedy. But Ann's death affected him more deeply, down to the core of his soul.

Abe remained at the shade tree for some time, pulling twigs from it. Using a string he had in his pocket, he tied them together in the form of a little homemade cross. Finally getting to his feet, he started back toward the farmhouse.

As he was about to reach the porch, David came out the front door, meeting him there. He told Abe, "Mom and my sisters have bathed Ann and dressed her in that beautiful blue dress you always like her in. I know Annie would've wanted you to see her this way. Won't you Abe? Won't you come in and see her now?"

"Yes David, I want to see her. You see, I have a present for her—something she'd like." He held out the little cross he'd made.

Tears formed in David's eyes as he spoke, "Abe, I'm thanking you for her. Annie always felt close to God. I know she'd like that, especially coming from you."

David held the door open as Abe went inside, past the entire grieving Rutledge family. As Abe entered her bedroom, David closed the door so he could be alone with Ann.

At first Abe had not wanted to see Ann in death, but now as he carried this little cross into her room, everything somehow all felt different. As he looked down at her, she seemed a bit smaller. The lingering effects of 'the sickness' had taken their toll on her body. Yet, even the dark shadows of cold, lifeless death could not take away from a sort of inner glow that was clearly more visible now. Her angelic beauty was more brilliant than ever. Focused on her expression, he whispered, "My beautiful angel—you always will be."

Sitting down beside Ann, Abe gently moved her hands across her waist, and whispered, "Annie, I've brought you a present. I know how much you've loved the Lord and how much He loves you." Opening her fingers, he placed the little wooden cross in her hands. "This is with all my love. I made it myself, for you to take with you and have for all time." Then he clasped his own hands together and prayed, "Thank you Lord for bringing Ann into my life."

Abe stood up, tears in his eyes again, as grief tore through his broken heart again. Somehow, even though her body was an empty shell now, he still felt warmth, coming from her, giving him strength. He whispered, "God bless you Annie, I'll love you forever." Turning toward the door, he left her room, taking every mental image from it in his mind and heart forever.

Later in the living room, Abe watched Ann's father pull out the family Bible and record Ann's death. Looking up at Abe, he said, "I wished I had been recording Annie's marriage to you, instead of my little girl's death." Having said what could never be, he handed the Bible to Abe.

Abe stared at that page for a very long time. It read: Ann Mayes Rutledge–died August 25th, 1835. Many times, he would come back and in the presence of Ann's mother, just stare at this page, gently touching the written words.

One can almost guess that in some way he was trying to retrieve something lost forever from his life. Deeply wounded inside, Abe knew these were the times that try one's soul.

CHAPTER 17
THE SADDEST PLACE ON EARTH

Two days later there would be a gathering at a little one-acre cemetery a few miles north of Sand Ridge. It was known as the Old Concord Burial Ground. For everyone it was a day of mourning, for this was the day of Ann's funeral.

The word had spread to all points around New Salem. Many citizens of the area showed up as Ann was loved and beloved by all who knew her. Through her whole life, Ann had given a full measure of love and kindness to all who knew her. Everyone there had felt her loss keenly. Grief was quite visible in the faces of all who were gathered there.

Abe would be the first one there and among the last to leave. Unfortunately, the Old Concord Burial Ground was a place he already knew well. One of his first jobs in the area was to split rails for a fence that bordered the cemetery on one side. At the time, Abe prayed he would never again have to see anyone dear to him to be buried there. Sadly though, this would be the first of other journeys to this place for him. Over time, Old Concord would become the last resting place for over 240 souls, many of whom Abe knew. In his mind this cemetery would become full of lingering sorrow for him. In a sense he came to feel this place was haunted.

On the morning of August 27th, when Abe first arrived he was easy to spot because of his six-foot, 4-inch height. He was first approached by David Rutledge, who embraced him in an emotional hug, opening up with his feelings, "My sister loved you

Abe. As for me, I will always look up to you as my would've been brother-in-law."

"We are brothers, David."

As they continued to console each other, David pulled something from his pocket. "Mom wanted you to have this," he explained, "it's a lock of Ann's hair."

Abe's eyes filled with sadness as he held it close to his heart. "It's like I'll have a part of Ann with me always." Putting it into his pocket, he continued, "I'll carry this with me for the rest of my life, till the day I die."

His words became a self-fulfilling prophecy. At Ford's Theater, a strange lock of hair was found in Abe's pocket. It was thought by all to have important significance to him. So it was, this lock of hair was placed in the pocket of the pants he was buried in. In this way, a part of Ann would remain with him forever.

As everyone gathered for Ann's funeral service, Abe found himself standing apart from the rest of the crowd. Seeing this, those closest to Abe gathered near him. On one side, next to him were Jack and Hannah Armstrong along with Billy Greene and Jimmy Short. On his other side, stood Judge and Mrs. Green with Mentor and Sarah Graham close to them.

It was Mentor Graham who had dropped everything, constructed Ann's coffin, and brought it out to the Rutledge farm in his wagon. Refusing to take even a cent for his work, he spoke highly of her, "She was a bright intelligent girl, who always seemed to have the Spirit of the Lord around her. Both Sarah and I loved Ann. Her passing is everyone's loss." With her gone, it did seem that some of the Lord's Spirit disappeared from New Salem.

Ann's funeral service was simple, a few words being spoken by the Rev: John Miller Cameron. He and James Rutledge had originally founded New Salem. In recent years he had moved several miles north of New Salem, but still remained close to the Rutledge family.

Over her grave, Rev. Cameron expressed his feelings, "We are all shocked and deeply saddened that one so young was taken from the world of the living. Our dear Annie was only 22 years old at the time of her death. Like a candle full of glowing life, her brightness has been snuffed out all too quickly."

As Rev. Cameron was talking about Ann, Abe was fast reaching a point where he felt like he had nothing left. A massive sense of aloneness seized him. The fleeting moment of his happiness with Ann was gone forever. He whispered softly, "There's nothing left for me." Though he tried to hold it back, the inner sadness building within him was too great. He began shaking as his inner turmoil worked its way to the surface. Bursting from him, a stream of unending tears flowed down is face. Crying aloud, many around him noticed Abe's visible grief.

Pulling Jack to one side, Hannah Armstrong whispered to her husband, "Poor Abe, he's crying his heart out. He must've loved Ann more than most of us knew."

"I knew," Jack revealed, telling her more out of ear shot from everybody else. "Abe is a man with such a kind heart, almost to a fault. His greatest strength is also part of what is his greatest weakness. With so much emotion building up inside him, I fear he might be on the edge of some sort of a breakdown."

At the end of his tether, Abe went to his knees at the foot of her grave, a broken man. In that moment he felt unable to stand, all mental and physical strength gone. As mourners left the cemetery, he protested to those wanting to help him up, "Just leave me be. Anyway my heart belongs out here with her." Continuing to cry uncontrollably, nothing seemed to assuage his grief.

Judge Green's feelings for Abe were never more visible than in this moment. Going over to him, putting a comforting hand on his shoulder, the Judge's heart went out to him, "Son, please, listen to me. I know it hurts, more than anything has ever hurt you. There are a lot of people out here that loved Ann. They also love you. I knew Ann well and I'm here to tell you she wouldn't have wanted us to just leave you out here, all alone."

Abe looked up into the Judge's face, agreeing with him, admitting, "Judge, I can hear Ann's voice now, in my head. She would've said, 'Abe Lincoln, listen to Judge Green.' I'm sorry, Judge. For a moment I felt like there was nothing left for me."

"That's not true," Jack Armstrong corrected him. "You've got a lot of friends here. You helped me when I was down. I'm here for you now." Extending his hand down toward Abe, he offered to help him to his feet.

"That goes for me too," added Billy Greene, who had come up next to him. "It was a long time ago, but remember, I said I would be your friend always. Well, I meant it."

Abe looked up though his tears at his three friends gathered around him, offering his gratitude, "Thank you all for being my friend."

"That's the spirit my boy. I want you to come home with Mrs. Green and myself. You can rest there till you're able to get on your feet again."

"I will, Judge."

"Jack and Billy will help you get up, and into my carriage." While they were doing that, Judge Green turned to Mentor Graham, who was standing nearby.

"Mentor," the Judge whispered in a concerned voice, "I'm worried about Abe. He looks like he hasn't eaten in several days.

"He hasn't. I just talked to David Rutledge and he said after his sister died, Abe has refused all food. It's as if he's losing the will to live. He told David repeatedly he wants to be with Ann."

"That concerns me a lot. I have known people who have quite literally died of a broken heart. Mentor, would you do me a favor?"

"Yes anything, Judge."

"Would you see if you can find Doctor Allen and ask him to come out to my place and see Abe."

"I know Doc's down at Rock Creek treating some cases of the sickness there. As soon as I take Sarah home, I'll go down there, get him, and bring him back with me."

"You're a good friend, Mentor."

"Thanks Judge, but I must tell you that I love Abe as well. He's become more than a student to me, actually more like a younger brother."

The Judge smiled. "Abe sort of has that effect on people."

Rejoining his wife, the Judge found Abe was now seated in his carriage. Getting in, he got one more closer look at Abe. As he studied his face, the Judge thought he had the appearance of one who truly needed the support of his friends more than any other time.

Within a couple of hours, they had made the six-mile journey southward, back to Judge Green's farm. Sitting in the Judge's office, Abe poured his heart out to him, "I can't help it, some part of me is always going to be buried out there with Annie. She was my life."

"It's hard when we lose someone we love." The Judge sympathized, trying to help him, "In my experience, true love never dies. Though she may be gone from this life, she will never really die as long as you keep her alive in your mind."

"That won't be hard as she occupies all my thoughts." Abe continued to brood, his mind completely weighted down with unending anguish. "All I hoped and prayed for was what I wanted for us. They were our shared dreams. Without her, life is all so meaningless." Abe's hopeless expression reflected that he was drowning in sadness.

"I see your pain," observed the Judge, sitting in a chair directly in front of him. "If ever two people were in love and worthy of each other, it was you and Ann. It was such an awful shame she died, far too young. My own heart breaks when I think about it. I knew her from the time she was just a baby and had come to love her too. Over the years, I came to know her mind and the way she thought."

"You did?"

"Yes, and it's because of that I can say with reasonable certainty, she would have wanted you to carry on and become the man you both dreamed of becoming. Search your heart and you will know what I'm saying is true."

"I will, Judge, but right now it's so hard."

The sound of the front door opening, and entering footsteps, interrupted their conversation. Both Abe and the Judge looked up in time to see Jack Armstrong and Billy Greene coming through the office doorway, stopping just inside. Jack spoke first, "We came to check on Abe and bring his horse back from the funeral." As Jack spoke, he did so directly to the Judge, avoiding eye contact with Abe.

Looking at both men, Abe asked, "Where is Diamond?"

"He's out in the barn, being fed as we speak." As Jack answered, he avoided eye contact with Abe.

"What's the matter, Jack? Why don't you look at me?"

"Because it hurts," Jack answered, finally making direct eye contact with Abe. "You're my friend, my very best friend. It hurts to see you this way. Don't you know that Hannah and I both love you?"

"A lot of people, all around New Salem, love you Abe." Billy quickly added. "Your loss is hurtful to all of us. To see you this way is painful. Going without sleep, not eating, you're fast reaching the point of collapse. This is why we're here, because we are worried about our friend."

"My boy," the Judge broke in, "you may not realize it, but in the past few years you've worked your way into the hearts of a lot of New Salem folks. Like it or not, you're part of a lot of families now."

Abe listened and saw this truth in all of their faces, feeling their sincerity as he responded straight from his heart, "I'm sorry, sincerely sorry to all of you. Believe me, more than anything, I want to be part of all your families giving the same love and friendship right back to everyone who has extended it to me. It's just…"

Tears filling his eyes, Abe lowered his head again, choking up, he still tried to explain, "It's just that my heart is so full of sadness right now, there's no room for anything else. I feel so worthless." His words were mirrored by the expression of grief that filled his face.

After a long moment of silence, in which Abe became lost in his own sorrow, one could've heard a pin drop in the room. Perhaps because of the sudden quiet, Mother Nature got everyone's attention with the sharp, rumbling sound of thunder in the distance.

Abe jerked, asking "What was that?"

Catching a view through his office window, the Judge commented, "Storm's coming in from the north. It's already clouding up and it's only afternoon." No sooner had he said that, and a second clap of thunder was heard, only closer this time.

This was the moment in which Abe became extremely uncomfortable. Sitting up, on the edge of his seat, his view took in all three men as he explained, "I can't bear the thought of it raining on Ann's grave. She's out there all alone, without me. I promised her I'd be with her forever. I just can't stand it, not for another minute. I've got to go to her."

Like some strange force had taken possession of him, a surge of adrenalin ignited Abe. He bolted from his chair and out the front door. Despite calls from all three men, he did not hear them, his mind focused on one objective. Headed for the barn, he saddled up Diamond, riding north in the direction of the Old Concord Burial Ground.

Inside the house another conversation was going on at this same time:

"Judge, I don't think I could stop him," admitted Jack. "At Ann's funeral this morning, young Nancy Rutledge pulled me aside and said it appeared to her that Abe's whole heart and soul was wrapped up in his love for Ann, that nothing else matters to him right now."

"I saw that too," observed Judge Green. "I agree with you, Jack. Knowing Abe and his force of will, nothing outside the power of God could stop him."

Billy asked, "Isn't there anything we can do? He's acting like a man possessed."

The Judge offered his opinion, "He's acting like a broken-hearted man, totally, completely in love. Such a man often acts without reason. It may be for the best. Just leave him be for right now.

Perhaps being alone, with Ann in his mind, just might give him some measure of peace. Let's give him twenty minutes head start, and then the both of you go out to the barn and hitch up my carriage with the covered top. Then the three of us will go up to Old Concord and see what we can do."

As Jack and Bill went out to the kitchen to get a small meal from Mrs. Green, the Judge remained in his office, alone with his thoughts. Picking up his Bible, he whispered a prayer, "Oh Lord, be with Abe. Please help us to bring him back and restore his health. Whatever happens, Thy will be done."

During the long ride to Old Concord, something happened inside Abe. He pushed everything else out of his mind except for the singular thought of getting to Ann. It was all that mattered to him. Without quite realizing it, he was beginning a journey leading to a breakdown.

Lightning would occasionally form into a frightening pattern and streak across the sky along the horizon ahead of him. Abe did not flinch, steadying Diamond, pressing the horse ever forward. With his wide-brimmed had pulled down tightly, Abe and Diamond plunged through the increasing winds that had kicked up.

It was becoming evening time when Abe finally got within sight of the one acre cemetery. Recognizing the primitive fence that bordered Old Concord, he brought Diamond to a stop. Dismounting, he tethered the horse's reigns firmly to one of the fence railings. He had already decided the rest of this journey was for him alone, on foot.

Advancing into the cemetery, Abe noticed it was becoming almost dusk along some areas of the horizon ahead of him. Blocking everything else out of his mind, there was no longer any future for him, only the here and now that existed around Ann's grave.

Getting closer to the wooden marker Mentor Graham had made for Ann, he looked up to see a truly amazing sight. Just beyond Ann's grave, a figure was moving in the dim light toward him. Abe yelled out, "Stop! Please stop!" Being less than ten feet from him, the figure turned around, revealing it was clearly Ann. Looking straight at Abe, she extended a hand directly toward him. Frozen in his tracks from the shock of seeing her, he still managed to ask, "Ann, is it you?"

Nodding 'yes' in response, that she was indeed her, it still seemed something was wrong. Perhaps it was from going too long without sleep. Abe was sure that what he was looking at was clearly a spirit being, all transparent. He could see her, yet he could also see through her. She looked crystal clear and radiant, more beautiful than she'd ever been. Extending his hand toward her, his voice was racked with emotion as he spoke, "I love you Ann. Oh Annie, I miss you so much!" His voice choked up as tears quickly filled his eyes.

At the same time, her image quickly vanished, as if it was never there. For a moment he thought all reason had left him and his sanity was slipping away.

"No! No!" He cried out, going to his knees. Wiping the tears away, Abe realized he was at the foot of Ann's grave, looking straight at her marker. Taking in a wider view, he was now conscious of other graves beyond Ann's, and a few trees further on back, along the horizon. Getting closer, another bolt of lightning tore through the sky above him, followed by an intense clap of thunder. To Abe, it just added to the feeling that his whole world was crashing in on him. Following the lightning flash, big drops of rain pelted him, only increasing his anxiety.

"Oh Ann, my Annie, I'm here now. You'll never be alone. I promised I'd be with you forever."

Stretching himself out, gently laying across her grave, he attempted to cover her with his own body. With his clothes absorbing the pelting rain that was beginning to come down, he thought his body was keeping the rain from seeping through the ground and into her coffin.

Laying there, feeling her presence from below the ground. In his mind, their two souls had merged now. For the rest of his life, nothing would ever make him forget the feelings that went through him that night. In that moment, he wanted to die, so his soul could be with Ann's soul forever. He asked himself, "Is such a thing wrong, that is to be with the one you love?"

Getting back up to his feet, standing at the foot of Ann's grave again, Abe focused on his dark decision. Staring at her grave, he whispered, "I'll be joining you soon." Reaching into his pants, he retrieved his pocket knife. Holding it in his hand, it was one of those knives of the 1830's with a long blade once it was unfolded. As he stared down at it, a lightning flash illuminated the sharp blade.

Just as Abe was preparing to use this knife on himself in the most deadly way, he heard a familiar voice shout a warning to him, "Abe, don't!" The hand belonging to the voice reached from behind Abe, jerking his hand away, taking the knife from him. The voice and powerful arm belonged to Jack Armstrong. Now he was behind Abe, standing there in a rain slicker.

Abe turned around, facing him. His wild-eyed expression was equally demanding as his words, "Give that back!"

"I will not," Jack responded defiantly, folding up the knife, putting it into his own pocket.

Settling down a bit, Abe pleaded, "Jack, I want to be with her."

"I know you do, but this way is wrong."

"I don't care. Life is meaningless for me without her."

"Abe, you're sick. The Abe Lincoln I know handed me a Bible one winter. Well, I read it, and what you were about to do was wrong."

"That's right, Abe," added the voice of Judge Green, stepping into view, also wearing a rain slicker and a wide-brimmed hat as well. "You know Ann was a God-fearing woman. She would've never tolerated you having such a thought of taking your own life. She told me on more than one occasion she prayed for you, that the good Lord would be with you. Think! Did you ever feel the strength of her prayers?"

The Judge's words hit home and genuinely moved him more than any other time. Abe would think long and hard about what both Jack Armstrong and Judge Green told him that night. In that moment though, as the two men faced him down, he swallowed hard as a surge of emotion rose in his throat. "I'm so worthless," he said, as the tears welling up in his eyes, streamed down his face again.

"Son, you're not well. Come home with us. Give your mind and body a chance to rest and heal."

Abe thought about it. He wasn't well. His appearance clearly showed that to others. His eyes had become hollowed out, deep set and blood shot. A pale sallow color had spread across his face as well. He looked like he was fast approaching death's door himself.

Becoming weaker by the second, he finally conceded, "I've gone over the edge, off the rails and I know it. For right now, I just want to do what's right."

Even though it was becoming dark, Jack had seen enough of Abe this day to know his health was failing. He asked, "How are you feeling right now?"

"Mighty weak. Mighty weak."

"Well here, put your arm around my neck, and I'll help you back to the Judge's carriage."

"Thanks Jack, you really are more than a friend."

"Abe, I'm your brother, just like I said before."

The three men, Abe, Jack, and the Judge, walked out of the rain-soaked cemetery, back to the fence line where Billy Greene was keeping all the horses calm. After Jack and Billy helped Abe into the Judge's carriage, Jack pulled Billy aside. He told him, "Poor Abe, he's more sick than any of us realized. Ann's grave has become the saddest place on earth to him."

CHAPTER 18
VISIONS

Arriving at Judge Green's farm, Jack and Billy helped Abe inside. The Judge had a dry blanket in his carriage which they had wrapped around a shaking Lincoln. Entering the Judge's office, which was the room nearest the front door, they carefully assisted Abe into the nearest chair.

Standing there, Jack explained to Abe, "Billy and I will be right down the hall in the living room, if you need us."

Billy added, "We'll be within ear shot, so we can hear you if you call us."

Abe looked up at both of them gratefully, "I'm thanking you both, most kindly. It's a lot more than I deserve."

"Not for a friend," responded Billy. "There are no limitations for a friend. Like Jack says, the three of us will be friends always."

Abe nodded yes, silently acknowledging Billy. Sitting there by himself, Abe's bloodshot eyes scanned the empty office. Anyone seeing him this way could see the agony he was going through.

Just coming in from the barn, the Judge easily sensed his young friend's torment. "Son, I know you're in pain, I see it written all over your face."

"I'm glad you know it, Judge, I need your help. I find myself quite alone in a way most people who've never been in love do not understand. My cup runneth over with despair."

The Judge pulled up another chair across from Abe, consoling him, "I know how much Ann meant to you. Everyone in New Salem knows it too."

"Up to the time I met Ann, my life had been full of struggle. In so many ways I was lost. She became my anchor. For the first time in my life I felt like I could really be somebody. She made me feel that way. But now, I'm lost again. Judge, I don't know if I can go on without her. I just…" He couldn't finish, grief overwhelming him again. From somewhere deep within himself, it spread outwardly, becoming visible in the tears filling his already bloodshot eyes.

Judge Green leaned forward, placing a comforting hand on Abe's shoulder, the Judge was silent. Even he knew words were inadequate this time.

Feeling desperation merge with his grief, Abe persisted and wondered out loud, "But what am I to do?" Something deeply troubling took hold of him as he explained, "I feel like I'm drowning inside. My head is pounding. I don't know what's real anymore. I'm seeing visions again.

"Visions? What kind of visions, son?"

"It was almost like when I was nine years old, when my mother died and came back to me in the middle of the night."

"What did you see?"

"Out at the cemetery this evening, before you got there, I sensed a presence close by. I was near the foot of Ann's grave when I looked up. There she was, just beyond her marker. Reaching out to me, she extended her hand toward me. It was though some force grabbed hold of me and I was frozen in my tracks. Less than twelve feet separated us, yet no matter how hard I tried to reach out to her, I couldn't quite touch her."

"Son, you've been under a tremendous strain. Our minds can play tricks on us in such situations."

"I wondered about that, if it wasn't some sort of figment of my imagination. But it was so real. She was right there in front of me, only she was not of the flesh."

"Not of the flesh?"

"She was all transparent, in spirit form now. Her image flickered. I could see through her, yet I could see her clearly and distinctly. Then her image quickly vanished, just as if it were never there.

I guess that's when I lost it. I collapsed across her grave, crying. I laid there so long I lost complete track of time. I must've got back to my feet shortly before you got there. What do you think? Am I losing my mind?"

"Son, I think you've gone too long without sleep and without something to eat."

Nodding in the affirmative, Abe conceded, "I know you're right about that."

Judge Green went out in the hall and called for Jack and Billy. They helped Abe to an upstairs bedroom, directly across the hall from Judge and Mrs. Green's bedroom. There, Abe's friends helped him out of his wet clothes and into dry ones. Sitting on the edge of a bed, Abe looked up as Mrs. Green brought him a bowl of hot broth. Mrs. Green fed him gently, just as if he were her own son. In a sense, he had become the Green's son.

For the next 48 hours, Abe lay there in and out of consciousness. He remained in the clutches of fevered dreams until the early morning of the third day, just before daylight.

Then a remarkable thing happened. Somewhere in that in-between stage of being asleep and just waking up, Abe felt a presence in the darkened room. At first, he heard a voice inside his head. It was Ann, whispering to him, *Abe, I've come back to comfort you.*

Still in bed, but raising up on his elbow, his eyes opened immediately and traveled about the room. Even though he saw nothing, he asked, "Ann is it you? Are you real?"

It is me, her voice whispered to his brain, *I'm as real as your mind will let me be.*

Shutting his eyes for a moment, he whispered, "I want you to be real. I want you to be real." Repeating himself, over and over, he meant what he said with all of his heart.

Feeling her spiritual energy in the room, it seemed to be getting stronger. Then he felt its power, her warmth, penetrate to the inner recesses of his brain.

When he opened his eyes again, he could clearly see her. Ann was sitting in the chair beside his bed, looking straight at him. She was no longer flesh and blood, but now more Ann the angel than she'd ever been. Transparent, surrounded by a warm golden aura, she whispered to him, *I'm here for you, to help you.*

"Oh, Ann, I need your help." As he said those words, he reached out to her.

She answered, *I want to help you too, but here's what you must do first. At the break of daylight, come to the Old Concord Burial Ground. All will be made clear to you there.*

Abe was transfixed, his gaze firmly locked on this figure of Ann as she appeared before him. The longer he stared though, her image grew faint and faded away into nothingness.

Ann was gone again. This was more than Abe could take. Raising his voice, he protested, "Ann! Don't leave! Please don't leave!"

Almost immediately, the door opened and Judge Green rushed in. "What's the matter, son?"

"Ann was here." Pointing to the bedside chair, emphasizing it, he added, "She was sitting in that very chair talking to me. Then suddenly, she just vanished."

"Abe, you've been very ill. It was probably just a dream."

"No Judge. This was no dream," Abe insisted. "She was here."

"Can you say that with absolute certainty?"

"She was more than real. In fact, she was just as real as you are right now."

"Why was she here? What did she want?"

"She wanted to comfort me. In doing so, she wanted me to come back out to Old Concord. I believe her spirit is still out there, at least for a while. So, you see, if I'm to have any peace at all, I've got to go back out there today and talk to her again."

The Judge had remained silent, carefully considering what Abe was saying, before responding. "I know one thing, if you don't keep up your strength, you may not make it. I seriously believe if you go out there without eating something, you stand a good chance of collapsing, even dying. Mrs. Green will prepare you some hot broth downstairs. I want you to have something inside you before making the trip back to Concord. If you do this, I won't be trying to stop you."

Abe listened and knew the Judge was sincere and well meaning. Respecting him, he agreed, "Very well, I'll have some of Mrs. Green's broth."

"I'm pleased, my boy," the Judge reacted satisfied with his response.

"One more thing, Judge."

"Yes, Abe. What?"

"I don't think I'd be alive right now if it wasn't for you and Mrs. Green. I think you're one of the finest men on the face of this earth."

"Thank you, son. That means a lot to me."

As Abe got dressed, Judge and Mrs. Green went downstairs. While Mrs. Green prepared breakfast in the kitchen, the Judge went out to the barn and had Henry McHenry saddle up Diamond. Coming back inside, he met Abe in the dining room. Mrs. Green was about to serve Abe a bowl of the 'life sustaining' warm liquid they'd all been talking about.

While Abe took the broth, Judge Green brought him up to date on a few things, "While you were ill, Jack had to go back to his farm up on Sand Ridge and Billy had to go back to New Salem. He's running the post office for you till you get back on your feet."

"They're two of my very best friends; actually, they're like brothers to me. Thank God for both of them."

"Speaking of the Lord, I want you to know something. God as my witness, I feel like I must tell you, I don't fully understand all of what's happening with you, but I'll stand by and support you, no matter what does happen. You see, I feel down deep inside me that God somehow has His hand in all of this."

"I believe that too," revealed Abe. "I don't fully understand what's happening either. Perhaps I'll get some answers at the cemetery."

After breakfast, as Abe was preparing to leave, the Judge patted him on the shoulder, wishing him the best, "God be with you son. Be safe."

"Thank you, Judge, please say a prayer for me."

As Abe waved goodbye and rode off toward Concord, Judge and Mrs. Green watched from the doorway of their home. Praying for the healing of his heart and soul, the Judge whispered, "Lord, please be with my son, Abe Lincoln."

Nancy Green was standing next to her husband at that moment and would remember his prayer all the rest of her life. Looking up at her husband, she asked, "Do you really believe Abe has seen Ann's spirit and talked to her?"

"It doesn't matter what I think. The important thing is that he believes it. As he explained it to me, his experiences were totally real to him. Perhaps going out to Concord again is the only way he will achieve a measure of peace. Whatever happens out there now, I feel it's going to become a matter between him and the good Lord."

During Abe's journey back out to Concord, his entire consciousness was full of thoughts of Ann. Since the hour of her death he had become more broken within himself. He reasoned, there's just so much a human being can endure. To lose the love of his love was just too much, he thought. No matter how much he tried to rise above it, this steady stream of kindred thoughts continued unabated all the way to the cemetery.

As he got closer, seeing Old Concord in the distance, Ann's voice invaded his mind. She spoke to his brain, *Abe–Abe, do not despair. Come, please come to my grave.*

Though he couldn't see her, Abe could hear her clearly and distinctly inside his head. He whispered, "Ann, I'm coming."

As Abe urged Diamond onward toward the fence he'd helped construct so long ago, he thought, Ann had always possessed a great gift beyond the normal senses. He had observed in her this gift from God in which she had the ability to see inside a person, into one's very soul. Now he was experiencing this gift, for he felt her presence growing stronger, reaching inside his brain.

After tethering Diamond to one of the fence rails, Abe proceeded forward, entering into the cemetery. Doing so, he immediately felt the spiritual elements that were awaiting him there. From the moment he crossed the uneven grounds of Old Concord, he was aware of Ann's presence. He caught her scent too, very much aware it was becoming stronger as he got closer to her grave. It was a familiar scent of fresh flowers that had always accompanied her in life. Now that scent was picked up in a gust of wind, blowing across him. It quickly permeated the entire cemetery. Even though he couldn't see it, he was convinced there was a living presence here.

Reaching the foot of Ann's grave, Abe lowered his head and whispered a few words of prayer, "The Lord giveth and the Lord taketh away. Blessed be the name of the Lord."

After that, there was absolute quiet for a long moment. The silence was broken by the sound of her voice calling him, *Abe*, but from far off, inside his head. Then he heard her calling him again, only this time much louder, from a shorter distance in front of him. *Abe, I'm here.*

Abe looked up and there she was: Though imperfect and transparent, it was the essence of Ann within a brilliant golden aura, completely surrounding her.

Seeing him, an expression of recognition formed in her glistening, incredibly blue eyes. She smiled, her lips moving now as she spoke, explaining, "Abe, I'm here because I missed you so much. But you, you're suffering, even now. I can see beyond the flesh. I see the heartbreak inside your soul. The Lord has let me come to help heal you."

Moving closer, she stepped from the aura, leaving it behind her. Extending her hand toward him, it was though some part of Ann's spiritual being was reaching across from another place, beyond the world of the living.

As he reached forward to touch her, Abe felt warmth well beyond any kind of warmth felt by mortal man. The sensation was more calming and healing than anything he'd ever experienced. Though he may not have quite realized it in that particular moment, something of Heaven's healing spirit was beginning to work its way inside Abe, mending him where he'd been broken. It was the starting of something he had so desperately needed.

Abe was now immediately in front of Ann's face, looking directly into the angelic brilliance that emanated from her. Her voice was soft and gentle as she continued, "I want you to stop grieving. I'm out of my pain now and in the hands of the Lord."

"What was it like?"

"After you left my bedroom, I felt myself letting go of my body. Then I realized I was not alone. I looked up, then the ceiling disappeared, and I could see the heavens above. They opened up and two angels descended and took me with them into what is beyond this life."

"What is beyond this life? Where is Heaven?"

"It's a place beyond what the human eye can see. God is there and He knows how you're suffering."

"Yes, I continue to suffer," admitted Abe. "Is this the end for me?" Deep depression was written all over his face.

"Death is not the end, but only the beginning. Life continues on in the hereafter, throughout all eternity."

"Oh Ann, I have to answer honestly. Without you, I'm truly a tortured soul. I don't know what I'm going to do."

"I want you to stop thinking about committing suicide. That would be so wrong. Stay the course. Accomplish all those dreams we talked about."

Listening carefully, he thought about everything she had to say. Then he said simply, "I want to do the right thing."

"If that be true, please listen to me," she urged him in her most commanding voice, once more getting his full attention. "The Lord wants to heal you because you're truly a good man. He has looked into your heart and soul as I have and knows the meaning of your worth."

"What does He want from me?"

"The Lord wants to use you as His vessel for good in the world. Troubled times are coming and He wants to use your strength against what may come."

"You're talking about something I'm not. I'm just an ordinary man full of weaknesses, just as any other man."

"I'm talking about the man you will become in the future, a good man full of wisdom and decency."

With tears in his eyes, he conceded, "For you Ann, I'll try to be that man."

"I'm so proud of you, Abe. The Lord sent me back to tell you this, and I can promise you, He will be with you every step of the way. You see, God often works through people to accomplish His will in the world."

"But Ann, will you be with me?"

"Yes, as I told you before, I'll be right here every time you think of me." With her spiritual finger, she touched his forehead again, above his sensitive left eye.

Then something got the attention of both of them. The golden aura behind her was becoming brighter as if it was beckoning to her. "I must go now," she said. When I step back into the light, it's not the end. It's but the next step in my own journey of life, one that will bring me closer to our Lord."

As she was leaving, Abe repeated his commitment to her again, "Ann, I'll love you always, forever and ever."

Just before stepping back into the aura, she looked directly at Abe, promising him, "When the time comes that you close your eyes for the final time on this world, I will be there to welcome you into eternity."

As her image disappeared into the brilliant aura, it immediately grew less intense, rapidly fading away into nothingness. However, its warmth remained, long enough to penetrate Abe.

Standing there motionless, Abe realized he'd been impacted with a feeling of spiritual peace. Even so, he was only just beginning to understand the enormity of the implications of what had happened. Something of the Lord was inside him now. He would never be the same: His mind and whole being was being reshaped and made anew by the Holy Spirit of God.

With Ann's spirit gone from the cemetery, Abe staggered over to a nearby dead tree. Leaning back against the trunk, using it as support, he slid down to the ground. He felt like he was in–what he would later term–a state of spiritual exhaustion. Seizing him, he felt incredibly tired, sleeping for at least an hour.

Awakening later in the afternoon, Abe did now know if what had happened was a dream or a vision. For the rest of his life though, he believed the experience had been real. It was also the beginning of a series of dreams or visions, and episodes of precognition he would have right up to a few days before he died.

After finally getting up on his feet again, Abe walked over to the foot of Ann's grave again and whispered, "Annie, I'll never forget you. You'll be with me in my heart always."

Standing there, he had become different in a good way. Something of Ann's spirit had mingled with the conscious thought within him. He felt transformed in a profound way.

Walking out of the cemetery, by the time he reached Diamond he felt stronger, both physically and mentally. Sure of it now, he was convinced that this new strength flowing though him was the work of the Lord. The day's events becoming a life altering experience, he rode from Concord, a man forever changed.

CHAPTER 19
DISCOVERING GOD'S PLAN

Getting back to Judge Green's farm, Abe was ready to discover God's plan for his life, or to be more exact, his *new* life. Telling the Judge and others from New Salem, who'd come out to visit him as he recovered, about his vision and subsequent transformative experiences, resulted in wide-ranging responses. Some believed him, but many thought he had suffered a complete breakdown. Others simply thought he'd lost his mind. However, all felt sorry for the town's favorite son.

The Judge counseled the good people of New Salem to give Abe the benefit of the doubt. He told them, "God often works in mysterious ways. Often they are ways us humans don't understand." In his heart of hearts, the Judge prayed for Abe, that He would help him through this, the most difficult time of his life.

To the Judge's mind, the Lord must have surely been listening. Within the next 24 hours it became an answered prayer in the form of Mentor Graham arriving, accompanied by Doctor Allen. It was good they arrived when they did, for even though Abe's morale was up, physically he was still incredibly weak. Mrs. Green had put Abe straight back to bed, upon his return from Concord. Her concern was mirrored in the impressions of others who saw him that week. Indeed, Abe still looked like he was at death's door and might be New Salem's next victim of 'the sickness.'

This was the situation that Mentor Graham and Doctor Allen had just walked into. While Doc visited with the Judge about Abe's condition, it was agreed for Mentor to go on upstairs and visit Abe at his bedside. He was determined in his own mind to try to help his young friend.

Hearing a knock on the door to his room, Abe's voice beckoned, "Come in, come on in."

The door opened back and Mentor Graham entered. Standing there, just inside the small bedroom, it took his eyes a moment to adjust to the dimly lit windowless room. Lit by a single candle lamp across the room, Mentor focused on a trance-like Abe, sitting on the edge of his bed.

Staring at the blank wall on the opposite side of the room, Abe barely looked up to acknowledge his guest. It was obvious all the turmoil from recent events were still swirling around inside his head. Ann was the light of his life, and now that light had been extinguished. Though he spoke, his eyes were still locked on grief-stricken images not actually there. His heart still ached for her. "The one person I want to have and hold in my arms, I can never have again. Mentor, do you know how it feels to have your life ripped open and all your hopes and dreams destroyed?"

"Yes, Abe, in a sense I do."

"You do?" At this point Abe looked up, making direct and sustained eye contact. His eyes were bloodshot from all the crying he'd done.

"Remember," Mentor explained, "I told you about Sarah and I losing our baby before you came here. It broke both our hearts. I couldn't teach for the longest while, but in time God healed both of us. The Lord brought two young people into my life who wanted to learn, you and Ann. Abe, you gave me purpose. I wanted to live again. Now, I want to help you."

"Mentor, I'm so sorry. I was so wrapped up in my own grief I'd forgotten about your own sorrow."

"That's alright, I understand how grief can be all consuming."

"Thanks Mentor, you're a good friend. You know, all of who I am was wrapped up in Ann. She was everything to me. After the funeral, a few nights ago, I went back out there in the rain. I had decided to kill myself, commit suicide with my pocket knife."

"Yes, I know." Reaching inside his coat pocket, Mentor pulled out Abe's knife, explaining, "Jack left it downstairs with Judge Green. The Judge gave it to me."

"I'm so ashamed you even know about this. I don't want it. You keep it. I'm still afraid I might use it in a moment of depression."

"Abe, you know how Ann felt, what she believed."

"Yes, I know. But I wasn't thinking of that. I just wanted to end it all. I felt like it was the only thing left for me to do."

"You can't. You shouldn't think such things."

"And why not?"

"Your life is not for you to take."

"What do you mean?"

"The Lord gave you life. It belongs to Him. It's His decision when you die, not yours. Don't you see? Ann's life, your life, my life, we're all in God's hands. The end of your life–your story–hasn't been written yet. Since God gave you life, it's something sacred, not for you to take."

"Then what can I do? Who can I talk to? I need help to get out of this depression I'm in. I feel like I'm drowning!"

Mentor could feel the storm raging within his friend's brain. This gave him an idea. He explained, "I want you to go along with something I'm about to tell you."

"I'll try."

"Imagine your inner self as a vessel upon a storm-tossed sea, about to break up. You are the captain of that vessel, trying desperately to hang on."

"I can imagine that."

"Now, think of the only power on earth that could help you regain control of your ship."

"What power is that?"

"The power of Almighty God. He can help you regain control of your ship, your life, and help you steer clear of all disaster."

Abe wished, "If I could only do that."

"All you have to do is open up your heart and let Him in. You might even be surprised if you let Him guide you." Moving closer,

Mentor sat down in the only chair in the room, directly opposite Abe, continuing, "With the Lord's help, you can overcome this depression. Please try this."

"For you, Mentor, I will try."

Taking Abe's hand into his, he revealed a vision of his own, "My dear young friend, I can see it very clearly now. God does have something for you to do. You must get well first and then fulfill that purpose."

Abe was beginning to open up, revealing his own vision. "When I went back out to the cemetery, I saw Ann. All angel-like, she was surrounded by a golden aura. She talked to me, and was just as real as the two of us talking right here."

"Abe, the man you need to talk to about this vision is right downstairs, visiting with Judge Green at this very moment."

"Who would that be?"

"Why Doctor Allen, of course. At one time, he was planning on becoming a preacher instead of a doctor."

"I've always known he was a religious man. Ann and I used to attend Sunday services in his home from time to time."

"He's much more than that. He has made a lifelong study of the Bible and spiritualism in particular. He's just the man you need to talk to about your vision. I'll have him come up to visit with you."

"Yes," agreed Abe, "I'd like to hear what Doc has to say."

As Mentor stood up to leave, he hesitated at the door, and revealed, "Just for the record, I believe you about your visions. You see, I know how your mind works. You have an ability few people have, a certain heightened sensitivity that allows you to see into that place where spirits become visible."

"Since her death I've felt Ann's presence around me. I not only believe it, I know she is real. This is the way it will be in my mind and heart, forever."

After Mentor left the room, these and other thoughts of their conversation would linger with Abe. Downstairs, Lincoln's condition was discussed with both Doctor Allen and the Judge. Offering his opinion, Mentor said, "Judge, we've got a mighty sick young man upstairs. He's going to need all the love and care you and Mrs. Green can give him. It's a shame. He's such a fine young man with a caring heart for everyone."

Hearing the school teacher's dire assessment, the Judge opened up with his true feelings to the two men, "You both should know, Abe has become like a son to Mrs. Green and myself. It's a bloody shame his real father is such a cold-hearted unfeeling man. I guess in the past few years I've sort of filled that role for him. The ironic thing is that I've come to love him, as if he really was my own son. I don't know what to do. He eats little, barely sleeps, just stumbles around when he is out of bed. It almost seems as though he's barely holding on to life. I'm beginning to think we might find him dead anytime."

"It's not so ironic that you love him," observed Doctor Allen. "I've come to know both you and Abe since I've been in New Salem. Your minds are similar, you think alike. You both are God-fearing, caring men."

"John, won't you see if there's anything you can do for him? I don't think I could bear to see him die."

"Judge, of course I'll go up and talk to him right away. If there's anything I can possibly do, I'll do it."

With that promise in mind, Doctor Allen ascended the stairs to see his patient. Opening the door, he saw Abe still sitting on the edge of the bed. As their eyes met, Doctor Allen announced, "I've come to help you."

"Come in Doc, I've been wanting to talk to you."

Entering, Doctor Allen sat down in the same chair Mentor Graham had occupied earlier. As they faced each other, Abe told him about his visions of Ann and communicating with her spirit at the Concord cemetery. As the good doctor was taking all of this in, Abe asked him the one question that had lingered on his mind, "Does the soul live on beyond death of the body?"

"Yes, I believe it does. In the Bible, it says concerning the death of the body, *from dust thou art and to dust thou shalt return*. As to the soul though, the conscious life force within the body, that's an entirely different matter. Let me be clear, I believe in the immortality of the human soul, that upon the death of the body it returns to Almighty God in Heaven."

"What else do you believe, Doc?"

"I believe one day you will be reunited with Ann, your mother, and all your other loved ones."

"Oh Doc, that gives me hope."

"And it should, Abe. I truly believe the soul–by God's good grace–lives forever."

"I want to believe it too."

"Our Lord was the beginning of all things. I've long felt that when we reach the other side, we will only be at the beginning of the great adventure we call life. We are all mere babies in what will become a spiritual walk that will last forever."

"I was so confused after Ann died. I didn't understand how I could see and talk to her. At first I thought I was losing my mind."

"Abe, do you ever read the Bible?"

"Some, but not like I used to. My mother on her deathbed urged me to read it often and obey God's commandments. I promised I would. So much has happened in my life though. I felt like I was prevented from doing it, but that's no excuse. Frankly, I'm ashamed I haven't kept that promise in recent years."

"Is there anything preventing you at present?"

"Nothing," Abe hung his head in shame.

"Then you can now. If you read the Bible on this subject, you will find that Christ appeared to his followers after his death on the cross. Others throughout the Bible also have appeared after their deaths. If you accept what it says, then you can begin to believe that life of the spirit will continue after death of the physical body."

"Doc, I have so many questions."

"Put your questions in the hands of the Lord. Open up your heart to Him. He will guide you every step of the way."

"How was it do you think I saw and talked to Ann's spirit?"

"I think of it as being through the framework of God's doorway that connects His spiritual dimension to our world of the flesh. You and Ann had achieved a powerful connection few ever do, even transcending death. Perhaps it was established through means far beyond human understanding. Abe, what happened to you is not up to us to reason why. It's within the Divine Intelligence of Almighty God. Accept it as a miracle. I believe there is a reason and purpose for everything that happens."

"I suppose you're right, Doc. It's just with Ann gone, I sometimes find myself feeling so alone. It hurts so bad, I don't know what to do."

"You should turn to the Lord in prayer. Restore God to your soul. Then you won't be alone. He will comfort you and help you, revealing to your mind whatever you need to know."

"As I think about it, I promised Ann on her deathbed I would live an honest and upright life, doing good for others. I'm going to stop wavering. I've decided–right here and now–I'm going to spend every last drop of energy I have, trying to keep that promise for the rest of my life."

"Abe, I see the sincerity in your face and hear it in your voice. Somehow, I know you will do everything you say you'll do. I admire you for that."

"Doc, you're a true friend."

"As not only your friend, but also your doctor, I want to help you get well." Leaning back in his chair, taking in Abe's whole expression, he added, "It just came to me, I think God has chosen you for His purposes. By doing what you say, I believe you'll be following through, doing His will."

Abe smiled, agreeing, "I like that. Just you saying it makes me feel good inside. It's the first time I've felt good in many days."

Doctor Allen leaned forward, putting his hand on Abe's shoulder in a comforting way. "That's the spirit. God wants you to know He loves you and wants you to live."

As he looked up at Doc Allen, tears formed in Abe's eyes. He asked, "How do you know that?"

"It just came to me: I'm supposed to tell you something that Jesus said to the apostles, *I am with you always.* God wants you to know He will be with you."

"Doc, are you sure?"

"If you will open up to the Lord and believe in Him with all your heart, He will never leave you."

"I want to know the Lord the way you do."

"After I go downstairs to see the Judge and Mrs. Green, I want you to pull out that old Bible I know you have up here somewhere. Start reading it. Then you will know the Lord in the fullness of time."

Abe felt an internal healing warmth, that he would later say was like a feeling of redemption, surrounding him. A measure of healing already going through him, he responded, "I'll do it Doc, I'll start reading my Bible this afternoon."

Doctor Allen observed something change in Abe's appearance. There was a glow emanating from his face. Hope had returned to a man who had lost hope.

One more thought came to the good doctor as he reacted. It would be an observation that would stay with Abe forever. "When you start reading God's word again, you'll start discovering God's path for your life."

Abe thought for a moment about this man of faith and told him, "Your words always give me food for thought."

The good doctor appreciated his patient more than ever before. "Please, from now on call me John."

"That means a lot to me, John."

From that day on, a special bond was established between these two men of similar spiritual beliefs.

Later, Doctor Allen made arrangements with Mrs. Green, giving her strict instructions for Abe's recuperation. He would be a positive factor in pulling young Lincoln back from the brink and in setting him on the right path into the future. Upstairs, a ray of hope was beginning to shine within his patient. The seemingly impossible was becoming possible.

Abe was alone, still sitting on the edge of his bed, wrapped up in the world of his thoughts, for a while. In complete silence, his mind ventured back to his childhood when he was nine years old: His dying mother, Nancy Hanks Lincoln took his hand. She whispered, "Abe, promise me you will follow God and keep His commandments. Read His words in my Bible and obey Him."

The nine-year-old boy promised he would, but the twenty-six year old man had forgotten. Tears filled his eyes as he thought of this memory. Sitting there, he whispered, "My mother, my angel in Heaven, I will follow God and obey Him, just as you taught me, all the rest of my life."

That very afternoon, Abe retrieved his old copy of the Bible that Judge Green had placed beneath his bed. He read a few passages from it, starting to renew the promise he had made to his mother so long ago. As he did so, Abe had a sense of the Lord's presence inside him. Just as Doctor Allen had said, he was beginning to discover God's path for his life.

Worn down and exhausted, he still managed to whisper a short prayer before he drifted off to sleep, "My Lord and my God, please be with me and guide me in all things throughout the rest of my life." When he awoke later, he did so with renewed strength and knew the healing powers of the Lord were with him.

Throughout the rest of his life, Abe kept the promise he had made. No matter what pressures were closing in around him, he found time to read the Bible and pray for the Lord's guidance. In making this direct contact with God, he rarely discussed religion with a minister and never became a member of any 'man made' church, as he put it. When asked he would say, "I'm a member of the church of the most high–the Church of Almighty God."

CHAPTER 20
FIRST STEPS

During the next week, despite showing signs of getting better, Abe was still suffering from a touch of 'the sickness' he'd caught himself. Worried, Mrs. Green would often have to spoon-feed hot soup to him. This paid off as he slowly gained some of his strength back. In addition, both she and Judge Green would take turns reading the Bible to him. So it was, they were helping Abe to heal both mentally and physically.

Doctor Allen explained it this way, "Abe needs more than just food for the body, he needs spiritual food for his mind as well." This proved to be true, as there was a deep hunger between the spiritual walls of his mind for the word of God.

After his breakdown, Abe did not leave his upstairs bedroom at Judge Green's farmhouse for almost a month. Even as he slowly rallied and regained his physical strength, there was still a grief-stricken expression that lingered on his face. Many who saw him, privately called him that young man of sorrows. Actually no one who visited with him thought otherwise.

Jack Armstrong and Billy Greene were frequent visitors to Abe's bedroom. Downstairs out of earshot though, they would visit with the Judge in his office. Whispering, they would ask, "How is he really? Has Abe lost his mind?"

The Judge answered, "Abe's not lost his mind."

"Then what is it?" Jack questioned.

"I've seen it before in others who've lost someone," the Judge explained. "Doc Allen thought Abe was showing symptoms of dying from a broken heart."

"Then what can we do?" Billy asked. "He's our friend."

The Judge looked at both of them and said, "We can all be his friend in this time of his grief, when he needs us most. We can try to cheer him up." The Judge's expression became very grave as he added, "We can also pray to the Lord to heal our friend."

Eventually, Abe was well enough to come downstairs and meet with Judge Green in his office. Rumors that he'd lost his mind had gotten back to Abe. Confronting the Judge about what some people were saying, he expressed his concerns, "Judge, I wished I could just stay inside, within these walls, and never have to face anyone again."

"Don't think that way, Abe. Those who have been ridiculing you don't know what they're talking about. Most people have never seen a spirit or ghost in their lives. They don't really know if such things exist. Yet you know, because you were given a special gift from the Lord and saw Ann's spirit."

"You believe me, Judge?"

"Yes, I've thought and prayed about this and I've come to think like Mentor and John Allen. We believe that God is going to be using you for His Divine purpose. Who are we, or any other man, to question our Lord? This is between you and Him."

"Then, what should I do?"

"Don't question what's happened to you. Go with the flow of those events you told me about, as God's vessel in this world. Son, I'll tell you what I see even now: I see an aura of good surrounding you. Actually, I observed it when you first came to New Salem. Ever since then, I've come to see it more clearly and believe it with all my heart. Now it's up to you to take the first steps in using that force for good in the right way."

"So what should those first steps be?"

"Beyond anything I could say, you know it was one of Ann's last wishes that you become the lawyer you were working so hard to become. I believe this is what you were meant to be."

The Judge's words struck home. Abe had already anticipated this was what he was going to tell him though, "I figured you might say that, but I've resigned myself to it. I can't fight both you and Ann."

"Son, you don't have to fight. Instead, pray on it for God's guidance and help. If you do so, His help will set you apart and make you a man among men."

These words meant a lot to Abe. "Thank you Judge, for making things so clear, for helping me get my life back on track."

"Son, just remember, take it one step at a time as you find your way back into life."

During September 1835, Judge Green revealed his fatherly instincts to Abe more than ever, in clear and unmistakable ways. Jack Armstrong commented, about his half-brother, "He was exactly what Abe needed at that point in time. There never was a kinder, more sensitive man than the Judge. Just as he helped me, he's now helping my friend Abe."

After a few more days passed, Abe was feeling well enough to mount Diamond and ride over to Sand Ridge to visit Jack Armstrong and family as well as Uncle Jimmy Short. Arriving there, he found Jack working out in the fields, barely within sight of his farmhouse.

"You're a sight for sore eyes," announced Jack once he realized who the incoming rider was. "I've been think'n of you mighty strong."

"So have I, Jack. It's just as good to see you. How's Hannah and the boys?"

"Let's go find out." Together, Jack and Abe walked across the rolling landscape to the Armstrong farmhouse.

Making conversation, Abe revealed, "I've learned a lot while staying at the Judge's these past few weeks."

Jack was curious, "What sort of things have you learned?"

Abe was not at all reluctant to tell him. "Ann's spirit came to me while I was there. She told me what God wanted me to do with the rest of my life. Between the Judge, Doc Allen, and Mentor Graham, I learned how to really open up my heart and pray."

"Sounds like a lot to take in."

"It was and is. Jack, I feel like I'm changing inside. I'm more spiritual than I've ever been. My personal relationship with God is far more intimate than anyone will ever know."

"Just from what you're say'n, Abe, I can tell you're changing."

"Don't you forget, you're partly responsible for the change in me."

"I am?"

"Yes, when you took my pocket knife from me in the cemetery and reminded me about the Bible, you saved me from taking my own life. I'm thanking you, with all my heart."

"Abe, I didn't want to lose my friend, my brother."

Stopping in their tracks, the two men turned to each other. Abe took Jack's hand into his and reassured him, "You'll never lose me, I'll always be your friend and brother." In that moment both men reaffirmed their lasting friendship–a friendship that would last beyond the grave.

Another twenty yards and they would be at the front door of Jack's farmhouse. In the doorway stood his wife, Hannah. She had a question written on her face, "What were you two talk'n about out there?"

Abe answered, "A lot, Aunt Hannah, a lot."

"There you go, call'n me Aunt Hannah, again. I hope you're stay'n for supper."

"I will, thank you most kindly."

Over a meal that included Hannah's wonderful homemade biscuits, Abe renewed lasting friendships with every member of the Armstrong family. After supper, their boys, Pleasant (almost seven) and little Duff (age two), pleaded, "Uncle Abe, please tell us one of your stories."

The festive mood seemed to change. Abe paused for a moment, his facial expression becoming more serious as he said, "Boys I want to do it a little differently this evening. Instead, I want to tell you a little story from the Bible and what it means to me. I want to tell you the story of how Jesus came to the door of someone who needed him. He says in the third chapter of Revelations: *Behold, I stand at the door and knock. If any man hears my voice and lets me in, I will come in and be with him.* This verse has changed my life."

Pleasant looked up questioningly, "What does it mean, Uncle Abe?"

"At least for me, it was how God started healing me. When I was sick I felt lost. I didn't know what to do. A friend suggested I start reading the Bible again. I did and came upon this verse. I figured it meant to open up the door that led to my heart. So opening that door, I invited God in. Ever since, I've felt like a different man. I feel like the Lord is with me whenever I need Him. All I have to do is pray and then I feel God's presence inside me, answering me."

Jack was also listening to Abe, finally breaking in, "Abe, is it really that simple?"

"For me it was. I've come to believe if any man is sincere enough and opens his heart up to God, He will come in and heal whatever troubles you. If you do this and humble yourself before God, you'll be a better person for it. The Lord will be inside you then, helping and advising you throughout your life."

The boys were satisfied and went on to bed. Abe went over to the front door, opening it. Standing there in the open doorway, he inhaled a cool breeze. He seemed to be wrapped up in his own spiritual thoughts within himself for a long moment.

Noticing the extended silence from his friend, Jack went over by him, interrupting his internal meditation, "Abe, I noticed you didn't tell the boys one of your whopper stories tonight. Why not?"

"Jack, I feel like I'm changing. I know, I've always been the one you could count on for a joke or a good yarn. But it's all different now. That whole part of me has sort of winked out since Ann's passing. She was the light of my life. As long as I had her I could be happy and laugh."

Jack placed a comforting hand on Abe's shoulder, consoling him, "Maybe someday you can again. I believe Ann would want you to laugh."

"Maybe someday," Abe conceded. Hearing a little noise behind him, he looked around to see Hannah working away, cleaning off the kitchen table. Abe reacted, "I've got to pay you all for such a fine supper. Besides, I need to work something out of me. Jack, I'm going outside and cut you a rick or two of firewood."

"Abe, you don't have to do that."

"Yes, I have to, for myself I have to do it."

After a bit, Hannah could hear Abe outside, chopping away with their axe. Going over by Jack in the doorway, she whispered to him, "He doesn't have to repay us."

"It's more than that, Hannah. I've seen him do this before. By cutting that firewood, he's clearing his head."

"He's still struggling within himself."

"Yes, he loved that girl so much. I keep praying for him that the Lord will ease his grief, but there's one other thing baring on his mind."

"What's that?"

"He's trying to figure out what God wants him to do."

Hannah stared at Abe working away, chopping wood over by the woodpile, then back to Jack, "I've got a feel'n that Abe's gonna turn out to be a better person than any of us ever thought about be-ing. The more I think about it, I do believe he's got some of Ann's spirit in his head with him. That's not all though. It's so clear to me now. He's got the spirit of the good Lord with him as well."

Jack marveled, "What a combination. Hannah, I think we're seeing the birth of a new man, right before our eyes."

The next morning Abe got up feeling refreshed, with renewed vigor and strength, ready to go see another old friend. Going on up Sand Ridge, he stopped off at Uncle Jimmy Short's cabin. It was good to see his old Indian scout from the Black Hawk war again.

All that morning Abe helped him gather corn. According to James Short, there was none better than Abe at husking corn from the stalk. Uncle Jimmy admitted, "I thought I was pretty good at this, but you always gather twice as much as I can."

"Jimmy, as I see it," Abe reasoned, "it's cause of my big hands. At least they're good for something—but not for much else right now."

Suddenly, Abe stopped, returning to Jimmy's porch. An expression of sadness formed across his face as he lowered his head, brooding.

Jimmy followed Abe, sitting down beside him. Talking softly, he tried to help, "I know it's rough. I'm all alone up here, having lost everyone I ever loved. So I kinda know how you're feel'n. I didn't know Miss Ann all that well, but what I did know, she was a mighty decent young lady, good to everyone."

"She was more than that. She was an angel–my angel."

"I wish to God I could help you, Abe. But I want you to know, in every way humanly possible I'll be here for you."

"Thank you, Jimmy. You're a very special friend."

Throughout the rest of the day and evening, Uncle Jimmy was right at Abe's side trying to help cheer him up. Abe was receptive at the old scout engaged him in colorful conversation, taking his mind off the heartbreak that was still trying to pull him down.

The next morning, Abe returned to Judge Green's farm. Sitting in the Judge's office, he announced, "I'm feeling strong enough to return to New Salem. I'm thinking Billy's probably more than ready for me to take my old job back at the post office."

"Are you sure you're ready, Abe?"

"I'm sure Judge. I've got my strength back. So the way I see it, I have to return to my old life while I'm up for it."

"I'm glad, my boy. I'll be pulling for you all the way."

"Judge, I'm more than behold'n to you."

"Mrs. Green and myself, we want you to know that you can consider our place your second home. The door will always be open to you."

A grateful Abe would never forget the Judge's words. He would often return to the home of his surrogate father for advice and guidance.

In the truest since of the word, the homeless person Abe had been, finally found a home. Out of his greatest grief, he had found the love of family and friends. Finding a measure of love and support from those mentioned, enabled him to return back to something close to a normal life again.

The last week of September, 1835 saw Abe back in his old job as Postmaster. He went through the motions of doing his job, but at the same time he was quiet and withdrawn. Frequently he would go walking down the road or off into the woods with no apparent destination in mind. Often times, an expression of sadness could be seen on his face. It was so obvious he was in a lingering state of depression. Many who knew him, now referred to Abe as 'that young man of sorrows.' Those who took more than a casual glance could see here was someone who was an empty shell of a man, often barely hanging on to life.

One thing though was a shining beacon of hope within him that kept him going. From time to time, he would hear Ann's voice in his head, speaking to his mind. During the night of October 14th, just such an event took place. He was awakened from his sleep in the rear of the post office. In that little room of what had formerly been the Berry-Lincoln store, he clearly heard Ann's voice, *Abe, please help my father and mother. My family needs you. They will sorely need your help in the morning.*

A commotion woke Abe up again about daybreak on the morning of the 15th of October. He could hear voices outside yelling, "He's back! I never thought I'd see him again." Getting dressed quickly, he went outside, only to come face to face with the one man he never wanted to see again–John McNamar.

"Lincoln, I told you I'd be back, though I'm quite surprised to see you still here."

"And you're more than three years later than when you said you'd be back."

"Well, I'm back and I'm going straight out to my property and marry Ann as soon as it can be arranged."

"You're too late, McNamar."

"Just what do you mean?"

"I mean Ann died on August 25th."

The news barely fazed him. He persisted on, not quite accepting one so young could die, "How is such a thing possible? She must've been only a little more than twenty."

"She was twenty-two to be exact. An epidemic of the sickness spread through the entire area around New Salem. It lasted most of the summer and is still going on in some spots. Many people have died. Unfortunately, Ann was one of them. I can show you her grave if you'd like to pay your respects."

At this point, the self-absorbed greed that always possessed John McNamar took him over. "I don't need to do that! Besides, I have other more important concerns." His reaction had the ring as if Abe had insulted him.

Abe asked him, "Then exactly, what are your concerns?"

"See here Lincoln, I've come all the way from New York. I've got my aged mother in one of those wagons across the street. I intend to go straight out to my property at Sand Ridge and take repossession of it today."

"But you can't, there's sick people living out there. It's Ann's parents and family."

"This may surprise you Lincoln. I don't care who they are! With Ann's death, my agreement with the Rutledges is severed. You can go out there and move them out if you like, but I'll have my property back today!"

"Are there no limits to your greed and selfishness?"

"I don't have to take that talk from anyone, least of all you Lincoln." McNamar walked off in a huff. He would make arrangements with the Inn for his mother to stay there. Later in the morning, he acquired a buggy with the express purpose of going out to Sand Ridge and evicting the entire Rutledge family.

At the same time, Abe saddled up Diamond and rode out to Judge Green's. Apprising him of the situation, the Judge took some deputized men out to the only road leading to Sand Ridge. It was there they waited on John McNamar.

It was early afternoon when McNamar approached in his buggy, only to be stopped by this group of men, all with loaded Kentucky riffles. Seeing Judge Green coming up to the side of his buggy, McNamar asked, "What's the meaning of this, Judge?"

"You're being turned back. There's possibly deadly disease out at your Sand Ridge farm."

"But it's my farm and I have the right to go out there if I want!"

"Let me tell you something about rights. First of all, you lied to a Justice of the Peace, namely me."

"What!"

"You gave me your word of honor you'd be back here within three months. That was over three years ago. Further, since you left the property abandoned, there is some doubt you still legally own it. Also, I happen to know personally from the lips of Miss Ann Rutledge, you didn't write her for almost that same length of time."

"That's not true. I wrote Ann over three months ago, that I was coming back to marry her."

"She never said anything about receiving any such letter."

"Judge, I swear I wrote her. It must've been lost in the mail between New York and here."

"It's possible, McNamar. But as to the ownership of the Sand Ridge property, I'll still have to research this matter. It could take several months for my ruling. Perhaps sometime after the first part of the year I'll have you an answer."

"Judge, I have my aged mother with me. What do I do in the meantime?"

"Where is she now?"

"Back in New Salem."

"Well, I suggest you turn this buggy around and get back to her. I'll contact you in New Salem when I'm able to make a ruling in this matter."

"Judge, I must protest! The law doesn't work this way in New York."

"McNamar!" The Judge was finally getting irritated. "May I remind you of one important detail? You are not in New York anymore! You are with frontier folk on the Illinois frontier. The law works differently out here. I'm the duly appointed Justice of the Peace of Sangamon County. Now of course, you could spend money and go down to Vandalia and see if someone at the State House would overturn my ruling. On the other hand, you could go back to New Salem and make arrangements for lodgings during the coming winter."

John McNamar had been humbled. He accepted the Judge's advice and went back to New Salem and stayed the winter there.

Later that afternoon, the Judge visited with Abe in his office back at his farmhouse. "Well, I stuck my neck out on this one. Abe, I would like for you to ride on out to the Rutledge farm and see how that poor family is doing. I think I can stall McNamar off till after the first of the year, but not much longer than that."

"Just as soon as I can get Diamond out of the barn, I'll ride on out there."

"Oh, just one other thing, McNamar said he wrote Ann more than three months ago he was coming back to marry her."

"I never saw any such letter come through the post office, nor did Ann ever mention the subject to me."

"That's what I thought. He could be lying, but check it out anyway when you get out there."

"I will, Judge."

Abe left shortly after that, riding up to the Rutledge farm about an hour later. Coming out on the porch to meet him was young David Rutledge. "Abe, it's good–mighty good–to see you."

Abe told him that John McNamar had returned to New Salem and was wanting to evict the Rutledges, and repossess his property. He further explained that Judge Green had come to their aid so that they would at least have time to find a new place to live.

David spoke for all the Rutledges, "Abe, I want you to know our whole family appreciates everything you've done on our behalf, but for right now it would be impossible for us to move anywhere."

"But why? What's holding your family back?"

"It's my father, Abe. He's dying. He's come down with the same stuff that killed Ann. He's fighting hard to overcome it, but he loses a little more ground each day.

"I did not realize his health had declined so much. I'm sorry David, I just haven't been able to face coming out here since Ann's death."

"That's just it. Out of all of us, Ann was that special light in his eyes. With her death, father has sort of lost the will to live." Tears filled his eyes as he delivered his final assessment, "I don't think he'll make it to the first of the year."

Sadly, David Rutledge's opinion turned out to be true. James Rutledge passed away on December 3rd, 1835. He was buried in the Old Concord Burial Ground, near Ann's final resting place.

Abe attended the funeral, once more embracing Ann's two brothers, David and John. As he comforted them and the entire Rutledge family in their deep grief, they loved him right back for his caring nature. To them, he had long since became another member of their family in their minds and hearts.

Before Abe left for New Salem, he pulled David aside and asked him about the letter John McNamar claimed to have written Ann, more than three months before his return.

When David was alone with Abe, he confessed knowledge of such a letter: "Abe, before I left for school, I had come to the post office to see you, but you were out delivering the mail. The daily coach had just arrived with a new packet of letters. I laid them on the counter for you, but not before I noticed McNamar's letter to Ann in the incoming mail. I retrieved it. It went through my mind all the sadness he had caused both Ann and you. I must confess, I've never liked the man. I know I shouldn't have, but I read the letter. Then something came over me. Knowing how Ann's whole heart and soul were wrapped up in you, I took matters into my own hands."

"What did you do, David?"

"I burned the letter and never told Ann or you, or anyone else about its existence. The way I see it, Ann was going through enough then. She did not need to have any thoughts of that horrible man on her mind. I told myself: if or when McNamar ever returned to

New Salem, I would have it out with him myself. Since he wants to cause my family more pain, I suppose I'll have to do just that."

"No David, according to Judge Green, McNamar thinks the letter was lost somewhere in the mail delivery from New York to here. It does happen fairly often. So let's just let him think that's what happened. I believe you thought you were doing the right thing–and maybe you were. For now though, Judge Green's acting as a go between your family and McNamar. In the meantime, Jack Armstrong and Jimmy Short have said that they will help you and your family move when you're ready." David agreed and took Abe's advice.

As for Abe, the next day he boarded the noon stage for Vandalia and his second session of the state legislature. During his time there his friendship with former Major, John Stuart, deepened. Once more, Stuart made the case for Abe to think about moving to Springfield someday. When the session adjourned on January 8th, 1836, Abe returned to New Salem.

Getting out of the coach, the first thing Abe noticed was how much New Salem had changed. 'The sickness,' in what we would now call a typhoid fever epidemic, had taken its toll all around town and the surrounding area. New Salem would never quite recover from the blow. Abe saw it clearly: the town was dying.

With this view in mind, many people wanted to find a better place to live. In early February, Abe surveyed and otherwise laid out plans for a new, more accessible town to be erected nearby, about three miles north of New Salem. The new town would become Petersburg, Illinois.

February also saw dwindling activity at the post office. So Abe took advantage of the extra free time and returned to the Graham home for a day's visit. Mentor was elated to see Abe again, "I'm so happy to see you back in New Salem."

"My dear old friend, I'm still craving to learn more in the pursuit of knowledge."

"I wish all my students were conscientious as you."

"Well, as you know I had outside forces spurring me on."

"By that you mean–"

"Yes, I mean Ann. I'm slowly pulling myself together, gaining more of my strength back every day. I've reconciled myself to the fact she's gone from this life. But, in a sense–in a spiritual sense–she's still with me."

"She is?"

"Yes, she is. Most recently, last October I heard her voice very clearly in my sleep."

"Abe, I'm beginning to believe that perhaps the good Lord intends for you to keep having this connection."

"I guess it's like Doctor Allen told me, there's a reason and a purpose for everything. I know this much, just being able to hear her voice every now and then helps keep me from going off the rails again."

"I'm glad to hear that, Abe. You know I still have your pocket knife if you ever want it back."

"No, you keep it, Mentor. It's like a sort of souvenir of the worst time of my life, a time I don't need to be reminded of."

"I do believe God is helping you, opening back some sort of door within your brain."

"Yes, I do feel the Lord has opened a door inside my mind, allowing so many things to flow into my brain."

"Abe, I see it, as if it were in a vision, God has a greater purpose for you. If you keep pursuing knowledge as you have been, I think you will have one of the finest minds of our generation."

"Beside Ann's spirit and the good Lord, I have you, Judge Green, and Doctor Allen to thank. All of you have helped me to become the man I am now."

Later, as Abe mounted Diamond to ride back to New Salem, he waved goodbye to Mentor and Sarah Graham as they stood on their front porch looking after him. As Abe disappeared into the distance, Sarah turned to Mentor and asked, "What do you think?"

He replied, "The good Lord is healing him."

The next day, Abe was behind the counter inside the post office, quite alone. Sorting through mail spread out on the counter, he became lost in thought when a voice broke into his private thoughts, calling him, "Abe, Abe."

Looking up into the face, he reacted, "Oh Doc, I mean John, what can I do for you?"

"I just got back from making my rounds, checking on my patients, and thought I'd come by and check on you."

"John, you caught me. I suppose I was day dreaming about Ann. She still comes to me as a voice inside my head, advising me."

Doctor Allen offered his opinion, "Did you ever think it's perhaps the Lord's way of getting inside your mind to help you?"

"No, I never really thought of it that way."

"Yes," continued the good doctor, "I think it's God helping you with your first steps in the spiritual walk that will take you on the journey through the rest of your life."

"I have been opening up my heart to Him, just like we talked about that day upstairs at Judge Green's farm. I'd like to think it's God's way of putting a little more of His wisdom inside me."

"Abe, I can almost guarantee you one thing. If you keep opening up to Him, He will walk with you on your path through life, wherever that takes you."

During the last two days, Abe had listed to Doctor Allen and Mentor Graham, taking the words of both men to heart. For the first time in months he slept well that night, feeling the true peace of mind only the Lord could give him. In the months and years to come, Abe would fondly remember and cherish the words of wisdom from his New Salem friends.

With still more time on his hands, the next morning he sought out Judge Green in his home office. The two men discussed Abe's future.

The Judge asked, "'What's been happening to you since we visited last?"

"Oh, the good ladies of New Salem have been trying to marry me off. They say what I need is a wife. I kinda went along with them for a little bit. But, I'm not ready yet. I don't know if I'll ever be. I still love Ann in my heart. No one else could ever really take her place. But that's not really why I came out here. I wanted to talk to you about my future."

"Yes, what about your future?"

"Judge, what do you think I should do?"

"Abe, it's like we talked before. You should pursue the goal that you and Ann had originally dreamed. You're no longer young Abe Lincoln of New Salem. You're fast becoming Lincoln the man, someone full of wisdom and something else. I'm not quite sure what it is, but I sense it's something good and decent."

"That other something is what I've learned during my last five years in New Salem, compassion and love. You can't see it because it's inside my heart and soul. But you can feel it, and as I continue to grow, just maybe others will feel it too."

"Abe, you've hit on something. There's a lot that needs changing in this old world. I think the good Lord wants you to be part of that change. You've already served two sessions in the state house. It's time for you to make 1836 the year you achieve the last steps in becoming a full-fledged attorney."

"It's what Ann always wanted me to do. You make a good case that the time is right for me to do it."

"Son, I believe it's through Ann's spirit, God is showing you this is the path you must take your life. Time is of the essence. As much as it pains me to say it, New Salem is dying. 'The sickness' almost destroyed it. People are moving every day. In fact, many are moving to that new little town you helped survey and lay out."

"What?"

"Yes, the new town of Petersburg, a few miles north of here. While you were in Vandalia, my brother Jack, Jimmy Short, and my man Henry McHenry helped move the Rutledge family over there."

"They did?"

"Yes, and I helped them to purchase land there."

"You're a good man, Judge."

"Well, I figured I owed a lot to James Rutledge, God rest his soul. His sons, John and David, are good boys. David is becoming a lawyer too. I think he might have a future in Petersburg. I guess this all brings me back to your future."

"Judge, will you help me with those steps in getting my license as a lawyer?"

"My boy, nothing would give me greater pleasure. The older I get, there's something I think about more often now."

"What's that Judge?"

"Life on earth is but a fleeting moment in comparison to the measure of time that is all eternity. So, let's do this thing quickly and make you a lawyer."

With this thought in mind, a sense of urgency became instilled in both Abe and Judge Green. True to his word, the Judge helped Abe with the necessary papers to be filled out. A little over a month later on March 24th, the first of three hurdles was overcome. His name was officially entered into the court record of Sangamon County as a man of good moral character.

Other events and outside forces seemed to pick up all around Abe and propel his life forward. All postal activity seemed to come to a complete stand still. The Judge had warned him, so it was no surprise when it came down officially, on May 30th, that Postmaster Lincoln was ordered to shut the New Salem post office down and turn over all records to the new post office in Petersburg, the new county seat of Menard County.

Though he was permitted by the old Lincoln-Berry store creditors to continue living in what was the New Salem post office, it would rapidly become a matter of survival that he find new sources of income. So now it was not only a matter of drive, but of necessity that he resolved to run for a second term in the Illinois legislature. Infusing himself with a rare combination of self-assurance and humility, he won re-election on August 1st.

On the heels of this triumph, a little over a month later on September 9th, Abe's application to practice law was finally approved. A ruling by two justices of the Illinois Supreme Court granted him a license to practice in all the courts in the state.

Not quite three months later, the tenth general assembly of the legislature convened on December 5th in Vandalia. It was the first session of Abe's second term in the legislature.

It was during this session; the friendship of John Stuart and Abe was cemented permanently as they joined in a common cause. They committed themselves to fight, step by step, to remove the state capital from Vandalia to the much closer town of Springfield. The representatives from Sangamon County, led by Abe, won the day, and on February 24th, 1837 achieved passage in the House. The next day it passed in the State Senate. Plain-spoken Abe Lincoln was now being recognized by others as a force to be reckoned with.

This was quickly followed by another triumph on March 1st. The third and final step in Abe becoming a fully accredited attorney happened when his name was entered on the official roll in the clerk's office of the Illinois Supreme Court.

Shortly before the session adjourned on March 6th, John Stuart confronted Abe with an offer he would find it difficult to refuse. "I want to offer you permanent employment as a junior partner in my law firm in Springfield effective as soon as possible."

"John, I'm flattered beyond words."

"I'm going to make this offer official in writing. You'll be getting a letter from me shortly."

Abe thought about this offer all the way on his journey back home. Inside the closed-up post office, Abe sat down in front of the fire place, thinking more about it. Staring into a place far from where he was, he whispered, "Ann, we finally did it."

When he had got off the stage, he'd taken a long lingering look down Main Street. It was like he and the Judge had discussed. New Salem was dying. Less than half of the stores were still open. The rest were either closed up or abandoned. It hit him then: he would have to go elsewhere if he was to survive.

Where should he go? He asked himself, Do I have the intelligence to succeed as an attorney in Springfield? These questions weighed heavily on his mind as he fell into sleep. It was within this state, before he could fully wake up, that he heard Ann's voice in his head, *Abe, be strong in your resolve to pursue your dreams–our dreams– in Springfield.* To hear her voice was just enough to erase any doubts he may have had as what to do. Through the years to come, he revealed only to a few who were close to him that hearing voices from his past–Ann and his mother for instance–spurred him on to the correct decisions.

Several days later, on March 15th, the twice a week stagecoach entered onto Main Street, stopping in front of the Inn. The driver, recognizing Abe, spotted him sitting under the old oak tree, across the Springfield Road. Calling to him, the driver said, "Abe, I got something for you."

"What is it?"

"A letter from Springfield."

Even before opening it, Abe knew what it was. John Stuart had kept his word. There it was, officially inviting Abe to join his law firm.

The next morning saw Abe riding north out of New Salem, toward the Old Concord cemetery. As he rode past Sand Ridge, seeing him out on the road, Jack Armstrong stopped what he was doing and mounted his horse, following him from afar.

Reaching the cemetery, Abe went to Ann's grave, whispering to her as if she were there. "Ann, I finally got the letter from John Stuart, my friend from the Black Hawk War, inviting me to join his law firm in Springfield. We've done it! I want you to know, I'm gonna do it, just like we said… I'm going to miss you so much." Tears filled his eyes as he wept silently.

Then, as if it were in response he heard Ann's voice in his head, *Abe, this is what we've worked hard for, for so long. Remember, I'll be with you, inside your head.*

Just as he pulled out an old weather-beaten calico handkerchief to wipe his eyes, a comforting hand gently touched his shoulder. Abe didn't even have to look around to know who it was. Somehow, he just knew. "Hello Jack, I'm glad you're here."

"Ever since Miss Ann passed away, Hannah and I've been come'n out here, take'n care of the cemetery."

Turning around, facing him, Abe expressed his gratitude, "Thank you Jack. Beneath your rough exterior, I think you've developed a mighty big heart inside yourself. I've been wondering whose been cutting all the weeds back and keeping it nice with flowers near the grave markers."

The flowers are all Hannah's work. She loves them just like Miss Ann did. I've been do'n all the rest. I've sorta become the caretaker of the whole cemetery."

"But why you, Jack?"

"I went to bed one night, think'n about all the mistakes and things I've done wrong in my life. Like we talked about, I started pray'n and opening myself up to God, ask'n what is one thing I could do that would be right? Well, I woke up the next morn'n and I didn't know what came over me at first. Think'n about it, I realized it was the Lord tell'n me this is what He wanted me to do."

"I guess that's why I'm out here, Jack. I was telling Ann what the Lord wanted me to do."

"What does He want you to do, Abe?"

"I'm leaving New Salem for good. I'm going to Springfield, to be a lawyer there. Even though I'll always feel like my heart is buried out here with her, I believe this is what the Lord wants me to do."

"Miss Ann always wanted you to become a lawyer. Somehow, I think she knows what you're do'n and is proud of you."

"I believe that too, Jack."

So, it was, a few weeks later, on Friday, April 14th, Abe visited Judge Green in his office to say his goodbyes. Just as they started to talk, Mrs. Green–Aunt Nancy–stepped into the doorway. She spoke with tears in her eyes, "Abe, I feel like I'm losing a son."

"No, you're not, Aunt Nancy, I'll be back through New Salem every now and then. No matter what happens, I'll always carry thoughts of you and the Judge right here in my heart."

"Son, I want you to know something very important, if for any reason this Springfield move doesn't work out, please contact Mrs. Green and myself. We will help you move back here."

"I'm right grateful, Judge. These past six years you've been my father. So, I'm gonna do everything in my power to succeed in Springfield. I want you to be proud of me."

"My boy, no father could be more proud of a son than I am of you right now."

By now both men had tears in their eyes, embracing each other. In this way they almost actually were father and son. As Fate would have it, life does sometimes turn out for the best.

"Abe," the Judge concluded, "several of your friends have gathered in the living room down the hall."

"But Judge, I hadn't really planned on seeing anyone before I left town. I was just gonna sort of slip out of town."

That familiar Santa Claus smile came over the Judge's face. "It's too late for that my boy! Come with me."

Walking down the hall, the two men approached the living room doors, which seemed to open back all by themselves. Gathered there within the large room, were some of the friends Abe valued most from the past six years. They all broke out singing, "He's a jolly good fellow which nobody can deny! So, say all of us."

Abe was truly moved, "I feel like I'm the luckiest man in the world to have such good friends as all of you."

For one last time the secret of Abe's New Salem experience was revealed. He had become everyone's brother, son, or uncle. They really were a family in ways words can never adequately express.

Coming up to him first were the Rutledge boys, consisting of Ann's brothers, David and John Rutledge, along with their cousin, McGrady Rutledge. Embracing Abe, David said, "I've always dreamed we could be law partners together, perhaps over in Petersburg."

"That would've been great," agreed Abe, "but sometimes Fate steps in and rules otherwise."

"Sadly, we can't always have our dreams," observed David, somewhat becoming reconciled to what would never be.

All three Rutledge boys wished him well anyway, saying, "You are one of the finest men we have ever known."

Pressing forward through the crowd, Abe then turned to the Graham family. Standing in front of him were Mentor and Sarah Rafferty Graham. Along with them was their little son, Septimus Graham. Barely two years old, Abe seemed drawn to the little toddler, who was already calling him, "Unca Abe."

This seemed to please Abe immensely, who replied, "Yes, I'm your 'Unca Abe,' and if you become half as brilliant as your daddy, you'll be a genius."

"Abe, I'm so proud of you, my brother," responded Mentor.

"You never stop amazing us," added Sarah Graham. "See our little son already loves you. After losing our last baby, Mentor and I were afraid to have another baby for a while. But seeing you accomplish what you have sort of inspired us in a strange way."

"Sarah," observed Abe, "I have found out sometimes it takes courage just to live. I'm so happy for you and Mentor and little Septimus."

Abe had barely turned, advancing a couple more steps, when he found himself facing Doctor John Allen. "John, my dear friend, it was you who pointed the way for me, back to God."

"Abe, I'm going to miss you greatly, but you're now on a spiritual walk that will take you far from New Salem."

"John, that's what I feel I'm on, even now." Profound thoughts, but Abe had found himself accepting, more every day, the destiny the Creator had placed in front of him.

Moving on past the good doctor, Abe was now confronted by his old friend from the Indian wars, Uncle Jimmy Short. He said, "Abe, I wished I could go with you and scout what lies ahead for you in Springfield. I'm sure gonna miss you."

"I'm gonna miss you too, Uncle Jimmy."

"Now you said it. I'm not old enough to be your uncle. I've just gotten white hair before my time. I'm gonna shave this beard off, so the next time you see me you'll know we're really about the same age." A few months later Abe would be surprised when Jimmy Short came to visit him in Springfield, clean shaven.

Going on past the old Indian scout, Abe now had a clear view of four people, whom he clearly felt their love for him. It was Jack and Hannah Armstrong with their two sons, little Duff and Pleasant.

Grabbing Abe's arm, Jack pulled him close, whispering, "I'm gonna be miss'n you. Things won't be the same around here without you. I feel like I'm losing a brother."

Abe could see the emotion in Jack's face and sought to reassure him, "I'll always be your brother no matter where I'm at."

Hannah took Abe's other hand, letting him know once again, "You'll always be a part of our family, Abe. We're so very proud of you, and what you've become. I know a lot more than most, how hard you've worked to become the man you are."

"Hannah, just you saying it means more to me than all the praise from all those rich folks in Springfield."

"Uncle Abe, Uncle Abe," interrupted Pleasant and little Duff. "We're down here, look at us. We love you too."

Getting down on one knee, Abe responded, hugging them, "How's my two favorite nephews?"

After getting back to his feet, Judge and Mrs. Green came up alongside of him. In his booming voice, the Judge announced, "I know all of you wish my boy, Abe, a fond farewell as he journeys to Springfield and a new life. He's truly a man among men, worthy of our love and support."

"Wait, please wait," Abe protested with visible emotion filling him. "Before you finish Judge, there are a few more words I'd like to say, something very important."

"Go right ahead, my boy. You have the floor."

"Thank you, Judge. You see, a time like this can't pass without me expressing how I feel. I want to tell you–all of you–you're the most special people on earth. When I came here six years ago I was a friendless youth, poor and with little education. You welcomed me into your homes. All of you made me part of your lives. But above all, you gave me your love. In turn, I want you all to know I love all of you. For as long as I live, you are my family. No matter where I go, all of you will always be in my heart."

After Abe spoke, a lot of emotion and honest feeling spread throughout the room. Judge Green expressed encompassing sentiments, "Abe, I think I speak for everyone here when I say you will be in all of our prayers, always."

Everyone in the room had been deeply moved by Abe's heartfelt words. They all gathered around him, hugging him affectionately. As he embraced each one of them, they all felt his love in return. It became part of a day that no one who was there would ever forget.

A short time later, as Abe rode Diamond back to New Salem, his heart overflowed with deep feelings for all those he came in contact with that day. In his mind, he would always know them as his family.

The morning of the next day, Saturday April 15th, 1837, Abe got up and took a look around the interior of the old Berry-Lincoln store for the last time. So much had happened there: when it later became the post office, and he told Ann he loved her for the first time. These were thoughts and memories he would cherish always. The time had finally come for him to leave this place. Packing up his saddle bags, filling them with his few law books, his late mother's Bible, and even fewer clothes he owned, he began thinking of what was ahead of him.

Feeling more positive, he went out to the barn behind the Inn and saddled up Diamond, preparing to leave. Rather than ride, he walked Diamond a little ways down Main Street to the turn onto the Springfield Road. As he made the turn, he saw a man in the distance, approaching on foot from the south. Though Abe couldn't make out who it was, the man waved at him as he got closer.

The mystery would soon be solved. As Abe started walking toward him, the man called out to him, "Abe, Abe!" The voice was familiar.

After a moment, as he came up, Abe recognized him, "Why Billy Greene, I wondered where you were when I went out to the Judge's place yesterday."

"I had to work all day on my dad's farm down Rock Creek way. But, I wanted to see you before you left town." Extending his hand, they shook hands warmly. Billy was positive in his words, "I'm real proud of you. I just know you'll be a success in Springfield. You must be happy about it."

Abe was more truthful about his feelings, "I don't think 'happy' is quite the word I would use. I'm grateful for the opportunity, but being happy is far from my true feelings. Inside, not a day passes I don't feel like the saddest man alive. Since the day of Ann's death, that is the real truth."

"I know it, Abe. I'm sorry, I was just trying to make you feel good."

"If I could even just see Ann one more time, maybe I might feel good."

"Who knows, maybe the good Lord will let you see her one more time." Honest and sincere, Billy's face was full of hope as he said those words.

Totally focused on him, Abe could see a well-meaning soul. "Billy, you're a good friend. You always will be."

Tears formed in Billy's eyes as his feelings found words. "I'm never going to forget you. Ever since we clerked together in that little Offutt store six years ago, you've always been so much more than a friend to me. Seeing you accomplish so much in spite of all Fate has thrown against you has inspired me. I'm going back to college in the fall and try to make something of myself."

"You will make something of yourself. Don't ask me how I know it, I just know it."

"Thanks, Abe. But back to you and your future, I hate saying goodbye."

"This isn't goodbye. Our paths will cross again somewhere down the line in our lives. After all, brothers never say goodbye."

With that, they shook hands and hugged each other like two men who really were brothers. Then, visibly sad, Billy Greene silently turned and walked on toward New Salem.

Abe turned southward and took a few more steps till he reached a point in the uneven path of the Springfield Road that was somewhat up on the high ground. Standing there for a long moment, a million lingering thoughts flowed through his mind.

It was then he felt a familiar presence all around him. Turning around, his view from this vantage point took in the whole of New Salem. For one brief instant of time, for a few flickering seconds, he thought he saw the spirit image of Ann staring after him. If she was there, he whispered, "I love you, Ann." Frozen in his tracks, the image barely had time to register to his mind before it vanished. In that moment, a great eternal truth came to him: No one ever truly dies as long as we keep them alive in our minds.

Abe had evolved and matured during his six years of life experience in this little village. He had been through a time that had tested him to the very core of his heart and soul. As he mounted Diamond, he glanced back at New Salem for a final time. Taking a deep breath, realizing a part of his life was gone forever, he nudged Diamond toward Springfield and the rest of his life.

CHAPTER 21
BEYOND NEW SALEM, A BRIEF HISTORY

Arriving in Springfield the next day, a new chapter of Abe's life would begin. It would see him looking up his friend from the Black Hawk War, former Major John Stuart, going into partnership with him in his law firm, just around the corner from the courthouse.

His new home was in striking contrast to New Salem. Even though it was only twenty miles south of the dying frontier settlement, it was bigger and larger in every way. With its multiple story buildings, Springfield had an official population of over 700 citizens in comparison to New Salem's dwindling fifty or sixty backwoods frontier folks. It would take a little getting used to some of the more sophisticated ways of people here, but Abe felt up to the challenge. It was going to be an 'experiment' as he put it.

The tall, lanky Abe Lincoln stood out in so many ways. Even the most casual contact with Abe left one feeling there was something different about him, that could not immediately be defined. This was so, because the difference was inside him, not visible to the human eye.

The Spirit of the Lord was inside him, lifting him up into becoming a more spiritual person. Inside, he was much more complicated than he appeared on the surface. He was becoming more comfortable with Doctor Allen's belief: he accepted that God did indeed have a higher calling in store for him. He wanted to play an active part in producing positive change in the world around him. In his heart, he had hungered for this opportunity. With each day's passing he was finding his own spiritual compass and becoming the man he would be the rest of his life.

Even though Abe was a citizen of Springfield now, memories of New Salem had worked their way into the fabric of his mind. Emotions ran deep, embedding feelings within him that he never lost or forgot. Certain cases in his law practice would occasionally take him back to those areas. The past and its attachments would never quite let go of him.

In the spring of 1838 while Abe was on one such trip, news reached him that the little son of his old friend and teacher, Mentor Graham, had taken gravely ill. He immediately put everything on hold and rode out to the great brick home he hadn't seen in many months.

Arriving there late one Monday evening, he went straight away to little Septimus' bedroom upstairs. Immediately, the love Abe possessed for little children came to the surface. Hearing the stories of animals out in the woods and seeing his Uncle Abe imitate them, brought brief but labored smiles to his face. Going without eating, he never left the boy's side for the next three days, that is until little Septimus passed away on Thursday evening.

When Sarah Rafferty Graham could take no more and retired to the kitchen, Abe followed her. Turning around she went into his arms and cried uncontrollably. He helped her to a chair, comforting her with words they both understood. "Sarah, losing someone you love is the hardest thing in all the world. But be comforted that you will have the memory of that little boy in your heart all the rest of your life."

Abe stayed with her until he felt he could leave her alone. Going back upstairs, he found Mentor still sitting by his son's lifeless body, praying for him.

Becoming aware of Abe's presence, Mentor looked up at him feeling more heartbreak than he'd ever felt. "He was my only son."

Abe told him what he believed, "His little soul has gone home to the Lord."

Both men looked into each other's faces and saw the same feelings mirrored there. Tears were in their eyes, as both men were crying. Abe struggled with the words as he spoke, "I loved that little boy too. After all, I was his Uncle Abe."

Mentor felt a complete sense of loss in that moment. He could barely think, asking, "Abe, what am I going to do?"

"You're going to go downstairs and comfort Sarah. She needs you more than ever right now."

Mentor nodded that he would, but then his face filled with grief again as he glanced over at Septimus.

"Don't worry my brother," Abe reassured him, "I'll stay with your boy, but there's something you should know."

"What's that, Abe?"

"I want you to keep remembering, your son is already with the angels in Heaven, even now as we speak."

Abe's words strengthening him, Mentor went downstairs to comfort Sarah, repeating them to her.

The next day, Abe helped Mentor construct a small coffin for Septimus. While Mentor helped Sarah clean and dress the little boy in his best clothes, Abe went out back and dug the grave beside the resting place of the other baby the Grahams had lost years before.

Before sunset, as Sarah looked on, Abe helped Mentor gently lower the little casket into its final resting place. All three wept greatly as they clung together, praying over the grave.

It was later on that night, Abe prepared to ride on over to Judge Green's place. Mentor followed Abe out to the barn and watched as he saddled up Diamond.

As Abe started to mount, Mentor spoke up, "I love you, my brother. I couldn't have made it these last few days without you."

Abe tried to get past the lump in his throat, but couldn't. Dropping the reins right there, he turned and folded his long arms around Mentor in an emotional embrace. Without saying a word, the deepest of heartfelt feelings were expressed between the two men.

Then Abe swung up in the saddle, riding off into the night. Before reaching the Judge's farm, Abe had whispered a silent prayer for both Mentor and Sarah. Brooding, he went off into silent thought as death had once more scarred this deeply feeling man.

Years later, Mentor Graham wrote of the week he lost Septimus. When asked about young Lincoln's character back then, he answered, "Abe was kind and always honest, but even more so, down deep in his heart, he was the most open–souled man I ever met. A pure and good man, that is how I'll always remember him."

Forcing his mind back onto all things legal and political, Abe's star continued to rise in these arenas. As the summer of 1838 approached, he decided to run for the legislature again. On August 6th he won for the third time.

Not only in Abe's life, but other people's lives, change was happening just as fast. In less than two years, 1839 through 1840, the whole town of New Salem would die. Doctor Allen and Billy Greene were among many who would move the short distance over to the new little town of Petersburg. Passing through, Abe took note of the ghost town and thought, New Salem would be forever frozen in his mind just as it was during the time he lived there. "It's funny how the mind remembers things," he would often say, "but those six years were the happiest days of my life."

Petersburg was the new county seat and all who lived in the area looked to it as the place to put down roots. During his years in New Salem, Doctor Allen had become a part time merchant of sorts. He had acquired over a thousand hogs in lieu of payment for his medical services. After selling the whole lot in the hog market, he suddenly found himself with a considerable profit. Never wavering from the devout religious man who had helped Abe, Doctor Allen married and moved to Petersburg, where he gave most of the money he made to the church. In 1839 he founded the Central Presbyterian Church of Petersburg which still exists to this day.

When asked, he said, "This is the task our Lord has set out for me to do."

From 1840 through the end of his life, Doctor Allen remained in Petersburg. Shortly before passing away, in 1863, he was heard to have said, "From 1835 on, I have remained a friend and supporter of Abe Lincoln. I have said many prayers for him through the years. God is with him, I know it to be so."

On his deathbed, he was heard by some to have said, "I can pass into the Good Lord's hands now, knowing the answer as to why I came to Illinois."

Someone asked, "Why was that?"

"So I could meet the finest man I've ever known and help him find his way back to God. I can die peacefully knowing a man of the Lord is in the White House."

Abe's reputation as a lawyer continued to grow in 1839, when on December 3rd, he was recognized to practice his profession in the United States Supreme Court. With this, awareness of him as an eligible bachelor spread among the ladies of Springfield. Among those taking an interest in Abe was Mary Todd of the aristocratic Todd family of Springfield. Ten years younger than Abe, she quickly became infatuated, even obsessed with him.

Abe eventually became engaged to Mary at some point in 1840. Almost from the beginning he wrestled with his feelings. Try as he might, he could never quite love her the same as Ann. Nothing could ever erase the intensity of Ann's memory in his mind. At length though, Mary's possessive and domineering ways became too much for him and he broke off the engagement on January 1st, 1841. As he left, she yelled at him, "Alright, go! Go and never come back!"

Throughout the rest of 1841, Abe was trying to find himself again. Nothing seemed quite right. As John Stuart was a cousin of Mary Todd, this breakup caused friction between the two law partners. Two things increasingly bothered Stuart. First, he never thought Abe was the right match for his aristocratic cousin. Secondly, as he came to know Abe better, Stuart confided to close friends he thought Lincoln was a little crazy for saying he had visions of dead people. This all led to their partnership being dissolved. Seeking out advice, Abe eventually traveled the road that led back to Judge Green.

It was in mid-February 1842, when Abe received the heart-breaking news: Judge and Mrs. Green had just entered the home of a friend for a visit when the Judge collapsed from perhaps a massive heart attack or stroke. Dying instantly, he was only 56 years old when he passed away on February 13th. Abe was actually on his way there, when a rider met him on the road with a message to come with all haste to meet Aunt Nancy at the farm.

A masonic funeral was quickly arranged, with Abe asked to give the eulogy. Abe had been profoundly shaken by the Judge's passing. So when it came time for him to speak, his voice was filled with emotion, "Judge Green was much more than a good man to me. He had become the only real father I've ever known. He introduced me to the law and set me on the path I'm now on. Beyond our relationship, he went out of his way to be fair and just to every person he ever knew. I think it is fair to say, no one could ever replace him. I, for one, will miss him forever." Unable to speak further, he sat back down, grieving visibly.

Later, Abe took Nancy Potter Green, the Judge's widow back to the farm in his buggy. Once there, they both grieved heavily together. Aunt Nancy told Abe, "The Judge was so very proud of you, loving you like a son." She hesitated and added, "No, not like a son, *you were* his son as far as he was concerned."

The Judge's death was a powerful blow to Abe. He became depressed and descended into an emotional turmoil for months. Just when he was beginning to recover he received an urgent knock at his door in Springfield. It was John Rutledge, one of Ann's brothers who had served with him in the Black Hawk War. John urged Abe to come with him at once.

Arriving in Petersburg on June 6th 1842, Abe was taken to the sick bed of Ann's favorite brother, David Rutledge. He had become severely ill with the same typhoid fever that killed Ann and their father seven years before. Abe sat with David all night, during which he reassured him, "I'll always love you as my brother."

"Abe, you meant the whole world to Ann and you mean the whole world to me."

Abe held his hand, never leaving his side all night. Just as the sun came up, David looked up and whispered, "Annie must've wanted her brother to come and be with her. If I do go, Abe promise me that my body will be buried beside her."

"David, I promise that, with all my heart. I'll see to it myself."

David smiled and closed his eyes forever. The young promising Petersburg attorney, David Rutledge was only 26 years old when he died the morning of June 7th 1842. True to his word, Abe saw to it that David was buried next to Ann.

Standing there in the Old Concord cemetery, Abe joined Jack Armstrong and Billy Greene at the foot of the new Rutledge grave. The three old friends talked, shared tears together and bared their souls to each other.

"David was a fine young man with a great future ahead of him," said Abe, as he reminisced about him. "He was far too young to die. He always wanted me to be his law partner. Sadly, that will never be."

Billy added, "I think we might all go mad if we think too much about the things that will never be."

Jack motioned to something behind them and asked, "Why don't we all sit down over there?"

Looking over in that direction, Abe immediately noticed something: The old dead tree that he'd once slumped up against was gone. In its place a new very sturdy wooden bench had been erected, positioned so that it faced toward all the graves nearby. Surprised, Abe asked, "How'd this get here?"

Jack and Billy both smiled as Jack explained, "We came out here, removed that old tree, and built this bench so folks would have a place to sit when they visited the graves of their loved ones."

Abe was quite moved. "I'm thanking you both, with all my heart for doing this. The three of us, we truly are bothers."

Sitting down on the bench between the two of them, Abe stared straight ahead. His steady gaze remained locked on Ann's grave for a long moment. Then slowly, and quite beyond his control, a wave of sadness gripped him. Shaking his head at first, trying to deny it, he found he could not escape the grief that was creeping up on him. Even though he put a hand over his eyes trying to cover them, a stream of tears flowed through his fingers.

Abe tried to apologize, "I'm sorry, but I can't help it. Even though its been seven years since she passed away, I still love her with all my heart. I know I always will. No matter where I'm at, just thinking of her brings it all back. Her name will always be sacred to me."

As the three men left Old Concord and Abe bid them farewell, Jack and Billy both noticed the dominant expression of sadness embedded into his face. For the rest of his life it never quite left him.

Abe had sunk back into a state of depression, but ten days later something happened to give him a glimmer of hope. Having received a letter summoning him to Mentor Graham's home, he arrived from Springfield on June 21st to be greatly surprised. Upon entering, he immediately heard a strange noise. Mentor led him into the living room where he came face to face with Sarah, sitting on the sofa, holding an infant baby boy.

Abe was astounded, "I can't believe it!"

Sarah assumed the obvious, "You thought, after losing little Septimus we would give up trying to have any more children."

"I'm ashamed to say it, but I did think you and Mentor would give up trying."

"We wondered after losing five children," Sarah conceded, "perhaps it was God's will that we not try. But we prayed on it, and then it suddenly came to us, there's always hope. I promised Mentor a large family and I prayed that God would let me fulfill that promise."

"Then the Lord answered your prayers," concluded Abe.

"We think so," agreed Mentor. "Abe, just look at him, black hair and sparkling hazel eyes, just like Sarah's father. But there's one problem. We don't have a name for him yet."

"That's easily settled, name him after somebody you admire, someone famous," suggested Abe.

Mentor and Sarah gave each other a knowing glance, then Sarah spoke up. "Abe, if we do that, we need your permission."

"My permission?"

"Abe," Mentor revealed, "we want to name him after you and we want you to be his godfather."

"But why me? I'm a nobody whose probably not ever going to amount to anything."

"Hush your mouth, Abe Lincoln!" Sarah chastised him. "If your Ann heard that, as much high regard as she held you in, she would be deeply hurt. You ought to be ashamed."

Hearing Sarah's withering criticism was all he could take. "I'm sorry. I'm sorry. I apologize. I can't fight both you and what Ann might think. Of course, I'm mighty pleased you would consider naming your son after me. You have my permission. I'll try to be the best godfather any little fellow ever had. But of course, you know what this will mean."

Mentor asked, "What, Abe?"

"This means I'm gonna have to go out and work extra hard so this boy will be proud of me."

"You should know something," Sarah told him. "We're already proud of you, more than you'll ever know."

"I'm deeply honored to hear you say that. One more thing though, what exactly is the little fellow's name gonna be?"

"The most wonderful name any boy or man could ever have," revealed Sarah. "His name is going to be Lincoln Graham."

So it was, as the years passed, Abe became very proud of his godson. As the Lord sometimes has His hand in these matters, Lincoln Graham lived a long life, well into the next century. In the fullness of time, God granted Sarah's prayer as she gave birth to nine more children who reached adulthood.

Abe returned to Springfield, his depression lifted. His outlook on life was evolving, that perhaps–even with disappointments–he could serve a useful purpose in the world. What Sarah Graham had said stayed with him, *there's always hope*.

Though initially he had no intention or desire to reconcile with Mary Todd, Abe did see her occasionally, attending some of the same parties and functions she did. But he held back making contact because he was quite aware of her negative traits. She was full of unreasoned jealousy, wild imaginings, and even beginning to show signs of possible mental problems.

Still though, remembering there is always hope, Abe decided to confront her at one fateful gathering in July 1842. He calmed her immediately by asking, "Can't we be friends?"

That opened the door and they started seeing each other again. Though her sister, father, and other friends were quite clear in their opinion: Abe was not a good match for Mary's rich and lavish lifestyle, she ignored them.

For one major reason, she put aside all others objections to Abe. She had become obsessed with him again. Into her twenties already, when most girls were married by seventeen or eighteen in her era, she became full of unreasoned fears she might become an old maid. To avoid that at all costs, she set out to entrap herself a husband.

Knowing that Abe did not drink, she urged him to take her to parties where liquor was served. At one such party she got him to drink repeated glasses of the punch that had been spiked with generous amounts of alcohol, quite unknown to him.

Poor Abe never knew what hit him. Mary Todd was in the process of springing her trap. After the party, instead of taking her home, the couple stopped off at his lodgings until quite late. After Abe had passed out, she summoned a mutual friend to take her home in his carriage. Abe awoke the next morning with no memory of the details of the night before. At this point he had no clue concerning Mary's devious plan. Many people in the know at the time asserted this is what really happened.

Later, Abe arrived at his law office, on November 3rd, 1842, only to find a sealed letter addressed to him, laying atop his desk. Opening it immediately, he was shocked at the contents. In it, Mary had written, 'Due to your actions of last night, my honor is now at stake. You must behave as a proper gentleman and marry me at once. To do otherwise could put your reputation as a promising attorney in serious doubt.'

Many who read this letter later, including members of the Todd family, attested to its validity. It was said that it was either burned by Abe's eldest son, Robert Todd Lincoln, or it was included in the Lincoln papers to be made public in 2026, a hundred years after Robert Lincoln's death.

Abe's movements for the rest of November 3rd are well documented. Rising from his desk, he was overheard saying, "I shall have to marry that girl." Walking out the door, he proceeded on foot to Chatterton's jewelry shop, located on the west side of Springfield's town square. While there, he purchased a gold wedding ring, ordering it to be engraved with the inscription, 'love is eternal.' He may have been thinking of Ann in that moment, for this phrase is one that he had used quite often in describing his feelings for his lost love.

On the morning of the next day, November 4th, as Abe was preparing to leave his place of lodging, his landlord's son noticed his dire facial expression, almost one of great physical pain and turmoil. Concerned, he asked, "Abe, where are you going?"

Abe glanced over at him, his expression changing into one resigned to a horrible fate or like a lamb being led to the slaughter. He repeated the young man's question, "Where am I going?" Then he answered, "To hell, I suppose!"

Later, that rain-soaked afternoon, Abe married Mary Todd in the parlor of her sister's home. There were thirty guests present. Mary's father and step-mother did not attend. Conversation and dinner followed the wedding.

After festivities concluded, a coach arrived to take the couple to their new residence, an 8 by 14 foot one-room apartment on the second floor of the Globe Tavern. It was smallish living quarters, with the couple eating meals in the Tavern's dining room downstairs. Total cost of rent and meals was four dollars per week.

It was at the Globe Tavern that their first son, Robert Lincoln, was born on August 1st of the following year, about nine months to the day. Photographs reveal that Robert had dominant Todd family genes, only vaguely resembling Abe around the eyes.

The following year, 1844, brought not only a new law partner, but a new lasting friendship into Abe's life, in the person of William 'Billy' Herndon. From a commoner background, who had worked long and hard to become a lawyer, he and Abe held similar beliefs, both personal and political.

Needless to say, Billy Herndon's personality did not gel well with Mary Todd. Later on in life, their disagreements led to much friction and a very public feud.

Abe's second son, Edward–or Eddie as he called him, was much closer in resembling his father. Eddie, who was born on March 10th 1846, was thin like his father. But the youngster was weak and sickly from the beginning, passing away before his fourth birthday on February 1st 1850.

The next eleven months was a period of emotional turmoil for Abe. First death, then life, and death again came into his life. As if to comfort Abe and Mary for the loss of Eddie, another son was born to them on December 21st 1850. This time, Abe named the boy, William Wallace Lincoln. Honoring his friend, Mentor Graham and his heritage, the child was named after the great Scottish hero. A warm and affectionate child, 'Willie' as Abe called him, had a personality very much like his father. Thinking of both sons, Willie and Eddie, upon Willie's birth, Abe was heard to have whispered, "Just as the Lord taketh away, He giveth also. Blessed be the name of the Lord."

During December 1850, another Lincoln became seriously ill. This time Abe had little sympathy. The person ill was the man who sired him, Thomas Lincoln. Through all the harassment and abuse during his youth, Abe had said nothing. But a permanent estrangement between father and son came to be, something that would last forever.

Thomas Lincoln was quite alone now, except for Abe's stepmother, Sarah Bush Lincoln. Disappointments and setbacks in life had permanently embittered him. Except for contact with Dennis

Hanks and the family of his first wife, he would have no knowledge of his son. Now though, hearing that the son he had called worthless, had made a name for himself as a prominent lawyer in Springfield, Thomas Lincoln decided to try and make contact with Abe. It was too late though.

Sarah explained to her husband, "I told you then, you would regret it one day the way you treated that boy. He needed you. He needed a father's love and encouragement, and you turned a cold shoulder to him. Why should he come and see you now?"

Thomas Lincoln persisted and talked to Dennis Hanks, "I'm deathly ill, please speak to Abe. I want to see my son and talk to him before I die."

Dennis Hanks dutifully contacted Abe at least three times about his father's declining health and his desire to see his son. Hanks finally said, "I believe it's just a matter of time and he shall die."

Hearing this, Abe replied, "Then he should look to the Lord for forgiveness and guidance. As far as me coming to see him, it would serve no purpose. Even if we did meet now, such a meeting would probably be more painful than pleasant."

The mental and physical scars this man had inflicted on Abe ran deep. He now saw Thomas Lincoln clearly for who and what he was: An alcoholic full of frustrations who had become a prisoner within his own illiterate self.

Abe briefly considered the old man's pleas. Thinking about it, in his mind this was still the man who turned his back on him when he was a boy. To him, the only man who ever treated him like a son had passed away eight years ago, in 1842. Rightly or wrongly, Abe made up his mind. He would not go see him.

Thomas Lincoln's health continued to spiral downward and he passed unto death on January 17th, 1851, dying alone in bed. The sin of what he had done to his son was repaid to him. Abe did not go to the funeral and only saw the grave ten years later when he visited his step-mother in Coles County, Illinois.

Throughout the early 1850's, dramatic changes were seen in the fortunes of three men who survived New Salem. John McNamar, thought to be the richest man in the area, was hit hard by poor investments. Those that he had once turned a cold, unsympathetic shoulder to, now did so to him. Losing his property on Sand Ridge, he reached a low point, when for about eight years he went wondering about Petersburg, begging and living on the charity of others. Eventually though he managed to claw out of the hole he found himself in, marry and have children. In his final years, his life consisted of a hermit-like existence on a small farm near Petersburg.

On the other hand, Abe's reputation steadily grew through a series of both legal and political triumphs. He bought a home, that still stands to this day, and was elected to the town board in Springfield. From 1856 on he began serving as a judge, presiding over Sangamon County Circuit Court. Over several years he acted as a judge in four separate counties in Illinois. By 1859, he presided over 34 cases in Logan County alone. At the time he got teary-eyed, remarking to friends who knew him, "In accepting this position, it sort of brings me full circle. I do so to honor the man who was the best example of what a judge should be. I hope Judge Green will be proud of me." For a while, it looked like he might become a judge full time, but events taking place in the world and the hand of Fate would deem otherwise.

The third man who rose above New Salem was Abe's close friend. Billy Greene went back to school, got a college education, then took over his late father's farm. He did well and invested the profits wisely. Acquiring land, more than one bank, he became a stock holder and then owner of one of the big railroads. Other business opportunities came his way, including ownership of gold and silver mines, and coal mines as well. A shrewd investor, he became one of the wealthiest men in Illinois. Through all of the years that passed, beyond New Salem, he remained one of Abe's closest friends and supporters.

It was during the late summer of 1857 that 'the sickness' returned to the New Salem-Petersburg area, striking down one of Abe's best friends. Jack Armstrong was lying on his deathbed, barely clinging to life. As Hannah listened, in his last hours he reminisced about

Abe, "I set out to give Abe a whipping and teach him a lesson the day I first met him. Instead he taught me a lesson for life, how to live it and be a better man to you and the boys. When you see Abe, tell him his brother Jack still loves him. Something else, I remember how much Ann and Abe were in love with each other. I saw how it broke his heart when she died, and he couldn't bare her being out in that cemetery by herself. Well I've been think'n, I want to be buried at Old Concord so my soul can help watch over Miss Ann till we all meet again one day in the hereafter."

About twelve days before, their son Duff had been arrested, accused of killing a man. As he lay dying, Jack urged Hannah, "If you have to sell everything we own to get our boy free, do it. I just know in my heart he's innocent. He couldn't have done such a thing. Hannah, I want you to go to Springfield, look up Abe and see if he can do anything to help Duff."

Jack died on September 9th 1857. He was only 54 years old at the time. Hannah saw to it that he was buried in Concord Cemetery near Ann. In this way he kept his word that beyond death he would find a way to look after Ann. After doing this, she did as he had asked and made the journey to Springfield to see Abe.

It was about a week after Jack's death that Hannah walked through the doors of the Lincoln-Herndon law offices in Springfield. At first, Abe didn't recognize her. He had been only 28 when he left New Salem. Now he was 48 years old. She had been beat down and dramatically aged by the last twenty years of rough frontier life. But when she spoke, her voice struck a familiar chord in his memory, "Abe, I need your help. Jack asked me to come and see you."

Momentarily, in his mind he had a brief vision of the lovely, young Hannah of twenty years ago. Then anxiety invaded that image and he asked, "Where's Jack?"

"Jack's dead. He caught 'the sickness' like your Ann did, and it took him a week ago."

"Oh no, my God no! I've lost a brother."

After ushering Hannah into his private office, she continued, "Jack wanted me to tell you something he always wanted you to know. As Ann lay dying, he prayed many times that the Lord would spare her. He often told me he wished to God he could have done something to save her, but now he wanted to be buried near her so that maybe somehow his spirit could watch after her for you."

"Bless his heart. Hannah, I loved Jack. I want you to know that."

"Yes, we both loved him."

By now they were both crying. One on one, they comforted each other.

At length, Hannah got hold of herself and explained why she had come to see him. "Now with Jack gone, I don't know what to do. Duff's got himself into a heap of trouble. He's been accused of murder and they're want'n to hang him. God as my witness, he's innocent. Please, Abe, can you do something?"

"Hannah, I'll take the case and represent him in court."

"But they say they'll hang him."

"No they're not. I won't let them."

Abe had turned into a tower of strength. In that moment, he remembered something Ann had told him, *You will touch many people's lives and lift them up in their hour of desperation.* He concluded, "Hannah, just as Ann was my angel in those dark days of my youth, you were my other angel who sewed my clothes and kept me fed. Now, let me be your angel and save my nephew, your son Duff."

The trial of Duff Armstrong for the murder of Preston Metzger was held in the second floor courtroom of city hall in Beardstown on May 7th, 1858. Traveling to the old red brick, two-story building on West Third Street, Abe thought how he was here more than 25 years ago as a captain of militia during the Black Hawk War. Now though, he was here to fight for the life of the son of an old friend.

By 1858, Abe was an attorney with a reputation as a formidable opponent. Having recently settled a case involving a major railroad in which he received a $5,000.00 fee, many wondered how this simple farm woman could hire this big time, Springfield attorney to represent her son. Over the course of the trial they would find out the answer to this question.

Abe entered the packed courtroom wearing an all-white business suit. His appearance drew everyone's attention as he questioned the prosecution's key witness, Charles Allen, "Mr. Allen, once more, could you tell us exactly what you saw?"

"I saw your client, Duff Armstrong, kill my friend, 'Press.' He hit him from behind with something. It was cold-blooded murder."

"By 'Press,' you mean the late Preston Metzger?"

"Yes, my friend, Preston Metzger. He was only twenty-eight, too young to die."

"You say you clearly saw my client strike him from behind?"

"Yes, I clearly saw him do it."

"Mr. Allen, what time of day was it?"

"It was 11 o'clock at night."

"Then you must have been pretty close to have seen what happened. Just how close were you?"

At this point, Charles Allen moved about uncomfortably in the witness chair before answering. "To the best of my recollection, I was about 150 feet away."

"Then, how could you have clearly seen what happened?"

"Because I could clearly see by the light of the full moon. It was directly overhead that night."

"Oh, I see," responded Abe, visible doubt crossing his face. Returning to the defense table, he retrieved a small booklet. Turning to Judge James Harriott, presiding over the trial, "Your Honor, I would like to submit into evidence a copy of *Jayne's Almanac* for 1857, covering August 29th, the night of the murder." It stated the moon at 11 PM that night was nearly moonset; meaning it was on the edge of the horizon, not overhead in the sky as the witness had stated. In fact, the area where the fatal fight took place was so thickly surrounded by trees, it would have been impossible for the witness to have seen anything from 150 feet away.

Later, Abe presented another copy of the almanac to Milton Logan, the jury foreman, who passed it along to the other jurors. This would prove to be a significant move in Abe's case for Duff's innocence.

In his defense summation, Abe walked slowly along, speaking to each individual juror. His voice was emotional, heartfelt, and above all genuine as he told the story of Jack and Hannah Armstrong, and their sons. In doing so, he laid his soul bare as he never had before in public. He said if it hadn't been for Jack's friendship that he would have starved to death. You see, a certain 'angel' woman in his house fed him and kept him adequately clothed, sewing up his ripped and torn clothes to keep them from falling off. He said, "That 'angel' woman is here in the courtroom today." Turning, and pointing directly at her, he continued, "She is Hannah Armstrong, mother of the accused. She was part of the turning point in my life, from being a nobody to becoming a person of worth. No more decent mother or finer woman has ever walked the earth." At that moment, tears were visible in both Abe and Hannah's eyes.

Focusing on the jury again, Abe told of how Jack and Hannah had been God-fearing parents to their boys and how he had personally rocked them to sleep at night. "Never was there a better picture of goodness and innocence in young boys," he said. "This boy, the accused, was raised right and is surely innocent of the crime. The facts prove it." By the end of his fifteen minute summation to the jury, there was not a dry eye in the courtroom. The jury and everyone there had been captivated and enthralled by his words.

One eye witness in the courtroom later remarked, "I've never seen an attorney exhibit such mastery and control over the emotions and feelings of a jury. Without exception, they all sat riveted, completely caught up in the power of Mr. Lincoln's every word."

After a brief recess, the jury came back, after deliberating and only one ballot taken, with a not guilty verdict. Upon hearing the acquittal, Abe reacting with a rare smile upon his face, turned to Duff at the defense table. The two men warmly shook hands.

Abe said, "You're a free man, Duff. Go home and live a good life."

"I owe you my life, Uncle Abe. From this day forward it belongs to you."

Looking around, Abe asked, "Where's your mother?"

"She stepped out the back door of the courthouse. She said she didn't want to hear the verdict, that if it was not guilty, have someone come and get her."

"I'll get her," replied Abe, as he went out the back door, looking for her.

Abe found Hannah in an open pasture area behind the courthouse. Walking up to her, taking her shaking hand into his, he said, "Hannah, you can take your boy home. He's free."

Shaking all over, tears rolled down her face. She managed to say, as she cried through the words, "Oh Lord! Abe, I love you for this. Words are not adequate. I know you get huge sums of money as an attorney. I'm happy to deed over our farm as payment."

"Hannah Armstrong, in your whole life you know me better than that. If I took your farm, I couldn't live with myself. I shant take a cent!" Abe took Hannah into his arms, adding "After all, we're family."

Later, as he left the courthouse, a young photographer, Abram Byers, spotted him, "Mr. Lincoln, would you mind posing for a photograph in my studio? It's close by, over on Monroe Street."

"Not at all, young man. In fact I'd be delighted."

The resulting full-face photo, the only one of Abe in a white suit, became his personal favorite up to that time in his life. His face truly reflected a man at peace after the emotional strain of what would be called the famous 'Almanac Trial.'

The next morning, Abe left his Beardstown hotel room for the return trip to Springfield. Deviating slightly, he stopped off to visit Concord Cemetery. Finding Jack's grave, he prayed first. Then, with tears in his eyes, he spoke softly to him, "My dear old friend, my brother, your son is a free man. I know now why you took that knife from me so many years ago. The Lord wanted me here to save little Duff. As you gave me a second chance at life, I set out to help Duff have a second chance at life. Oh how much I wish you were here now. Perhaps one day in the hereafter we'll see each other again."

Back in Springfield, when they were alone, Abe had a conversation with his law partner, Billy Herndon. Coming back from the 'Almanac Trial,' several friends from the New Salem area had recently come through the doors of their law offices. Over hearing various conversations finally got to Herndon's curiosity. Having become close personal friends, he felt like he could approach his now famous law partner with some intimate questions behind closed doors. He asked, "Abe, what about your past?"

"Billy, ever so often it's good to talk about the stories that have shaped our lives. We can't go back, but we can remember them in our mind's eye."

"I've heard a name mentioned frequently by the old timers that have come here to visit you. Her name was Ann Rutledge. That Armstrong woman spoke of her several times when she came here to visit you. Was there such a person? Is it true, did you know her?"

"Yes, it's true indeed. She was my first love, a handsome, beautiful girl. She would've made a good and loving wife. Sadly, though it was not to be. If she had lived, we would've married. It's been 23 years since her death, and I still think of her quite often. Even with all that has happened, I can't get her out of my head, especially now."

"It sounds like Ann Rutledge was a very special person to you."

"She WAS my life, once. The name of Rutledge is sacred to me. After all these years, I still keep track of her family, and friends as well. If any of them were in need–for anything–I would be there to help them."

"Abe, that's what I've always liked about you. If someone is a friend, they're a friend for life."

"I guess that's an essential part of what makes me the man I am. It works similar with something else."

"Yes?"

"It's a funny thing about love, at least how it works for me."

"How has it worked for you?"

"Once I've loved, that emotion and all the feelings attached to that emotion stay with me forever."

"If others knew, some might say you've loved too much."

"Perhaps, but I can't help being who I am."

"Abe, it strikes me we've been friends and partners for fourteen years now. In that time I've learned quite a bit about you."

"You know more than most. I'll tell you what, Billy, if I ever become famous, I want you to be the one to write a book about me."

"I'd be honored to, my friend."

"Just in case that were to happen, I'm gonna write up a list of names, people you can go to for the real truth about me."

"What kind of book would you want me to write?"

"One that is true, with no legends or lies."

As it turned out, one day William Herndon did write that book, one much to the hostile feelings of the Todd family and their friends. It was a book that told the truth about Ann Rutledge and brought her out of the shadows of a forgotten past.

As time passed, and the summer of 1860 approached, Abe was drawn irrevocably by the hand of Fate into the Presidential race, receiving the Republican Party's nomination for president on the third ballot. In the November 6th election he defeated his old political opponent, Stephen Douglas, once his rival for the hand of Mary Todd, becoming the first Republican president of the United States.

Abe never forgot his friends, those that helped make him the man he was. Once more, he made the journey to the old two-story brick home that stood west of New Salem. Entering through the doorway, he warmly embraced Mentor and Sarah Graham, as well as his godson, Lincoln Graham. Mentor was emotional, "It was the proudest day of my life to see you, my brother, elected president."

"Mentor, you always believed in me. I've never forgotten that. I want all of you to come to Washington and be there when I'm sworn in."

Sarah's health was not good then and eighteen-year-old Lincoln Graham was needed to stay and help run their farm. But Sarah told Mentor, "I want you to go. Abe wants you to be there. He needs you there." Listening to his wife, Mentor Graham traveled with the Lincoln family on the same train that took them to Washington.

Before going outside to the inauguration, Abe and Mentor talked to each other privately. Abe recalled, "A long time ago, you told me that you believed God would select a task that only I was equal to do. Now I believe I know what that is. What do you think, Mentor?"

"I think the Lord has chosen you to lead the nation through the coming storm."

As the two men went outside for the inauguration, Mentor Graham was seated beside Abe on the platform. Early on, he leaned over to Mentor and whispered, "I still need your prayers. Please pray for me."

"I will Abe. I'll pray for you with all my heart. I truly believe God will impart His wisdom into you and guide you."

"Thank you, my brother. I needed to hear that."

Then Abe stood up, took the oath of office and became the sixteenth president of the United States. It was indeed the proudest hour of Mentor's life, seeing his young student rise to the highest office in the land. If there was one moment he'd lived his whole life for, this was it.

Before he left Washington, Mentor embraced and said goodbye to young William Wallace Lincoln. Noticing 'Willie' was thin–perhaps too thin–like his father, he voiced his concern to Abe, "Willie looks on the weak side. Please keep an eye on him."

After that, Abe focused on Willie even more so over the coming months. The concern proved to be warranted. Little Willie's face soon developed an uncomfortable resemblance to 'the sickness' that took Ann and her brother David so many years before.

One evening as Abe sat beside his son, Willie looked up from his sickbed and said, "Daddy, if the Lord allows me to live, I know what He wants me to do with my life."

"What's that my son?"

"I want to teach the Bible to others or perhaps become a preacher."

"I'll support you all the way, if that's what you want to become, my son. Just get well."

It's very sad to report that his condition only continued to worsen, his breathing becoming heavier and more labored, till he passed away at 5 P.M. on February 20th 1862. The passing of eleven-year-old William Wallace Lincoln once more broke Abe's heart. He agonized, "My poor boy. God has called him home. I know in my heart that he is much better off with the Lord in Heaven. Yet, I loved him so." Staring down at his lifeless form from the chair beside his bed, he whispered, "It's so very, very hard to see him die."

Standing up, Abe emerged from his son's bedroom with tears flowing down his face. Walking down the hallway to his office in the Executive Mansion, he encountered his secretary, John Nicolay. "Well, John," he said, "my boy is gone, actually gone! It's almost more than I can stand."

Pausing to wipe his face with an old red bandana, sort of a handkerchief now, he'd kept from the Black Hawk War, Abe's face changed. Taking on a very determined expression, he said, "John, I want you to bring me as much work as you can. I must keep busy."

Beyond Willie's funeral, Abe became consumed by the Civil War in the weeks and months to come. The events of the war took over his life, day and night, as they closed in around him.

On one such day in early September 1863, Abe became aware of a familiar voice among raised voices coming from outside his office. Listening carefully, he could hear his other secretary, John Hay, explaining, "Ma'am, you can't see the President without an appointment."

"You don't understand! I know the President. He will see me."

Over hearing this, Abe came to the doorway and immediately set a tense situation at ease, "That's alright John, I'll see this person. I know her." Taking her into his office, he closed the door.

Turning to her, he welcomed an old friend, "I would know that voice and your face anywhere. Hannah Armstrong, I'm so glad to see you."

"Abe, I might not have recognized you."

"How come?"

"You've grown a beard. Why?"

"Oh, I know. I was always clean shaven, until a couple of years ago. A little girl wrote me that as president, I'd look so much more impressive with a beard. Others have liked it, but I swear I'm going to shave it off the day I leave office. It itches too much. I hate it! But now, let's get down to business. Why have you come all the way to Washington to see me?"

"It's my boys again."

"How are your boys, Hannah? Never were there two finer boys than Pleasant and Duff."

"That's just it, things aren't good."

As tears welled up in her eyes, Abe took her hand and embraced her. Extracting an old red bandana from his coat pocket, he dabbed her tears away. "Now Hannah, sit down here and tell me all about it."

Focusing on the old bandana, she asked, "Isn't that the old bandana that Ann Rutledge tied around your neck about the time of the Black Hawk War?"

"Yes, it is. It's hard to let go of the memories of those you love. I've always kept it and I always will. Sometimes I look at it in the quiet moments and it makes me feel like she's still close to me."

"Abe, you're a good loving man just like my Jack was. I knew I was right to come and see you." Pulling a letter from her purse, she continued, "This is for you, it's from Pleasant."

Noticing the stains on the envelope, Abe reacted, "There's blood stains on this letter."

"Yes, my boys loved you, Abe. After you got Duff off that murder charge, he and Pleasant both said they'd fight for whatever their Uncle Abe believed in. So when the war came, both Pleasant and Duff enlisted in the 85th Illinois Infantry. Pleasant was severely wounded in the fighting around Nashville back in March. He was being brought back with the wounded aboard a steamer when he died."

"No, no! My poor nephew. I remember him sitting on my knee, listening to my stories." Tears filled Abe's eyes as he slumped into a nearby chair.

Hannah took the chair opposite him, continuing, "My boy remembered those stories too. It's all in this letter to you. A nurse wrote it down as he lay dying. He said in the letter, 'stay strong, Uncle Abe. I only wish I had more than one life to give. I would gladly die again, for all you stand for is right, just, and good.' That's where the letter ends." Tears were in her eyes again.

"Hannah, I feel like any words of mine would be so weak and fruitless regarding so costly a sacrifice that our boy Pleasant has made. I pray that our Heavenly Father may comfort you in your grief."

"Bless you Abe, you know how I feel, having lost two sons yourself."

"Yes, it's a pain no parent should ever have to endure, to see our children die before we do."

"Pleasant was only thirty-four years old when he died. I can't even go and say a prayer over his grave. I don't know where they buried him. But I do know he left a young wife, Martha, and a young son, Hugh, only two years old. He would've been Jack's grandson."

"Hannah, we must see that boy and his mother are taken care of."

"Yes, that's part of the reason I've come to see you. Duff's been fighting for the cause and is in the army. He said he owed you his life and would give you the last full measure of his devotion. Right now, he's seriously ill in an army hospital in Louisville Kentucky. Abe, I've already lost one son, please don't let me lose another."

"And you won't." Abe went over to his desk and pulled out a sheet of official stationary, labelled *Executive Mansion* at the top. Writing something on it and signing as A. Lincoln, President and Commander in Chief. Turning to Hannah, he said, "With this piece of paper I've just ordered the immediate discharge of your boy, Duff. He and Pleasant have sacrificed enough upon the altar of freedom for our country."

"Abe, what's going to happen to our country?"

"I don't know. It's in the good Lord's hands. The killing continues."

Looking at him, she noticed his eyes looked so very sad in that moment. As she prepared to leave, the words just came out of her, "Abe, I fear I may never see you again. I just have this feeling someone's going to kill you."

"If they kill me, at least I'll never die another death. Then at last, I'll be able to see your Jack, my Ann, and my boys Willie and Eddie again. Looking at it that way, it won't be so bad. Will it?"

"Heaven must be a wonderful place." That was all she could say as she left.

From that meeting, Duff Armstrong was discharged from the army and returned to Illinois. He kept a promise to take care of Pleasant's little boy, whom he raised as his own. On April 18th 1864, Pleasant's widow, Martha, married Duff. He eventually fathered five children before dying in 1899.

Hannah Armstrong never saw Abe again. After Abe's death in 1865, she remarried and moved to Winterset, Madison County, Iowa. Among friends and relatives there, she became famous with her tales of the old New Salem days and made beautiful quilts for twenty five years until her death in 1890 at the age of eighty. It was her last wish though, that her body be returned to Illinois and that she be buried near her first husband, Jack Armstrong.

During the troubling years of 1864 and 1865, there was much slaughter and loss of life in the Civil War. Taking more responsibility upon himself than any one human being ever should, pushing himself beyond the limits of human endurance, Abe was fast approaching both mental and physical exhaustion.

Hungering for the advice and personal close friendship of someone he could completely trust, Abe found that someone in the person of an old friend, Billy Greene. Commuting to Washington, Billy was now an influential businessman back in Illinois, being in charge of a significant portion of tax collections for the war effort there. As such, he was in the nation's capital one or more times each year.

As Billy put it to Abe, "We've been friends for over thirty years, since the Offutt store days in New Salem, back in '32."

"That's right Billy, it's been a long time. Memories of those days still roll over in my mind." Even as he said it, Ann's memory sprung up in his mind. "Thinking about it, in these troubled times I often find myself asking, what would Ann have me do?"

"Remember, Abe, I knew her too. She had already come to know that you had this overpowering sense of what was good and right, inside you. I can almost hear her tell you, *Think about a thing, reflect upon it, then let your conscience be your guide*. Only then will you know what you're doing is right."

"Just hearing those words again, especially now, I feel her spirit is close, around me."

Even unto the end of his life, Abe never quite lost that aura of depression, or melancholy as they called it in those days. Perhaps it was this unfulfilled part of him that hung on within him until the last.

At this point he confided in Billy, "I had a dream last night. I could hear noises, much crying and weeping, coming from downstairs, here in the Executive Mansion. I got up and went downstairs, where I saw two young soldiers, one at each end of a flag draped casket. I inquired of one of the soldiers, *Who died*? He answered, *The President's been shot*. I looked in the opened coffin and saw myself. Then I woke up. But before putting my glasses on, I glanced in a mirror. I saw two images of myself, one sharp and distinct, the other faded."

"What does it mean?"

"I think it means, I completed my first term as president, but the faded image means I won't complete my second term."

"Abe, please realize it was just a dream."

"No Billy, I think such things are warnings from God for me to prepare myself, that my work on earth is almost done. Out of all that has happened these past four years we are seeing a new nation, one in which all men are created equal, one in which there is no more slavery. In accomplishing this vision, in doing all I've done, I've become so very, very tired."

"You've done it though, what no other man could've done."

"Yes, but at a terrible price with so much loss of life. It seems like death has been all around me for so many years that it has become a way of life for me. Here we are, at Mid-March of 1865, as I grow older and the war nears its end, I feel like the task God gave me is near complete."

"Then we'll have peace in the land again?"

"Yes, but with that peace there will also come bitterness. The people of the South are a proud people. There are those among them that will not accept defeat so easily and go quietly into the night. Among them will be some full of anger who will want to do bodily harm to me."

"Perhaps you should consider having more security, more guards around you."

"No, I don't believe that would stop them. If someone wants to kill me, they'll find a way. After all, it was God who made me president. He can take it away in the blink of an eye. Besides, something else has been on my mind, even more so lately."

"What could that possibly be?"

"Something Ann said to me a very long time ago. It almost seems like a dream to me now. But once, having my complete attention, she said that when I close my eyes for a final time on this world, she would be there when I opened them again in the hereafter. I'm actually looking forward to that moment, now more than ever."

Less than a month later, Abe's dreams and History would come together in the flash of one inevitable moment. With the war's end a virtual certainty now, the evening found Abe conceding to spend the evening viewing a play with Mary at Ford's Theater. The subject matter–a comedy–was cheering him up. About midway through it, he leaned over to her and asked, "Now that the war is over and death has taken two of our sons, can't we try to find some peace between us and grow closer to each other?" She started to answer, but a loud POP! went off behind them. Abe never heard her reply.

Mary Todd Lincoln was haunted by that moment all the rest of her life, replaying it many times in her mind. Quite often, she told their son, Robert Lincoln, that she never got the opportunity to ask Abe's forgiveness for the many moments of pain that her foolish behavior may have caused him. She remained guilt ridden for the rest of her life as her behavior became more eccentric and approached the edge of sanity.

Robert Lincoln distanced himself from his mother for most of the rest of her life. He had often witnessed her verbal abuse of his father up close as he was growing up. It sickened him. Smart and driven like his father, he was off to college at seventeen, getting out from under the roof of his parent's Springfield home. Finally though, after doctors declared she had suffered a complete mental breakdown and was considered to be insane, he signed the papers committing her to a mental institution ten years after his father's death.

On that tragic April 14th night, Abe was carried across the street to the Peterson house, where he was stretched across a bed. Mary Todd's continual screaming and wailing caused Secretary of War Stanton to have her removed to an adjoining room.

Robert Lincoln was quickly located and summoned. Arriving shortly before midnight, he would remember every minute of the next twelve hours for the rest of his life. Sitting at his father's bedside, he held his hand in a firm grip all the rest of the night. Robert was twenty-two at the time and a student at Harvard law school. Even though he resembled the Todd family, on the inside he was his father's son. He always wanted to be an attorney, just like his father. Abe was proud of his oldest son and Robert was proud of his father. He whispered to Abe all night, with words of affection and love. At one point he was heard to have said, "Daddy, I'll love you forever."

Somewhere across that void, between life and the edge of death, Abe heard his son's words. At least, Robert thought this to be so. He said later, "Every time I spoke to him, my father's hand would tighten around my own, as if to respond."

At 7:22 A.M. on April 15th 1865, Abe took one last deep breath. With tears in his eyes, Robert Lincoln still clinging to his father's hand looked up at Secretary Stanton. As their eyes met in that moment of truth, Stanton reacted, "Now he belongs to the Ages." Abe was fifty-six years old at the time.

The news of Abe's death spread quickly. When word reached him, Mentor Graham refused to believe it. He thought it to be a fiction spread by Lincoln's enemies. Only gradually did he and Sarah accept the news, both of them grieving heavily.

After giving birth to fifteen children, coupled with the suffering of many years of rugged frontier life, Sarah's health rapidly disintegrated in the years following Abe's death. Married to Mentor for 51 years, she passed away in 1869.

With their children moved away, Mentor could no longer bring himself to live in the large brick home by himself. Leaving it, he moved in with the family of his son, Lincoln Graham, in Petersburg. It was there he continued in the teaching profession until 1879.

Picking up roots again, he felt a calling to see the American West. Making the trek, he moved with his son's family, finally settling in South Dakota.

In 1886, on the occasion of the dedication of the Statue of Liberty, as the Graham family sat around their dining table, Mentor gave his grandchildren a lecture about the cost of liberty, "The greatest man I ever knew gave his life for that liberty, to preserve the country we have today, as truly one nation under God. There is a cost sometimes, the ultimate sacrifice that some of us have to make for whatever we believe in."

"Grandfather, did President Lincoln really feel that way?"

"Yes, he did. Long before he became President, when he had just begun studying the law, I asked him what he wanted to do in life."

He answered, "I'm always going to be honest and true in whatever I do. If I'm able to become a lawyer and a public servant, I would rather be killed than betray my principles. If I can't stand up for what I believe in, what would be my worth as a man?"

Mentor Graham passed away a few weeks later on November 15th 1886. He was more than 85 years old at the time. Above his grave, in a little Presbyterian cemetery, there was only a wooden marker at the time. It said, *Mentor Graham, the teacher of Abraham Lincoln.*

It had been among Mentor's last wishes, that if it were possible one day, he would like to be buried next to his beloved wife. After more than fifty years, his granddaughter, Mary, who became a teacher herself, fulfilled his last wishes. His metal casket was unearthed and brought back to Illinois, where he is now buried next to Sarah.

At the time of Abe's death, he was still law partners with Billy Herndon back in Springfield. When Abe left for Washington in 1861, he told Billy, "Just leave my name on the shingle outside the door *Lincoln and Herndon, attorneys at law.* When I finish my term as president, I'll be coming right back here. It'll be as if I never left."

"Just as you've said, partners for life."

"Oh Billy," Abe added almost as an afterthought as he started to leave, "just in case I don't return, for any reason, go ahead and look up that list of folks I gave you for the book about me. I know if you base it on the information they give you, it'll be the true story of my life."

"Abe, you have my solemn promise, I'll do it."

Billy Herndon kept his promise. One of the first persons he interviewed was Billy Greene on May 30th 1865. In the process of telling the truth about Abe's life and the story of Ann Rutledge, Herndon incurred the wrath of Mary Todd, the entire Todd family, and their friends as well. They tried to suppress his book, portraying it and his speeches as the ravings of a drunken alcoholic who was delusional. Over the course of time though, the merits of his work won out, backed up with interviews from seventeen eyewitnesses who had known Abe from his New Salem days. As Herndon said, "You cannot bury the facts. The shining light of truth will always come out."

As for Billy Greene, the remainder of his life was happy and successful. He married Louisa White and together they had nine children. For many decades he was one of the primary sources of information about Abe and all of the New Salem folks. He not only gave numerous interviews, but took writers out to where the town had actually stood. By then, the ravages of time had taken their toll and it had largely disintegrated into the dust.

Over the years, Billy was asked many questions even some that bordered on minor trivia. One reporter asked him, "Did you ever figure out if you were related to the famous judge, Bowling Green?"

He answered, "Yes, actually the Judge and I sat down once and traced it back, figuring out we were distance cousins. Only my side of the family spelled our last name 'Greene' while his side spelled it like the color, leaving the last E off. But if anybody asks me, I say we were first cousins. In spirit, we were anyway."

Another reporter asked him, "What was the President really like?"

He became very emotional as he answered, "He was my best friend for thirty-four years. Even more than that, he was like a brother to me. In life, he was unchangeable. If he loved you, he never let go of that love. He loved you till the day he died. Here we are twenty-five years after his death and I miss him just as much as if he died yesterday."

Shortly before his death he was heard saying, "I'm going to a place where I can see my old friend Abe Lincoln again." Billy Greene passed away on June 30th 1894, at the age of 82 years, five months and three days.

Those that knew Abe among the Rutledge family were also dying out in the decades after Abe's death. Ann's mother, Mary Rutledge, lived well into her nineties, passing away in 1878. In her last years she often spoke of Abe to her grandchildren, saying, "My little Ann had the good fortune to fall in love with the greatest man of our times. They were truly good for each other."

After Abe's death, reporters tracked down John Rutledge, Ann's brother. They asked him, "What do you know about President Lincoln?"

"I knew him long before he was President. He was my Captain during the Black Hawk War. I trusted him with my life. Later, Abe and my sister were going to get married, but she died. You ask what I really know about Abe Lincoln? He was a kind and loving man, generous to a fault. A better man never lived on the face of the earth."

Eventually, Ann's favorite cousin, James McGrady Rutledge was located. Nearly 85 years old at the time, he said, "I had a long friendship with Abe Lincoln during his years in New Salem. Had she lived till the spring of '36, he would've married my cousin, Ann. He was deeply in love with her. Sixty-four years after her death, I still remember how Abe took her loss so very hard. If one has to pick such a person, in my lifetime he was the greatest man that ever lived. I loved him and had the great honor of voting twice for him as president." 'Mac', as Abe called him, passed away in April 1899, having witnessed a simple farm boy advance and achieve the highest elected office in the land, changing the course of History in the nineteenth century.

The shifting sands of time over the decades have radically altered the appearance of the land around what was once New Salem. After Jack Armstrong's death and his wife Hannah moving away, the Old Concord Burial Ground lost its caretaker. Unkept, the ravages of time and nature closed in on this place containing so much sadness. A virtual forest of weeds and vines grew up around the cemetery, completely concealing it. By the final decade of the nineteenth century, even the memory of such a place had been erased from the view of man.

Certain events occurring in 1890 though, have caused a controversy that rages on to this day. In May of that year a scheme was concocted by the co-owners of the new Oakland Cemetery in Petersburg, D.M. Bone and Samuel Montgomery. As their new cemetery was not able to compete with the nearby, more established Rose Cemetery, they came up with the idea that if they only had someone famous buried in their cemetery, it might draw future customers to buy burial lots. From the beginning, what was about to happen was stemming from pure financial greed.

Who was famous in the area? Pondering that question, the two cemetery owners came up with the name of Ann Rutledge, the lost love of President Lincoln. As matters developed, Montgomery, who was a Petersburg furniture dealer and sometimes undertaker, became obsessed with the idea of removing Ann's body from its present resting place and reburying her in his own cemetery. It did not seem to bother him that such a deed may have been morally or legally wrong.

First, Montgomery contacted Ann's younger sister, Nancy Rutledge, since she was first thought the only surviving member of the immediate family in 1890.

Though living in Iowa at the time, she was immediately opposed to moving Ann's body, saying, "She should stay where those of her family are buried. After all, my father and my brother are on either side of her. It was their wishes to be laid to rest by Ann. I stand firmly behind them." Later, she added, "Abraham Lincoln personally saw to it that my brother David's desire to be buried by my sister was carried out. I feel in my heart he would frown on any attempt to move her."

Samuel Montgomery was undeterred, responding openly, "President Lincoln has been dead for twenty-five years. Since he never married Ann Rutledge, he would've had no say so in the matter. We on the other hand, have to think of the welfare and prosperity of Petersburg. To have Miss Rutledge buried here will undoubtedly bring needed tourist trade to our little town."

Going around Nancy Rutledge, Montgomery went outside her immediate family and approached Ann's cousin, McGrady Rutledge, who lived near Petersburg. His feelings were consistent with Nancy's though. He opposed the moving of Ann's body believing the last wishes of his uncle, Ann's father, should be honored.

Montgomery exhorted to pressure tactics, bullying and threatening Mac, who was then 76 years old. The greedy furniture dealer continued to paint a picture that Mac would be hated by every citizen of Petersburg for opposing the moving of Ann's body, because the city would lose thousands of dollars in potential tourist trade.

McGrady Rutledge finally folded under this constant pressure and agreed to show Montgomery where Ann was buried.

When it came down to it, Montgomery and his associates did not know the exact location of Old Concord or where Ann was buried within that cemetery. All they knew, more by legend, that it was somewhere north of Petersburg within a few miles.

In the early morning of May 15th 1890, Montgomery took one of his furniture wagons, an open buckboard type, along with McGrady, out in search of Old Concord. Accompanying them was two of Montgomery's employees, equipped with shovels.

One of the would-be grave diggers, a man named Hollis, brought his nine-year-old son, James. What happened next would leave an indelible impression on the youth, who would recount the events of that day many times over the years.

When they finally arrived at Old Concord, McGrady had a difficult time in recognizing the place since the cemetery had been left unattended for many decades. An encroaching mass of underbrush and wild trees had advanced unchecked, growing up among the graves. Many headstones and markers had been toppled over or broken. All were weather-beaten. Others had disappeared altogether.

Searching, McGrady Rutledge came to where he thought Ann's grave was. Mentor Graham's hand-carved wooden marker had long since vanished. Indicating this was the spot, Montgomery immediately set his two grave diggers to work. Digging down about seven feet, their shovels made contact with a broken off chunk of rotted wood. Clearing away more dirt, they quickly uncovered a much-decayed wooden coffin.

This was the moment of truth. Without any kind of official document or signed permission paper (by Nancy Rutledge) to do so, Samuel Montgomery ordered his men to break open what remained of the coffin's lid and exhume the body. They would be startled at what they found.

After removing the last barrier of wood that made up the lid, they found no body, or at least what most would call a body.

Within the passage of fifty-five years, nature itself had consumed the flesh of Ann's body.

McGrady barely whispered, almost to himself, "From dust thou art made and unto dust thou shalt return." These were the words that God spoke to Adam and Eve in casting them out of the Garden of Eden, as recounted in the Book of Genesis.

Outside of a few bones found and a few strands of her beautiful hair, no trace of Ann's body was ever found. It had vanished.

McGrady thought, the important part of Ann–her soul–had long since gone home to God. No man, no grave robber would ever get his hands on her.

Montgomery got a small box from his wagon, in which he put two of her bones and a small tin of dirt from inside the casket. Though the sides of Ann's casket were still reasonably intact, the ends of it had completely rotted away, allowing the interior to become one with the earth.

The little boy, James Hollis saw all of this take place. As the boy grew into an old man, he was still speaking of it, right up into the 1950s, giving his last interview on the subject matter in 1958.

After re-sealing Ann's grave, Samuel Montgomery returned to Petersburg. The next day he buried the small box in the cemetery he owned. He and his partner claimed that Ann's body was now buried in Petersburg. He got his wish in a sense, for he did sell additional lots in his cemetery and thousands of tourists have made the journey to Petersburg to see what they thought was the final resting place of Ann Rutledge.

In 1921 a huge granite monument (more than five feet tall) was erected at the new gravesite in Petersburg. Lines of the famed poet, Edgar Lee Masters, are etched into the granite. Since then, for almost a century, thousands of visitors have passed by the iron fence surrounding the monument to pay their respects and say prayers for Ann Rutledge.

The events of that May 15th day haunted McGrady Rutledge most every day of his remaining nine years of life. While Ann's grave was open though, he did retrieve four buttons from the dress she had worn in that coffin and a lock of her hair with a yellow satin bow. These items eventually went to his daughter and were passed down to other members of the Rutledge family.

As for Nancy Rutledge, Ann's younger sister, she continued to contest Montgomery's false claims that he had reburied Ann's body in Petersburg. She did so right up until her own death in 1901 at the age of 79, still saying, "Sam Montgomery was nothing but a greedy undertaker, who only had his own financial interest at heart."

Many still speculate and wonder, is not the essence of Ann Rutledge still out there a few miles north of Petersburg in Old Concord Cemetery? McGrady Rutledge told his children there was no body inside the coffin. Ann's remains had disintegrated into the earth. In recent years, tests of soil samples from around Ann's original gravesite reveal a high pH level. This indicates the soil there, over time, could decompose organic and mineral matter. This could include bones as well. Knowing this, it becomes very reasonable to believe her body has become one with the soil of Old Concord.

Certainly, Ann's extended family members believed that something of her still remains at Old Concord. In 1996, they did something about it and caused a two-sided granite headstone to be erected there. On one side it says:

ORIGINAL GRAVE OF
ANNA MAYES RUTLEDGE
JAN 7 1813–AUG 25 1835
WHERE LINCOLN WEPT

On the opposite side, etched into the granite for all time, it says:

ANN RUTLEDGE
I CANNOT BEAR TO THINK OF HER
OUT THERE ALONE IN THE STORM
A LINCOLN

Dear Reader, if you ever get the opportunity to take the journey yourself, here's how to reach Old Concord: Take Route 97 going north through Petersburg until you reach the Lincoln Trail Road.

Turn right on it, going east for about a half mile, till you reach a muddy or grassy lane between two fields. On foot, follow this lane for about a quarter mile. In the midst of the two fields, you'll see a fenced-in area and a flag atop a pole. This is Old Concord.

The day I was there, the wind was blowing hard and the flag was rippling in the wind. Being back away from the highway, it is a quiet peaceful place. There are the physical remains of 244 souls that we know of, buried there. These are the souls of the very embodiment of the pioneering-spirit that made America great. Among the markers and weather-beaten, tilted stones are the graves of Ann Rutledge and Jack Armstrong, other Rutledge and Armstrong family members, some Clary's and many unknowns known only by History itself.

Standing in front of Ann's grave, the feelings of long ago caught up with me. I felt like I was standing on hallowed ground. I could sense Abe's feelings, where he soaked the earth with tears straight from his heart. Even years later, he always said his spiritual heart was out at Concord with Ann.

Walking the grounds of Concord, threading my way through the irregular rows of faded markers, I also came upon Jack Armstrong's grave. For a moment there too, I could feel Hannah's sadness as she stood looking down at her husband's grave.

Looking around, I thought one can feel so much more in the atmosphere than the occasional breeze that blows by. If one is perceptive enough, one can feel Ann's spirit and Abe's mournful presence.

My view began taking in the whole of Old Concord. I felt the deepest, most spiritual impact upon me. I said a prayer for all of those buried here. May they all rest in the arms of the Lord, in eternal peace.

AUTHOR'S NOTES

W hy did I want to write this book? Beyond being a Lincoln buff for over fifty years, I was ready to make a three-year commitment necessary in doing this story justice. For me, as a writer it is important to have that level of passion for any project I undertake.

I believed a story of real depth about Lincoln's six years in New Salem and how the events of those years affected the rest of his life needed to be told in the way I have recounted it. That is to say in an almost docudrama style through the medium of historical fiction.

I wanted to take those years of his life and peel back Lincoln's story within them, like layers of an onion, revealing the essence of not only his heart and soul, but also that of others involved in his life. In doing so, it became an emotionally involving project for me, one in which I have sought to bring these figures of the past back to flesh and blood life.

As opposed to the big events of history, the search for truth is far more revealing in day to day encounters between people. I have long felt, in telling a really moving story, it is in the little details of their lives that we get to the emotional core of their characters.

Getting inside Lincoln's mind and inner thoughts has been one of the great challenges for this novelist. Doing so, in an authentic way, has been the result of careful research and study. Of course, I hope to have done so in a manner that has made Abe, Ann, and others come alive for you, the reader. The end result becomes a perfect merging as a novel and a history.

Going back in time, life on the American frontier of the early 1830s was quite a bit different than what we know today. If reading about Lincoln has sparked your interest and you want to see a window into the past, do yourself a favor and take a trip to New Salem. It is a brilliantly researched restoration of the frontier village where Lincoln lived from 1831 to 1837. William Randolph Hearst purchased the land on which the village originally stood and then donated it to the state of Illinois for the expressed purpose of a Lincoln memorial. New Salem is now a state park with all of its original structures brought back to life in a close approximation of what they looked like in the 1830s. This glimpse into the primitive conditions of life back then is truly an eye opener.

As I went into New Salem and the surrounding area for the first time, an unusual feeling took me over. It was though a presence from those long-ago times had permeated many of those structures there, the Old Concord Cemetery, and inside Lincoln's home in Springfield. Others, perceptive enough, have spoken of being aware of this presence. For me at least, this whole area borders on hallowed ground.

Feeling a genuine connection as I wrote this book, I sought to honor both Abe and Ann, and all the other individuals who lived the events within these pages. Collectively, they were the soul of America as it existed then. We should honor them for their part in giving us the country we are blessed with today. It is also my hope, over time, we will all resolve to live better lives, truly worthy of their sacrifices and our great heritage.

In the writing and research of this book, and bringing it to completion in its present form, I wish to address the following: I soon realized that in telling the story of New Salem, as it was populated by approximately 150-200 highly colorful individuals, it would be very difficult to do adequate justice to all of them. Any attempt to do so could easily result in a thousand page plus novel. Regrettably, to make the story more readable and flow better, I would have to omit some characters and incidents that might be important to certain readers. For these decisions, in the interest of sheer story-telling, I take full responsibility.

Getting to the heart of the story and how New Salem influences threaded throughout the rest of Lincoln's life, characters and incidents within these pages were the result of much research. In this process, I have carefully drawn from original and eyewitness sources obtained through interviews, letters, diaries and memoirs, many of which were out-of-print, thought lost, or unavailable. A majority of incidents present within these pages were recounted and verified by twenty-two residents of New Salem, several of whom being mentioned in this book.

In addition, a number of scenes depicted were found in material collected and compiled by Abe's law partner, William Herndon. Examination of these documents reveal unanimous agreement by seventeen eyewitnesses that Ann and Abe were deeply in love, were engaged, and had confirmed to them their intentions to be married in the fall of 1835 or spring of 1836.

A selected bibliography for your review is available at the end of this book. You, dear reader, will have to be the judge if I have made good use of this information.

In the process of going through countless volumes and original material step by step, I felt I had opened a window that through which I was being drawn ever closer into Abraham Lincoln's real world. At times it was though I could feel the presence of his spirit, whispering into my ear from time to time, guiding me through one of the most heart-breaking stories ever told.

In conclusion, talking about the craft of writing, I write in the hope of enriching the lives of my readers, to provide a transformative experience that is genuinely moving. It is my earnest hope that you will find this a meaningful portrait of a simple man who became driven to achieve uncommon greatness.

Thank you, dear reader for taking the time to peruse my thoughts on writing in general and in particular, *Young Lincoln*.

ACKNOWLEDGEMENTS

From conception to completion I have found there are so many to thank for their help and encouragement along the way.

To begin with, this book would never have gotten off the ground without the interest of my wife June and her daughter Mary. As I was considering doing a Lincoln story, one day in early 2016 they urged me to go to Illinois and do on site research in New Salem and the surrounding area. This fact finding trip became the initial step in this book's journey from a dream into becoming reality.

Later we visited Springfield, the Lincoln Presidential Library and Museum, Lincoln's home on 8th Street (where he lived from 1844 to 1861), as well as many other out-of-the-way places which were sources of information.

In doing this intensive on-site research, I remember the two of them, June and Mary, helping me at every turn. I still retain this mental image of Mary climbing ladders, retrieving out-of-print books and valuable research material, well beyond my reach. Without their help you might not be holding this book in your hands.

In doing research in Lincoln's New Salem state historic site, as it is now officially known, there are many people to thank for their aid and knowledgeable assistance. Among them were Jack Alexander at the Visitor Center, which is a veritable museum of artifacts and all-encompassing information, Terry Jones and the historical interpreters, all in period clothing, that frequent the entire village. You instantly feel like you're back in the primitive 1830s living conditions. I experienced so much in this environment that has found its way into the pages of Young Lincoln.

For this Lincoln buff, New Salem was a place to be remembered. I highly recommend a trip there for all who would fancy a journey back in time, retracing Lincoln's steps. New Salem is located two miles south of Petersburg, IL and twenty miles northeast of Springfield, IL on Route 97. For more information, call 217-632-4000 or go online to www.lincolnsnewsalem.com.

For the purpose of accurately reflecting the emotional core of Young Lincoln, a search was undertaken for a gifted artist who would create a cover that would achieve maximum impact and interest among potential readers. Seeing the end result, this cover reflects the very soul of my book. In achieving this, I want to convey my very special thanks to Dell Harris for the wonderful cover art he has done.

In producing my book in its final form, I wish to express my thanks to Yorkshire Publishing and the guiding hand of its Director of Publishing, Samantha Ryan, who has always been supportive. Throughout the publishing process, her entire staff has been most helpful.

In bringing this manuscript to completion through several drafts, I'm extremely grateful to Shelly Reynolds for her participation in this project. Her typing of these multiple drafts was efficient and skillfully done. Through this phase, Shelly's insightful comments were always a definite positive in the book's evolution. For that and all her hard work, I wish to express my heartfelt thanks.

Beyond those specifically mentioned here, I want to make note of others, without whom I might not be the man–or writer–I am today. From my grandparents who raised me, on down through my son and my daughter, my three wonderful granddaughters, and the rest of my extended family, their love and affection has helped make me who I am.

In this same group, the encouragement and sincere friendship from a few very special people has lifted me up and kept me going. I hope, in some small way, this book honors all of you. Even though words are sometimes inadequate, I still wish to express my love and undying gratitude to all who have supported me through the years. You have inspired me as I continue on this long winding road as a writer.

May God bless and be with all of you.

– Sam Rawlins
2019

BIBLIOGRAPHY

A commentary on this book's research:

This book had its beginnings in my own personal interest into Lincoln's life many decades ago. I soon became aware of certain primary sources. The first and foremost of which is the work undertaken by William (Billy) Herndon, which began less than a month after the President's death. Endeavoring to keep his word to his late law partner and friend, he began a series of interviews and correspondence to over 250 sources, or informants as they have been termed. Though some of these documents were tragically lost in an office fire and others lost to mice while in storage at his farm, the vast majority were acquired by the Library of Congress in 1941.

The Herndon documents along with those of his later collaborator Jesse W. Weik are housed as the Herndon-Weik Collection on a number of long reels of microfilm. A word of warning though to the would-be researcher or writer, the many hand-written documents are often hard to read or are out-of-focus on microfilm, but the assistance of the Manuscript Division staff can be most helpful. Elements of this material, along with newspaper and magazine articles are interspersed among the published works consulted for my book in the following list of sources:

Alger, Horatio, Jr. *Abraham Lincoln, the Young Backwards Boy; or How a Young Rail Splitter Became President.* American Publishers, New York, 1883.

Angle, Paul M, "Here I Have Lived: A History of Lincoln's Springfield," *Abraham Lincoln Association, Springfield*, 1935.

Angle, Paul M, "More Light on Lincoln and Ann Rutledge," *Bulletin, Abraham Lincoln Centennial Association,* September 1928.

Angle, Paul M, "Lincoln's First Love," Bulletin, Abraham Lincoln Centennial Association, December, 1927.

Armstrong, Hannah. Interviews with William (Billy) Herndon, 1865-1866.

Arnold, Isaac N. *The Life of Abraham Lincoln* McClurg & Co., Chicago, 1885.

Ashmun, George, "Abraham Lincoln at Home," *Springfield Daily Republican*, May 23, 1860.

Atkinson, Eleanor, *Lincoln's Love Story.* Doubleday, New York, 1909.

Bale, Ida. *New Salem As I Know It.* (pamphlet), Petersburg, 1939.

Baringer, William E. *Lincoln's Rise to Power.* Little, Brown & Co., Boston 1937.

Barrett, Joseph H. *Life of Abraham Lincoln.* New York, 1865.

Barton, William E. *The Life of Abraham Lincoln.* The Bobbs-Merrill Company, Indianapolis, 1925.

Barton, William E. *The Women Lincoln Loved.* The Bobbs-Merrill Company, Indianapolis, 1927.

Barton, William E. *The Lineage of Lincoln.* The Bobbs-Merrill Company, Indianapolis, 1929.

Barton, William E., "Sister of Lincoln's Sweetheart Recalls Romance Death Ended," (Interview with Ann's youngest sister, Sarah), *San Diego Sun.* California, January 11, 1922.

Barton, William E., "Abraham Lincoln and New Salem," *Journal of the Illinois State Historical Society,* 1926-1927.

Beveridge, Albert J., "Lincoln as His Partner Knew Him," *Literary Digest International Review,* September 1923.

Beveridge, Albert J. *Abraham Lincoln, 1809-1858.* Houghton Mifflin Company, Boston and New York, 1928; 2 vols.

Browne, Francis F. *The Every-day Life of Abraham Lincoln.* Brown & Howell Company, Chicago, 1923.

Burba, Howard, "A Story of Lincoln's Boyhood," *American Boy*, February 1905.

Carnegie, Dale. *Lincoln the Unknown*. Dale Carnegie Publishers, Inc., New York, 1932.

Carpenter, Francis B. *The Inner Life of Abraham Lincoln: Six Months at the White House.* Hurd & Houghton, New York, 1867.

Chandler, Josephine C. *New Salem: Early Chapter In Lincoln's Life. Petersburg*, 1930.

Charnwood, Lord. *Abraham Lincoln.* Henry Holt & Company, New York, 1917.

Cogdal, Isaac. Interview with William (Billy) Herndon in which he verified that in 1860, Abe had confided to him, the story of his love for Ann Rutledge. 1865-1866.

Coggeshall, E.W. *The Assassination of Abraham Lincoln.* W.M. Hill, Chicago, 1920.

Crook, William H., "Lincoln's Last Day," *Harper's*, September 1907.

Crook, William H., *Memories of the White House: The Home*

Life of the Presidents from Lincoln to Roosevelt. Little Brown & Co., Boston, 1911.

Dall, Caroline H., "Mr. Herndon's Account of Abraham Lincoln and Ann Rutledge," *Boston Daily Advertiser,* December 15, 1866.

Dall, Caroline H., "Pioneering," *Atlantic Monthly*, April 1867.

Davis, J.M., "Lincoln as a Storekeeper and as a Soldier in the Black Hawk War," *McClure's*, January 1896.

Duncan, Kunigunde, and D.F. Nickols. *Mentor Graham: The Man Who Taught Lincoln.* University of Chicago Press, Chicago, 1944.

Erickson, Gary, "The Graves of Ann Rutledge and the Old Concord Burial Ground," *Lincoln Herald,* Fall 1969.

Flindt, Margaret, "Lincoln As a Lover," (Interview with Nancy Rutledge). *Chicago Inter-Ocean*, February 12, 1886.

Fowler, William W. *Woman on the American Frontier.* Scranton, 1877.

Gibson, Robert. *The Theory and Practice of Surveying: Instructions Requisite for the Skillful Practice of This Art.* New York, 1814. A copy exists with Lincoln's name and handwriting in several places.

Gordon, J., "Abraham Lincoln in His Relations to Women," *Cosmopolitan*, December 1894.

Gore, Spencer, "Early Physicians in My County," Journal of the Illinois State Historical Society, 1931.

Graham, Mentor. Letters to William (Billy) Herndon, May 29, 1865 and July 15, 1865.

Greene, William (Billy) G. Letters to William (Billy) Herndon, May 30, 1865 and June 7, 1865.

Greene, William (Billy) G. Interview with William (Billy) Herndon, October 9, 1866.

Gridley, Eleanor. *The Story of Abraham Lincoln.* Monarch, Chicago, 1902.

Hammond, Jane E., "Memoirs of the Rutledge Family of New Salem, Illinois." Manuscript form, Library of Congress, 1921.

Hanks, Dennis. Letters to William (Billy) Herndon, June 13, 1865 and March 22, 1866.

Helm, Katherine. *The True Story of Mary, Wife of Lincoln.* Harper & Brothers, New York, 1928.

Herndon, William (Billy). Herndon's lecture, "Lincoln and Ann Rutledge and the Pioneers of New Salem," 1866.

Herndon, William H. and Weik, Jesse W. *The History and Personal Recollections of Abraham Lincoln.* The Herndon's Lincoln. Publishing Company, Springfield, Illinois 1888; 3 vols.

Herndon, William H. and Weik, Jesse W. *Herndon's Lincoln: The True Story of a Great Life.* Chicago, New York, and San Francisco, 1889; 3 vols.

Hertz, Emanuel. *Abraham Lincoln: A New Portrait.* Boni and Liveright, New York, 1931; 2 vols.

Hertz, Emanuel. *The Hidden Lincoln: From the Letters and Papers of William H. Herndon.* Viking, New York, 1938.

Hickox, Volney, "Lincoln at Home: Reminiscences of His Early Life," *Illinois State Journal,* October 1874.

Hill, Frederick T. *Lincoln the Lawyer*. Century, New York, 1906.

Holland, Josiah G. *The Life of Abraham Lincoln*. Gurdon Bill, Springfield, 1866.

Howard, James Q. The Life of Abraham Lincoln with Extracts from His Speeches. Columbus, OH, 1860.

Lamon, Ward Hill. *Life of Abraham Lincoln from His Birth to His Inauguration as President*. Osgood, Boston, 1872.

Lamon, Ward Hill. *Recollections of Abraham Lincoln, 1847-1865*. Edited by Dorothy Lamon Teillard, Washington, D.C., 1911.

Laughlin, Clara E., "The Last Twenty-Four Hours of Lincoln's Life," *Ladies Home Journal*, February 1909.

Lewis, Lloyd. *Myths after Lincoln*. Harcourt, Bruce and Company, New York, 1929.

Lincoln, Sarah Bush, (Abe's step-mother), Interview with William (Billy) Herndon, September 8, 1865.

Lincoln, Waldo. *History of the Lincoln Family*. Commonwealth Press, Worcester, 1923.

Linder, Usher. *Reminiscences of the Bench and Bar of Illinois*. Legal News Co., Chicago, 1879.

Maltby, Charles. *The Life and Public Services of Abraham Lincoln*. California, 1884.

Masters, E.L. *Lincoln the Man*. Dodd, Mead, New York, 1931.

McHenry, Henry. Letters to William (Billy) Herndon, May 29, 1865 and January 8, 1866.

McHenry, Henry. Interview with William (Billy) Herndon in October 1866.

McNamar, John. Letters to William (Billy) Herndon, June 4, 1866 and November 25, 1866.

Miller, R.D. *Past and Present of Menard County, Illinois.* Clarke, Chicago, 1905.

Morrow, Honore, "Lincoln's Last Day", *Cosmopolitan Magazine* February, 1930.

Nelson, G., "The Genesis of Restored New Salem," *Journal of the Illinois State Historical Society,* December 1943.

Newton, Joseph. *Lincoln and Herndon.* Torch Press, Iowa, 1910.

Nicolay, John G., and Hay, John. *Abraham Lincoln: A History.* The Century Co., New York, 1890; 12 vols.

Nicolay, John. *A Short Life of Abraham Lincoln.* The Century Co., New York, 1902.

Nicolay, John. *Personal Traits of Abraham Lincoln.* The Century Co., New York, 1919.

Offutt, Denton. *A New and Complete System of Teaching the Horse on Phrenological Principals.* Appleton's Queen City Press, Cincinnati, 1848.

Oldroyd, Osborn H. *The Assassination of Abraham Lincoln.* Oldroyd, Washington, D.C., 1901.

Old Salem Lincoln League, *Prospectus of the Old Salem Lincoln League for Restoration of New Salem, the Early Home of Abraham Lincoln.* Petersburg Illinois: The Old Salem Lincoln League, 1918.

Onstot, Thomas G. *Pioneers of Menard and Mason Counties.* Franks, Peoria, Illinois, 1902.

Pond, Fern Nance, "The Memoirs of James McGrady

Rutledge," *Journal of the Illinois State Historical Society*, April 1936.

Pond, Fern Nance, "Lincoln Lived Here," *Saturday Evening Post*, February 1941.

Pond, Fern Nance, "Abraham Lincoln and David Rutledge," *Lincoln Herald*, June 1950.

Power, John C. *History of the Early Settlers of Sangamon County, Illinois.* 1876.

Pratt, Harry E., "Lincoln in the Black Hawk War," *Bulletin of the Abraham Lincoln Association*, December 1938.

Rankin, Henry B. *Personal Recollections of Abraham Lincoln.* Putnam, New York, 1916.

Rankin, Henry B. *Intimate Character Sketches of Abraham Lincoln.* Lippincott, Philadelphia, 1924.

Raymond, Henry J. *The Life and Public Service of Abraham Lincoln.* New York, 1865.

Reep, Thomas P. *Lincoln at New Salem.* The New Salem Lincoln League, Petersburg, Illinois, 1918, 1927.

Renwick, Percival. *Abraham Lincoln and Ann Rutledge, an Old Salem Romance.* Pamphlet, 1932.

Rice, Allen T. *Reminiscences of Abraham Lincoln by Distinguished Men of His Time.* North American Review, New York, 1888.

Ross, Harvey L. *The Early Pioneers of Pioneer Events of the State of Illinois.* Eastman Brothers, Chicago 1899.

Rothschild, Alonzo. *Lincoln, Master of Men.* Houghton Mifflin Company, Boston and New York, 1912.

Rutledge, Robert B. (Ann's brother). Letters to William (Billy)

Herndon, November 1st 1866, November 18th 1866, and November 21st 1866.

Rutledge, David H. Letter to his father James and his sister Ann, July 27, 1835. Obtained by William Barton during interview with Ann's youngest sister, Sarah.

Saunders, James Rutledge. "The Rutledge Family of New Salem, Illinois." Compiled from the Rutledge family Bible and other family records. California Interview, January 1922.

Scripps, John Locke. *Life of Abraham Lincoln.* Chicago, 1860.

Short, James (Uncle Jimmy). Letter to William (Billy) Herndon, July 7th 1865.

Spears, Zarel C., and Barton, Robert S. *Berry and Lincoln: The Store That "Winked Out."* Stratford House, New York, 1947.

Speed, Joshua. *Reminiscences of Abraham Lincoln.* Louisville, 1884.

Stephenson, Nathaniel (compiler). *The Autobiography of Abraham Lincoln: consisting of the Personal Portions of his Letters, Speeches, and Conversations.* Blue Ribbon Books, New York, 1926.

Stevens, F., *The Black Hawk War.* Chicago, 1903.

Stuart, John T. Interview with William (Billy) Herndon, 1865-1866.

Stuart, John T. Interview with John Nicolay (Abe's Presidential secretary), June 23rd 1875.

Tarbell, Ida M. *The Early Life of Abraham Lincoln.* S.S. McClure, New York, 1896.

Tarbell, Ida M. *Ann Rutledge: In the Footsteps of the Lincolns.* Harper & Brothers, New York, 1924.

Tarbell, Ida M. The *Life of Abraham Lincoln.* The Macmillan Company, New York, 1917.

Tarbell, Ida M. "Lincoln's First Love," *Collier's,* February 1930.

Thayer, William M. *The Pioneer Boy and How He Became President.* Walker Wise and Co., Boston, 1863.

Townsend, G.A., "A Talk with the Late President's Law Partner," *New York Tribune*, February 8th 1867.

Townsend, William H. *Lincoln and His Wife's Home Town.* The Bobbs-Merrill Company, Indianapolis, 1929.

Wallace, Joseph. *Past and Present of the City of Springfield and Sangamon County, Illinois.* Chicago, 1904.

Ward, William H. (editor) *Abraham Lincoln: Tributes from His Associates–Reminiscences of Soldiers, Statesmen and Citizens.* Crowell, New York, 1895.

Warren, Lewis A. *Lincoln's Parentage and Childhood.* Century, New York, 1926.

Weik, Jesse W. *The Real Lincoln.* Houghton Mifflin Company, Boston and New York, 1922.

Whipple, Wayne. *The Story of Young Abraham Lincoln.* Goldsmith, Chicago, 1934.

Whitney, Henry C. *Life on the Circuit with Lincoln.* Estes and Lauriat, Boston, 1892.

Whitney, Henry C. *Life of Lincoln.* Baker and Taylor, New York, 1908; 2 vols.

Wilson, James Grant, "Recollections of Lincoln," *Putnam's Magazine*, February 1909.

Wilson, R.W. *Lincoln among His Friends.* Caxton, Idaho, 1942.

Wright, Annie F., "The Assassination of Abraham Lincoln," *Magazine of History*, February 1909.

Wright, Erastus, "Lincoln in 1831," *Bulletin of the Abraham Lincoln Association*, December 1927.

Wright, Richardson. *Forgotten Ladies: Nine Portraits from the American Family Album.* Lippincott, Philadelphia, 1928.

Zane, Charles S., "Lincoln as I Knew Him," *Sunset Magazine*, October 1912.

Also by Sam Rawlins

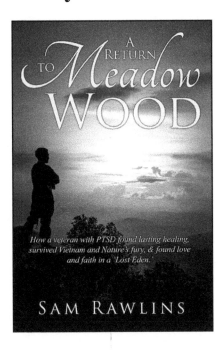

A RETURN TO MEADOW WOOD

If you enjoyed **YOUNG LINCOLN**, you may find this powerful story of love and faith a rewarding book.
Spanning from the Vietnam War to the present, this is the inspiring tale of a veteran suffering from PTSD in search of lasting healing.

Available in hardcover, paperback and e-Book

CPSIA information can be obtained
at www.ICGtesting.com
Printed in the USA
FFHW022340050419
51542254-56993FF